RICOCHET THROUGH TIME

ECHO TRILOGY, BOOK THREE

LINDSEY FAIRLEIGH

RUBUS PRESS

Editing by Sarah Kolb-Williams
www.kolbwilliams.com

Cover by We Got You Covered Book Design
www.wegotyoucoveredbookdesign.com

ISBN: 9781539567714

ALSO BY LINDSEY FAIRLEIGH

ECHO TRILOGY

Echo in Time

Resonance

Time Anomaly

Dissonance

Ricochet Through Time

KAT DUBOIS CHRONICLES

Ink Witch

Outcast

Underground

Soul Eater

Judgement

Afterlife

ATLANTIS LEGACY

Sacrifice of the Sinners

Legacy of the Lost

Fate of the Fallen

Dreams of the Damned

Song of the Soulless

THE ENDING SERIES

Beginnings: The Ending Series Origin Stories

After The Ending

Into The Fire

Out Of The Ashes

Before The Dawn

World Before

World After

For more information on Lindsey and her books:

www.lindseyfairleigh.com

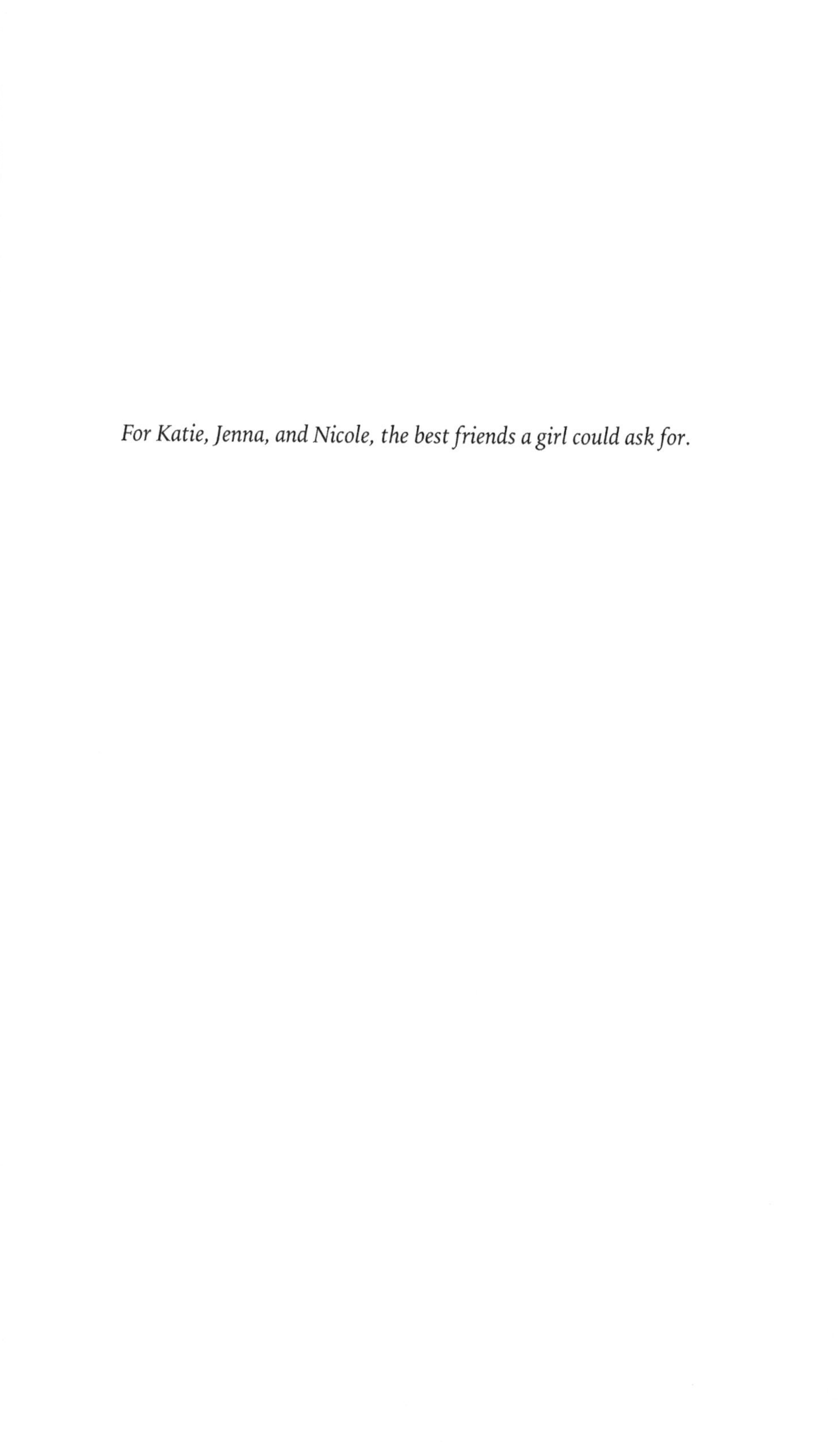

For Katie, Jenna, and Nicole, the best friends a girl could ask for.

PART I - TIMELESS

LEX

1

REVIVE & REVILE

"It's time." Neffe's words settled over us, a muffling cloak stealing breath and silencing tongues in the sterile room.

The group of doctors and nurses surrounding Tarset's bed of stony, opalescent At tensed collectively, prepared. Waiting. In just a moment, Neffe would give the word and they would jump into action, attempting to save Marcus's frozen-in-time little girl.

Nik stood at the head of the bed, his mother, Aset, at the foot with Neffe. The two ancient, beautiful women were codirectors of their highly trained and even more highly experienced orchestra of Nejeret medical savants. A pair of them stood on either side of Tarset, others standing behind them, ready to tap in once the little girl had been awakened from her eternal slumber and transferred to the waiting hospital bed just a few feet away.

Generic blue scrubs were the outfit of the day for a team that was anything but generic. This group of people was about to attempt to revive a four-year-old girl who'd been on the verge of death four *thousand* years ago, frozen in At ever since. They would do everything they could to counteract the effects of the ancient poison killing Tarset and achieve the impossible, returning this tiny, dying child to health. But they were Nejerets, mythic gods of time; impossibility lay at the heart of their very existence.

Marcus and I stood with our backs against the wall near the doorway to Neffe's state-of-the-art laboratory, taking up as little space as we could. Staying out of the way. Keeping our mouths shut. Letting the experts do their work. Trying to *not* have a damn freak-out.

"Nik." Neffe's voice was sure, commanding. "When you're ready, please begin."

My hand sought out Marcus's, our fingers lacing together in a painfully tight grip. We watched, helpless and useless, as Nik cupped either side of Tarset's head, closed his eyes, and inhaled deeply. He held his breath, looking so strange without his standard garb—no black clothing or leather or spikey hair. Now, his myriad of graying tattoos and silver piercings looked out of place next to his blue scrubs. *Now*, breath held and clothing matching those around him, he appeared the quintessential team player, a regular joiner.

I suppressed a highly inappropriate laugh and swallowed, cotton mouth making the action ineffective.

As Nik began his exhale, color bled back into Tarset's opalescent body. First her hair blossomed to onyx black, then her skin to an ashen hue. The blanket covering the rest of her body, a relic woven millennia ago, faded from shimmering moonstone to vibrant crimson, yellow, and teal.

"Wait . . ." Nik's voice was strained, quiet.

Though Tarset appeared to be made of living flesh now rather than solidified At, her body showed no signs of life.

"Almost . . ."

A tiny, pained noise came from Marcus as he stared at his unresponsive little girl. I gave his hand a squeeze.

This was it—the moment of truth. In just a few seconds, we

would know whether Tarset had even the slightest chance of recovering from the ancient poison Apep had tainted the Oasis's water source with thousands of years ago, or if her damaged organs would give out and she would be truly gone.

I'd made a promise to her mother, Seshseshet, to save Tarset. To look after her. To raise her as my own daughter. To give her a chance at a normal life in a world that would seem foreign and alien. But at least it would be a life, a chance to grow up. At least it would be a promise kept.

A few weeks back, we'd revived the kitten I'd frozen in At with Tarset so long ago. Rus had been a gift from Heru, Marcus's ancient counterpart, given to me during my first homesick night in ancient Egypt. The fuzz ball was, once again, the rambunctious creature he'd been millennia ago, though his first few days had been a little rough, and that was poison free. Tarset's transition into modern times would be far bumpier. Which was precisely why the room was packed with a small army of highly skilled Nejerets waiting for Nik to finish the transformation process.

Sweat beaded on Nik's brow, and I was fairly certain he'd yet to take another breath. "And . . ." he said on the final stretch of his exhale. "Done."

The room exploded with activity. The four Nejerets standing on either side of Tarset's ancient bed gathered her up in a choreographed movement and swiftly shifted her to the hospital bed. Before their hands were even free, other Nejerets moved in, intubating, inserting needles, injecting antidotes, setting up IV bags, and placing electrodes. When one moved away from the bed, another would swoop in, weaving between the others and a vast array of bulky machines in a fluid, expertly executed dance.

As the machines came to life with beeps and whirrs, Tarset seemed to revive as well. Her cheeks filled with color, and she coughed on the breathing tube, her small, fragile body writhing on the mattress.

"Administer two milligrams of pentobarbital," Neffe ordered.

Seconds later, Tarset's body grew still and quiet, her limbs askew. Her chest rose and fell in time with the whoosh and beep of the ventilator set up near her head.

"BP is sixty over forty—low, but stable," one member of the team said mechanically while another delivered a pinky-sized vial of blood to Neffe.

"Take another sample after the transfusion," Neffe told the Nejeret, then looked at Aset. "You're up." She gave her aunt's arm a squeeze, and the two small but brilliant Nejerettes exchanged a nod.

Neffe turned and headed toward the doorway. She paused at the threshold to place her hand on Marcus's shoulder, flashing him the tiniest of smiles. "So far, so good, Father." Her caramel eyes were bright with excitement, her cheeks flushed.

"Thank you," Marcus said, his voice husky.

Neffe pulled her hand back and hurried through the doorway into the lab.

"Sir." Carlisle, Marcus's "man," stepped into the doorway in Neffe's place, his features tense. "I know this isn't the best time, but—"

Marcus tore his gaze from the activity surrounding Tarset to look at Carlisle, who leaned back a few inches.

"What is it, Carlisle?" I asked softly.

With a quick nod to himself, Carlisle regained his bearings and shifted his focus to me. "Apologies, Meswett"—he bowed his head, just a little—"but a couple of people were detected attempting to breach the wall at the north end of the compound. Dominic is detaining them as we speak." British aristocracy dripped off of him with every word and movement.

Marcus looked from Carlisle to Tarset and back, his expression torn. I could only imagine what he was going through. I was barely a month pregnant and I already felt like I'd slaughter anyone who even mentioned harming our twins.

"I'll handle it," I told my husband—my bond-mate. "Stay here with Tarsi. I'll check in soon." I leaned in to brush my lips against his cheek, then caught Nik's eye across the room and nodded toward the doorway. He was on his way before I'd even taken my first step.

Carlisle led Nik and me through the lab toward the stairwell leading up to the main floor. We were in the basement of the Heru compound's mansion of a main house on Bainbridge Island. Dozens of other buildings populated the complex, including homes for other Nejerets in Marcus's line, garages and outbuildings, a training facility, and, I had no doubt, some sort of detention or holding cells.

"Where's Dom holding them?" I asked.

Carlisle paused with his hand on the handle of the stairwell door and looked at me. "The dungeon, Meswett."

I grabbed his arm. "I'm sorry—did you just say 'dungeon'?" This was the Pacific Northwest, after all. Our oldest buildings were a century and a half, *maybe*. Hardly built during the age of *dungeons*.

"Yes, Meswett." Carlisle glanced down at my hand. "Might we continue?"

"Sure."

He pulled the door open and waved me through the doorway. I hurried up the stairs, Nik and Carlisle close behind me.

"This way," Carlisle said once we'd emerged in the hallway on the main floor. We crossed the entryway and passed through the tall front door. A posh electric golf cart waited in the driveway, what the inhabitants of the Heru compound used to get around within the walls when they didn't feel like using their own two feet.

"So who are these intruders?" I asked as we jogged down the stone steps at the front of the house. I figured it had to be someone notable, or Carlisle would've waited until Marcus was free.

The look Carlisle shot me confirmed my suspicion, but it was the names he uttered that turned my blood into lava. "The young Nejeret Carson," he said, holding out his hand to help me onto the cart.

I waved him away, but he remained there for a moment longer, his eyes meeting mine.

"And Genevieve."

2

CATCH & RELEASE

I have trust issues. I know this. Earning my trust is like pulling teeth, and regaining it once it's lost is like trying to shove those pulled teeth back into their respective holes, dead roots and all. It's probably my biggest flaw. But what can I say? I've been conditioned to expect those who love me most to lie to me. My parents did it, my grandparents did it, my friends did it . . . even Marcus did it.

All that dishonesty makes a girl wary. And, at times, pissed off.

Last winter, I'd been a normal grad student at the University of Washington, well on my way to earning my PhD in archaeology. I'd been a bit of a loner, my only true friend in the program being a fellow archaeologist, a classicist named Carson. Or I'd thought he was my friend.

It turned out Carson was an agent of Marcus's, planted at the U to keep an eye on me on the off chance that I manifested into a full-blown Nejerette. But what Marcus hadn't known was that Carson was a double agent, so to speak. He'd pledged his loyalty to Marcus, claiming to be of his bloodline. And maybe he was—none of us knew for sure. But Carson's true loyalty belonged to the Kin, a hidden, subversive group of Nejerets opposed to the Council of Seven's rule for reasons we didn't fully understand yet.

Carson had kept his head low, earning his way into the close circle of Marcus's trusted few by capitalizing on his friendship with me and manipulating the emotions of my young Nejerette half-sister, Kat. He'd fooled us all, and in the end, he'd shown his true colors by shooting Dom, holding Kat hostage with a gun to her head, and stealing the At orb containing the twisted soul of one of the most ancient and powerful beings in the universe—the Netjer Apep.

And who'd helped him accomplish that great feat of betrayal? None other than Kat's mom, Genevieve. And now they were both here, within our walls. Our home. My deceitful former UW peer and Kat's traitorous mother were somewhere nearby, just under my feet. I had no idea what I would say to them when they were finally in front of me. Accusations and blame were the only things that came to mind.

Carlisle brought the electric cart to a halt in the compound's enormous warehouse of a garage. It wasn't far from the main house as the crow flies, but the route to get there was circuitous, and the cart wasn't the speediest four-wheeled creation.

I'd been clenching my teeth so hard that my jaw groaned when I finally spoke again. "There's a dungeon below the garage?"

"Can you think of a better location?"

"I—" Was any location a good location for a dungeon? "Well, no," I admitted.

Carlisle scooted out of the driver's seat and rounded the front of the cart, stopping on my side. "Please, Meswett . . ." He held his arm out toward the back wall. "It's just this way."

"Have they explained their intentions?" Nik asked as we wove between vehicles of all sizes parked in orderly rows and closed in on a metal fire door painted an ashen gray.

I blew out a breath. This whole thing felt surreal.

"So far as I know," Carlisle said, "they have not explained their reason for being here." He fit a silver key into the lock and turned the handle, pushing the door inward to reveal a short hallway with another door at the end.

This new door was also metal, but the similarity ended there. It was shiny and paint-free, had no visible hinges, locks, knobs, or handles, and was paired with a small screen in the wall immediately to the right. Some sort of high-tech biometric scanner, I assumed.

Carlisle stepped up to the screen in the wall by the second door. He stared at it for a few seconds, saying nothing.

"Identity confirmed—Carlisle Walker the Third." The voice was vaguely artificial, but still pleasant. "Passcode, please."

"Five-three-eight-U-C-L," he said clearly.

"Voice recognized. Passcode confirmed."

The door slid open, revealing a compact elevator car with stainless steel everything. We loaded in and, as soon as the door slid shut, started descending.

"So," I said, drawing out the word. I felt like I was shouting in the deafening quiet. Who knew I'd ever wish for elevator music? "Are there any other secret elevators hidden around the compound?"

"Not at present, Meswett," Carlisle said, clasping his hands behind his back. "Though there is one on the outside, in case an emergency evacuation is necessitated. It links to a system of tunnels under the compound. The entry security for that elevator is much stronger, of course."

"Of course," I said dryly.

Our descent was quick and ended not with a ding, but with a

gentle shush as the door opened. Carlisle led us into a hallway that was nothing like what I'd expected. Plaster coated the walls and the arched ceiling, friezes faintly engraved and painted into the surfaces to display hieroglyphs and figures in a notably Egyptian style. The color palette, limited to grays and silver, gave the wall decoration a distinctly modern bent. It was the perfect marriage of ancient Egypt and Marcus's personal stylistic taste, and it was so unexpected that it knocked me temporarily speechless.

Not Nik, though. He whistled. "Well, this is interesting . . ."

"Heru has always taken comfort in surrounding himself with reminders of his home."

As we made our way down the hallway, I studied the scenes depicted on the walls. Most made little sense to me, though I was certain every detail had been chosen purposefully and held deep significance to Marcus. He never said, did, or created anything without purpose.

"What stories do the friezes tell?" I asked, eyes scanning the images. Yes, I was avoiding the confrontation with Genevieve and Carson. And yes, I knew it was inevitable. But delaying it just a smidgen longer was so very tempting. I couldn't resist.

"They contain our history." Carlisle paused and waved his hand over a scene on the left side of the hallway. "This one in particular is a vignette of Heru's childhood growing up in the Netjer-At Oasis." It was a beautiful image, with buildings in shimmering silver in the background and two children standing on either side of a noble-looking ancient Egyptian woman. All three were staring up at a glorious male figure, who dwarfed them.

"Mut," Nik said softly, brushing his fingertips over the depiction of the woman. There was fondness in his voice, and sorrow.

I rested my hand on his arm and studied his features. An aching sense of loss was painted across his face, transforming him from tough ancient being to little boy in an instant. "Your grandmother?"

When he nodded, I returned my attention to the graceful figure—Marcus and Aset's human mother.

"She was an incredible woman. So warm and giving, but also strong enough to stand up to Osiris when necessary." He let out a whisper of a laugh. "Their marriage was arranged by Nuin, but the way everyone told it, grandfather never minded one bit."

"Marcus never talks about her," I said, my voice hushed.

"I'm not surprised." Nik turned and draped an arm over my shoulder. "Don't take it personally, Lex. Her death—it destroyed him. He spent decades shying away from mortals to keep himself from feeling that way again." He glanced at me, sympathy filling the pale blue depths of his eyes. "Immortality takes a while to get used to. Watching beloved humans die . . . it's not easy, not for any of us. You'll see." Though his words carried the promise of terrible pain, his open expression told me he'd be there to help me through it.

I offered him a weak smile and a reluctant nod, then turned to Carlisle. "Alright, let's get this over with, shall we?" Facing traitorous Carson and Genevieve would be way better than thinking about the inevitable day when my human parents would die . . . and my sister . . .

Anything would be better than thinking about that.

A few minutes and several turns down different hallways later, we reached what appeared to be a dead end. Like the other walls, the one at the end of the corridor was covered in gleaming silver hieroglyphs. But unlike the other walls, this one contained only a single, large image—a human male, limbs extended Vitruvian-man style. The figure still appeared Egyptian, stylistically, but the image was far more gruesome than any ancient Egyptian art I'd ever seen. The man appeared to have knives stabbed into his feet and wrists, holding his limbs in place, and where his eyes should have been were nothing but gaping black holes.

I tilted my head to the side, watching as Carlisle pushed on the figure. It depressed, sinking into the wall, and a moment later, the entire wall slid to the side, revealing a wrought iron gate.

"That last image was rather unique," I said to Nik while we waited for Carlisle to unlock the gate.

Nik nodded slowly. "It's Marcus—or, Heru."

I gaped at him.

Nik glanced at me sidelong. "That's how we found him, Mother and I, when Apep-Set jumped him back during the whole Council succession thing—you know, 'The Contendings of Horus and Seth' . . ."

My eyes bulged. Set—or rather, Apep—had done *that* to Marcus? "At least that psycho's locked away for good," I said, crossing my arms and shaking my head. About a month ago, Nik had sealed Apep's sickly soul in a prison of At about the size of a baseball, and until my kids were born and came into their godly power, nobody else on this earth but Nik could let Apep out. Maybe I'd have felt a little more comfortable if we still had possession of the Apep orb, but we didn't. Because Carson stole it. The bastard.

"Maybe Carson's here to return the orb." Nik laughed under his breath. "I bet he grovels real nice."

"Guess we're about to find out," I said as Carlisle pushed the wrought iron gate open. I took a deep breath, then followed him down the stairs.

He led us into a fairly authentic dungeon setting. The dingy, rough-hewn stone walls, iron-barred cells, and pervasive chill in the air seemed both ridiculously out of place and laughably expected. But then, dungeons like this had been the way of things for millennia for Marcus; I supposed it didn't make sense for him to change his ways now just because the world had gone ahead and changed all around him.

"The cell at the end," Carlisle said, though the direction was unnecessary. Dominic and a full retinue of guards crowded the space at the end of the dungeon.

Dominic spotted us and hurried our way.

"What have they told you?" I asked my half-brother, rushing ahead to meet him.

"Nothing." His dark eyes met mine, and he combed his long fingers through his night-black hair, slicking the lengthy strands back. His face was tense, his irritation clear, making his sharp features even more angular. "Where is Marcus?" he asked, his French accent heavier than usual.

"With Tarset."

"Is she—"

"She's still alive. On life support, but still with us." I cleared my throat. "Neffe seems hopeful."

"Well, that is something, at least." With a hand on my lower back, Dominic guided me toward the cell at the end. "Gen demanded to speak to Marcus, but hopefully you will be good enough."

I snorted. Not likely, considering Genevieve's none-too-hidden feelings toward Marcus. Not that her jealousy meant she didn't like me, exactly. At least, not that I was aware of—or had been aware of before she'd gone turncoat. It was just that she'd been carrying a torch for Marcus for years, and if she wanted to talk to him, well, she wanted to talk to *him*.

"Also," Dominic said when we reached the iron-barred cell door, "Carson is injured."

I stared through the bars into the dimly lit cell. Within, Genevieve was huddled on her knees on the floor, Carson curled into the fetal position, his head resting on her lap. Blood soaked her lilac tunic and white leggings, as well as Carson's blue T-shirt. My stomach twisted at the sight; it had been sensitive lately, an early gift from the twins.

"Injured, indeed," I said quietly, crossing my arms.

Genevieve's head shot up at the sound of my voice, and she speared me with bloodshot eyes. "He needs a doctor! Where's Neffe or—"

"She's busy," I said. I glanced at Dominic, hesitant to dismiss aid outright. "How bad is it?" After everything Carson had done, I really didn't mind him being in pain for a while. But that didn't mean I wanted him to die.

"Gunshot to the shoulder," Dominic said with a lazy shrug. "He has lost some blood, but he will live."

"Okay." I flashed Genevieve a grim, humorless smile. "He'll have to wait. Why did you come here?"

"To warn Marcus . . ." She trailed off, shaking her head. "I want to see him."

"You *think* you want to see him," I said, "but trust me, Gen, you don't."

"But—"

"You came back here thinking . . . what? That things would go right back to the way they were? That he'd still love you like a little sister?" I took a step closer to the cell door, stopping when Dominic placed a hand on my shoulder, holding me just out of arm's reach from the bars. "After everything you've done, Gen, after all the betrayal, did you really think he'd forgive you?" I leaned forward. "Tell me why you're here. Prove to me—to Marcus—that there's a reason he should still give a damn about you."

Genevieve's resolve was wavering; it was written all over her face.

"Did you really come here to warn Marcus?" I asked. "About what? Are we in danger?" I would do anything to protect my twins—*anything*. Even kick another mother when she was down. "Is Kat in danger?"

Genevieve's love for her daughter had always been her weakness. Kat was her whole world and, in a twisted way, had been her reason for betraying Marcus and the Council of Seven.

She hung her head, her limp chestnut waves falling around her face like a curtain. "Apep . . ." She spoke so quietly that without my heightened sense of hearing, I wouldn't have heard her. "Someone released him. He's free."

3

SAFE & SOUND

The last time I saw Apep, the last time I actually spoke to him, was in the Nejeret Oasis a little over a month ago. He'd been possessing Marcus, dead set on killing me to release Re's borrowed sheut, a source of unimaginable godlike power. The time before that had also been at the Oasis, just about four thousand years earlier. He'd been possessing Nuin's daughter, Ankhesenpepi, and was laughing as I lost control of Re's sheut, destroying the Oasis and nearly killing everyone living there in the process. And the time before that, he tried to tear out my heart to send a message to Nuin but settled for shattering nearly every bone in my foot instead. The time before that, he shot me. And the time before *that*, he tortured me for months in the At. On and on, he never let up. He never relented.

And he never would, not so long as he was free. Which, according to Genevieve, he was.

After Genevieve dropped the bomb, there was a collective gasp. A full second of what-did-she-just-say and did-I-hear-that-right.

Then the dungeon exploded with sound. Voices and footsteps surrounded me as the guards circled up. It was organized chaos at best, with me at the eye of the storm.

I covered my ears and ducked my head, huddling in on myself.

This couldn't be happening. Apep's unhinged soul couldn't be free from its At prison. It was about as close to impossible as things came in our crazy world. Nik was the only person currently alive with a sheut, a mere shadow of the one I'd borrowed from Re, allowing him to manipulate solidified At, the very fabric of space and time. He was the only person capable of releasing Apep. But he would never, *ever* do such a thing.

And even if I'd misjudged Nik's character and convictions horribly, he shared his body with the soul of Apep's opposite, Re, the Netjer who'd sacrificed his own life and power for the mere chance that Apep might be stopped. There was no way Re would've let Nik release Apep. There was no way Apep could be free.

Because if he was, I'd never be safe again.

Apep was a Netjer, a true god of which we were diluted imitations in comparison. He was one of the two original powers in this universe, alongside Re, and together, the two had created *everything*. Even Apep's disembodied soul was frighteningly powerful, possessing the ability to take over another being's body. It was what he'd done to my biological father, Set, and what Re had done to Nik. Only unlike Re, Apep didn't share; he'd wrested control of Set's body from its rightful owner and had worn his skin for thousands of years like a favorite suit. The things Apep had done to me, masquerading as my father . . . the ways he'd broken me . . .

All the noise in the dungeon, the moving bodies, the possibility that the impossible had happened—it was too much. I gasped for breath, my lungs desperate to suck in all of the oxygen in the dank room. My head spun, and I squeezed my eyes shut to steady the tilt-a-whirl the world had become.

Apep . . . he can't be free . . .

. . . I can't go through this again . . .

. . . I can't fight him again . . .

As quickly as the cacophony all around me began, it cut off.

"Lex . . ." Dominic's voice cut through my rising panic, his arm curling around my shoulders. "You are alright, sister."

I whimpered.

He squeezed my shoulders. "You are safe."

Nik's voice joined his, close and right in front of me. "You are, Lex. You're safe."

Eyes squeezed shut, I shook my head vehemently. I hugged my middle as if that measly effort might protect my children.

"You're safe," Nik repeated, his tone even, soothing. "I promise, Lex. Open your eyes and see. Apep can't get to you now. Nobody can."

I cracked an eyelid open. Nik's face was the first thing I saw, his pale blue eyes locked on mine.

Slowly, cautiously, I opened my eyes the rest of the way and straightened to peer around. The Nejerets guards had settled into their defensive postures in a ring around me, but I viewed them through a shimmering cloak of solidified, crystalline At. I followed it upwards with my eyes, where it arched overhead into our own private little dome.

On my next inhale, I found I was able to breathe a little easier. Apep wouldn't get to me today. More importantly, he wouldn't get to either of my children, either.

"Thanks," I said.

Nik nodded once, straightening to his full height.

"So, what do we do now?" I glanced around, gesturing to the otherworldly dome with one hand. "It's not like I can stay in here until the twins are born, because clearly even a solid wall of At won't keep us safe . . ."

While I spoke, the color faded from Nik's eyes until his irises resembled moonstones, a perfect match to the At surrounding us. "What you say is true, my Alexandra," Nik said. Or, rather, Re said, using Nik's lips and teeth and tongue to form the words.

Re-Nik raised his hand and brushed the backs of his knuckles over my cheek. "We had wondered how it would come to pass, but it seems so obvious now that the Kin finding a way to free Apep would be the cause."

I stared at him, my eyebrows drawn together. "What are you talking about? You wondered how *what* would come to pass?"

During my time in Old Kingdom Egypt, when Re had been residing in his former host, Nuin, I'd had plenty of practice wading through his half-answers and vague explanations. And yet Re was still as confounding as ever. I'd all but given up on attempting to understand the murky motivations behind everything he'd done during his time on earth, let alone his time before it. He was a Netjer, a god, and he operated on an entirely different plane of existence. But he had my trust, unequivocally. In his own odd, godly way, he'd earned it.

Which is why I didn't freak out when Re-Nik didn't answer my questions, only stared at me with those secretive eyes.

"Okay . . ." I took a deep breath through my nose. "Next question—what do we do now? Apep's going to come after me—after the twins—isn't he?"

Re-Nik nodded slowly. "Without a doubt."

When it became apparent that those three words were all he intended to say, I ground my teeth together. He knew more, that much was clear. And while it drove me nuts that he wouldn't share, experience told me that he was holding back for a reason. Probably some preservation-of-the-timeline, fate-saving reason. Fine. I could deal with that. For now.

I sighed and rubbed my forehead. I was suddenly exhausted.

Without warning, Re-Nik's features transformed as the pale blue color bled back into his irises. His eyes tensed and his mouth curved downward in a frown. "Sorry, Lex." Nik reached out and gave my arm a squeeze. "I know this is frustrating, but it'll all make sense soon." He offered me a conciliatory smile. "Promise," he added with a wink. Somehow, I managed to convince myself I was only imagining the shadow of doubt in his gaze.

Dominic's arm slid from my shoulders, and he took two steps toward Genevieve and Carson's cell. "You must remain in here, Lex, but there is no need for me to." He looked at Nik, his dark eyes determined. "Allow me to pass so I might interrogate them. We must be as prepared as possible for what is to come."

. . . *for what is to come.* More ominous words had never been spoken.

Nik agreed, and Dominic passed through a slim opening in the barrier. It closed the moment he was clear of it. I moved to the spot he'd passed through to watch the proceedings.

Minutes passed, and though I couldn't hear either his or Genevieve's words, I was able to watch the tension enter Dominic's body, stiffening his posture and making his movements minimal, precise. He was the third-deadliest man I knew, behind only Marcus and Nik, and was essentially cloak and dagger personified. I actually felt a little sympathy for Genevieve and Carson.

For months, ever since I'd found out who and what I was—the Meswett, prophesied savior not only of our people and our world, but apparently of the whole damn universe, courtesy of the godly Netjer twins I was carrying—I'd felt like a prisoner in a gilded cell. My choices were no longer mine. My future belonged to everyone but me.

My eyes became unfocused as I watched the strange tableau beyond until all I could see was the wall of shimmering At. My not-quite-gilded cage. Worse.

After fifteen minutes of waiting and watching the interrogation from within our soundproof bubble, Nik and I conceded that our presence in the dungeon was less than pointless; really, we were in the way. We made our way out of the gloomy dungeon, Nejeret guards ahead of and behind us.

"Do not be afraid, my Alexandra," Re-Nik said as we ascended the stairs. The change in cadence and tone of Nik's voice was unmistakable.

I raised my eyebrows. "You left pretty quickly back there."

"I wished to consult the At," Re-Nik said, nodding to himself.

"Learn anything?" I worried the inside of my cheek.

Thanks to ma'at still being out of whack—something that wouldn't return to proper balance until my children were born —the At was unstable to the point of being unusable. Nejerets hadn't been able to view more than a few seconds in the "echoes" for months now. But Re was different. Or rather, his connection to that plane of existence was different, because his was the soul—the ren—of a Netjer, rather than the lesser ba of a Nejeret. While we were all but locked out of the At, Re could still transcend to that other plane at will to view the reflections of past, present, and future possible events.

"I learned little of value," Re-Nik said, shaking his head. "The At is currently misaligned in this location . . . a time anomaly, it would seem."

I frowned. I'd been a time anomaly once, my presence in an ancient, foreign period masking all that was truly happening, leaving the echoes of Egypt during that time grossly misshapen in the At. My presence had inadvertently led to the fall of the Old Kingdom. How many people can say that? It was quite the accomplishment.

"What does that mean?" I asked.

Again, Re-Nik shook his head. "Only time will tell." His words were far from comforting.

Once we were aboveground, following the trail that led back to the main house, I felt less and less safe with each successive step. Even within the impermeable At shell, even with the gang of guards stretching out ahead of and behind us and stalking through the woods on either side of the trail, it became glaringly obvious that any sense of safety was an illusion.

"Re," I said hesitantly, "if someone was able to free Apep, wouldn't the same someone be able to get through any other barrier of At, too?"

"Indeed." Re-Nik walked along beside me, hands clasped behind his back.

I inhaled and exhaled deeply, and some of the rising panic abated. "And considering Apep's penchant for possessing the most powerful being he can find, wouldn't it also be safe to assume that he possessed whoever released him?"

"Yes," Re-Nik said with a thoughtful nod. "That seems like a logical assumption to me."

I clenched my jaw so hard my teeth ground together. His blasé attitude was becoming irksome. "And since I think we'd all agree that Apep's headed straight for me—for them," I amended, pointing to my belly, "there's not really anywhere or way for us to hide." I rapped a knuckle against the thin sheet of solidified At. "This won't even be able to protect us."

Finally, Re-Nik stopped and faced me. He placed his hands on my shoulders and leaned in, just a little, opalescent eyes searching mine. "I know you are afraid, my Alexandra. Just as Nik and Dominic and all of those bound to you by oath are afraid." Compassion filled his alien eyes, and his lips curved into a gentle smile. "I, too, am afraid. But we must not let it get the better of us. We will acknowledge our fear, then set it aside and do what must be done, regardless."

Ever so slowly, I shook my head, eyes stinging with the strength of my frustration. "But what's the point? There's nothing we can do!"

"Rubbish," Re-Nik said in response to my hysterics. "This shield of At might not keep Apep out, assuming Apep has indeed possessed the mystery Nejeret with a minor sheut enabling him or her to manipulate At, but it *will* warn us of Apep's arrival, and—"

"You mean when Apep breaks through the shield, kills the Nejeret he's possessing, and comes after me and my children?" I clarified, eyebrows raised. "Fat lot of good that two-second warning will do."

"Ah, but you didn't let me finish." Re-Nik moved his right hand from my shoulder to my belly. "The children you carry and the Netjer sheuts interwoven in every fiber of their beings—they will sense the danger, and this warning will give them the time they need to defend themselves *and* you."

"But—but—but," I stuttered. "I'm barely a month along! They're just fetuses! How could they possibly do anything to defend themselves, let alone *me*?"

Re-Nik sighed heavily, his hands falling away from me. "Your children may still be forming, but their sheuts are as old as time and more than capable of acting on instinct."

My slow headshake continued. "That doesn't make any sense."

"It most certainly does. And more importantly, it is what *is*. When they sense that your life is in immediate danger—and there is no doubt in my mind that once Apep shows up here, you will feel that very thing—their sheuts' innate survival instinct will kick in and you will be carried away to safety."

I stared at him, mouth agape, and hugged my belly. My kids weren't just going to be gods whose very existence would restore balance to our failing universe. They *already were* gods. And they hadn't even been born yet.

4

FLIGHT & FIGHT

The moment I walked through the doorway from the basement laboratory into Tarset's recovery room, the moment I saw Marcus hunched over the bedside, I could breathe a little easier. It was a basic, physiological reaction to seeing him.

Marcus and I shared a bond that went beyond love. We were, quite literally, addicted to each other, courtesy of a rather obscure pheromone emitted by my kind. It was rare that one of us found our biological and spiritual match, as Marcus and I had, and as wondrous as our bond was, it could be as much a curse as it was a blessing. It opened the door to unimaginable pleasure, but also to the very real possibility of death. Were we to be separated for longer than a few days, we would go into bonding withdrawals and, in time, we would die. People say they can't live without the one they love all the time; they rarely mean it quite so literally.

"Go on," Nik said, and the sheet of shimmering At evaporated into a wispy smoke containing all the colors of the rainbow. "I'm going to speak with Neffe. I'll seal you in here."

"Thanks." I took a step toward Marcus, who still hadn't

raised his bowed head, then glanced back at Nik. "We'll only be in here a moment." I didn't want to interfere with Tarset's treatment. "Will you tell Dom to meet us upstairs in the conference room? And anyone else you think needs to be there? And can you alert the Council of Seven to be ready for an emergency meeting?"

"I'll take care of it," Nik said with a quick nod. "Just knock on the At when you're ready for me to move you upstairs. I'll hear it."

I watched him erect a barrier in the doorway, then pass through the solidified At like it was as insubstantial as air. Once upon a time, when I'd possessed Re's sheut, I could've done the same thing. Of course, that same sheut had also threatened to tear me apart from the ba out.

Sometimes, when I slept, I dreamed of the explosive episodes when my borrowed sheut threatened to rip free of me; I always woke screaming in pain and covered in a sheen of sweat, Marcus holding me close, murmuring to me in our people's ancient language, the original tongue. I didn't miss the power one bit, not when the cost was so high. Now, I was perfectly happy to be a regular ol', sheut-free Nejerette. With two gods growing inside her.

"Why are we calling an emergency meeting?"

I spun around and stared at Marcus, taking in the weariness lining his chiseled features. I dreaded telling him about Apep, knowing how much more stress and worry it would pile on his already burdened shoulders. We were at war with the Kin, that much had been decided weeks ago, not that we'd made much headway in defeating them. Or in even finding them. But this escalation—the Kin releasing Apep—it was so much worse than anything we'd planned for so far. And Marcus, as our people's general, would be responsible for seeing us through this horrendous situation.

I opened my mouth and the words caught in my throat.

Apep's free, I didn't say. Couldn't say. Not when, right before me, Marcus sat at his daughter's bedside, watching her struggle to stay alive.

"Tell me, Little Ivanov." He scrubbed his hands over his face, his stubble scratching against his palms. "I won't break."

I swallowed roughly and nodded, offering him a weak smile. And here I was the one always getting on his case for treating me like a fragile thing; hearing him say those words almost teased a laugh out of me. Almost.

"How is she?" I asked, moving across the room to stand at Marcus's side. I rested my hand on his shoulder and leaned down to press a kiss against the top of his shaved head.

"Stable." He covered my hand with his and tilted his head back to look up at me. "They're keeping her in an induced coma. Neffe tells me she's out of the woods . . . for now." He grasped my fingers and brought my hand to his lips. "Tell me."

I sighed and perched on Marcus's knee, and it felt like my spine caved in on itself, just a little, as I recounted everything I knew about the situation so far. I watched his expression as I spoke, taking note of the subtle changes to his features as they tensed along with the rest of his body. His eyes, however, retained that weary glint.

"And if he really is possessing the Nejeret who freed him, we're pretty much screwed," I said, voice heightened by the threat of hysteria. "Can you imagine the damage someone with Nik's power could do if they decided to use their sheut as a weapon? They could destroy this place in a matter of minutes. If Apep's possessing someone like that . . ." I shook my head, limbs twitching and heart fluttering with the desire to run, to flee, to go *away*, anywhere but this place where Apep would know to find me.

"We won't let that happen," Marcus said with so much conviction that part of me believed him. Maybe. Just a little. I wanted to believe him so badly.

"Well, Re says the twins' sheuts should kick in with some sort of automated defense and 'carry me away to safety' as soon as they sense that Apep's an immediate threat, so that's something at least . . ." I let out a despondent laugh. After everything we'd been through this past year, I'd had the audacity to hope that the threat posed by Apep had truly been neutralized.

But based on Marcus's lack of shock, part of him had expected something like this to happen. I leaned forward, more or less collapsing against his chest and nuzzling his neck. His spicy scent soothed me enough that the tide went out on the ocean of panic threatening to sweep me away.

Marcus's arms curved around my back, and he held me close. "We'll figure it out, Little Ivanov. It's simple, really—all we have to do is kill the person who released Apep, then have Nik imprison Apep in At once more . . . then lock the whole thing away in a vault that nobody will ever get into again."

Another of those desperate, verge-of-tears laughs bubbled up from my chest. "So simple . . ."

My sarcasm wasn't lost on Marcus. Hands gripping my upper arms, he pushed me away enough that he could see my face. His eyes burned with conviction. "Apep will *not* harm you or our children. I swear to you . . ." He clenched his jaw. "I won't allow it. You're too important."

I squeezed my eyes shut, and a tear broke free. It snaked down my cheek, only stopping when its path was barred by Marcus's lips. "You know," I said, my voice unsteady, "I wish the universe would be done with me already. I don't want to be important anymore." It wasn't something I'd ever wanted. I just wasn't a fate-of-the-universe kind of girl.

"Not important to the universe, Little Ivanov." Marcus pulled away, the corner of his mouth twitching. "Though you are *that*," he conceded with a nod. He slid his hands up over my shoulders and along the curve of my neck until he grasped either side of my head. He drew me closer, his burning golden eyes engulfing my world. When he spoke next, his lips were a hairsbreadth from mine, so close I could feel the ghost of their touch. "I meant: you're too important *to me*."

"Oh," I said. It was all I could get out before his lips were on mine, his tongue gently wrestling mine to silence.

At the sound of a throat clearing, we froze. My eyes opened wide.

"Sorry," Nik said. "I, uh, thought you heard me . . ."

Marcus and I broke apart, and I sprang off his lap, smoothing down my jeans and T-shirt and looking anywhere but at Nik. My cheeks were ablaze.

Marcus, however, remained seated, crossing his leg in that über-masculine, relaxed way. His gaze was palpable as it trailed over my face, and when his eyes met mine, I caught the hint of a smile.

He stood smoothly and started across the room. When he reached me, he stretched his arm across my abdomen, curling his fingers around the side of my waist, and leaned in close to brush his lips along the length of my cheekbone. "You're blushing, Little Ivanov. Whyever might that be?"

"I, um . . ." I choked on my response. He was tracing the waistband of my jeans with his fingertips, causing a tingling warmth to cascade throughout my body.

"Hold onto that thought," he said, pulling past me and continuing toward the doorway.

His footsteps stopped, I assumed because he'd reached Nik. I *assumed* because I wasn't ready to turn around and face them all wobbly kneed and googly eyed. But as embarrassed as I was that Nik had caught us making out—right next to Tarset's bed, no less—I was immensely grateful to Marcus for being able to distract me from our dire situation.

"So this is how it starts," Marcus said, his voice low and quiet. "Did you know?"

My ears perked up. *This is how* what *starts? War? The end of the world?*

"I think Re suspected," Nik said. "But he doesn't share everything with me."

"I see. Is everyone gathered?" Marcus asked.

"For the most part. We're waiting on a couple Council members to link up, and Dom is on his way now."

"Good," Marcus said. "Let's head up. Lex?"

I inhaled deeply, then blew out the breath. Turning, I forced a tight smile. "Ready when you are."

Nik faced me, flashing his pearlescent eyes. Re was back in control. He gestured to my abdomen. "Your children's defensive reaction should be proportionately relative to the severity of the perceived threat. If the twins sense a more minor danger—such as Apep lying in wait in his host but not overtly attacking you—they'll likely not react so drastically and merely become upset, thus alerting *you* of the danger by making you feel off, possibly even nauseated."

Frowning, I nodded slowly. I was fairly certain I knew what that would feel like. A couple weeks ago, a harmless-looking pocket watch came into my possession, bringing with it a nauseating sense of complete and utter wrongness. The watch had been crafted from an obsidian-like material Kat had dubbed "anti-At"—the physical manifestation of the universal force polar opposite to At. When given physical form, anti-At became a ravenous, soul-sucking material that consumed all it touched. Any Nejeret unlucky enough to come into contact with it would slowly unravel from the ba out, all threads tying them to the timeline rotting away until it was as though they'd never even existed.

The anti-At pocket watch had been a "gift" from the Kin, and the closer I'd come to it, the stranger I'd felt. My discomfort had been a warning from the twins, and once we'd enclosed the watch in a shell of solidified At, the sensation had abated. It was no longer a threat.

"And conversely," Re-Nik continued, "the twins should not have any reaction if they don't sense danger. It is the most definite way to tell if someone is a threat to you or them."

"So, what—you want to use me as some kind of an Apep detector?"

"Precisely, dear Alexandra," Re beamed at me using Nik's lips and cheeks and eyes. It was a little disconcerting, seeing the godly pride I'd come so used to seeing on Nuin's face altering Nik's features. "Wouldn't it be nice if we could expand our protective barrier to include all of our trusted people instead of carrying it around with us everywhere we go?"

"Or we could just run," I suggested. I looked at Marcus. "You've got a helicopter. Let's fly somewhere . . . get away. If we go now—"

"It won't do you any good," Re-Nik said, drawing my attention back to him. "Apep can sense the sheuts your twins carry. Their power calls to him. Wherever they go, he will find you."

"But—"

"Apep *will* track you down, and the twins *will* jump you to a safer time and place," Re-Nik said, talking over my objection. "It is already written in the timeline, my Alexandra. It is what *is*."

"Oh," I said numbly. "Oh, I see. Well then . . ." I frowned. "Did you know?" I looked from him to Marcus and back. "Those things you keep saying—'this is how it starts' and the like . . . did you know this would happen?"

"No, Lex," Marcus said. "I knew—"

"Heru . . ." Re-Nik's voice was ripe with warning.

Marcus exhaled heavily, rubbing his hand over his shaved head. "I knew nothing of this—of Apep or Carson or Genevieve." He stared at Re-Nik, his gaze hard, challenging. "I only knew you would travel through time once more."

My mouth fell open. "And you didn't tell me?"

"Aset warned me the stress would be unsafe for you and the children so early on in the pregnancy."

"What about the stress of traveling through freaking time?"

"We only did what had to be done to keep you and the little ones safe," Re-Nik said. "Your health and comfort have always been our top priority."

I made an ugly scoffing noise but couldn't bring myself to actually speak. I was too pissed.

Marcus cleared his throat. "Should we get on with this, then?"

I nodded once, unable to even look at him, the liar.

Re-Nik encased us in a bubble of solidified At, and the three of us made our way up to the conference room on the second floor of the house. By the time I'd finished clearing Neffe, Aset, Carlisle, and my heads of guards, Sandra and Vali, who'd all been waiting for us in the conference room, Dominic had arrived.

Nik shrouded the room in a film of impenetrable At, and the nine of us took our seats around a circular mahogany table, the six virtually present members of the Council of Seven visible on the monitors hanging at even intervals on the walls around the room. Among them were my great-grandfather, Ivan, and my biological father, Set, the latter of which who shared a screen with my grandfather, Alexander. Set and Alexander were currently in Eastern Washington, watching over my family—my parents, sister, and grandma—as they packed up enough of their lives to move here for the duration of my sister's and my pregnancies.

I glanced over my shoulder at burly Ivan, with his sculpted goatee and diamond-hard eyes. He gave me a somber nod in greeting. Alexander and Set shared the screen on the wall directly opposite Ivan, sitting shoulder to shoulder and looking cozy as could be. I no longer thought of Set as the man he'd been while possessed by Apep; though others still had issues separating Set's actions from Apep's, he was, to me, once again, the kindly man he'd been millennia ago, when his body had been his and his alone.

I shifted in my chair, my focus flitting to the open doorway. A thin sheet of At provided us more than enough privacy, though it felt like a flimsy wisp of a barrier to me. It was nothing but a false sense of security. A glorified alarm system. Despite Re's assurances that the twins' latent power would kick in the moment they sensed danger, I couldn't help but feel that once we were alerted to the danger, it would be too late.

"We'll get through this, Little Ivanov," Marcus said, his voice barely a whisper. He was seated on my right, Re-Nik on my left. Marcus claimed my hand under the table and gripped it tight. When I tried to jerk my hand free, he held on. "*We* will get through this."

I gritted my teeth and managed a tight, close-lipped smile. I still couldn't bring myself to look into his lying eyes. "Of course we will," I murmured.

"We all know why this emergency meeting has been called," Ivan said. "Dominic, if you would begin."

All eyes shifted to my half-brother, seated on Marcus's other side, and a breathless hush fell over the room.

"Yes, of course," Dominic said. "The prisoners told me much, most willingly." His dark eyes turned to Marcus, then settled on me. "They claim they did not know it would come to this. Both believed the Kin's false goals of taking down the Council, of establishing a new world order, with a democratic system of Nejeret ruling over humans from the shadows to usher in a modern golden age. Neither was aware of an extremist faction within their ranks." He paused to meet the eyes of every Nejeret seated around the table, virtual and otherwise. "I believe them."

His chest rose as he inhaled deeply. "It would seem that Carson witnessed a member of the Kin called Bree—apparently a Nejerette with a sheut, like Nik—free Apep from his prison and welcome him into her body. Carson fled and alerted Gen of what he'd seen, and together the two came straight here to warn us." Dominic's eyes honed in on Re-Nik. "You allowed others with sheuts to be born. You did not do a good enough job of policing the timeline."

"Watch yourself, Dominic," Ivan cut in. "Do not forget to whom you are speaking."

"I could never forget," Dominic said, his voice low and cold. He blinked, then seemed to shake himself out of a trance and once again scanned the faces surrounding the table. "There are more Nejerets with sheuts than just Nik and this Bree, not to mention whoever created the anti-At pocket watch. Gen claims that dozens, if not hundreds, of the Kin's members have sheuts. Their power sounds slight in comparison to what the Meswett could do with the full Netjer sheut, but their minor sheuts do afford them a variety of special abilities, nonetheless. Somehow"—he shot a quick glare at Re-Nik—"they seem to have found a way to hide themselves from our ever watchful and diligent *Great Father*."

"Dominic," Ivan warned.

A thought struck me, and I sat up straighter. "Can one of them travel through time?"

Dominic's eyes narrowed infinitesimally. "How did you know?"

"A time anomaly—that's how they could be hiding from us. One of the Kin's members being from another time would conceal them from us for, I don't know, however long they've been building up their army of über-Nejerets. And it would be effortless—no need for cloaking in the echoes or anything like that. The time traveler just needs to be slightly out of time, and they and everything they influence around them won't show up in the echoes."

"I am in agreement with Alexandra," Re-Nik said. "It is the

only way they could have remained hidden from me for any amount of time."

Dominic looked from Re-Nik to me and back. "Their leader, Mei, is supposedly ancient and somehow managed to go undetected until she discovered her ability to travel through time. For whatever reason, she started forming the Kin in utter secrecy hundreds, maybe thousands of years ago. Gen and Carson were unsure. As the Kin's numbers grew, so did Mei's power. Gen claims Mei had no interest in freeing Apep—"

"Then why hasn't she gone back in time to stop it from happening?" I asked.

"Unless she can't," Re-Nik said. "Because she's dead . . ."

I looked at him, eyebrows scrunched together.

"Mei's body was found only moments after Apep was freed," Dominic said, confirming Re's supposition.

I felt sick, and slightly breathless. Just when I'd grown used to my current perception of the world, immortal beings with powers over time and all—godly children *and all*—the universe had to go and throw a viper into the mix. I was done. I didn't want to know any more. No more surprises. No more revelations. No more.

"From all that Gen and Carson have told me—we do not know how many people might be working with this Bree or how long it will take Apep to settle into her body." Dominic looked at me, his dark, deep-set eyes filled with compassion. "Assuming Apep's goal is unchanged and he will, once again, attempt to possess the being currently holding what was once his sheut, we must expect him to come for you, Lex. And as such, we must prepare for the worst—that Apep is only minutes from our gates now, and that his and Bree's companions are numerous and possess every possible sheut ability imaginable."

My tongue turned into a cottony thing, so dry it stuck to the roof of my mouth. I wanted to throw up.

"Do not fear, my Alexandra," Re-Nik said, leaning closer and rubbing my arm in what I supposed was meant to be a comforting gesture. Maybe it would have been if I could still feel. But I was numb, absolutely and completely.

I once had an odd conversation with an anatomy grad student over drinks, something that had stuck with me, though I hadn't realized it until now. He told me that nature had the kindness of a mother, because when faced with deadly physical trauma, an animal—any animal—will go into shock. Their brain will sort of shut off the part of them that feels afraid, that worries, that thinks about the winter stash of nuts that will go uneaten or the babies that will starve in their absence. When faced with certain death, they go numb, mentally, physically, emotionally. Nature, benevolent mother that she is, provides them at least this comfort in the end.

I couldn't help but wonder if Mother Nature was reaching out to me now, a preemptive attempt to cloak me in peace before the inevitable.

"Lex." Marcus squeezed my other arm, not enough to hurt, but enough to shake me from my languid acceptance.

Damn it, I'd never been a quitter. I wasn't about to start now.

"When the time comes," Re-Nik said, his expression earnest, "the twins will protect you. They will whisk you off to safety. It is already written into the timeline. You must simply let it happen."

I drew in a shallow breath, then another. Another. I had a bone to pick with him, Aset, and Marcus, all of whom had lied to me about my supposedly fast-approaching travels through time, but this was neither the time nor the place for that. I shelved my hurt and betrayal, tucking this latest edition in beside all the others I'd collected this past year, and focused on another worry. "What about the rest of you?"

While I might be whisked off to safety by the godly children in my womb, people I cared about would be left behind. Marcus and Dominic and the others—young, innocent Kat and poor little Tarset—they would be here, facing down an unknown number of super-Nejerets with unimaginable powers.

I looked at Marcus for the first time since we left Tarset's room, feeling like a doe staring down a mountain lion. "You have to get everyone away from here—away from me. You can't fight these people, Marcus. *Don't* fight them. You have to run."

A hard glint flashed in his eyes, a dark promise eclipsing their golden glow. "What would be the fun in that?"

"TALK TO ME, LITTLE IVANOV." MARCUS PLANTED himself behind me, placing his hands on my shoulders. We were in our suite's sitting room. I'd been staring out the tall window for some time, watching dusk fall over the forest and the Puget Sound beyond, stewing in a mess of hurt feelings.

I gave his hands the slip and sidestepped to the next window over. Usually, I would go for a walk by myself to clear my head, but that was out of the question now. A bald eagle soared over the treetops outside. I envied it for its freedom.

"Lex . . ." Thankfully, Marcus stayed where he was. A good thing, because I'd have slapped him if he tried to touch me again right now.

I crossed my arms over my chest. "Is it just chemicals? Is that all we are—a pair of perfectly matched pheromone producers?" When Marcus didn't say anything, my head drooped. "How long have you known I would be traveling back in time again?" *How long have you been lying to me?*

"Since you came back from Kemet," he said, using the ancient name for *Egypt*. "When you unblocked my memories, you unblocked all of them . . . not just the ones you've been a part of so far."

I laughed under my breath and shook my head. "I feel like

I've been the butt of some sick joke between you, Aset, Nik, and Re."

"Nobody is laughing at you."

"No, you're just whispering about me in dark corners, planning my future—"

"What need do I have to plan your future, Lex, when it is my past?"

I looked at Marcus, drawn by the heat in his voice.

He moved to stand in front of me, his perfect face a thundercloud staring down at me, threatening a storm. "I live in fear every second of every day that each moment will be the last I share with you. And at the same time, I worry I'll slip up and reveal something to you that will change things. Your future is my past, Little Ivanov. That's all I've known since you returned to me. *Your* future is *my* past, and anything I tell you about what's to come—any way I try to prepare you—might change how you act in that future. In *my* past. The very same past that has led us here to this moment. It is a loop that *cannot* be broken. This timeline—*our* timeline—must be protected."

I sucked in a halting breath, then gave in and leaned against him. "I understand."

His arms wrapped around me, encasing me in a false sense of security.

"I'm still mad at you," I said against his shirt.

He chuckled, resting his chin atop my head. "I would expect nothing less."

5

FOOL & FOIL

I'd never felt less safe in Marcus's home. It was the knowing, I supposed. The sense of dreadful inevitability. The sun shining brightly through the living room's broad picture window mocked me with its cheerful light. Usually I found Marcus's taste in furnishings and decor too modern and cold with all of its sleek, clean lines and wide array of gray tones. But not this morning. At present, gray and cold fit my mood perfectly.

I sat on the end of the couch furthest from the snickering sunshine, one leg tucked under me, the foot of the other ticking the passing seconds just above the ashen hardwood floor. Thora, my brown tabby, and Rus, my ancient fluff ball of a kitten, basked in a rectangle of sunlight a few feet from my toes.

Kat, my half-sister, sighed, and I cast her a sideways glance. She was sitting on the far end of the couch, elbow on the squared-off sofa arm, cheek resting on her palm, and one slipper sitting on its side, forgotten on the floor. She looked even more miserable than me. Poor thing. Her mom was upstairs, locked away in the conference room with Dominic. In the days since Genevieve and Carson arrived, Dominic had taken to interrogating Genevieve in the house, far away from Carson's prying Nejeret ears.

I was a wreck, constantly worrying about what would happen tomorrow . . . later today . . . in five minutes. At some point, I would be yanked away from this time and place; that much was all but written in stone. I just didn't know *when* it would happen, and the anticipation was killing me.

Even so, I couldn't imagine being in Kat's shoes—or shoe, in the case of her abandoned slipper. She was one of a kind, and not in any enviable way. She was, like me, a newly minted Nejerette, and she was, like me, a daughter of Set. But unlike me, Kat was also a product of gross incest—Apep-Set having seduced his own unwitting daughter, Genevieve. The reality of Kat's bloodline had come to light several months ago, revealed by Marcus in a last-ditch effort to rescue my ba from Apep-Set's prison in the At. Only someone so genetically close to Set could break through his prison's walls.

Unfortunately for Kat, eighteen at the time, she was still a few years away from manifesting, which meant her Nejerette traits had to be triggered early by forcing her into the At. Her body was forever stuck at its current level of maturity. She hadn't cared. Once she'd heard that she was my only shot, she'd volunteered—against her mom's wishes, of course—knowing full well that she would be the world's first eternal teenager. She'd saved me, dooming herself to be forever eighteen in the process.

And just a few weeks later, Kat's mom had left to join the Kin. Genevieve's reasons were noble enough, I had to admit—from Dom's interrogations, I knew she'd thrown her lot in with the Kin in order to create a more tolerant world for her daughter. Kat wouldn't talk to anyone about it, but it was clear that Genevieve's return was torture for her. She refused to visit her mother, no matter how many times Dominic relayed

Genevieve's requests. It was painful to watch. I couldn't imagine living it.

Figuring it was just about time for us both to suck it up and stop wallowing—or, at least, to make a show of it, I cleared my throat and forced a wooden smile. "Hey, Kit-Kat . . ."

I waited for her to glance my way. I could practically see the dark cloud raining down on her.

"I'm going to head down and check on Tarsi. Come with me?" The four-year-old was still comatose, but neither Neffe nor Aset could say for certain whether Tarset could or couldn't sense us when we visited her. I chose to assume she knew we were there and therefore visited her often, sometimes reading to her, sometimes just talking to her, and sometimes simply sitting there, holding her hand. It helped to pass the time. But even more so, it felt right.

Kat's long mane of curly chestnut hair was knotted into a messy bun atop her head, and the stray curls sticking out here and there would've lent her a wild, wacky appearance had the usual sparkle shone in her brown eyes. But the glassy, dull gleam, the faraway stare despite looking directly at me, made her simply look wrung-out.

"Sure," she said with a halfhearted shrug.

Stretching and groaning, I hauled myself up off the sofa, earning disinterested glances from the cats for disturbing their sunbathing. Kat rose as well and had to fish around the floor for a moment to recapture her lost slipper. She dragged her feet as she followed me into the entryway, the rubber bottoms of her slippers marking her path with a shsh-shsh-shsh.

"Lex!"

I sucked in a breath and clutched at my chest with one hand, flinging my other arm out in front of Kat like my mom always did when she had to brake suddenly.

Nik came barreling down the stairway, taking the steps four at a time and reaching the bottom in barely three strides. "Get into the basement and lock the door!" he ordered as he flew past us.

Kat and I stumbled backward a few steps, and Kat's hands latched onto my arm.

Marcus and Dominic were halfway down the stairs, Neffe and Aset close behind them. The two ancient Nejerettes hauled a distraught Genevieve between them, twisting in their hold and gasping, "I didn't know! I swear, I didn't know!" She spotted her daughter clinging to me at the bottom of the stairs and redoubled her efforts. "I swear, Kat! I had no idea!"

"Now, Lex!" Nik took hold of my arm, practically dragging me to the basement door.

"What's going on?" Panic threaded through my words. I didn't fight against Nik, but I couldn't help but stare back at Marcus as I passed him. "Is this it? Is it Apep? Is it time?"

Someone banged on the front door hard enough to rattle it on its sturdy hinges, and I had my answer. Nik had enshrouded the entire house and its immediate grounds in a shell of solidified At, and the only way anyone would've been able to get to the door would have been *through* the At.

"Yes," Marcus said, pushing me after Nik. "Now go!" As we'd talked strategy over the past week, Marcus had revealed that it seemed to take the twins' innate defense mechanism a little while to warm up, especially earlier on in my pregnancy. Our first priority was to buy them time once we knew Apep was here, his threat to me—to the twins—imminent.

I watched, wide-eyed and gaping, as the shimmering iridescence of At crept across the surface of the door like the deepest of freezes, transforming it into the otherworldly material. A moment later, the entire door dissolved into a glittering dust that floated away in the warm, midday air.

Carson stood in the open doorway, my old grad school peer. My academic competitor. The adorable, goofy, sweet young man who'd tricked me into believing he was my friend. The Nejeret who'd been in a healing trance just days ago. The one actual living person who I blamed for this entire, hopeless situation.

When his eyes met mine, an all-too-familiar inky darkness churned just below the surface, and my knees gave out.

"No . . ."

Nik shoved me behind himself, though I would've gone willingly. Hell, I *was* going willingly, but my foot tangled with Kat's, and we both stumbled to the floor.

Carson—or rather, Apep—twisted his lips into a cruel sneer, his bright blue eyes laughing at us. At me. "Hello, *Mother.*"

"M—mother?" My stomach twisted, and I pressed my palm against my belly to stave off a rush of nausea. Was I looking at some time-traveling version of my grown-up unborn son?

Some distant, less dumbfounded part of my brain puzzled out his meaning. Carson wasn't my son. And he wasn't here to kill me, or to kill my children. He wanted to possess them—to ooze into their still-forming bodies, eject their emerging souls, and hoard their sheuts, their power, for himself. He wanted to *become* my child. To become the most powerful being in all the universe. And I would be his mother.

The prospect was more terrifying than death.

I was on my knees and pulling Kat up with me when a strange, butterfly-like sensation tickled me from deep within. It was closely followed by a gut-twisting cramp. I doubled over but didn't give up the retreat. I crawled toward the basement door, Kat pushing my rear to propel me ahead.

Behind me, Kat yelped, and a moment later, the grunts of a scuffle give way to heavy breathing and a whole lot of nothing else. I risked a backward glance, daring to hope it was over and that Apep-Carson had somehow been subdued. Damn hope gets me every time.

Wearing what appeared to be a glimmering, almost transparent suit of armor, Apep-Carson stood before a trembling Kat. He was holding a pistol, the nozzle pressed against her forehead. Marcus stood just out of arm's reach of Kat, hands upraised in surrender, Nik stood a few feet away from me, and Dominic lay sprawled on the ground near the missing front door, framed by a seeping puddle of blood.

I slapped a hand over my mouth.

Dominic wasn't moving. I couldn't even be sure he was still breathing, and with all that blood . . .

And Kat—this was the second time Carson had held her at gunpoint. It didn't matter that he was possessed by Apep this time. I could only imagine how terrified she was.

"Let me pass or I'll kill sweet little Kat here," Apep said, using my former friend's lips.

The combination of emotions I felt toward him and Carson at that moment knotted in my stomach, and I groaned under a violent wave of nausea. I gritted my teeth when another cramp throbbed in my belly, and some remote part of my mind realized that maybe it wasn't the terror of the situation or the fear for Kat's and Dominic's lives or the disgust and betrayal that was causing my gut-wrenching discomfort.

Smoky threads surrounded me in reds and blues and yellows, wrapping around me like a ghostly cocoon. *It's the twins,* I realized. They were reacting to the threat, trying to carry me—and, with me, themselves—away to safety.

Apep-Carson took a step forward—toward me—forcing Kat to step backward awkwardly. Another step. Another.

"Nik . . ." Marcus's voice contained a warning.

"I know," Nik snapped. "I'm not fucking blind!"

The gossamer rainbow surrounding me was growing denser, but it was still somewhat transparent. I was still here. The twins were still vulnerable to Apep. Their built-in defense mechanism was taking too damn long.

"Don't you go anywhere yet, *Mother*." Apep-Carson was close. Too close. Maybe a couple yards away.

Nik made as though to step between us, but Apep-Carson

tutted him. "I really wouldn't, if I were you," the possessed Nejeret said, his tone dripping with condescension. Another step. "You won't stop me."

"Who said anything about stopping you, shit-stain?" Nik growled, lurching to stand before me. A sheet of At sprouted from both of his hands, curving around me until I was locked away in an impenetrable shell, surrounded by nothing but silence and that thickening, otherworldly mist.

I watched, sealed away, as Genevieve launched herself not at Apep-Carson, but at Kat. She shoved her daughter to the side with the force of her impact.

Not a second later, blood and hair and bone and other things sprayed from the back of Genevieve's head.

It was the last thing I saw before the misty rainbow smoke thickened to opacity, and the world fell away.

"No!" I screamed. Because I was safe now, but everyone else I'd just left behind might very well be dead. I slapped the inside of my crystalized pod with both hands and howled in outrage, in pain, in desperation. *"Noooo!"*

My cocoon vanished between one slap and the next, and I fell forward on my hands and knees. The swirling colors of the At burst to life around me, and I floated there, breathless and terrified for the others. A moment later, an unrelenting black abyss consumed me.

6

LOST & FOUND

When I came to, I found that I was lying on a forest floor, an unkempt older fellow peering down at me, his face barely a foot from mine. Beyond him, pine trees stretched high overhead, their needles glowing emeralds in the bright sunlight. It looked like home. Aside from the guy standing over me.

I drew back, as much from his stench as from the surprise, and smacked the side of my head against a tree trunk. I sat up and scurried backward a few feet through the overgrown underbrush. My hair caught in the rough bark, and I lost a good chunk out of my ponytail in the process.

"Ouch!" I yelped when I felt a string of sharp stings in my palm. I halted my retreat, yanking my hand from the ground and settling on my butt. I glanced down at the line of tiny, bloody pearls beaded on my palm. Damn blackberry vines . . . they were everywhere, hidden among the ferns and bushes.

"I thought you was dead," the stranger said.

Forgetting about my stinging palm, I looked at the man crouching a few yards away.

He wore buckskin from neck to toe, the outfit boasting more

fringe than a neo-hippie would know what to do with, and had a long, bushy salt-and-pepper beard. A leather satchel crossed his body, and I could've sworn he was wearing an entire raccoon on his head. The thing went far beyond an iconic coonskin cap; the fur of the entire critter was on his head, from the fluffy ringed tail pulled over his shoulder to the pointy little black nose sticking down his forehead and almost reaching his bushy eyebrows. Little forelegs dangled on either side of his face, clawed feet and all.

There was no doubt in my mind that I was in the past. Still in the Pacific Northwest, though, from the looks of the forest. And if the stranger's garb was anything to go by, he was a fur trapper. That placed me in the late eighteenth or nineteenth century, well before the small battle that was taking place in my time in Marcus's foyer. If it was even still going on. If any of them were even still alive.

I stared at the trapper's hat, focusing on the raccoon's little claws.

Genevieve was dead, that was a sad certainty. Possibly Dominic, too—there'd been so much blood. And the others? Marcus and Kat? Nik? Aset and Neffe? There was no way to know. The horrifying possibilities surrounded me, blocking out where I was. *When* I was. Blocking out the stranger standing nearby. Blocking out everything except for the terrible prospect that they were all dead.

The trapper touched his hat, his eyes sliding down to the underbrush. "My summer cap . . ." His eyes met mine, almost defiantly. "I got me a coyote I wear when the weather turns. Shot and skinned the beast myself."

"I—" Barely a crack of sound came out. I cleared my throat. "I have no doubt," I said cautiously. "You look like a very formidable man." Something to keep in mind when I let my thoughts stray into the land of ifs and could-bes, when I felt the numbness of shock threatening to creep over me. They might very well all be dead. But they might not be. I simply didn't know. I *wouldn't* know until I made it back to them, however the hell I was supposed to manage that. But their fate wasn't the most urgent matter right now. My kids were—my kids, and the very real threat this fur trapper could be.

The trapper narrowed his eyes. "You got a strange way of talkin'." His eyes slid down the length of my body with only a hint of lechery. "And a strange way of lookin'."

"I, um . . ." I shot a quick glance down at myself. Jeans and a T-shirt—how to explain jeans and a T-shirt to a fur trapper from the Western frontier?

"You escape from the Indians? Or are you some kind of wandering whore?" His eyes narrowed, drawing the raccoon's nose down along with his eyebrows. He snapped his fingers, his face lighting up. "I got it—you're one of them Mercer Girls, ain't you? I heard tell some of them've got a wild way about 'em."

"I, um . . ." *Mercer Girls*—the term was familiar, but I couldn't quite put my finger on it. My mind kept circling back to that foyer . . . to the blood . . . "Yes!" I said when it finally clicked.

The Mercer Girls had been transported to Seattle from the East Coast in the 1860s by one of the founders of the University of Washington to help balance out the population of settlers by bringing in single, *reputable* young women of a marriageable age.

"I . . . wanted to explore a bit," I said. "Get out of Seattle and experience the true Wild West, so . . ." I gestured around me with my bleeding hand. "Here I am."

The trapper stared at me without speaking a while longer. "You shouldn't be out here. Where's your things?" His focus shifted to my hand. "You're gonna need to clean that, lest it get inflamed. Ain't no doctors out here."

"My things—" I shook my head. "I don't—they're gone. Someone took them . . . after I set up camp last night. I was . . . washing up on the beach, and . . ."

My companion grunted. "Unsavory folks have been known to

hide out in these here parts. Not many are too keen to make the trip onto the island—'cept for the Indians and a couple other trappers. We got a 'live and let live' deal here, we do, so it ain't likely to be any of them that done took your possessions . . ." He coughed and spit something dark and slimy. "What's your name?"

I stood there, mouth open but silent for several seconds. "My, uh, name is Alexandra," I said. "Larson," I added. "Of Boston." I was fairly certain that was where the Mercer Girls had originated.

"Yeah, well, I'm Tex," my companion said. "Of Texas."

I gave a small bow of my head. "Nice to meet you, Tex," I said, hoping decent manners might decrease the likelihood that Tex would assault, rape, or murder me. Of course, if he intended to do any of those things, I figured he'd have done it while I was unconscious.

"Why don't you let old Tex here fix up that hand for you," Tex said, taking a step toward me. He extended one arm as though to calm a skittish critter. "Then we'll get you somewhere safe."

I held my hand to my chest, curling my fingers over the injury. My palm throbbed in protest. "It's just a few scratches." And had my pregnancy not suppressed my Nejeret regenerative abilities, I'd have been well on my way to being healed by now. But I wasn't, which was a frightening reminder of my current rather fragile state.

"Inflammation don't care a thing about that," Tex said. "A scratch is all it takes." He took another step toward me while reaching through the front opening of his buckskin jacket. "But if we give it a good wash with this," he said, pulling out a gourd canteen small enough to be considered a flask, "I think you'll survive."

I uncurled my fingers enough that I could see the four angry, red punctures seeping blood onto my palm. They were small, but the thorns had gone in deep, and just that small motion of moving my fingers increased the throbbing pain. "What's in there?" I asked, pointing to the flask with my chin. If it would prevent infection, I wouldn't say no to his offer.

Tex blinked, and his beard shimmied as he worked his mouth. "Why, whiskey, of course." He said it like it was the most obvious thing in the world. The sky is blue. Fish live in the water. There's whiskey in the flask.

I cringed. Whiskey would sting like a bitch.

Tex pulled the cork with his teeth and spat it out to take a swig. The cork dangled by a thin leather cord. "Well . . ." He cleared his throat roughly. "What's it gonna be?"

I extended my hand, trembling not from fear of pain but from the force of my bottled-up emotions. "Alright, go ahead." I yanked my hand away almost as soon as the liquid touched my skin, burning worse than fire. My eyes watered, and I gritted my teeth. The deed was done.

Tex's soulful brown eyes shone with mirth. "I reckon you've had just about enough of adventuring and exploring right about now."

I nodded. He had no idea just how tired I was of all of my "adventuring." I just wanted to settle down with Marcus *in my own time* and raise our kids together to be the ma'at-balancing gods they were destined to be. Maybe spend a few months each year in Egypt or Italy, uncovering the past the old-fashioned way —with a trowel, brushes, and dental tools—rather than viewing it in the echoes.

Now, I didn't know if any of that would ever be a possibility, and thinking about it opened up the doors for all the other things that could've been but now might never be. My chest ached, and my eyes stung. *If Marcus is dead . . .*

"Well, now . . ." Tex patted my arm. "This ain't no place for tears." He handed me the flask. "Best bolster your resolve. Go on"—he flicked his fingers at the flask—"take a drink."

I nodded and brought the flask to my lips.

You're pregnant!

I froze. With shaking fingers, I recorked the flask and handed it back to Tex. "I appreciate the offer, I really do, but I shouldn't. Spirits go straight to my head." I flashed him a weak smile.

"Well, be that as it may," Tex said, tucking the flask away in his jacket and giving the panel a soft pat, "you know where find this if you decide your resolve is in need of some bolsterin'."

"Thanks." My eyes met his. "Really, Tex, thank you. I don't know what I would've done if you hadn't found me."

"Aw, well . . ." Tex hunched his shoulders and made a rough noise in his throat. "I may not be a gentleman, but I know a lady when I see one, I do. You've got a kindly way about you, Miss Larson, and with a sweet face like that, well . . . you don't belong out here."

"Trust me, Tex," I said, brushing off the back of my jeans with my good hand, "I couldn't agree with you more." I just wanted to go home. I needed to *know*.

"Well then, let's get you up to Port Madison—traders come in and out of there every couple of days. One of them is sure to be willing to escort you back to civilization."

Port Madison—that was the reservation just across the Agate Passage from the northern tip of Bainbridge Island. You could see the shore from the beach just outside the compound's walls. If we were near Port Madison, then I was closer to home than I'd thought. The realization spurred a surge of excitement, followed by a deluge of grief. Being "home" wouldn't do me any good. It was just about the worst case of right-place-wrong-time imaginable.

Regardless, I had to start looking for Marcus—*this* time's Marcus—somewhere. I only had a matter of days before the bonding withdrawals would set in, and based on the almost-nothing Marcus had told me about my pending travels through time, I *would* find him, each and every time. I figured I might as well start looking in Port Madison.

I bowed my head to Tex. "I'd appreciate that."

He turned and started picking his way through the underbrush.

"You don't, by any chance, know of any prominent men in the area with the name Bahur?" I ventured as I followed, making about three times as much noise as him. "Or Horus?"

"I can't rightly say I do," he said over his shoulder. "You hunting for someone? That what brought you all the way out here, Miss Larson?"

"No, I—well, yes, I suppose I am." Crouching down, I picked up a several-foot-long stick, intending to use it to push bushes out of my way as we trailblazed. I don't recommend tromping through the woods in sandals. "How about Heru?"

Tex's head tilted to the side, and he looked at me sidelong. "What sort of a name is 'Heru'?"

I pressed down a blackberry vine as thick as my thumb. "Egyptian." The plump berries bunched together along the vine were a deep purple, practically falling off with their ripeness. They filled the forest with their sweet aroma, mixing with the scent of decaying pine needles in the most intoxicating way.

Tex whistled. "Can't say as I've ever met an Egyptian. But seeing as they're supposed to have darker skin like the Indians, I reckon they must be related in some way." He nodded to himself.

"I suppose," I said, not wanting to start a debate about evolution, human migration, and the origin of the human species. I really wasn't in the mood.

"So what are you tracking this feller down for? A matter of the heart?" For a rustic old trapper, Tex sure was a chatty guy.

"It's more of a matter of life and death," I said with appropriate gravitas. Once the bonding withdrawals started, it would be only a matter of days until they actually killed me. I placed my hand on my abdomen. Not just me. "I have to find him."

"Is that so? Well then, we best hurry." Tex sort of hopped-leapt over a waist-high fallen log, then turned and held his hand out to help me over.

We'd reached a beach, the sparkling Puget Sound stretching out beyond the rocky shore, the tide line strewn with driftwood, seafoam, and kelp. Two seagulls swooped low overhead, calling out to one another.

Across the water some ways, a mass of vibrant evergreens grew out of the sea, several thick plumes of smoke steadily climbing among the dense trees. Before them, a massive wooden longhouse stretched along the top of the beach. I had to be looking at the Port Madison Indian Reservation, a Squamish settlement so unobtrusive in this time that it was barely visible from across the Agate Passage.

I stopped and stared out across the water, dumbfounded. So far as I could tell, I'd landed exactly where I'd been on the northwest tip of Bainbridge Island, just a hundred and fifty years in the past. I'd walked this beach dozens of times. I'd been closer to home than I'd thought; I'd been right on top of it.

"My canoe's just there, around the bend," Tex said, pointing down the beach. "There's a feller who sometimes trades at Port Madison—calls himself the Collector. He makes his rounds out here, going from reservation to reservation, trackin' people who come out here to get lost. He ain't no Indian, but he's darn near as good as one when it comes to trackin', and he keeps his ear to the ground where civilized affairs is concerned. Makes a good deal of money off huntin' people, I reckon he does." Tex glanced at me over his shoulder. "Might be worth asking around about him. And iffen he's in the area, it might be worth tracking him down to see if he's willin' to help you find your Egyptian . . . for the right price, of course."

"Of course," I said, taking a deep breath and letting it out slowly. I would allow myself a full freak-out later. I could ugly-cry and hyperventilate for days. Once I found Marcus. I just had to stuff my panic and fear and terror and worry somewhere deep inside me until then.

Picking up my foot, I jogged after Tex, thinking how lucky I'd been that our paths crossed.

7

HONEY & VINEGAR

"You just wait here, Miss Larson." Tex climbed out of the canoe and dragged it up onto the rocky shore, me still in it. "I'll ask around about the Collector. He don't linger much when he passes through, so if he's in the area, you ain't got time to waste dillydallyin' around here."

I nodded absently as I stared around at historic Port Madison. Technically, I specialized in "Old World" archaeology, mostly studying those ancient civilizations bordering the Mediterranean Sea, but that didn't decrease my interest in this slice of "New World" history. I'd known almost as much as there was to know about ancient Egypt when I'd traveled back to that time; comparatively, I knew next to nothing about the history of the peoples native to my beloved Pacific Northwest, beyond what I'd leaned in my single PNW archaeology course. I was both humbled and mortified by my ignorance.

"Just wait here," Tex repeated. "I'll return momentarily."

I watched him walk away, heading straight for the enormous longhouse up shore, then sort of climb-fell out of the canoe. This "Collector" guy might've been my best bet for finding

Marcus in the here and now, but he sure as hell wasn't my only option.

I watched Tex disappear through the longhouse's left-most door as I climbed the beach, heading toward the myriad of tents and wooden structures erected all around it, most covered with woven mats made from some plant fiber that reminded me of the reed mats that were everywhere in ancient Men-Nefer. I wondered what they used—some sort of bark? Or dried cattail, maybe? This village felt just as ancient as Men-Nefer; the absence of modern technology was just as glaring, the noises just as pure, devoid of the hum of motors and the buzz of electricity. And the people were just as busy, bustling around, carrying out daily tasks.

They wore an unexpected combination of Western and Native clothing—long cotton dresses or skirts with high-collared white blouses for the women and woolen trousers with white button-down shirts and suspenders or vests for the men, all accessorized on varying levels with woven belts, pouch purses, or shawls. Most of the men wore Western-style hats while many of the women tied their hair back with brightly patterned headscarves.

I passed by wooden racks of drying fish, cookfires and roasting spits, lean-tos containing looms or bushels of harvested cattails beside baskets and mats in various states of done-ness, stopping to speak to each person I saw along the way. I asked them if they spoke English, and if they did, then if they knew of a man named Heru—or Marcus or Horus. I struck out, big-time.

As I neared the longhouse, I couldn't resist the chance to take a peek inside. One of the few things I knew about the history of the Squamish people and the Port Madison Reservation was that this longhouse—called "Old Man House"—had been burned to the ground, supposedly as a preventative measure to stop the spread of infectious diseases. It was iconic—the largest longhouse in what was, in this time, the Oregon Territory—and stood on land that archaeological records showed had been occupied continuously for thousands of years. I couldn't skip the chance to see this historic sacred communal space firsthand. It was against my nature.

I was maybe a dozen steps away from the central doorway when Tex rushed out through it. I stopped in my tracks and blinked in surprise. I'd expected him to come back out the same way he'd gone in.

He planted himself directly in front of me, hands on his hips and face stern. "Didn't I tell you to wait at the canoe?"

"I thought I'd ask around while I waited for you." I tried to step around him, but he sidestepped to block me.

"The Collector was just here yesterday. We can't afford to waste any time lollygaggin' around here iffen we're to have any chance of catching up to him."

I raised my eyebrows. "We?"

Tex shrugged, then pushed past me and headed back down the beach toward his canoe. "I got business with him anyway, so it ain't no skin off my back."

I jogged after Tex.

"Assumin' you're still interested in utilizing his services," Tex said as he trudged along. "Otherwise, I'll just leave you here to wait for a trader to ferry you back to the city."

"No," I said, catching up to him. I fell in step beside him. "I want his help." I *needed* his help. Tracking down Marcus truly was a matter of life and death.

"Best be on our way, then," Tex said with a nod.

We neared a group of three women sitting on more of those cattail mats about halfway down the beach. Several woven baskets were spread out between them, all filled with salmon or their discarded heads and guts, and a wooden rack with three horizontal bars was set up beside them, cleaned fish hanging up to dry. They hadn't been there when I'd passed this section of the beach on my way up. They glanced our way as we approached, though their knives continued to work, cleaning and gutting with remarkable efficiency.

The oldest of the trio, a middle-aged woman wearing a long, red-and-black-patterned skirt and a white blouse, stood as we passed, pointing her knife in our direction. Well, more in Tex's direction than mine. She said something to Tex in her native tongue.

Tex stopped and turned to her, his hands once more migrating to his hips. "It ain't nothing to you who she is or what her business is with me." He turned to continue on his way, but I lingered a moment before following.

The woman's face darkened, her eyes narrowing. She said more in that incomprehensible language, all gibberish to me except for "Collector."

Tex froze, only a few steps away. "You don't know what you're talkin' about." Under his breath, he muttered, "Superstitious, primitive, backwards people . . ."

The Squamish woman let out a string of angry words and reached for me, her strong fingers latching onto my arm. I recognized three syllables: Netjer-At. It was the ancient Egyptian name for my people, translating to "god of time."

"Now you listen here," Tex said. "The Collector promised—"

"You *know,*" I said to the Squamish woman, staring at her. I was totally knocked off guard. "You know about my people?"

Her grip on my arm loosened and she bowed her head, a faint curving of her lips the first hint of the break in her stormy expression. "Yes. And I would ask you to speak with my father," she said, her English flawless. "He can explain much better." She leaned in close, her gaze flicking to Tex. "You are in danger. I concealed my words because I did not wish to frighten you, but whatever he promised you—it is a lie." She met my eyes, hers holding even more warning than her words. "The Collector is looking for a female Netjer-At. It is said he has been waiting for her for many lifetimes, searching this place, where the flow of time is disturbed." Her eyes never left mine. "Her name is Alexandra. Are you she?"

I stared at her, stunned. "How—how do you know my name?"

"Others are looking for you as well." She pulled back and glared at Tex. "Others who know you . . . who would help you, not deliver you to the Collector, however handsome the payment may be."

I looked at Tex, blindsided. "You were going to—to what? *Sell* me? But you were kind to me." I looked from him to the Squamish woman and back. "Why? Why didn't you just bash me over the head and drag me to this—this . . ." Dread replaced the hurt, and the blood drained from my face.

I knew who the Collector was. It had to be *him*—Set, my father, possessed by Apep's twisted, power-starved soul.

Tex mumbled something about honey and vinegar, then kicked a rock the size of a golf ball with the toe of his boot.

I barely heard him. "It's Set. That's the Collector's name, isn't it?"

"Please." The Squamish woman tugged on my arm. "Come into D'Suq'Wub, where you will be safe."

"But I won't be." The sun was already dipping back down toward the horizon; I'd spent valuable hours to get here, to Port Madison with Tex and his deceptive promises, and I only had so much time until the withdrawals kicked in. If Apep-Set found me before I found Marcus, the twins' sheuts would kick in again, and I'd be dragged further back in time. I'd have to start my hunt for Marcus all over again.

"He can sense me," I told the Squamish woman. "He already knows I'm here." I placed my hand over my stomach, hoping the sudden spike of terror didn't alert the twins that it was already time for another time jump. "He's coming for me. I have to go." I tried to pull my arm free. "Let me go, I have to—"

"Not yet." The Squamish woman's expression remained

compassionate, but her voice was laced with a hard vein of determination. "You must speak with my father, the chief of our people. He knows more of this than I do. He will help you. You will see."

"No, but—" Hope blossomed in my chest. What if she was right? What if her father, the chief, *was* Marcus? Or even Nik? Nik had never mentioned having fathered any children, but the guy had been alive for thousands *and thousands* of years; plus, he'd all but vanished for millennia, only reemerging with his mother a few months ago, my time. I didn't know why he and Aset had vanished, only that they had. I felt a surge of hope. If this chief *was* Marcus or Nik . . .

"Alright," I said, nodding once. "Take me to him."

A grin spread across the Squamish woman's face. It faded when her hawkish gaze slid to Tex. "You. Come. My father would have words with you, as well."

Tex's eyes widened and he spun on his heel, making a run for it. He made it all of five steps before the other two women in the salmon-cleaning circle caught him in a fishing net with a single, well-timed toss. Tex struggled against the hand-tied netting until he felt the pointy end of a fishing spear jabbing into his lower back. I stared at the woman holding the spear, blown away by how fast it had all happened.

"You will come with me and speak with my father," the first woman reiterated, then looked at me. "Let us hurry."

I nodded. When she released my arm, I followed without hesitation and we made our way back up the beach toward the longhouse.

"I am called Kikisoblu," she said.

"I'm Lex—Alexandra—but then, you already knew that."

Kikisoblu let out a dry laugh. "I was told to expect you. I grew up hearing from my father and grandmother about a woman with your name who would come here from another time, seeking sanctuary, but they were just stories. I have seen your likeness drawn on a cave wall, but that was just a picture. I must admit I did not truly believe you were real until this moment."

Both her father *and* grandmother had told her about me—told her to *expect* me. I felt almost certain that her father had to be Nik, her grandmother Aset. After all, nobody knew what they'd been doing all those years they'd been hiding, let alone *why* they'd hid. Maybe I was about to find out. Hope fanned to anticipation, to expectation. If Nik was there, in the longhouse, then I would be able to find out what happened in the foyer after I jumped back in time. Re could look into the future At. His soul was special—a ren—and he could see through the instability of the At in my native time; he could view the echo of the moment I'd left. He could tell if Marcus was still alive. If Dom had survived his wounds. If Kat and the others had made it through whatever happened *after*.

"Kikisoblu, what's your father's name?"

She looked at me as we neared the narrow doorway at the center of the longhouse's expansive face, her eyes widened in surprise. "Why, my father is Sealth, of course, for whom the great city of the white men across the sea has been named."

My hope deflated. Chief Sealth, namesake of Seattle, had been a central figure at this time, someone kids like me who grew up in Washington State learned about in elementary school alongside George Washington and the like. Cameras, however rudimentary, had existed during this era. I'd glued photographs of Chief Sealth onto a trifold poster board for a middle school project and had memorized and recited his most famous speech. Most of those photos had been of him as an extremely elderly man. Which meant Sealth couldn't be Nik, let alone Marcus. He couldn't even be Nejeret, because Nejeret don't age.

So how did he know about *me*?

8

BEND & BREAK

Kikisoblu led me into Old Man House—D'Suq'Wub—ahead of Tex and the woman escorting him at spear-point. The interior of the longhouse was dark and relatively empty, most of the inhabitants utilizing the favorable late summer weather to work outside. This central portion was sectioned off from the rest of the building with wooden walls roughly a dozen yards from the doorway on either side. A sunken rectangular fire pit stretched nearly the length of the room, a single cookfire in the very center of the space providing the only luminescence beyond the late afternoon light leaking in through the doorway and the small opening in the roof over the fire.

An elderly man sat on a woven mat on the opposite side of the fire pit, a vibrant red blanket draped over his broad shoulders. Two internal totem poles flanked him, one an enormous figure of a man, the other a woman. Both had been carved nude and with serious expressions, seeming to stand guard against the wall behind the old man. Behind Chief Sealth.

The iconic Squamish chief was such an enormous figure in the history of this area, his ideas, deeds, and words living on long after he was gone, that it seemed incongruous to my mind for him to appear so old, so frail. His heavily lined face and the turned-down corners of his mouth gave him an appearance of absolute solemnity, but the sparkle in his eyes hinted at the kind, wise nature I remembered from my studies.

As we approached, he held out a hand with huge, gnarled knuckles. "Please, sit." His voice was deep, but soft, and a kind smile transformed his wizened features. "I have been expecting you for a very long time, Alexandra of the Netjer-At people." Much to my surprise, he spoke in the original tongue—Nuin's ancient language—which was known to all of my people. But not to many humans.

I stared across the fire at Sealth, stunned. "How—" I shook my head. "You are not Netjer-At," I said, responding in the same language. "How do you know the original tongue?"

"Sit," Sealth repeated, pointing with his chin to the mats layered on the floor near his right knee, "and I will tell you my story." He smiled once more. "Or, at least, part of my story."

I did as he'd bid, rounding the long fire pit and folding my legs beneath me. My fingers fidgeted with the hem of my jeans.

Sealth seemed to be ignoring Tex, standing on the opposite side of the fire with a spear at his back, and waited only for Kikisoblu to settle in beside me to begin his tale.

"When I was a young boy," he said, still speaking in my people's ancient language, "first watching Vancouver's ships, my mother told me a story." His eyes twinkled with remembrance. "She told me it was a story that must never be spoken of except among my own children, as our bloodline had been chosen as the keepers of the tale. It was the story of the lady in the cave. Of the woman who watches time pass. Of the one time does not touch. It is the story of the woman who waits."

I held my breath, not wanting to shatter the delicate spell Sealth was weaving with his words.

He leaned forward. "Of the woman who waits for you,

Alexandra. And of the man who searches, hoping to steal you away before she can find you."

A young woman knelt on the far side of Sealth, and he accepted a small wooden bowl from her. She bore a strong resemblance to Kikisoblu. Sealth nodded to her and sipped from the bowl, then offered it to me.

I hesitated, but thirst quickly overwhelmed any fear of disease. I hadn't drunk water since arriving in this time; Tex had only offered me whiskey, and I'd been so preoccupied that I hadn't thought to ask for anything else. I took a sip, fully intending to pass the bowl on to Kikisoblu, but the water tasted so fresh and clean, and that single sip only reminded me how parched I was. I tilted the bowl back further and took several long gulps.

Sealth watched me, laughter in his eyes.

I lowered the empty bowl. "I did not realize how thirsty I was . . ."

Sealth reclaimed the bowl and handed it back to the young woman.

Meeting her eyes as she stood, I gave her a nod of thanks.

She bowed her head, then retreated to the back wall, where she dipped the bowl into a large, water-tight woven basket.

"The lady in the cave," Sealth said, reclaiming my attention. "She came to my grandmother's father one day when he was stalking a doe in the woods. My great-grandfather claimed the woman was the spirit of the doe. She offered him a trade—he and all of his descendants would enter her service, and in exchange, she would share her knowledge of the troubled times to come."

I accepted the refilled bowl from the young woman with another nod of thanks, then looked at Sealth once more.

"My great-grandfather agreed and, in so doing, bound our future to the woman's . . . and to yours. We gather information for her, keeping her apprised of the Collector's activities and of any Netjer-Ats who enter our territory, and in return, she advises us so that our people might survive."

"And have you met her?" I asked. "This 'lady in the cave'?" It had to be Aset. I crossed my fingers. It *had* to be.

Sealth nodded once, slowly. "The first time my mother brought me to the cave, it was the same day I first saw Vancouver's ships. My mother told me about the woman as we stood on the beach, staring at the strange, monstrous crafts floating on the water. She said we must go to the lady in the cave so she could advise us. And when we went to the cave, the woman greeted us by walking through a solid sheet of stone."

My heartbeat picked up. *It has to be Aset and Nik!* If I could get to them—to this cave—then I could find out what happened to the others after I left. I had to know. I was terrified to know.

"I was but a boy, and yet the woman held my hand in hers and kissed my forehead and told me not to fear the men on the ships. She told me more would come, but that she would help me guide my people through the gathering storm.

"The second time I went to the cave, I carried with me news of my mother's death. I was still a young man, not yet married or the father of children, but she told me of a great enemy from the north, of the tribe who would make good on their past threats to our people and our ancestral land. She told me I must convince my people to let me lead our warriors against this threat, that it was the only way we would survive.

"I did as she bade, and when I returned to her victorious, she taught me this language. Eventually, she told me what I must do to prevent my people from being washed away by the great and powerful wave of the white man spreading across this land. She told me that because they are countless, like the many blades of grass in a vast field, and we are few, the scattered trees standing tall across the field, we must learn to bend like the grass when the winds blow strong or we will break completely."

I cleared my throat. "The Point Elliott Treaty and the reservation—is that why you agreed to it? Why you convinced the other leaders to agree, as well? Because of what she told you?"

Sealth nodded sagely. "It is. I only hope she spoke the truth and that my people will continue on, bending, but not broken."

"She told you about me, did she not? About where and *when* I come from?"

"She did."

"Then know that she spoke the truth to you. Your people still live, even in my time. You are not the same you once were, but then, nothing ever is."

Sealth's eyes were shimmering and glassy. "I am immensely relieved," he said. He shook his head, reminding me of a great lion waking from an afternoon slumber. "But we are wasting precious time now. You have heard my story, and hopefully my family has earned your trust. We have been devoted to you and to the lady in the cave for generations."

"You have my trust," I said. "And my gratitude."

"Good." Sealth gestured with both hands for me to stand. "Please, go with my daughter." He switched to his native tongue and exchanged rushed words with Kikisoblu. Once I was standing, he returned his focus to me. "She will take you to the cave."

Sealth's attention shifted past me, and I glanced over my shoulder at Tex. "I will deal with this one."

9

UP & DOWN

I thanked Kikisoblu as we walked away from Old Man House. She'd given me boots made of supple leather, an enormous improvement over the sandals I'd been wearing. We made our way into the fringe of the woods bordering the beach, thick with pine trees, ferns, nettles, and dense underbrush. Well-worn trails cut through the woods, their paths cushioned by a thick layer of fallen pine needles.

"Think nothing of it," Kikisoblu said, taking the lead as we entered a narrow trail.

Just as I stepped over a rogue blackberry vine crossing the path, a pang of nausea struck me hard in my belly. I bent nearly double.

"Alexandra! Are you alright?"

I held a hand out to my side, keeping Kikisoblu at bay while I emptied the contents of my stomach onto the forest floor. I feared the nausea wasn't primarily because I was pregnant—not to mention exhausted and freaked out and worried as all hell—but because the twins sensed Apep closing in on me.

But after few more heaves, I felt the stomach-twisting sensation abate. I straightened. "I'm fine." My focus shifted to the trail winding an uphill path through the woods. "I really need to keep going."

"Come," Kikisoblu said. "Let us hurry." She started up the path, looking back at me every few steps. I was hot on her heels.

As the sun neared the horizon, its golden glow flickering between the trees, exhaustion settled into my legs and renewed thirst turned my saliva into a sticky paste. Hundreds or maybe thousands or millions or billions of steps later, Kikisoblu stopped. I looked up for the first time in ages to see that there were no blinding slivers of sunlight peeking between the endless sea of evergreens. I'd been too busy staring at the path, coaxing my feet to take just one more step, to notice that dusk had fallen.

I bent over, hands on my knees. "Why are we stopping?" I asked, chest heaving between each word. I spit tacky saliva onto the ground; it was so thick and glue-like that swallowing it no longer seemed possible.

"Because we are here."

"What?" I straightened, and the forest swam around me. I brought my hand up to my forehead and closed my eyes. "Whoa . . ."

Kikisoblu rushed back down the trail, her steadying grip on my elbow the only thing keeping me from swaying my way down to the ground. "Perhaps I pushed you too hard, but I thought—"

"No, no," I said, waving my hand. "You had to. We needed to get here as quickly as possible." With a deep breath, I opened my eyes and raised my head, wondering where exactly the lady and her cave were.

Dread washed over me as I stared at my guide. Had I done it again? Was I both grand-prize winner and runner-up for most gullible person in the world? First with Tex, and now with Sealth and Kikisoblu—had I put my depleted faith in the wrong person once more?

"The cave is just around the bend in the trail," Kikisoblu said, moving closer and curling her arm around my waist. "I will help you the rest of the way." She guided me along the trail slowly. "There is a spring just outside the cave. You will drink from it and be refreshed. And the lady in the cave is a great huntress, so surely there will be some rabbit or venison roasting over the fire . . ."

My stomach lurched at the thought of roasting meat, and I returned to staring at my feet, giving each a mental pep talk when it was its turn to shuffle forward.

"Look! See—the cave is there, just right there," Kikisoblu was all but dragging me onward.

Somehow, I managed to haul my gaze up from the ground.

The mouth of a cave blocked off by an iridescent wall of solidified At was several dozen yards away. Right before our eyes, the sheet of otherworldly material shimmered, then dissolved in a puff of foggy, rainbow tendrils.

Aset stood in the mouth of the cave, Nik a shadow standing behind her.

Adrenaline zinged through me and I lurched forward, a joyous, desperate laugh spilling out of me. I made it about three steps before my knees gave out and the darkness of unconsciousness promised to cushion my fall. I was out cold before I even hit the ground.

"HERE," ASET SAID, HANDING ME A CUP MADE OF solidified At. She sounded exactly like the woman she would become in another century and a half, slightly accented English and all. "This tea will act as a restorative." I was sitting with her and Nik around the cookfire in their cave, Kikisoblu asleep on bedroll a yard or two from the fire's edge. She'd already been fast asleep by the time I regained consciousness. The first thing out of my mouth had been, "Are they still alive?"

Aset had assured me that Marcus, Dom, Kat, Neffe, and Nik and herself had survived—*would* survive—the encounter with Apep-Carson. While Re hadn't been able to see exactly what happened in the echo of that time and place, thanks to the time anomaly caused by the ripples from my temporal jump, he was at least able to see that they were all still alive and kicking a year later. And the cherry on the sundae: the twins and I were there, too.

My relief was palpable, far more real and comforting than the furs nestled around me or the warmth and crackle of the fire. I felt a hundred times lighter. I was ready to take on anything, including time itself.

I sniffed the steaming liquid in the cup Aset had handed me, then wrinkled my nose. It smelled like mildew and bad breath, and I had no clue what the little floating flecks of leaves or chunks on the bottom of the cup were.

"It will steady your stomach and return some of your strength." Aset smiled, nodding. "I promise. Drink."

"It smells awful."

Aset snorted. "That may be, but it will do you good. Then we can get some broth in you, and then some meat." She settled her stern physician's stare on me.

Wide-eyed, I took a sip. The tea wasn't so hot that it burned going down, but a few flecks of the herbs floating around stuck to my tongue. I pinched them off with my fingertips and flicked them away. Thankfully, the concoction didn't taste as bad as it smelled, and much of the bitterness was cut by a generous helping of honey. I took another sip and found the taste almost pleasant. My third drink was practically a gulp.

"Careful," Aset said, retrieving the cup from my clutching grasp. "Not too much at first. Let it settle . . ."

I stared longingly at the tea.

"We've been waiting for you for so long," Nik said. He was crouching by the fire to the right of me, periodically adding herbs or roots to a cast-iron pot hanging just over the flames and stirring the contents with a heavy wooden spoon. It smelled savory and spicy, and the scent of the simmering broth made my stomach groan. "Mother was growing tired of the hunter-gatherer lifestyle—she's really more of a city girl—and I think I've been sedentary for so long that my muscles have atrophied entirely. If I go a decade or two without setting foot in the At again, it won't be long enough . . ."

My eyes skimmed over him, his buckskin tunic and pants covering a physique that was the picture of health and vitality. The only difference between this Nik and the one from *my* time was the lack of visible tattoos and piercings. It was good to be Nejeret; we aged well.

"He exaggerates, of course," Aset said with a huff of amused disapproval. She patted my knee. "We'll be just fine in our cozy little cave for a little while longer." She returned the cup to my beseeching hands.

I took a long draw of the tea, choking back dozens of questions about why they were here in the first place. I had a much more pressing issue. "I have to keep moving," I said. "Apep can sense me. He's sure to be coming for me already. We can't stay here, and I need to find Mar—Heru."

Aset scooted closer to sit beside me on my nest of furs. It had been a cozy way to return to consciousness, nestled in all that soft warmth. "You have a long journey ahead of you, Lex, with many jumps backwards in time. This was the first jump for you. But for us, it was the last time we'll be tasked with finding you. We've done this many times before." She held her wrist out in front of me, displaying a quartz-like bracelet engraved with row after row of hieroglyphs. "This is our map to finding you. Every time and place we've found you is etched into its surface. Trust us, Lex. We know what we're doing."

I stared at the impossible bracelet, seeing it for what it truly was: a fragment of my future . . . and their past. "This is why you vanished so long ago," I said, finally understanding. "Why everyone thought you were dead—because of me." I felt sick with guilt and other things.

"It has been a grand adventure, dear Lex. Fret not." Aset lowered the bracelet and gave my hand a squeeze. "And as for Apep—"

"He won't be able to sense you through all the At I've laced through the cave's walls," Nik said. "It's why we chose this place to begin with, and Re and I have been very careful to cover our tracks both here and in the At—Apep doesn't know we're here."

"But Marcus—" I squeezed my eyes shut and shook my head. "*Heru*. I need to find him."

"You need to take care of yourself, first," Aset said. "Then we'll bring you to my brother."

My eyes sought hers, and I clutched onto her arm. "So you know where he is?"

She nodded. "Nik and Re keep a close eye on him in the At."

"Where is he?"

Aset offered me a mollifying smile. "He's currently at Fort Nisqually."

I'd been to Fort Nisqually once on a grade school field trip. The frontier fort had been relocated and reconstructed in Point Defiance Park in Tacoma, where it served as a living history museum displaying life on the Western frontier. I didn't know the original location, other than somewhere in the south Sound area. It would take days to walk there.

Panic fluttered in my chest and I stared at Aset, eyes bulging. "I have to go—now. If I wait too long . . ." When I traveled back to Old Kingdom Egypt, it had only taken a day or so for bonding withdrawals to begin, and the symptoms had increased in intensity shockingly fast. Only being close to Heru had alleviated the pain.

"It's only a day by canoe," Nik said, setting down the wooden spoon in a small At bowl near the base of the fire. I was pretty sure he'd just conjured the bowl a moment earlier for the sole purpose of holding the spoon. "Barring poor conditions, of course." He looked into the fire, his eyes growing unfocused. Several seconds later, he blinked and looked at me. "We should be fine."

"But you don't *know* that," I said, leaning forward. "I'm a time anomaly. The actual weather might be totally different from what's reflected in the echoes, and—"

"Lex," Aset interrupted. "Do not forget—we've done this with you many times already." Her eyes were penetrating, the dancing flames making her irises resemble polished tortoiseshell with the ever-changing play of golds and browns. "The era and situation may be different, but we do know what we're doing . . . more so, I dare say, than you."

I took a deep breath, holding back tears of frustration. My life was in her hands—hers and Nik's. I trusted them both implicitly, but that didn't stop the frustration from churning within me.

Aset patted my knee once more, then tapped the bottom of my cup with her nails. "Drink up. We'll have you strong enough for the trip by morning. With any luck, you'll be marching into Fort Nisqually before you've even noticed any withdrawal pains."

I took another couple sips of the cooling tea while I mulled over her words. Blood going cold, I lowered the cup. "Marcus—Heru, in my time—when we first met, he didn't remember me from his past. I *have* to find him because of the bond, but I can't *go* to him, because then he'll remember me—which he didn't. I'd be changing the past . . . and our future because of that."

"Actually, you won't," Aset said. "A little bonus from the

twins' sheuts: anyone near you when you're pulled back in time will forget you when you're gone. Their memories of you will be blocked, just as you had to do to Heru and all of our people at the Oasis so long ago."

My shoulders relaxed. "So I just have to make sure I'm close to him when the time comes?"

"Precisely," she said.

I chewed on my lip. "How long?"

"How long what, Lex?"

I inhaled deeply, letting the breath out in a sigh. "How long will I be here—in this time?" I felt compelled to ask, but I dreaded the answer. I wasn't ready to go through the whole process of finding them and Marcus—Heru—again. Not yet.

"A while," Aset said. "The last time we saw you, your pregnancy was starting to show, so I would guess you'll be here for a couple months."

The breath I'd been holding rushed out of me. "Well, at least there's that . . ." I took another sip, reaching the dregs, and set the cup down. "Where's my next stop? I'm assuming I'll just keep moving backwards, since you said this is the last time you'll see me until, well, the first time *I* see *you*."

Aset and Nik exchanged a look.

"What?" I eyed them. "What is it?"

"You shall see us next in Iceland."

"We shouldn't say more, Mother," Nik said.

"I know." Aset's eyes were troubled when they returned to me. She lifted her shoulders, then let them fall, looking defeated. "As frustrating as this is for you, Lex, it is for us as well. But the timeline—"

"Must be protected," I said, thinking of Marcus and the argument we'd had in our suite what felt like a lifetime ago. "I know."

What I learned of my future, especially when that future was fated to play out in the relative past, could change my actions.

Any information might compel me to act differently, reshaping the sands of time into a new, unknown design. I might undo *everything* Re had worked so hard to orchestrate as Nuin, and then through Nik. I might help Apep win. I might unmake the whole damn world and leave the universe in shreds of writhing chaos.

I let my eyes slide closed, rubbed the back of my neck with one hand, and sighed. I was so over time travel.

10

LAND & SEA

Dark clouds had moved in, signaling a rare summer storm, but the weather held, not breaking until we were rowing toward the beach. My withdrawals, however, were another matter entirely. A dull throbbing had begun in the base of my skull just after we cast off that morning, emanating up to my temples and down my neck to my shoulders.

I huddled on the middle bench of Aset and Nik's canoe, a coyote fur draped over my shoulders, countering the cool sea breeze. I ducked my head to avoid the increasing rainfall and dug my fingertips into my shoulder muscles in an attempt to alleviate the ache. My stomach cramped and churned, and a low groan emanated from my chest. I'd never been one to suffer from motion sickness, but with the twins snug in my womb, all bets were off.

"You'll be indoors soon, Lex," Aset said from behind me. "We have money for you. You'll be able to purchase a warm bath and some new clothes on top of whatever my brother provides. Just hold on a little bit longer . . ."

I rocked my whole body instead of nodding.

"The next time we see you in, oh, a hundred and fifty years or so, you're not going to have any idea who we are," Nik said from his seat in front of me. He glanced over his shoulder. He was talking about *their* future, not mine, about the first time I met them—Aset in the hospital and Nik on the bus. "That should be interesting."

Aset tsked.

"Mother's going to have to suffer through university in order to get a job at your hospital, but she has a while to wait," Nik continued. I appreciated the distraction of his words, though my pained brain had a hard time making sense of what he was saying. "I can't believe women still aren't allowed."

"Please," Aset said. "They wouldn't be able to teach me anything I don't already know, anyway." She grunted with the effort of her next row.

"Maybe you'll end up teaching them." I squeezed my eyes shut as soon as I started speaking, unprepared for the reverberation of my voice in my skull. But I was determined to keep the conversation going. Silence had stretched out the journey for too long already, making the nauseous moments expand into relative eternity. "You'll have to keep a low profile when you go to college. Heru is a professor—in the future, I mean. He goes by the name Marcus Bahur."

"Of course he'll be a professor," Aset said. "My dear, oblivious brother is so good at unintentionally making our mission more difficult. I look forward to the day when Nik and I can emerge from hiding and reclaim our lives. To live without fear that any of our kind will discover us and ruin our hard-laid plans . . ."

Shame welled inside me, and I twisted to look back at her, which was a mistake. The rain-spattered sea surrounding us spun, the shore, foothills, and mountains beyond bobbing and swaying far more than the movement of the canoe warranted. I gritted my teeth. "Aset . . . I'm so sorry."

She froze, her paddle dripping over the water's choppy surface. "For what?"

"For you having to hide for so long. I just—I'm sorry."

Aset was quiet for a long time, the splash of her and Nik's paddles dipping into the water mixing with the pat-pat-pat of rain hitting the water's surface. "You have nothing to be sorry for, Lex. You rescued me not once, but twice. As I told you so very long ago—my life is yours."

I gripped the side of the boat. "What do you mean *twice*? I only freed you from Apep when he abducted you and—" I just couldn't bring myself to actually say what he'd done to her when he'd been possessing the Nejeret who'd fathered Nik. Because I hadn't rescued her, not really—the deed had been done. Aset had been abused and tormented for days on end, and Nik had been conceived.

"I—" Aset met my eyes, only to look away hastily when she resumed rowing. "I spoke without thinking. Please, Lex, you must disregard my words."

"But—"

"Let it go, Lex," Nik said. "You'll understand in time."

"Oh." I pressed my lips together, sealing in the questions fluttering around in search of freedom, and shivered. I wrapped the fur more tightly around myself.

Ahead, tiny rocks in a rainbow of grays covered the shore. Scattered driftwood formed a haphazard line higher up on the beach, just before the mass of rocks gave way to low sandstone cliffs. A lush forest cascaded over the crest of the cliffs; ferns, moss, and bunches of blackberries dangled over the precipice. Even a few slender pines bowed outward over the rocky beach below before straightening and reaching for the sky.

When the bottom of the canoe scraped against the rocks under the water, Aset's delicate hand settled on my wrist. "This is where we will leave you, dear Lex."

"What?" I spun on my bench, ignoring the dip and twirl of

the shoreline. "But—we're not there yet. I don't know how to get to Fort Nisqually, and—"

"Do you see that path over there?" She extended her arm, pointing off to the right of the canoe where a trail led up along a deep groove worn into the sandstone. "It leads directly to the fort, joining with a wagon road near the entrance. It is well traveled, so you have no fear of losing your way."

I turned back to her, imploring her with my eyes to stay with me just a little bit longer.

She smiled, her expression filled with confidence and encouragement. "You'll be fine, Lex. I promise."

I'd never navigated my way through a past time period on my own. When I first landed in Old Kingdom Egypt, Aset had been there to guide me to Nuin, and when I jumped back even further to rescue her from her abusive captor, a young Heru had been there, helping me make sense of things. Even when I first arrived in this time, Tex had been there to guide me—however devious his intentions had been—to a place where I'd found more reliable help.

Now, I would truly be on my own.

EVEN IN THE DOG DAYS OF SUMMER, FORESTS IN THE Pacific Northwest retain quite a bit of moisture. Maybe it's the near-unbroken canopy of piney branches that help the woods hold that precious water in. Maybe it's the abundance of rain that falls throughout the other nine months of the year. Maybe it's the fact that the woods covering the Olympic Peninsula are technically a rainforest—a notoriously wet place any time of the year. Maybe it's all three put together.

Regardless, on the rare summer days that it rained, that residual dampness expanded. To mud. Not sloshy mud puddles that pock parched earth, but yard-long patches that are equal parts water and dirt, where the end of one "puddle" signals the start of another until it seems like there's no end to the sticky, mucky, mud-pie mess. By the time I'd reached the top of the shallow cliff and taken barely a dozen steps into the woods, I'd given up all hope of trying to pick my way around the muddy patches.

I touched the drawstring purse hanging from one of my belt loops. It was large enough to hold a softball and was currently half full with heavy gold coins—eagles, Nik had explained. They'd sent me off with about five hundred dollars. Accounting for inflation, I calculated I was carrying roughly ten thousand dollars' worth of gold in my native time's terms. It felt like a blaring beacon calling out to any and all unsavory folks in the area.

I curled my fingers around the small purse and scanned the trees and dense underbrush on either side of the path. There was no one in sight, and the splat drip-drip splat of merged raindrops falling from the branches overhead drowned out the usual sounds of the forest around me. I proceeded along the trail, throwing furtive glances around, one hand clutching the heavy purse, the other partially outstretched to help me balance each time I slipped in the mud. With my low-tread leather boots, my balancing act wasn't always successful.

It took at least an hour to reach the wagon road, and by the time a break in the trees was in sight at the end of the trail, the lower half of my jeans was caked in mud, along with my right arm and half of the coyote pelt draped over my shoulders, thanks to one rather glorious spill.

"Oh, thank God," I muttered when I first caught sight of the road. It didn't look any less rain-soaked than the trail, but I was betting the hard-packed dirt was at least covered in that waterier, less pesky variation of the mud puddle. And—bonus—

walking the rest of the way to the fort in the open rain would wash some of the mud off me.

I picked up the pace as the pathway widened and gave way to harder packed earth. A flash of bright white lightning lit up the road ahead, and several seconds later, thunder rumbled among the trees. The rain, which had dwindled to a weak drizzle, picked up to a downpour.

I jogged the final few steps to the road, relishing the chance to clean up. It was like the universe had heard my desire, my need. It was like, for once, the universe had *listened*. I rushed into the center of a road that was barely five feet across and stood, arms outstretched, eyes closed, and face tilted up toward the dark gray sky, gratefully accepting its offering.

"What in tarnation—" The shout was cut short by a shrieking neigh.

I spun around, arms instinctively covering my face from the flailing horse hooves not a foot away. I stumbled backward and lost my footing in a deep puddle, landing on my butt with a splash.

"Christ almighty, woman!" I could hear the splat-splat of the rider's boots as he approached, but I couldn't see him through the curtain of mud-soaked hair hanging in my face. "I done nearly killed you. What were you thinking flying out of them woods like that?"

I held my arms up on either side of me, letting the water drip off of my dangling fingertips. "What were you doing riding like a bat out of hell *like that*?" I retorted.

"So you speak English." He grunted. "And pretty damn good, for a squaw."

"I'd appreciate you not using that term." I shook off my hands and wiped the gritty hair back from my face. "I'm not Algonquin—and some find it quite offensive," I added, glaring up at the rider. He wore leather chaps over brown wool trousers, a tailored wool coat over a shirt and leather vest, and knee-high leather boots. A wide-brimmed hat finished off the outfit, making him appear very much the gentleman cowboy. My eyes widened when they reached his ageless, bearded face. He wasn't human; he was Nejeret.

He whistled. "Well, now . . ." His eyes scoured my face, and I had no doubt that he was looking for something familiar, for a hint at my immortal bloodline. "I find myself wondering what a Nejerette like yourself is doing running around in the rain out here, wearing God knows what." He held out a hand to help me up.

I pushed myself off the sodden ground with one hand, using the other to straighten my coyote pelt and reassure myself that the purse was still there. "And I find *my*self wondering what a Nejeret like *your*self is doing out here trying to run people down." I shot him another glare, more than a little pleased to discover that I had a few inches on him.

The unfamiliar Nejeret used his rejected hand to raise his hat. He ran the fingers of his other hand through his short mop of hair, smoothing it back. "I do apologize for that, Miss . . . ?"

"Alexandra."

"Alexandra . . . ?" He settled his hat back on his head, his eyebrows raised in question.

"Just Alexandra is good enough for now," I told him.

"Well, every lady is entitled to a bit of mystery." He bowed his head and held out his hand once more. "I'm Dorman." He glanced up at me and winked. "Just Dorman is good enough for now."

I placed my hand in his as though to shake it, but he turned my hand over and raised it to his lips. The whiskers of his mustache tickled my knuckles.

"It's very nice to meet you, Alexandra." He released my hand and straightened, his entire demeanor changing. He seemed very much the gentleman now, not so much the cowboy. "Now, is there some way I might assist you? I am expected elsewhere, and I'm running a tad late"—he flashed me a crooked smile—"which is precisely why I was in such a hurry. But you do seem like you might be in a bit of distress, and I've never been one to abandon a damsel in her time of need."

I snorted a laugh, liking this Nejeret in instinct. "I'm hardly a damsel."

His eyes widened, hopeful. "Maiden?"

I gave him a *look*. "Mr. Dorman—"

"Just Dorman," he said with a cheeky grin.

"Alright, *Dorman*. The only thing I need from you is for you to point me in the direction of Fort Nisqually. Is it this way or that way?" I asked, pointing up the road with one hand and down it with the other.

"Well, isn't that mightily serendipitous," he said. "It just so happens we're headed to the same place. I would gladly escort you to Fort Nisqually and would greatly appreciate the pleasure of your company." He winked, a charming grin splitting his short beard.

I found his good nature addictive, and I couldn't help but return his grin.

Dorman's eyes crinkled at the corners. "Shall we?" he asked, offering me his elbow.

I gave him a look that said, *Don't push it, buddy*.

He shrugged and pulled back his arm, then reached behind himself for his horse's reins and clicked his tongue. "C'mon, Isis, your master will be glad to know I've brought you home safely."

I stared at him, my heart thudding in my chest. *Isis*—it was the anglicized version of Aset's name. It could just be a coincidence. Or not.

"Isis is an interesting name for a horse." I licked my lips. "Who's her master?"

Dorman eyed me. "Whyever do you ask?"

"I—" I hesitated. "I'm looking for someone."

Dorman cocked his head to the side, still eyeing me curiously. “Pray tell, who are you looking for?”

I held my breath, hesitating. “Heru. I’m looking for Heru.”

With another whistle, Dorman let out a low chuckle. “Serendipitous, indeed.”

11

SEE & KNOW

"Here," Dorman said, stopping and shrugging out of his coat. "It's a fair bit drier than your fur there . . ."

"Thanks." I accepted the coat. It was just a touch ripe, but it mostly smelled of earth and horses and campfire. I handed him the soaked coyote fur before slipping my arms into the sleeves of the wool coat and hugging it closed over my chest. It wasn't quite long enough to entirely conceal the purse hanging from my belt.

"I figure you'll make less of a stir among the soldiers if you're not quite so wild-looking."

I flashed him a wide, grateful smile. "Such a gentleman."

He handed me back the coyote fur. I wasn't sure, but I thought his ears might have reddened.

Continuing on our way, we rounded one sharp bend in the road and the open gate to Fort Nisqually came into view a hundred yards or so away. Its wall of standing logs stretched out on either side of the entrance, spiked tips pointing skyward. Lookout towers with horizontal slats for rifles or arrows, possibly both, stood tall at either corner, and a uniformed watchman peered over the wall near the gateway, a rifle slung over his shoulder.

"What you got there, Dorman?" the rifleman called when we were nearly to the gate. "You finally find yourself a woman to clean your drawers and ride you like a little pony?"

I glanced sidelong at Dorman. His expression had darkened. "Best watch yourself, Turlow. You offend the lady's honor any further and I might find myself in a position where I need to defend it. Now, you and I both know you don't want that, don't we?"

Turlow's only response was to sneer and spit a long, dark globule over the wall. He wiped his chin as we passed through the open gate.

"Charming fellow," I said under my breath.

Dorman's lip curled. "Just a moron flapping his mouth, is all. Don't you mind him." He veered to the right, aiming for the largest building within the walls, which was situated in the center of the fort—a whitewashed, two-story house surrounded by a deep covered porch. He headed straight for the hitching post out front, standing between two shade trees. He tied Isis's reins around the wooden pole, then met my eyes and nodded toward the front door. "After you."

My heart was beating a steady, expectant rhythm against my sternum, and I suddenly felt parched despite the rainstorm. I stared at the door. "He—he's in there?"

"Should be." Dorman headed for the three steps leading up to the porch and scraped his muddy boots on the edge of the bottom stair. He eyed me over his shoulder. "You look like you're going to be sick."

"I'm fine," I said, taking a deep breath. I straightened my spine and followed him to the porch stairs, pausing at the foot of the steps and staring down at the clumps of mud from Dorman's boots. I didn't think any amount of scraping would get my own mud-caked boots clean at this point.

"Just take 'em off."

"Won't that be weird?" I asked, slowly ascending the three wooden stairs. "Me, walking around barefoot while you all have shoes on?"

Dorman frowned. "I can see how that might make one feel out of sorts." And much to my surprise, he bent over and tugged off one of his boots.

"Oh, no, you don't have to—"

"Nonsense." He smirked at me. "I donned fresh socks this morning, so hopefully the smell won't knock you dead."

I laughed. The shrillness of it struck me.

"C'mon, little lady," Dorman said, snapping his fingers. "Those boots ain't going to take themselves off . . ."

"Oh, right." I lifted first one foot, then the other, and pried the sodden leather off my feet. I placed the boots on the porch, just to the side of the front door, and tucked the mucky wool socks inside. Straightening, I brushed my hands off on my jeans.

Dorman opened the door. "Ladies first," he said, standing to the side.

I took a deep breath, then another. My bare feet were cemented to the deck's wooden boards.

Until I heard *his* voice. "Do not be absurd," Heru said. "He wouldn't seek refuge with Set. Doing so would be risking death. He's danced back and forth over the line for far too long. He must know his father would never forgive such unreliability."

My feet started moving of their own accord, carrying me over the threshold and toward Heru.

"I suppose . . ." It was a woman's voice, and one that I recognized instantly—Neffe.

Moving on silent feet, I followed the sound of their voices past a narrow staircase and up a hallway that led to the back of the house.

"Why would he come here, then?" A third voice, accented with French and all too familiar. Dominic was here, too.

All three of them were in the room at the end of the hallway. I sucked in a breath, my heart soaring even as my headache gave a renewed, enthusiastic throb. Dizzy, I placed my hand against the wall, steadying myself.

Dorman touched my shoulder. "Are you unwell?"

"I'm fine," I breathed, resting my forehead against the back of my hand while I waited for the dizzy spell to abate. "I'll *be* fine." I was so close . . .

"If you say so." Dorman moved past me to the doorway at the end of the hall. I closed my eyes and took deep breaths.

"Pardon the interruption," Dorman said, "but I've got news. And, well . . ." He cleared his throat. "There's someone here to see you, Heru."

"The woman you were speaking with outside? For whom you felt the desperate need to remove your boots?"

"I'm surprised she survived the smell," Neffe said.

"Perhaps he is lovestruck." Dominic kept his voice was quieter than the others. "Torturing us, just so she would feel more comfortable?" Had I been human, I doubted I'd have been able to hear his words. The corner of my mouth lifted into a fond half smile; he was such a gentleman.

Dorman made a choking noise. "No. She's, well . . . it's not what you're all thinking."

The others snickered. "I'm sure," Neffe said.

"Alexandra," Dorman called down the hallway. "Come along."

Inhaling deeply, I pushed off the wall. The worst of the withdrawal spell had passed, leaving only a tinge of dizziness and the hint of a throb at the back of my skull, though I knew from experience that I wouldn't start to shake the withdrawals until I was in the same room as my bond-mate, breathing the same air. I made it to the end of the hallway, still hugging Dorman's jacket around myself. My legs were shaking, but steady enough; it was more nerves than anything else.

When I reached the doorway, I paused behind Dorman and peered into the room over his shoulder. It was a long, narrow study, with a desk near the far end and bookshelves filling the wall space between windows. Neffe, Dominic, and Heru were seated around a pedestal table about four feet in diameter nearer to the doorway, several hand-drawn maps sprawled on the tabletop between them.

I stepped into the room, looking first at Neffe's face, then Dominic's. Finally, I forced myself to look straight at Heru. Those familiar golden eyes were opened wide, those strong, striking features locked in an impossible expression.

Heru stood, the abrupt motion rocking his chair backward. If Neffe hadn't reached out to steady it, the chair would've tipped over completely. "You," he said, recognition written all over his face.

And I thought my heart might explode. Somehow, against everything I'd been led to believe, Heru knew me.

He *knew* me.

12

MEET & GREET

Heru stood on the other side of the table, his face washed out and his eyes opened so wide that the whites were visible around the entirety of his golden irises. He wore an outfit very similar to Dorman's—wool trousers and jacket, cotton shirt, and leather vest—minus the chaps and hat and entirely composed of gray tones. His obsidian hair was shoulder-length and smooth as glass, holding only a slight wave.

"Give us the room," Heru said, not taking his haunted eyes off my face.

"Father . . ."

"Now."

With the scratch of chair legs and a small parade of footsteps, we were alone. I was struck dumb. All I could do was stare.

How was it possible that he knew me—*remembered* me? According to Aset and Nik, whoever was nearest me when I jumped back in time would have their memories of me blocked. I didn't just have to stick close to Heru to soak up his bonding pheromones; I needed to make sure he was near me when I jumped—to make sure he forgot me.

So, had I failed? Had we been apart during one of my upcoming time jumps, leaving his memories of me intact?

"You know me?" I said, voice as wispy as my understanding of the situation. "You *remember* me?"

Heru stared at me. Color returned to his face, but the look in his eyes—it was still as though he was looking at a ghost. He shook his head. "No, but . . . I dreamt of you. So often . . ."

I drew in a breath and opened my mouth to speak, but no words came forth.

Heru took a step, then another, slowly making his way around the table. He stopped in front of me, well within arm's reach, and raised his hand. His fingertips trailed down the side of my face, from temple to jawline. "You're really here."

I nodded, eyes drifting closed as I leaned into his touch. Remotely, I noticed that the ache at the base of my skull had faded and the world had returned to its usual, steady state.

"But who are you? I've thought you were a fantasy for so long . . . just a figment of my imagination."

"I'm not." I opened my eyes, turning my head to press my lips against his palm. "I'm real."

Heru's breath hissed in through his teeth, his eyes blazing.

"There's so much to tell you." I shot a quick glance over my shoulder. Nobody had left the house through the front door, so I figured Dorman, Neffe, and Dominic had to be in one of the front rooms, being quiet as mice while they listened to us. I couldn't risk them overhearing my story. It was going to be hard enough making sure I was near Heru for the next jump back in time, let alone three other people. And Nejerets had *long* memories.

"Just you," I added.

Heru's eyes searched mine, back and forth. After a long moment, he nodded. "Neffe," he said, raising his voice just a hint as he addressed his daughter on the other side of the house, "go look after Isis . . . and take Dorman and Dom with you." His hawklike gaze never left mine.

We stood in silence, staring at one another while we listened to the others leave the house. The silent staring continued long after they'd gone.

Finally, Heru spoke. "You look as though you've been through the wringer." He pinched a dripping tendril of hair between his thumb and forefinger, the corner of his mouth twitching.

I exhaled a laugh. "If you knew what my last day and a half was like, you'd understand."

His expression returned to its usual, commanding state. "Tell me."

"I—" My eyes wandered to the chair behind him, and the weakness in my legs seemed to multiply threefold.

"Sit, yes, of course." Heru took a step back and held his arm out to the chair. "Would you like to change into dry clothes? Are you hungry? Thirsty? Surely some whiskey would dull your discomfort . . ."

"No whiskey," I said too quickly. At the slight narrowing of his eyes, I explained, "I'm pregnant. Alcohol would be bad for . . ." I trailed off, realizing what I'd just told him.

"You're with child?" He stared at me, his expression unchanged and his eyes unblinking. "Is it mine?" He frowned and shook his head as soon as the words were out of his mouth. "Apologies. I have no right or reason to ask such a thing. I don't even know your name." His frown deepened. "Tell me, mistress: how is it possible that you are with child when you are clearly a fully manifested Nejerette?" It was a valid question; the females of our kind were notoriously infertile, a byproduct of our superhuman regenerative abilities.

"Well . . ." I moved forward and more or less collapsed into the proffered chair. "It's a long story." My eyes drifted to the chair he'd abandoned. It was an invitation. I wouldn't force my story—*our* story, really—on him. But if he wanted to know, I would tell him. Ancient Heru had reacted poorly to learning we were fated to bond, but this Heru was different . . . older. This Heru remembered me, just a little.

Eyes trained on me, he nodded and eased into the chair. "You have my ear, Miss . . . ?"

"Alexandra." I held his gaze, preparing to drop my first bomb. "Ivanov," I said, using my Nejeret family name. I took a deep breath. "Alexandra Ivanov."

Heru leaned back in his chair, his fingertips running over the stubble growing along the line of his jaw. "You're of Ivan's line . . . via Alexander?"

I nodded. "He's my namesake. I'm his granddaughter. You can call me Lex."

"If you're Alexander's granddaughter, how is it I've never heard him speak of you?" Another valid question, considering they'd been close friends for many centuries.

Well, it just so happened I had one hell of a valid answer. "Because I haven't been born yet," I said.

Heru leaned forward, elbows on his knees. "I beg your pardon?"

My stomach knotted. It was time for the second bomb. "I'm from the future."

13

BOUND & FREE

"And that's how I ended up here," I said, folding my hands together in my lap. I'd shed Dorman's coat some hours ago, near the beginning of my retelling. It was humid in the room and warm enough that my jeans and T-shirt felt mostly dry.

Heru's eyes were still cast in my direction, but his focus was distant. Not surprising, considering I'd pretty much unloaded my whole life story on him. I'd told him way more than I'd planned to, including that in the future we were a bonded Nejeret pair. Hell, I'd just let the guy know he was the father of my children. He deserved a moment of silent processing. He deserved a *year* of silent processing, but we didn't have that much time.

Maybe it had been a gamble telling him so much. Maybe he would dismiss me as insane. Maybe he would see me as a lying, manipulative Nejerette who'd come to him and told him tall tales as part of some diabolical plan. Maybe, but I didn't think so.

Heru blinked, and his thousand-mile stare vanished, replaced by the intense focus I was so familiar with. He stared at me, seeming to see into me. "This thing you would have me believe—"

"My life story?" I offered with a shaky smile.

"Yes." Heru's eyes searched mine, and he leaned forward. He extended his hand, almost like he was reaching for me, but stopped short and set it palm-down on the table instead. "Have you any proof that what you claim is true?"

I nodded and scooted forward on my chair, perching on the edge of the seat. "If you go into the At, looking at this moment, this place, you won't see me. I'm a person out of time. We call it a 'time anomaly.'"

His eyes narrowed. "*Or* you could be extremely talented at cloaking." He nodded to himself. "Which would befit a daughter of Set, both the trickery and the talent."

I sat up straighter, my eyes narrowing to match his. "I wouldn't do that. I *haven't* done that. Hell, I wouldn't even know how to do that." I laughed bitterly. "My Nejerette traits manifested less than a year ago. I might be a quick learner, but I'm not *that* quick."

"I meant no offense," Heru said coolly. From the way he was looking at me, studying me, I had the impression that he was testing me.

"I'm sure," I grumbled.

"Do you have any other proof?"

Shrugging, I shook my head. "I don't think—" I sat up straighter. "Yes. Yes, I do," I said, reaching into my shirt through the collar to fish out my phone. I'd stored the dormant device in my bra to keep it safe during the canoe trip, and it had seemed wise to keep it there during the rainstorm.

Heru, who'd been watching my down-the-shirt phone retrieval with amused interest, craned his neck once the device was visible. "What kind of a contraption is that?"

"It's a phone—a cellular phone," I said, holding down the power button until the screen lit up and launched into its loading sequence. I'd powered it off shortly after Tex found me the previous afternoon. I set the phone on the table halfway between Heru and myself.

Heru scooted his chair closer and leaned over the table. "I've never seen anything like it."

I, too, leaned in. "In basic principle, it's similar to a telegraph —it allows you to send messages instantaneously over long distances." I tapped the glassy face of the phone. My background picture appeared, a photo of a rare snuggly moment between Thora and Rus, and a moment later, the icons for the apps popped into place. "The main difference is that these messages use actual voices."

"I don't understand."

"This"—I picked up the phone, then set it back down—"allows people to actually speak to each other from opposite sides of the world. You could have a conversation with someone in China—for hours, if you wanted—as though you're sitting in the same room as them. Some phones even allow you to *see* the person you're talking to."

Heru stared at the phone, wonder etched all over his face. He'd lived for thousands of years and, as such, had seen the ebb and flow of technology progressing firsthand. But still, he shook his head in disbelief. "How is such a thing possible?"

I shrugged. "Honestly, I don't know." I tapped the camera icon in the bottom right corner of the phone's display. "It can also take pictures—um, photographs. See?" I leaned closer to him and smiled into the camera, then tapped the screen to capture the shot. Heru's dumbfounded expression was priceless.

I showed him the image, barely hiding a smile.

He touched his fingertips to the likeness of his face on the screen. "That's incredible." He slid his finger to my face, and the photo swiped right off the screen, only to be replaced by another, this one taken a century and a half in the future.

In the new photo, Marcus and I were lying on a white and

green checkered picnic blanket on Bainbridge Island's rocky northern shore. Marcus was scowling while I cheesed it up big-time. He had an extreme aversion to photographs, a fairly common trait among our kind.

"This was taken a little over a week ago." I smiled wistfully, remembering that perfect sunny day. "We had a picnic, just you and I. So much was going on all around us with Tarset and the war on the Kin, and I wanted to surprise you. You'd been working nonstop, more stressed than I'd ever seen you, and . . ." My voice became husky. I cleared my throat, staring up at the ceiling while I blinked unexpected tears away. "It was a lovely afternoon. A perfect moment. I had to capture it with a photo."

"And yet remembering it saddens you." I could feel the trail of his gaze tracing over my face.

"It was our last moment of pure happiness before things went so wrong. And now I'm here, but you're there, and I don't even know if you're really okay, and there's nothing I can do about it but let our kids toss me further and further back in time like a damn skipping stone." I wiped away the wetness under my eye, angry at myself for letting the tears escape. "I don't even know how I'll get home." I just had to trust that the twins would bring me back when the time came.

Heru captured my hand before I could return it to my lap. "I may be there, in the future, but I am also here, with you, *now*." His thumb rubbed slow circles over the back of my hand.

Shaking my head, I let out a desolate laugh. "Yeah, but you don't believe me, not really. I thought that maye, since you sort of, somehow remember something of me, but . . ." I blew out a breath, frustrated, exhausted, and so over this. "You must think I'm insane."

"Well, Alexandra Ivanov—Lex—either you are insane, or I am." He smiled and shook his head, his open expression a rarity, even in my time. "And I'm inclined to believe your tale, so it must be me."

My gaze locked with his. "You believe me?" Tears streaked down my cheeks, and I made no attempt to stop them. "You really believe me?"

"I do." He laughed out loud, a wondrous, joyous sound. "And I'm to be a father!"

"Well, it's not like it's the first time . . ."

"Oh, but Alexandra, in so many ways, it is." He stood abruptly, releasing my hand to pace around the room. "To create a child with my bond-mate—to *have* a bond-mate! Such a thing I've never wanted, and yet how many times have I found myself lying in bed after waking from a dream of you, my mysterious fantasy woman, wishing you were real? How often have I lain there thinking that should our paths cross in the real, waking world, I would gladly hand you a piece of my soul?"

I stared at him, utterly speechless. Marcus was rarely so expressive. Only when he was caught up in an extreme tsunami of emotions did he allow himself to shed his usual aura of restraint and share his true feelings with such aplomb. I could count the number of times such a thing had happened on one hand.

He crossed the room to kneel before me and take my hands in his. "I have been searching for you for so long. You've been haunting me, day and night. You are with me always. Now I understand why."

I swallowed roughly. "You heard what I said about the bonding block in your mind, right? That we cannot ever—that if we were to reestablish the bond on your end by, um . . ." Blushing, I looked away and tried again. "We're bonded, you and I. That happened thousands of years ago, and nothing can change that. But the bonding block I placed in your mind so long ago is the only reason you haven't succumbed to withdrawals. While I have to stay close to you, now, to stave off the bonding withdrawals, you won't be able to experience our bond until we meet again in the twenty-first century. Were the bonding block to fail and our bond be fully reinstated on your end, you would—" I took a deep breath, then met his golden gaze. "You would die, Heru. You would die long before I'm born, and none of this—*us*, our children—would ever happen."

Some of the glow faded from his eyes. "I had not considered all angles of the situation, but I can plainly see the logic in your words." A faint, rueful grin curved his lips. "Though I cannot say I'm overly pleased with the reality of the situation."

I smiled, grateful for his acceptance. Heru might have been a millennia-old god of time, but he was also a damn good man.

He squeezed my hand. "Now, Little Ivanov—"

With my next inhale, I choked a little. "How did you know?"

Heru's brows drew together. "Know what?"

Smiling, I shook my head. "Little Ivanov—it's what you call me in my time."

Heru grinned, broad and true. "Is it, now? Perhaps that will help you see me as the same man you first bonded with, despite being a few years younger."

My smile faded as I stared into his eyes. I raised my hand, touching my fingertips to the side of his face. "I always know who you are. You are Heru. You are mine."

His eyes blazed hotter than any sun. He leaned in, and I wet my lips in preparation for his kiss.

"Wait," I said when he was a hairsbreadth away, our breath commingling in the space between us. My chest rose and fell quickly, and it was an effort not to close the distance and just kiss him already. "This is probably a terrible idea. Kissing leads to other things, and other things lead to—to—"

Heru's hands were making a slow path up the outsides of my thighs. "Hmmm . . . I'd very much enjoy hearing about these 'other things' . . ." His hands were on my hips, kneading through the denim.

"I—I—"

The front door crashed open, and we both jumped. "Father!"

Heru pulled back a few inches. "What is it, Neffe?" In one smooth motion, he stood.

I felt suddenly naked in the absence of his heat. But I also felt fantastic, rejuvenated by my time with him. I figured I must have absorbed a pretty healthy dosage of his bonding pheromones during our little flirtation of a kiss. That on top of the relief I felt at having confided in him—and knowing he believed me—lifted my spirits immensely.

"Dom found him," Neffe said from the doorway behind me. I forced myself to *not* look at her; I didn't want to give her any reason to remember my face. Like I said, our kind have long memories. "He found Samuel."

Heru stood behind his chair, his hands gripping the top rail. "Where?"

"North," Neffe said. "According to Dom, he's searching for someone—a woman. Dom witnessed an echo of a conversation between him and a Squamish hunter, and Samuel threatened to kill the poor bastard if he didn't tell him where the woman had gone."

Heru's eyes shifted to me. "How fascinating."

"That's not even the whole of it." With the sound of boots on hardwood, Neffe took several steps into the room. I could see her in my peripheral vision, dressed much like her father in wool and leather rather than the dresses with their heavy woolen or cotton skirts typical to women of this era. I smiled, just a little. Trust Neffe not to roll with the tide. "He told the hunter that finding 'her' was the only way to prove to 'the Collector' where his loyalties truly lie."

"So he *was* planning on seeking refuge with his father." Heru's focus shifted back to Neffe. "Take Dom and Dorman, and find him."

"You're not coming?"

"No, not this time."

"Standard procedure after we track him down, then? Or did you need us to keep him alive?"

"No." Heru tucked his hands into his pockets and shook his head. "No, I have no need of him. He's made his bed . . ."

"Very well." There was a long moment, and the silence quickly grew expectant.

"Is there something else?"

"Father . . ." Neffe hesitated. "It's her, isn't it? She's the woman Set's after?"

"Yes, Daughter." Heru's stare became diamond hard. "And that is the only time I would hear you speak of it—of her—*ever* again. Am I understood?"

There was only the slightest pause before Neffe answered. "Yes, Father." She made her way to the hall but paused in the doorway. "Will you be here when we return?"

Heru's eyes slid back to me, and his jaw tensed. "No, I don't think I will."

"As I suspected. Safe travels, then, and find me when you're ready."

"Of course." Fondness softened the determined set of Heru's features. "Be safe, Daughter. And good hunting."

"And you, as well." With the sound of quick, confident footsteps, Neffe was gone.

Heru waited for the front door to open and close before speaking to me. "By now, I'm sure Set is well on his way here. We must leave as soon as possible."

I nodded, surprised by how quickly this was all happening. I'd spent hours yarning my tale, weaving a sense of normalcy when our situation was anything but.

"I'll fetch you a hot meal and, while you eat, procure you some new clothing." He started for the doorway, retrieving a black bowler hat hanging from the corner of one of the chairs, then paused. "Women's clothing is difficult to track down out here . . ."

I shook my head. "It's fine. I'd prefer to wear something like what Neffe has on, anyway."

"As you say. Can you ride?"

I bunched up my shoulders until they were near my ears. "I honestly don't know. I've never tried."

"I'll keep that in mind when purchasing your horse." He unsheathed a dagger fastened to his belt and handed it to me. "In case there's any trouble while I'm gone." When I nodded, he turned and passed through the doorway.

"Wait!" I stood and followed after him. "I have money." I touched the drawstring purse hanging from my belt loop.

Heru glanced down at the small leather bag. "Is it gold?"

"Yes, eagles. I have plenty to pay for—"

He raised a hand, waving away my offer. "Hold onto your coin purse. Gold is valued in almost any time period and may very well save your life, down the road."

"But—"

"Trust me, Alexandra, I have more than enough to fund our flight. Save your money for a time when it is a necessity, not merely a convenience."

"Alright." I lowered my hand.

"That's settled, then. Remain here. I'll return shortly." And then he passed through the front door and was gone.

14

FEAST & FAMINE

I returned to my chair and sat, tapping the fingernails of my right hand on the table while I waited. Time seemed to have slowed, stretching out each minute until they felt like miserably long hours. After only a couple of minutes—so said my phone—I powered it off. Otherwise, I'd just keep checking the clock. At least this way I could preserve the battery a little longer.

I started when someone knocked on the front door, jumping to my feet as it opened and moving to stand against the wall by the study's lone doorway. I peeked around the doorframe to see Heru enter the house with a woven picnic-style basket in one hand, its contents covered by a thin linen towel, a small, covered cast-iron pot hanging by a handle in the other hand, and a corked earthenware jug tucked under his arm.

He kicked the door shut and eyed me from the far end of the hallway. "I startled you. Apologies."

I met him halfway. "I'm just jumpy."

His lips curved downward the slightest bit. "With good reason." He allowed me to take the jug when I reached him but nothing else. "When next I return, I'll knock twice, then once, then twice again, and you'll know it is I."

"Thanks." I felt silly, being so skittish.

Heru led the way back to the study and set the basket on a chair before using his free hand to roll up the maps and tuck them in a tall vase in the nearest corner. "You look like you haven't had a solid meal for a while, so I brought a little bit of everything the kitchen had."

Returning to the basket, he pulled back the cloth cover, revealing a small linen-wrapped bundle, an earthenware crock about the size of a mason jar filled with summer berries native to this area—blackberries, salmonberries, blueberries, and tiny little wild strawberries—a trio of miniature crocks containing what looked like butter, honey, and jam, and a small, corked earthenware jug a mere fraction of the size of the one I'd already set on the table. He fished another linen towel from the basket, folded it into a neat square about six inches by six inches, and set it on the table. It was just large enough for the cast-iron pot.

"Mostly, this is what remains from breakfast and midday. We were lucky they'd yet to feed the pigs." Heru set his hat on the corner of the nearest chair and ran his fingers through his sleek black hair, combing it back from his face. It was so long and shiny and silky looking—the definition of touchable. His eyes narrowed infinitesimally. "What?"

I blinked. "What, *what*?"

"You are staring at my hair."

Heat burned in my neck and cheeks. I'd been imagining what it would feel like to run my fingers through those silky black strands while he kissed my neck, along my collarbones, and made his way lower . . .

"I, um . . ." I dropped my gaze to the floor and cleared my throat. "I've only ever known you with short hair."

"Truly?" He touched the ends of his hair, where it brushed one shoulder. "It feels as though I haven't worn my hair shorter than this for ages." He laughed through his nose. "I think it's been a thousand years, maybe longer . . ."

"I could see how shaving it every couple days would be a hassle back in, well, now."

"A hassle, indeed." He returned to unloading the basket, setting the linen-wrapped bundle on the table and following up with the tiny jars of condiments. "The biscuits are cold but not yet stale. If they're too hard, just soak them in the stew and they'll soften right up. There's also berries and cream," he said, unloading the crock and small jug. "And, of course, water." He uncorked the larger jug, then folded up the linen towel that had lined the basket and placed it on the lid of the cast-iron pot. "Be careful with this. It's hot."

I ogled the feast spread out before me. "Thank you. This looks wonderful."

"The land is abundant in these parts. So untouched . . ." Sadness cast a shadow over his eyes. "Were that this place could stay this way forever."

"You really love it here, don't you?"

Heru met my eyes, then looked away, gazing through the nearest window. "I have called many places home, but few have actually felt like it. Here, I feel a sense of belonging I thought lost with Oasis."

I turned away from him and busied myself by moving things around the table in a fairly random fashion. "I'm sorry about that—what happened. What I did." I bowed my head. He hadn't remembered what had truly happened after Nuin died—that I'd unleashed the full power of my borrowed sheut, quite literally bringing the walls down all around us. But he knew now, because I'd told him. "It was our people's home, and because of me, they've been cast out for thousands of years." My only consolation was that I hadn't killed everyone at the Oasis in the process of destroying their home.

"Perhaps we will return one day." Heru rested his hands on my shoulders, and I leaned back against his body, forgetting, just for a moment, that we were in the past. That he wasn't Marcus. He wouldn't be Marcus for another one hundred and fifty years. And yet, he would always be the man I loved. The man I'd bound my soul to.

Heru's arms wrapped around me, crossing over my chest. "I feel as though I've held you this way a thousand times, and as though this is the first time I've ever held you before. What are you, to be able to make me feel such things?" He'd asked me something very similar once, when walking me home through the snow on our first date.

I smiled at the memory and whispered, "Yours." My stomach rumbled, and I choked on a laugh. "And also, I'm starving . . ."

"Of course." Heru's arms slid off me. "I apologize for keeping you from your meal." He was gone from the room in an instant.

I followed him back down the hallway. He didn't leave through the front door, but turned left at the foot of the staircase and entered the dining room beyond.

"What are you doing?" I asked.

"Gathering what you'll need to sate your rabid appetite."

I eyed his broad shoulders as he crouched to search a cupboard in the sideboard, doubting that whatever he found in there would do anything to truly sate my appetite—only he could do that. But *that* was something that wouldn't happen until I'd returned to my own damn time. Damn it. I'd played this game before. It was no fun, and guaranteed misery and bad tempers all around.

I crossed my arms over my chest and leaned against the wall while I watched Heru rummage.

"Huggins is a terrible housekeeper," he said, his voice muffled by the cupboard. "Ah—that'll do well enough, I suppose." He stood and kneed the cupboard closed, a mismatching china plate and bowl in one hand, a crystal goblet in the other. He transferred the goblet into the bowl and opened the drawer above the cupboard, pulling out a tarnished silver butter knife, a soup spoon, and a three-pronged fork.

He moved back across the room and offered me his findings, which I accepted with a slight clink-clinking. "I trust you can manage from here?" he said, heading for the door. "I should only be an hour, maybe two, and I'll be within the walls the whole time. If you have need of me, you need only call out my name. Wherever I am, I'll hear you. You can be certain of that."

"I'm sure I can manage eating all by myself," I said dryly.

Hand on the doorknob, Heru glanced back at me, his lips twitching. "One would hope." He opened the door. "I'll gather what we need and return straightaway." And then he was gone.

I saluted him through the door with my small horde of dishes, then headed back to the study to dig in. I was just finishing my second bowl of stew when the hairs on the back of my neck stood on end and I had the oddest sense that I was being watched. I wiped the bottom of the bowl with a piece of biscuit, popped it into my mouth, and stood, doing a cursory scan of all three windows in the study. All appeared empty of peeping faces, showing the placid, idyllic scene of life inside the fort.

Unsettled, I retrieved the knife from the table and moved around the perimeter of the study, examining the books and odds and ends on the shelves between quick glances to this window or that. I was standing behind the desk when I heard the faintest sound of scratching at the front door.

A moment later, the door creaked open—no secret knock.

I gripped the knife tightly, keeping it snug against my leg. I held my breath, hoping that whoever had entered the house wouldn't realize I was back in the study but would do whatever they'd come in to do and leave. I thought my hopes thin, considering the scent of food that had to be wafting out of the room.

At the first bootfall, I considered scurrying around the desk and hiding underneath. But I dismissed it, thinking that would make too much noise. The wood floors were creaky, and whoever was in the house would know someone was back here . . . assuming the person even cared.

"Mistress . . ."

My heart gave a heavy thud-thump, and I squeezed my eyes shut for the briefest moment.

He cared.

I licked my lips and swallowed, preparing to respond as the sound of several more footsteps drew the intruder nearer. Oh, who was I kidding? *I* was the intruder. For all I knew, this guy was the owner of the house—possibly the Huggins fellow Heru had mentioned while digging through the cupboard.

"Mistress?"

"I'm back here," I said, voice wobbly. "In the study."

I was surprised to recognize the man who appeared in the doorway. It was Turlow, the leering rifleman from the lookout at the gate. Dressed in a shabbier version of Heru and Dorman's attire, he was of average height and build, with shaggy brown hair and a short, scruffy beard. He snagged the hat from his head and wrung it in his hands as he took his first step into the room.

I backed into the desk, keeping my body turned to conceal the knife. "Can I help you with something?"

He took another step, his eyes skimming me from the floor up. I felt the urge to shake off the touch of his gaze. "You sure are pretty . . . real pretty."

"Thank you," I said, my tone bland. Head high, I took a few steps toward the table, toward him, hoping the gesture showed some don't-mess-with-me confidence. "Now, if you don't mind, I'd like to finish my meal in peace."

He took another step but halted when I held up my free hand.

"Do you think—" He took a scooting step closer. "It's just

that it's been so long since I've seen a pretty lady—or any lady—and I so do miss the delicate feel of a woman's skin. May I—could I hold your hand, just for a moment?"

I stared at him, flabbergasted. The request seemed innocent enough, but something about him disturbed me. His mere presence struck a discordance deep within me. "No, I think not." I sidestepped around the table to put something tangible between us. "Now if that's all, I'll bid you good day, sir." It sounded both period-appropriate and clearly dismissive to me. Stern, but not too harsh.

Apparently my gauge was off, because Turlow hunched over, raised his hands to his face, and started weeping.

Well, crap. Now I'd gone and made a grown man cry. I pitied him. For about three seconds.

Without warning, he lunged across the table, reaching for my purse and knocking the jug of cream and crock of berries to the floor in the process. I reacted without thinking, swatting his hand to the side and spearing it with the knife.

I stared down in shock.

Turlow's hand was pinned to the table, the knife sticking straight out of the back of it. He opened his mouth and let out a shriek so harsh and pained that I was forced backward. I stumbled into the bookcase behind me and knocked a shelf free. Leather- and cloth-bound books and assorted trinkets clamored to the floor.

"Alexandra?" The door crashed open. "Alexandra!" Heru rushed into the room, scanned the scene, and struck, knocking out a shrieking Turlow with a single right hook.

The scruffy man dropped to the floor, tugging the knife free of the table on his way down.

"What happened?" Between one breath and the next, Heru stepped over Turlow's body and crossed the room to me. And my breaths were coming pretty damn fast at that point. "Are you alright?" His hands were on my face, my neck, his eyes scanning all of me that he could see and leaving behind none of that icky, slithery feeling. "Did he hurt you?"

"He—" I shook my head, my eyes locked on the unconscious man just a few feet away. "He tried to rob me."

"Perhaps he noticed your purse when you first entered the fort."

I nodded dumbly.

"It will stand out less once you're outfitted in your new attire."

Once again, I nodded.

"Alexandra . . ." Heru gave my shoulders a gentle shake. "You are quite pale. Are you truly alright?"

I tore my eyes away from the bloody knife protruding from Turlow's hand. "Yes. Yes, I'm fine. I'll *be* fine." I pressed my hands against my suddenly churning stomach. The twins hadn't liked that little bit of excitement one bit. "I just need a moment away from"—I waved one hand at the man on the floor—"this."

"Yes, of course." With one hand gripping my elbow, the other wrapped around my shoulders, Heru guided me down the hallway to the sitting room opposite the dining room. He led me to an upholstered armchair and, with a hand on my shoulder, enticed me to sit. "Give me just a moment to handle Turlow, then we'll be on our way. I have all that we need, save for your mount."

"Can't we just ride Isis together?" I asked, nervous about attempting to command such a large creature.

"We could, but it would slow us down . . . more so, I think, than will your limited equestrian proficiency." His eyes crinkled at the corners. "You strike me as a quick learner."

I shrugged, unsure of anything at the moment.

Heru crouched before me. "Fear not, Little Ivanov. I will be by your side." He looked into my eyes, the black-rimmed gold of his irises shining with promise. "So long as you are here, with me, I will not let you fall."

My throat constricted, and my eyes stung.

"All you must do is trust in me."

Nausea forgotten, I nodded once. "Always."

15

HIGH & DRY

"Lex." I was being shaken by the shoulder, yanked from sleep. I recognized Heru's voice through the haze of exhaustion that comes from being jarred out of the deepest of sleeps.

I groaned, curling in on myself. I was so incredibly tired. For days, we hadn't stopped to rest for more than what the horses' needs necessitated. Only when I nearly toppled from my saddle had Heru relented on driving us onward. We could afford a few hours, he'd said. He would wake me if there was trouble.

Which meant: there was trouble. Apep-Set was here.

"Lex! We have to get going—now."

A tear snuck between my lashes and snaked across my temple. "No."

"Lex, please. The horses are saddled and packed. We must—"

I shook my head and caught his hand, pulling it from my shoulder as I gathered it between both of mine. "No, Heru. Not this time." I opened my eyes to see his heartbreaking expression. Defiance shone in his stare, the golden hue of his irises silvered by the moonlight, but resignation was clear on his face.

He knew. It was time.

"I can't do this anymore. The running . . . the never stopping." I shook my head again, my chest convulsing with suppressed sobs. We'd been at it for weeks. "It can't be good for the babies."

Heru gathered me up off my sleeping roll. "I knew this day would come, but I cannot say I'm prepared. I'd hoped for just a little while longer . . ."

"I—I'm sorry," I cried against his shoulder. He smelled of woodsmoke, dirt, and sweat, and of *him*. His scent surrounded me, soothing my raw desperation as much as his words or gentle caresses ever could. "I—I tried to—"

"I know, Little Ivanov. I know." He stroked my unkempt hair and pressed a kiss to the top of my head. "Do you know how close Apep-Set must be to trigger the time jump?"

I shook my head, fingers clutching the lapels of his wool coat. "Last time he was right in front of me, but that was a couple months ago." I sniffled. "The twins should be stronger now, don't you think?"

Heru's arms tightened around me. "Let us hope, for both our sakes, they need not let him draw quite so close to you this time." Heru would need to hold Apep-Set off long enough that his presence—and my fear—triggered the twins' sheuts into jumping me backward in time. He would then need to incapacitate Set, allowing for his own escape. He was the better fighter of the two, always had been, so once I was out of the way, I had little doubt that he would handle the situation well enough. Of course, that didn't stop me from worrying.

After another kiss atop my head, Heru was back to stroking my hair with one hand, the other drawing slow, soothing circles on my lower back. "Rest now, Little Ivanov. Save your strength for whatever you must face next."

Not fifteen minutes later, the careful footfalls of someone picking their way through the fallen leaves and scant underbrush to the east of our clearing reached our sensitive ears. I was already dressed in my wool and leathers, my drawstring coin purse tucked safely underneath my jacket. I'd stowed a small stash of dried meat and stale corn cakes, a wooden canteen filled with drinkable water, and a set of flint and steel in the leather satchel slung across my body. I was as ready as I could be for whatever lay waiting in Iceland, my next destination.

I'd never felt less ready for anything in my life.

"I know you're there," Heru called out, placing himself between me and the sounds of steady movement in the woods beyond.

The noise paused, my heart beating thunderously in the relative silence. I tried to regulate my breathing, or at least breathe more quietly, but it proved pointless. Every inhale and exhale sounded like a screaming gale to my ears.

"Of course I'm here," Set said. Or rather, *Apep* said. His accent was much as I remembered it the last time I'd heard him speak, with Carson's voice rather than Set's—very British and very proper. "Can you not feel her—the power of the sheuts radiating from her . . ."

"Power that will never be yours," Heru said.

Apep-Set chuckled, the sound sending goose bumps cascading over my skin. "You amuse me greatly, cousin. Accept the reality of the situation. I am here. It is over. You've lost, and I've won." His silhouette became visible, moving between the barren, moon-shadowed trees.

Heru turned partway to glance at me, his eyebrows raised in question.

I shook my head and pressed my hands against my slightly protruding belly, the baby bump undetectable under my layers of clothing. Nothing yet from the twins, not even a stirring.

"I've won *everything*," Apep-Set said, continuing his gloating diatribe. He stepped over a fallen log and into the clearing, then paused to take in the scene. "How quaint." He was maybe thirty yards away, far too close for my liking.

With his next, cautious step toward us, my heart rate doubled. Not a second later, I felt a fluttering sensation within, closely followed by a roil of nausea and a cramp that bent me nearly double. I hugged my middle as tendrils of misty At surrounded me, glowing with every color of the rainbow. They grew more robust, curling loosely around my legs and arms, my torso, and lastly my head.

"No!" Apep-Set yelled, launching forward at a dead sprint. "*Noooooooo . . .*"

In a blink, Apep-Set and Heru were gone. *I* was gone.

The world lurched, and a moment later, an orchestra of stars burst into existence all around me, a brilliant, blinding symphony of light. I dropped to my knees on cold, jagged rock. I leaned forward, holding myself up with one hand, and emptied the contents of my stomach over a cliff. When there was nothing left to bring up, I wiped my mouth with the back of my hand and sat on my heels, staring out at an ocean far darker than the dazzling night sky above.

It was done. I was in Iceland, and Heru was gone, waiting for me to find him once more.

Surrounded by the cold solace of the infinite universe spreading out above the sea, I buried my face in my hands, hunched in on myself, and let myself cry. Zero shame. I'd earned this, damn it. Because I was exhausted, and now I would get to do it all over again.

"I see her. There!" I barely heard the words—spoken in the original tongue—through the whip and roar of the salty wind and the crash of sea so far below. "Hurry, Nik! We do not have much time."

"Oh, Lex," Aset's voice was gentle as her son scooped me up like a small child trembling from bad dreams. My reality had become the stuff of bad dreams.

I bounced a little as Nik carried me away from the cliffside, but I didn't mind. His heat seeped in through my leathers, and I soaked up the warmth. Moments later, I was tucked into a cocoon of furs and thick woolen blankets, thawing my icy fingers over a crackling fire while Aset fussed around me, pinching me here, prodding me there. They'd set up a small camp in a barren dell not far from the seaside cliffs.

"You have not been receiving adequate sustenance," Aset said, her tone clearly disapproving. She spoke to me in the original tongue, as our respective accents and versions of English were different enough to make communication in that language difficult.

"Mother, you are wasting time."

"Ah, too true, my son." Aset extended her arm behind her, to where Nik was crouched by the fire, feeding a few small pieces of wood into the flames. "Hand me a horn of broth, then start packing. We must leave this place soon."

"Wh—where are we going?" I asked between chattering teeth. "And where exactly are we now? And when?"

"Oh, dear Lex." Aset handed me a large horn cup filled with a steaming broth, the rich, herbaceous scent making my mouth water. "We are in Iceland—the Látrabjarg cliffs—and it is March of the year 1624." She brushed a grimy chunk of hair out of my eyes. "Unfortunately, Nik and I must be leaving you soon, for we dare not test the reach of the twins' memory-blocking power."

I shook my head, my eyes opened wide. I must have heard her wrong. They couldn't be leaving me alone here . . . not yet. "Heru—I have to find Heru."

"No, dear Lex." Aset's warm amber eyes glowed with sympathy in the firelight. "You will not be in this time for much longer, anyway, certainly not long enough to reach my brother." She took a deep breath. "Something went, well, not wrong exactly, but . . . your last temporal jump fell a bit short of Heru's location. Perhaps the twins overreached." She shrugged. "There is no way to know, only that this is where we were meant to meet you, according to this," she said, holding up her wrist with the At bracelet.

"It is what *is*," Nik said, his eyes rainbow moonstones in the firelight; Re had taken over.

I stared at them, not blinking and far from understanding. "What are you saying?"

"Heru is not here on this distant isle." Aset smiled, like doing so might help me process her meaning. It didn't. "So you must see now that you cannot remain in this time for much longer."

Heart thudding in my chest and breaths coming faster, I alternated between looking at Aset and looking at Re-Nik, hoping something in their compassionate expressions would explain exactly how I was supposed to get myself out of this tangle. Because this was one hell of a whoopsie.

I swallowed roughly. The broth that had smelled so appetizing only moments before now turned my stomach. "And Apep . . . ?"

They exchanged a veiled glance.

"He must be on his way here now." I studied their faces, not understanding their hesitancy to respond. "That is why you have to get going, right?"

"No, Lex." Aset's features filled with pity and something that looked an awful lot like wariness. "Apep may have sensed the presence of the sheuts you carry, and it is likely that he is already heading this way, but he will not reach this place for weeks."

The meaning of her words was lost on me.

"Apep is currently in Paris," Re-Nik said. "Because your brief presence in this time has created a barely perceptible time anomaly in the At, he has had no way to prepare for your arrival by making a preemptive voyage here. Unfortunately, this time you are on your own."

"Then . . ." I looked at Aset, searching her gentle amber eyes. "How am I supposed to leave?"

"A leap of faith, dear Lex," Aset said, light and shadows dancing over her features, making her expression impossible to read. She placed a hand on my wrist. "You must force the twins to make their next jump back in time. It will not be pleasant, but, as Re says, it is what *is*."

"Which means *what*, exactly?"

She cleared her throat. "You must leap, as I said."

"I do not understand . . ."

"Off the cliff."

I stared at her, not blinking, not speaking. I was barely even breathing.

"You must give us some time to make our departure. We will leave you the broth and the fire and the furs to keep you warm while you pass the time. It should not be so bad. Nik and I have already seen you in your next destination, so rest assured that you will survive this."

"You—you want me to jump off the cliff?"

"Yes."

I pointed up the hill. "*That* cliff? The one with the jagged rocks and crashing waves at the bottom?"

"Yes."

I pressed my lips together, a million things to say but momentarily struck dumb.

"But you will want to change into this, first," Aset said, handing me a leather-wrapped bundle about the size of a pie box. She placed it on the ground between us. "Within, you will find a shift and a gown suitable for your next destination. The gown is simple but well-made and will allow you to blend in." She laughed softly, but it sounded forced. "You would certainly stand out in your current attire."

"And then I jump off the cliff."

"Yes, Lex. You change, and then you jump off the cliff."

"I see." I turned to the side as my stomach heaved, but thankfully nothing came up. I'd already lost it all over the edge of the cliff.

The damned cliff.

I STOOD ON THE EDGE OF THE PRECIPICE ALONE, THE stars' bright glow dimming as the edge of the horizon grayed, a harbinger of the approaching morning. My midnight woolen skirt flapped around my legs. The stone beneath my feet felt like ice, numbing me from the ground up. My hair whipped in every direction, dark ribbons with a mind of their own.

I couldn't do it.

Far below, the ocean waves taunted me, crashing against the cliffs relentlessly. They would withdraw, revealing the poorly concealed rocks jutting up from the ocean floor, only to surge forward once more, a writhing behemoth waiting to consume my broken body.

I couldn't jump.

My heart was in my throat, and my lungs were filled with panic instead of air. My pulse whooshed in my ears, accompanying the mocking waves so far below.

I couldn't do it this way, looking over the edge. Taking a single step. Falling.

I turned away from the cliff and marched back several yards. Bowing my head, I curled my fingers into fists and took a deep breath. Then another.

With a howl—a roar—I spun around and ran straight for the cliff's edge.

And leapt.

16

BOREDOM & SURPRISE

Well, I jumped off a cliff and didn't die. So that's good.

In spite of Aset's assurances that I would arrive safely at my next destination, as I hurtled toward the crashing waves and jagged rocks at the bottom of the cliff, I was convinced I was done for. I may have even had a small heart attack. But I didn't die.

I emerged from the miasma of swirling At in the middle of a rolling field of tall, golden grass. It was such a serene pastoral scene—lovely squat trees lining the field in small clumps and a clear blue sky overhead, the sun shining and cheerful—that I gave in to the weakness in my knees and collapsed to the ground. I rolled onto my back, splaying my arms out to either side, and allowed myself a moment to simply breathe.

A few perfect puffy white clouds hung overhead, floating lazily across the sky. Beneath me, the earth was dry and warm from soaking up the sunshine, and as my heartbeat slowed and the adrenaline left my system, my cozy earthen cradle lulled my overtaxed mind and body into a peaceful daze. I closed my eyes, basking in the sun's gentle caress and listening to the soft shush-shush of the swaying grass and the friendly, chirping songs of the birds perched in the trees nearby.

For seconds, minutes, or hours—it all felt the same to me—I drifted in that lazy half-sleep.

"Non ti muovere." Though I didn't understand the words, I recognized the voice—Heru.

My eyes popped open, and I started to sit up. I halted abruptly when the tip of a sword pierced my skin just below my collarbone, but my eyes continued their journey upward, seeking out Heru's face. He was little more than a dark silhouette, but the sight of him still elicited a gut reaction from me, and the corners of my mouth lifted.

His hair wasn't quite as long as it had been in the nineteenth century—or *would* be—but it still reached past his chin and swayed gracefully when he moved. He wore clothing that gave little indication to the time period—leather trousers, a loose-fitting white linen shirt, and a structured leather coat that appeared almost armor-like, despite hanging open.

I lowered myself back down to the ground to put some distance between my skin and that sharp blade. "You cannot possibly know how glad I am to see you," I told him in the original tongue, wagering it was our only common language in this time.

He tilted his head to the side and stared down at me. The point of his blade didn't move closer to me, but he didn't pull it away, either. "Have we met before?" he asked, also speaking in the original tongue.

I studied his shadowed features for a moment, then settled on a more cautious route than full disclosure. "Perhaps we have met, and you have forgotten me."

His gaze traced the lines and contours of my face, then continued onward down the length of my body until he reached my bare feet. "Not likely." His focus returned to my face. "Had we met previously, I would most certainly remember a woman such as yourself."

A blush crept up my neck and heated my cheeks. I shook my head. "Not if I made you forget," I said, testing the waters. How much could I tell this Heru without scaring him off? I couldn't rely on using photos from my phone as proof this time—the battery had died weeks ago, even though I'd rarely turned it on.

Heru's eyebrows rose. "You claim to have such power over the memories of others?"

"Perhaps." I looked from him to the point of his sword and back.

"And might this power be connected to your ability to appear out of thin air?"

My eyes widened. I hadn't realized he'd seen my arrival. "Yes, the two are connected."

"Curious." Finally, Heru withdrew his sword and sheathed it in the scabbard hanging at his hip, though his attention never left my face. "I will take you to my home, and you will explain how such things are possible." He offered me his hand, and I reached out, letting him pull me up to my feet. His skin burned against my frozen fingers, and I found myself reluctant to release his hand.

Heru released mine and touched the backs of his fingers to my arm, then to the side of my neck. "You are nearly frozen. How can that be?"

"I—before I appeared here, I was somewhere quite cold."

He glanced up at the clear, sunny sky, then looked at me, slowly shaking his head. "I find myself quite eager to hear your tale, mistress Nejerette. You are quite the intriguing one."

"So . . . you believe me?"

"I cannot explain how you came to be here, and I am not willing to discard that which I have witnessed with my own two eyes simply because your sudden appearance defies all logical explanation." Heru turned and started across the field. "Come."

I stared after him for a moment, then followed, jogging to catch up. The earth was soft beneath my bare feet, a stray twig or stone poking me only a few times.

"You seem to have lost your shoes, mistress," Heru said when I fell into step beside him.

"Lex," I said. "My name is Lex."

He frowned thoughtfully. "A curious name for a curious woman."

"It is short for 'Alexandra.'"

"And your shoes?"

"Oh. I, um, sort of left them behind." In my frantic mind, I'd been thinking ahead to the eventuality that the twins' power *didn't* kick in before I hit the churning sea, and on the off chance that I survived the fall, I thought my boots would only drag me down. "It is complicated," I added.

"I have no doubt. I am Heru."

"I know who you are," I admitted. "Can you tell me where we are? And *when*?"

He laughed, the sound low and deep. "As I said, I find myself quite eager to hear your tale. But to answer your questions, the year is 1481." He stopped and turned around, motioning for me to do the same. "And we are on the hills just south of the river Arno."

I turned around. "Oh," I breathed, dumbstruck as I took in the sight of fifteenth-century Florence spread out below. Smoke billowed up from chimneys on thousands of clay-tiled roofs within the sprawling walled city, and a string of gracefully arched bridges spanned the curving river, reminding me so much of the At bridges in the Oasis. "This is incredible."

"Is it?"

I nodded, tongue paralyzed.

"How fascinating." Heru placed his hand against the curve of my lower back, and electricity zinged up my spine. "Let us away, mis—Lex. My home is not far, and I think sitting by the hearth would serve you well."

"Yes, of course." I turned back around and didn't balk when Heru offered me his arm. I hooked my hand in the crook, grateful for the added support. Honestly, I wasn't sure I had the strength to keep going without it. I felt dead on my feet, and from the sidelong glances Heru kept throwing my way, I looked it, too.

Some fifteen minutes later, we approached a large, three-story Tuscan farmhouse constructed of gray stone. It was surrounded by all sorts of cultivated, growing things—an orchard curving around one side, a vineyard stretching out down a rolling slope beyond the fruit trees, and a lush vegetable garden surrounding a circular stone fountain. An older man and woman, both gray-haired with skin as tan as leather, moved among the rows, crouching down as they tended their garden. It was a beautiful scene, though I imagined theirs had to be a hard way of life. Hard, but fulfilling.

I fully expected to pass this little bit of rural heaven right on by and head for Heru's no doubt grand estate. Which is why I kept walking down the dirt road when Heru veered off to the right. His pull on my arm redirected me, and I found myself drawn along a wide pathway lined by verdant olive trees that led straight to the stone farmhouse.

"*This* is your home?" I asked, unable to hide the hint of skepticism from my voice.

"At present." Heru eyed me. "Are you disappointed?"

"No, I-just—" I smiled. "This is incredible . . . just not what I expected."

Heru grunted a laugh. "I admit, I have a reputation for having a taste for luxury, and it's true that I rarely deny myself anything, but every few decades, I find myself losing interest in even the most extravagant of pleasures."

"Ennui," I said in English.

"*Ennui,*" Heru repeated. "I do not know this word. To what language does it belong?"

"English," I said. "Though not precisely the English you would be familiar with. It refers to a sense of deep dissatisfaction and weariness, which seems an appropriate thing to feel when one's life spans as much time as yours has."

"Ennui," Heru repeated, then nodded. "When the *ennui* becomes unbearable, I find myself yearning for this life—the chance to work with my hands until they become callused and to live off food that I coaxed from the earth with water and attention . . . to feel a sense of purpose and accomplishment . . ."

"It brings you back to the Oasis," I guessed, recalling the way he'd worked with his family there, sunrise to sunset, keeping their home running and their land productive. "To how your life used to be."

Heru stopped just before the pathway opened up to the garden and turned to me, a hand gripping either of my arms. "How could you possibly know that?"

Because I was there, I didn't say. It seemed like the wrong way to start my rather complicated story, assuming I even chose to share it with him. Again. "It will make sense once you know who I am and how I came to be here," I said. But suddenly, the idea of explaining everything—explaining *us*—to him all over again seemed so far beyond my current capability that I started to tear up.

Heru's eyes searched mine, golden and penetrating. "Perhaps, but as eager as I am to hear your tale, it will have to wait." His gaze slid lower. "You have yet to heal," he said, and I realized he was staring at the cut below my collarbone. The one caused by his sword. I'd forgotten all about it.

"Yes, well . . ." I looked away, staring without seeing at the older man weeding on the far side of the garden. Explaining the reason I wasn't healing like a normal Nejerette would be just as complicated as everything else he wanted to know.

"You are wearier than I realized."

Heru guided me past the garden and onto a patio paved with uneven, time-worn stones. He led me through the broad, arched doorway set in the center of the wall and into a high-ceilinged room with exposed beams, whitewashed walls, and terra-cotta floor tiles. There was a large stone fireplace set in the interior wall, the broad wooden mantel stretching across the top matching the rough beams overhead. A pair of padded wooden armchairs were arranged near the fireplace, a small, squat table between them holding a ceramic pitcher and a pair of matching goblets. A carved wooden bench that looked like it doubled as a chest set against the far wall appeared to be the only other seating in the sparsely furnished room.

Heru paused, his gaze lingering on the armchairs before the dormant fireplace, then shook his head almost imperceptibly and turned instead toward the steep, narrow stairway leading up to the second floor. Gently, he pushed me ahead of him.

I started up the stairs, feet dragging. The worn stone steps were neither standard height nor as even as I was used to, and I missed a step twice, the second time tripping on my skirt when I tried to catch myself. Heru reacted with inhuman speed, his arm snaking around my waist to keep me from falling forward onto the higher steps. His body pressed against me from behind, his hand splayed over my belly.

I held my breath, waiting for the inevitable. Because there was no way he couldn't feel the slight but noticeable bulge in my abdomen now that his hand was actually *on* it.

"Forgive me, mistress, but can it be possible—"

"Yes," I said, tensing. "I am with child."

He was quiet for a few seconds. "Indeed, you are." He righted me quickly but kept a firm hold on the side of my waist and on my elbow. "Then it is even more pressing that you rest."

We reached the hallway at the top of the stairs without further incident and passed by mirroring doorways on the left and right. A second doorway on the right revealed another, narrower staircase.

Heru stopped before the opening. "Apologies, but the other rooms are occupied by my daughter and her family, and I feel most comfortable housing you in my own personal quarters. I could carry you up, if you prefer it . . ."

"No, no, I can make it."

It was slow going, but I made it up those damn stairs. And when I crested the top, my knee gave out.

Heru caught me before I hit the floor and picked me up easily with an arm under my knees and one behind my shoulders. "Almost there," he whispered.

He laid me in a bed—his bed, I realized in the sluggish recesses of my mind—and while I fought that final losing battle with exhaustion, I thought I felt his fingertips trailing over my forehead and across my cheekbone, brushing hair from my face.

Whether or not it was a trick of my tired mind, his gentle touch was one hell of a nice send-off into the land of dreams.

"AND THAT IS WHEN YOU FOUND ME," I SAID, RUBBING the tender skin around the cut under my collarbone absent-mindedly. Speaking in the original tongue had come to be our go-to method of communication. The language was constant, as unchanging as the people who spoke it. "As I said, it is a long, complicated story."

I hadn't told him everything—far from it, in fact. He knew I was from the future, that I was Alexander's granddaughter, and that I was pregnant. And he knew that I was running from Set. He also knew I needed sanctuary, and that I'd sought him out as the one most likely to be able to keep me safe—on my grandfather's recommendation, I'd claimed. He didn't know about *us*, or that the twins were his, let alone that they were fated to restore balance to the universe, thus saving us all from the unrelenting chaos Apep yearned for so desperately, and he didn't know anything about Apep or Re.

I supposed he saw me as something new, possibly something precious—hope for our kind, that we might one day be a viable species able to reproduce without relying on interbreeding with humans. Perhaps I would tell him about *us* in time, once I knew it wouldn't lead him to throwing me out or running away from fear of bonding with me. I couldn't risk either, and I still didn't have a solid feel for this Heru.

He set a large ceramic mug filled with steaming mulled wine before me on the kitchen's heavy-duty farm table—mulled wine I'd demanded he bring to a simmer to burn off most of the alcohol. "I do not like that," he said.

I leaned over the mug and inhaled deeply; the smell was an intoxicating blend of sweet and spicy. I blew on the steaming liquid, impatient to try it. Heru's elderly daughter, Francesca, named for her mother's mother, or so she'd told me shortly after I'd risen the afternoon following my arrival, touted the miraculous healing properties of her mulled wine. To hear her tell it, it was a bona fide cure-all. Considering that she had to be nearing her eighties and was still an active gardener, showed no signs of arthritis, and appeared to have all of her original teeth, I was forced to give her thinking some merit.

"You do not like what, Heru?" I leaned back in my wooden chair, resigned to wait for the wine to cool. "That you nearly ran me through?"

He stared at me with those too-familiar golden eyes, then turned away to tend the hearth fire. He fed it several logs before giving the leg of pork on the spit a good basting and a turn. "You still have not healed, even after resting."

I shook my head, my hands curling around the mug of mulled wine to absorb its warmth. "I explained to you why . . ."

"You should be in bed, resting until your children are born."

Tired of waiting, I took a tentative sip of the mulled wine, then whimpered and spit it back out. Still too hot. I touched my fingertips to my tongue, hoping I hadn't burned it too badly. "It is hardly like I have a say in the matter. As soon as Set shows up, I will have to leave, just as I came . . ." I snapped my fingers. "Poof."

Heru eased onto the bench that ran along the side of the table and took my hand in his. "While you are here, mistress, in this time and place, you do have a say." He raised one hand but hesitated, his fingertips hovering millimeters from the side of my face. Though he didn't know about our bond, he still felt its pull, and he'd have to be blind and deaf not to sense my own attraction to him.

His fingertips grazed down my cheek, and my eyelids fluttered closed. "It will take Set at least a month to journey here from London, possibly longer. You will have time to rest." Heru's thumb brushed across my lips, and I inhaled a shivering breath. "You will let me take care of you. After all, that is why you came here in search of me, is it not?"

My eyes snapped open, and I sat up straighter. His hand fell away. "I will do what is best for my children," I said. "Nothing more, and nothing less."

Heru's nostrils flared and his lips quirked, hinting at amusement. "You are quite spirited; I shall grant you that much."

Eyes narrowed, I pulled my mug closer and leaned forward, once again basking in the mulled wine's spicy scent.

"Have you anything else to wear?"

I lifted the cup to my lips and took a sip, pleased to find the liquid didn't burn this time. Much. I took another sip, then shook my head. "I have money, though—gold." I patted the hidden pocket in my skirts, eyes widening when I found it empty. "No . . ."

The purse had been my lifeline, my backup plan in case Aset, Nik, and Heru were nowhere to be found. "It's gone!" I pushed back my chair and started to stand. "I must have dropped it when I jumped from—"

"Calm yourself." Heru's fingers closed around my wrist, preventing me from standing all the way. "I removed your purse when you were sleeping."

"You have it," I said, eyes unblinking.

"As I just said."

I sank back into the chair. "Well, you could have said something earlier."

His eyebrows rose, and he leaned away from me. "I left it on the table beside the bed. It was there when you woke."

"Oh, well . . ." Avoiding his gaze, I brought the mug of mulled wine up to my lips once more. "I was a bit distracted by the food." An array of fruits and cheeses and cured meats had been set out on a small table beyond the foot of Heru's bed while I slept, and when I awakened, I'd demolished most of it.

Heru laughed. "I was pleased you enjoyed the spread. Franci takes pride in her cheeses."

"She should." I tilted my mug his way. "And in her mulled wine. It is delicious."

Heru took a sip from his own mug and wrinkled his nose. "I prefer it a bit more potent."

"Then heat yourself another batch." I snagged his cup by the handle and dragged it across the corner of the table to sit beside mine. "I claim this mug as my own."

Heru's lips quirked. "Quite spirited, indeed."

17

PEACE & LOVE

My time in fifteenth-century Tuscany was idyllic. Days were spent exploring the rolling hills surrounding the farmhouse or helping in the garden when Heru deemed a task not overly strenuous. And during the evenings, Heru and I would sit around a long table under the covered patio behind the house, sharing stories and laughing over food and drink with Francesca, her husband Giovanni, their eldest son and daughter-in-law, and *their* three adolescent children. None questioned my presence—I was simply a visiting Nejerette. An "old friend" of Heru's.

This place, this life . . . it was paradise. Except for one thing: Heru didn't know who I was, not really. He came to care about me on his own, which made his affection all the sweeter for having nothing to do with our bond. I enjoyed where we were, *how* we were, and I'd fully intended to maintain the status quo. I truly had. But things got out of hand, words were exchanged, and one thing led to another . . .

I sat on the edge of the garden fountain, the scent of the herbs in the garden plot behind me fragrant as the heat from the sun-soaked earth rose to greet the stars. I wore only my long linen shift, as I'd grown comfortable doing in the quiet evening hours after the rest of the family had retired, and I luxuriated in the freedom of movement it afforded. I hadn't been made for fussy gowns; I found all the buttons and ties and frills cumbersome. And more so, I felt immensely grateful and pretty damn lucky that I'd managed to skip over the periods when corsets were *en vogue*.

Tracing the outline of the full moon reflected in the water's surface, I thought back on my afternoon with Heru. We'd taken a leisurely stroll to the hilltop to the north, where I'd first arrived, and had flattened some of the tall, golden grass under a heavy wool blanket for a midday picnic. The view was unbeatable: early Renaissance Florence buzzing and humming and puffing smoke, a thriving organism on the cusp of a new century, practically bursting with the promise of greatness. These were the days of Leonardo and Michelangelo and Botticelli. Of the Medicis and Machiavelli. Of the curiosity and creativity that lay at the heart of one of the greatest cultural, intellectual, and philosophical revolutions in Western history.

"Do you know Da Vinci?" I asked Heru while I loaded a slice of bland Tuscan bread with a hearty layer of tangy coarse-ground mustard, a piece of prosciutto, and a thick slice of hard, nutty cheese—all made under Francesca's artful direction, of course.

"Leo? We are acquainted." Heru munched on pickled vegetables, his avoidance of my gaze teasing.

I slapped his arm even as I took a healthy bite of my open-faced sandwich. "Well . . . ?"

The corner of Heru's mouth quirked. "I take it that Leonardo di ser Piero da Vinci is still something of a notable figure in the future?"

I nodded while I chewed, then raised my hand to cover my mouth. "He is fascinating to many and has become an obsession for some. Books, movies, TV shows . . ."

"You have, once again, reverted to speaking gibberish, mistress."

I sighed, popped the rest of my bread-meat-cheese combo into my mouth, and shrugged. It was how so many of our conversations ended, derailed by something either Heru or I mentioned that was utterly unfamiliar to the other.

With another, very contented sigh, I eased back on the blanket and used my arm for a pillow, resting my other hand on my belly. Even the yards of fabric that I begrudgingly wore each day did little to hide the bump now. I was well into my second trimester, and it showed. I could even feel the twins moving around, every so often.

"I want to stay here," I said, "on this hillside—in this moment —forever."

"You could . . ."

I gazed up at Heru, finding his handsome features arranged in a careful, guarded expression. "I could not." I smiled sadly and reached up to stroke the side of his face. "No matter how much I might like to stay here with you, Heru, I cannot."

He stared off at the distant reaches of the city beyond. "I would love you for all eternity, if only you would let me."

"Heru . . ." I let my hand fall away, returning to my belly and the twin souls within—the entire reason I was even here to begin with. They mattered more than anything else in the world, certainly more than this temporary slice of bliss, however reluctant I was to let it go. I closed my eyes and tears snuck free, gliding over my temples.

"Of course, you must return to the father of your children," Heru said, his voice devoid of emotion. "He is a lucky man."

"He is you," I said before I could stop myself. My eyes popped open, and I looked at him, horrified that I'd let the truth slip out.

Much to my surprise, the corners of Heru's mouth ticked upward and his lips curved into a very self-satisfied smile.

I stared at him, blindsided by his reaction.

"I worked it out weeks ago," he confessed, still staring off at Florence. "It was the only plausible explanation—we had bonded in the future, and once your time became unsafe, you fled to another, safer time,

where you would be free to feed the bond while our children grew within you."

I shook my head, ever so slowly. "Why did you not say anything?"

Heru was quiet for a long moment until, finally, he looked at me. "I suppose I was afraid you would confirm what I already knew to be true." He laughed to himself. "It does not matter now. I know that you cannot stay with me, and I shall cherish you all the more while you are still here, dear Lex, for knowing you will leave me soon." He leaned over me, propped up on one elbow, and planted his other hand beside my head on the blanket. "I shall not waste a single moment."

As his face drew closer to mine, my breaths grew shallow, my heartbeats more urgent. I was desperate for him to kiss me. It had been so long since I'd felt the press of his lips against mine. "We should not." My voice was breathy. "It is unwise . . ."

"Perhaps, but I think I may yet have a chance of convincing you to stay." Heru's mouth hovered over mine, and I licked my lips in anticipation of just one forbidden taste. "Tell me you will stay, Lex." His lips brushed over mine, the faintest pressure, and he pulled back.

I whimpered, following him up, but he rested his hand on the crook of my neck, holding me down with the gentlest force.

His eyes burned with a thinning rim of golden fire. "Lie to me."

"Yes," I breathed, paying his price willingly. "I shall stay. Always . . ."

He descended on me, a hawk swooping down on its prey, and his kiss was neither gentle nor quick. His lips were greedy, his tongue impatient as he poured weeks of wanting into that one, single kiss. His restraint was minimal; mine was nonexistent. I hooked my hand around the back of his neck, pulling him closer, refusing to let him go. I wanted so much more than this one, need-filled kiss. But it would have to be enough.

In truth, it was probably too much.

Heru broke the kiss, pulling back and leaving me gasping, far from sated. His golden irises had been swallowed entirely by pupils swollen with lust. "Perhaps you were correct; that was unwise," he said, his chest rising and falling heavily. "I can see that now." When I nodded, he flopped onto his back on the blanket. "The things I wish I could do with you . . . to you . . ."

My hand sought his, and I laced our fingers together. "Tell me?" I watched his profile, saw the moment realization washed over him, quickly followed by a new, more potent wave of desire.

Heru turned his head to look at me, his midnight eyes boring into me. "Do you truly wish to know?"

"I—" My whole body throbbed in wanting, aching for the man lying beside me. For the man who couldn't touch me. I swallowed roughly, parched for far more than drink. "Yes. Tell me."

"Well then, close your eyes, mistress, and I shall do as you command."

My eyelids fluttered closed, and I inhaled shakily.

"I would trace the collar of your gown with my lips." There was a strained note to his voice, a huskiness I was all too familiar with. "Yes . . . be my hands and lips, Lex. Do what I would do but cannot . . ."

I hadn't even realized I'd started running my fingertips over the sensitive skin below my collarbone, following the embroidered edge of the dress's collar. I withdrew my hand but, after opening my eyes and meeting Heru's, settled it once more on my chest. My hands were his. "Keep going. Please?"

He licked his sculpted lips before curving them into a sultry grin. "As my mistress wishes . . ."

SKIMMING MY FINGERTIPS ALONG THE FOUNTAIN'S onyx surface, I blushed even recalling the things he'd said—and I'd done—on that hilltop. We'd been foolish, playing with fire, but somehow we'd managed to emerge unscathed. *This* time.

We couldn't do it again. Not ever. It was too dangerous.

From behind me, I heard Heru approach the fountain. "I would take you to bed on this night," he said. His fingers traced fire along the line of my shoulders, tempting me to dance with those deadly flames once more.

I shivered, goose bumps forming all over my skin.

". . . would doing so not condemn us both to death." He sat beside me on the fountain's rim. "I have been replaying our *kiss* in my mind all evening." And I knew that by "kiss" he meant everything that had followed that brief, lip-locked moment. "Tell me of the first time our lips touched."

I tore my gaze from the water's faintly rippled surface and looked at him, eyebrows drawn together in confusion.

"*Your* first time," he clarified.

"Oh . . ." The few tendrils of hair that had escaped my loosely pinned bun caressed my back and shoulders. "I always think of it as the time I uncloaked an echo of you in the At—it was when I first learned you were Netjer-At." I smiled fondly. "But *you* claimed that one did not count, since it was only our bas, not our actual bodies." My smile faded as realization dawned. Going into the At together wouldn't have been a possibility in my native time, because it was so unstable—but we weren't in my native time. The At here was pristine, only skewed due to my out-of-time presence.

"Heru . . ." I stared at him, my pulse speeding up as an overlooked possibility occurred to me. "What happens to our bas in the At has no impact on our physical bodies, correct?"

His fingers closed around my wrist, his thumb tracing the pulse along the inside. His eyes were lowered, but the moment they met mine, I knew he was on the same page. Hell, from the looks of it, we were on the same damn word of the same damn line.

Heru stood and held out a hand to me. "If it is not inconvenient, mistress, perhaps you would accompany me upstairs?"

I nodded, eyes wide and heart thundering. I placed my hand in his, and we raced up the two flights of stairs to his Spartan bedroom. I'd barely sat on the bed before Heru's ba pulled mine into the At.

. . .

WE CRASHED INTO EACH OTHER AMIDST AN OCEAN OF COLOR. THE vibrant swirls of the whenless, whereless At surrounded us, dulling in comparison to the torrent of emotion cresting between us. Heru tore at my imagined gown, and I treated his unreal clothing with equally vicious disregard.

No time was wasted on buildup, on gentle kisses or teasing caresses—we'd had enough of that on the hilltop. My lips moved against his with crushing desperation, and he responded with equal, unrestrained ferocity. My arms wrapped around his neck as his hands gripped the backs of my thighs, hoisting me up. I wrapped my legs around his hips, hooking my feet together and pressing them into his backside to get closer to him.

Heru broke our kiss only once, hissing in a breath when he first slid inside me.

In that moment of stillness, in the timeless eternity, the controlled chaos of the At all around us, I felt utterly at peace. There was a deep sense of rightness in being joined with Heru, there in the place where our bodies held no sway over what we were feeling—over who we were to each other. There, in the At, Heru and I were simply a man and a woman, no pheromones driving our need, no ancient prophecies pushing us together.

We were Heru and Lex, two people who cared for each other beyond words. Just two people, loving each other. We were, I finally realized—finally accepted—so much more than perfect chemistry.

I smiled, just a little, and was pleased by the answering warmth in Heru's tiger eyes.

The moment I rocked my hips, he groaned and leaned in, capturing my lips once more. It was eons until he released them. And I savored every single second.

18

FAR & AWAY

I woke the next morning feeling more unsatisfied than ever. Damn it.

I rolled onto my back, legs tangled in the skirt of my shift, and reached out for Heru. I felt nothing but soft linen sheets and hard mattress. My eyes popped open, and I turned onto my side, propping myself up on my elbow. As I scanned around the bedroom, disappointment settled in my stomach. I was alone. Heru's sword belt and scabbard weren't hanging from the corner of the wardrobe, meaning he'd left the farm, and the jug and tray of bread, cheese, and fruit on the table told me he'd expected me to wake before he returned.

Flopping onto my back, I stared up at the exposed beams and white plaster ceiling. I felt Heru's abandoned side of the bed once more, trying to gauge how long he'd been gone based on the residual warmth—or lack thereof. Long enough that the bed was cold. I huffed out a breath and rolled to my other side to sit up.

And realized I was about to pee my hypothetical pants.

"Oh, no," I said, standing and rushing to the chamber pot behind a simple wooden screen in the corner of the room. "A little warning before you smoosh my bladder would be nice, guys," I muttered to the twins.

After a quick wash using the basin on the washstand by the wardrobe and bar of house-made soap scented with lemon and lavender, I headed over to the table and plucked a nugget of hard, aged cheese from the tray, popping it into my mouth. There was a folded piece of thick paper propped up in front of the jug, my name scrawled on the front in Heru's long, slanted hand. I poured some unfermented grape juice into a pewter goblet and sipped from the cup as I picked up the note and read.

He'd written in English, since hieroglyphs would have taken forever to draw out, but it meant he'd purposely kept the note simple. His English and my English didn't really get along. The note told me he'd gone into Fiorenza—the contemporary name for Florence—to retrieve a gift he'd commissioned for me, one apparently made by Leonardo da Vinci himself. I could hardly be irritated about that.

Although it was the beginning of my twenty-eighth day here, and Heru had estimated it would take Apep a little over a month to journey here from London. He was cutting it a bit close . . .

The door at the foot of the stairs opened, and heavy footsteps ascended the stairs at a quick clip.

"I did not expect you to return so—" My words died on my tongue as I stared at the man cresting the top of the staircase. "Nik!" I took two halting steps toward him. "What are you doing here?"

Nik blinked, and his irises faded from pale blue to the iridescence of moonstones. "Apologies for barging in, dear Alexandra," Re-Nik said, "but we only recently discovered the urgency of the situation."

I craned my neck to see the empty stairway behind him. "Aset?"

"She is downstairs, convincing Heru's kin that we are not here out of malicious intent."

Considering the menacing figure he cut in his crimson doublet and black jerkin and hose paired with the long, thin sword in the scabbard at his hip, I could understand their concern.

"Please"—he waved his hand in the general direction of the wardrobe—"you must dress. Apep is hardly an hour's ride away, and Heru is still in Fiorenza. You must make your way to the city quickly if the twins are to have any hope of blocking his memories when they pull you from this time."

I rushed to the wardrobe and pulled out the first gown I saw—the simple, midnight-blue wool dress Aset had given me centuries in the future. The silver-embroidered belt that had once rested at my waist had to be shifted higher to accommodate my growing belly, but it didn't look overly ridiculous.

I stared at the stockings rolled up in the top drawer beneath the cabinet. "Warm or cold?"

"I am afraid I do not—"

"Am I dressing for warm or cold weather, Re? Where am I headed? And when?"

"Ah, right . . . you will land in Fiorenza again, but I believe you arrived shortly after the New Year, so—"

"Cold," I said, taking the thickest pair of stockings from the drawer and pulling them on up to my knees. I sort of hop-stepped around to the far side of the wardrobe to retrieve the knee-high leather riding boots Heru made me wear when we walked around the vineyards and explored the surrounding hills—to stave off snakebites, he'd claimed. I didn't mind; they were incredibly comfortable.

I also retrieved one of Heru's cloaks, a dark gray wool of such a fine weave that it almost glinted silver in the sunlight streaming in through the room's narrow twin windows. I slung the cloak over the crook of my arm, then grabbed my drawstring purse from the floor of the wardrobe cabinet and tucked it into my skirt's hidden pocket.

"Alright," I said, taking a deep breath to calm the wobble in my voice. Though I'd known this day would come, and soon, I wasn't ready to say goodbye to this place—to this Heru. Not yet. Another deep breath, and I nodded once. "I am ready." Maybe by saying the words, I'd make it real. I'd make me ready.

Re-Nik continued to block the way, his eyes scouring the room.

"I am ready?" I said, far less sure this time. "Am I missing something?"

"It is not here," Re-Nik said, more to himself than to me.

"What is not here?"

"The sword."

"A sword?" I raised my hands, palms out. "I have no need of a sword, Re. I have never used one before. It would be useless in my hands."

"It must be elsewhere in the house." He turned and jogged down the stairs.

I followed him, moving just slightly slower to avoid tumbling the rest of the way down. "Are you even listening to me?" I stood in the hallway outside of Francesca and Giovanni's bedroom while he did a quick search. "Re?"

"You had the sword when you arrived last time; therefore, you most definitely *do* need a sword."

I placed my hands on my hips. "Well, Heru keeps a spare downstairs in the chest, just in case, so you can stop violating Franci and Gio's personal space already."

Re-Nik straightened from peering under the bed and smoothed down the front of his jerkin. "I see. Well, by all means, Alexandra, lead the way."

Picking up on the urgency in his tone, I lifted my skirts and hurried down the hallway toward the stairs to the ground floor. Once I'd reached the bottom, I rushed across the sitting room to the bench-chest and lifted the seat with a grunt. The thing was sturdy and weighed a ton.

Sure enough, resting on top of a pile of folded blankets, quilts, and table linens was a scuffed and age-darkened leather scabbard. I'd never actually lain eyes on the backup sword, so I was surprised to find it was long, thin, and slightly curved . . . very Japanese, and very unlike any European swords of this time. It had a simple leather-wrapped hilt and a steel pommel inlaid with a silver medallion displaying a falcon—Heru's ancient symbol.

"Just so you know, I have no idea what to do with this."

Re-Nik reached into the chest to pick up the sword. "I had feared this would be the claymore Heru has been toting around for centuries. Thankfully, this is the right one." He pulled on the hilt, sliding the blade free of the scabbard a few inches. It gleamed like it was made of solid, polished opal. But it wasn't. It was made of something far rarer—At. "A tad showy for everyday use. I can understand why Heru keeps it stowed away, though it is highly functional. There is nothing this sword cannot cut through."

He sheathed the sword and handed it to me. It wasn't nearly as heavy as I'd expected—not even close to as heavy as it would have been had it been made entirely of steel.

"Where—how—" I stared at Re-Nik. "You made it, didn't you?"

The ancient, literally dual-personality man nodded. "I created it after I saw you last and realized it had to come into Heru's possession at some point. He discovered the blade in Hatnofer's coffin nearly a century ago." Re-Nik stared up at the ceiling and tapped his forefinger to his lips. "I wonder who might have placed it there?"

"That is so convoluted."

"It is what *is*." He shrugged. "The timeline, you know . . ."

"I thought I heard you two," Aset said, rushing into the room. "Time is running short, Lex. You must be on your way."

I nodded, agreeing completely, but I held the sword out at a loss for what to do with it. Re-Nik stared at it as well, looking equally lost. "Do I just carry it?"

"You are hopeless," Aset said. "Both of you." She strode across the room, took the sword from my hands, and unbuckled the belt. With deft fingers, she slid the end of the belt under the one I was already wearing high on my waist, draped the leather over my shoulder, and buckled it in front of my chest, just over my heart. With the sword belt slung across my torso, the scabbard hung down my back at an angle, awkward, but not uncomfortable. "It may bounce a bit when you walk, but it should stay put, and this way you will not feel unbalanced or worry about the sword belt slipping off entirely. I'll have a proper harness for you when next we meet."

I grasped her hands. "Thank you, Aset." I looked at Re-Nik. "Thank you."

Aset covered my hand with hers. "Yes, yes, and now you must go, Lex."

When we hurried out of the house, Francesca and her family were nowhere in sight.

"Where is everyone?"

"Resting," Aset said, her eyes opened too wide and not remotely innocently.

I grabbed her wrist, forcing her to face me. "Did you hurt them?"

She took a step back. "Of course not! My own brother's family?" Leaning forward, she winked. "I knocked them out with valerian in their wine. By the time they wake, you shall be gone, as will their memories of you."

"But I will be too far away from them." It hadn't even crossed my mind that the memory wipe wouldn't reach them. I was still caught on the part where I was supposed to be leaving. "They will remember me, and Heru . . . they will tell him, and—"

Re-Nik touched my shoulder. "No, dear Alexandra, they will

not remember you. The twins' power grows with each passing day, and human minds are far more susceptible to manipulation than those of our people. All will be well."

So this was really happening. There was nothing to hold me back now.

We said our goodbyes, and, numbly, I started along the pathway lined by olive trees toward the road to Florence. A horse would've been faster than my own two feet, but riding would've put the twins at risk—too great a risk for a little more speed. I walked fast, in a full-on, somewhat waddly power walk, and with each step along the curving dirt road, the reality of the situation sunk in a little bit more. I was leaving my peaceful sanctuary. The respite was over.

And if I wasn't fast enough, if Apep-Set reached me before I reached Heru, I wouldn't have the chance to tell Heru how much I cherished the time I'd spent here, with him. I wouldn't have the chance to thank him. To tell him I loved him—this version of him—and not just because I loved the man he would be in six centuries. I loved him, as he was, right now. He'd stolen my heart all over again.

"Of course it has to be a hundred damn degrees out," I grumbled as I rounded a bend, wiping the back of my hand across my sweaty brow. The river Arno came into sight, and beyond it, walled Florence, the city of lilies. I'd yet to explore it in this time; Heru had deemed it too dangerous—there were other Nejerets in the city, and our kind have long, near-perfect memories. I hadn't minded spending all of my time in the countryside with him, anyway.

"Alright," I said with a huff of breath. "Move your ass, preggo. It's the final stretch . . ." It was a mostly straight, slightly downhill shot to the gate now.

I was halfway there when the hairs on the back of my neck stood on end. I froze. Was it a warning from the twins? Could they sense Apep? Was he closing in on me already?

A quick scan of the lanky, leafy trees bordering the road revealed nothing out of sorts, but the tall, bushy underbrush could've been concealing anything.

I moved off to the side of the road and crouched down, tossing the cloak over my shoulder to free my hands and placing my right palm on the cracked, dusty earth to keep me from toppling forward. I closed my eyes, inhaled and held my breath, and listened. My Nejerette hearing picked up everything—every scurrying critter, every flap of a bird's wings. In the distance, the sounds of the medieval city, the clanking and shouts and creaking, built to a dull roar.

I exhaled shakily, then breathed in and held my breath once more, focusing on tuning out the far-off cacophony.

The soft shush of fabric brushing against the edge of a bush.

I turned my head, honing in on the scattered woods extending beyond the opposite side of the road, slightly ahead of my position. Were he behind me, I would've considered making a run for the gate.

The snap of a twig.

He definitely wasn't behind me.

Slowly, I stood and reached over my shoulder with both hands. My fingers closed around the hilt of the sword, and I drew it in one surprisingly smooth motion. The solidified At rang out as it slid free. I held the sword out before me, hoping the mere sight of it would hold Apep at bay long enough for the twins to jump me further back in time.

"What a pretty toy you have created, carrier of my sheut," Apep said using Set's voice. The quiet words, uttered in the original tongue, slithered over my skin. "I think I shall pry it from your hands after I have ripped my sheut out of you."

I could see him now, picking his way through the woods. He wasn't being careful any longer.

"Try me," I said, surprised by the steadiness of my voice.

He threw back his head and laughed.

"Lex!"

At the sound of Heru's yell, I looked down the hill. He was running, but still so far away. And Apep-Set was far too close.

My deranged, possessed father emerged from the woods on the other side of the road and stopped, clasping his hands together behind his back. "Is this not exciting?"

I risked a glance down the hill. Heru was still several hundred yards away. Was he close enough? If I let the twins jump me back in time now, would he remember me?

Part of him would. But then, part of him *had* to. I felt like an idiot for not connecting the dots earlier.

I stepped onto the dirt road toward Apep-Set and grinned.

This was how it happened . . . how it was supposed to happen.

I took another step, feeling the twins' power welling in my abdomen in response to their closer proximity to Apep. Iridescent flames danced over the skin of my arms extended before me.

This was why I'd haunted Heru's dreams for centuries. I took one more step across the road, staring directly into Apep-Set's horror-filled eyes. Heru was too far away to forget me completely. Because he had to be.

The vibrant, misty colors of the At burst into existence all around me, and the road to Florence fell away. I hadn't screwed up the timeline. I'd protected it. Fulfilled it.

As Re loved to say—it is what *is*.

19

DUST & BONE

I passed through two more stops in my whirlwind tour of European history fairly quickly—Florence in the fourteenth century, then twelfth-century London, smack-dab in the middle of Richard the Lionheart's reign—bringing me to tenth-century Scotland, or *Rìoghachd na h-Alba*, as it was called these days. Once again, I'd concealed parts of my story from Heru initially, specifically the *us* parts, and once again, he'd puzzled it out—though this time I was strict about practicing restraint. We were as celibate as a cohabitating monk and nun. Who made goo-goo eyes at one another. And snuggled. And shared a bed.

Heru was fast asleep when I rose one morning and snuck from his bed. I retrieved the gown I'd worn the previous day, the velvet a muted purple that reminded me of the rising and setting sun, and slipped it on over my head. The heavy fabric fell around me, draping over my protruding belly. I gathered up the worked silver belt that I wore with all of my gowns, folding the delicate links over each other and wrapping them in my skirt to mute their noise. It was time for my weekly—or weekly-ish—checkup with Aset.

Tiptoeing, I slipped out of the bedchamber, inching the heavy wooden door closed slowly enough that the iron hardware wouldn't clink together. I'd learned the previous times I'd snuck out not to close the door completely. The latching of the mechanism within was a surefire way to wake Heru.

Aset, Nik, and I always met somewhere new. There was ever a risk of being caught, but as my belly grew, accommodating the twins within, Aset became more and more adamant about meeting up.

I felt like I was about to explode. I thought it couldn't possibly be much longer until the twins arrived—an event I was both looking forward to and dreading. Their birth would mean an end to all of this running, this constant looking over my shoulder, this fear that every little nick might become infected or that I might catch some disease that my muted regenerative abilities wouldn't be able to fight off. I still didn't know how it would happen, but once the twins arrived, we *would* return home. Nik had told me as much in the cave all those months ago. I would have the chance to raise my children with the man I loved and, assuming Apep had been recaptured in my time, finally—*finally*—stop being so damn afraid all the time. I was so tired of being afraid.

One hand curled under my belly, I snuck along Castle Uaireigin's drafty third-floor hallway toward the stone stairwell that led to the second-floor landing. I paused at the top of the stairs, taking a deep breath and digging my knuckles into a particularly achy spot in my lower back. The heavy achiness was getting worse every day, cramps on steroids. Just another, albeit smaller, reason I was ready for this to be over.

Quietly, I made my way down the stairs. At the landing, I turned away from the gallery open to the great hall below and headed toward the servants' stairwell at the back of the castle. I'd been living in Castle Uaireigin for nearly three months, and I was familiar enough with the servants' schedules by now to know they'd either be busy in the kitchens at this early hour, working out in the stable yard, or still sleeping, waiting for the sun to rise, the roosters to crow, and their day of servitude to begin anew.

If I was careful, I could slip down the stairs and behind the tapestry at the bottom, ducking into a hidden passageway before any of them noticed me. I knew I could do it; I'd already done it nearly a dozen times before.

I'd spent most of the third trimester of my pregnancy here, in the heart of the Middle Ages—the Dark Ages—but it wasn't as bad as it sounded. I'd grown accustomed to the increasingly simple ways of life as I jumped further and further in time. The simplicity was almost addicting, and the ladies' fashion of this time was surprisingly comfortable—pretty much like wearing a floor-length nightgown and a robe. And right now, comfort was as important to me as anything. Because I was so damn uncomfortable.

Over my three previous stops in time, I'd grown moderately proficient with the sword Aset and Nik encumbered me with in Renaissance Italy. I hadn't been practicing much with it lately; Heru refused to train me when I was so off-balance. Probably a wise decision.

It was a little disconcerting to dive further and further back in time—back in medical advancement—even as I drew closer and closer to my due date. At least I had Aset. Her knowledge and skill with healing was far beyond that of the humans of this time. Knowing she'd be there when I needed her most was one of the few things keeping me sane in what had become an increasingly insane period of my life.

I made it downstairs and into the secret passageway without a hitch. Once I was concealed, I paused to press both of my thumbs against the base of my spine. This aching—how did it keep getting worse? I exhaled heavily, hurting and tired. I'd slept horribly the night before, plagued by strange, incoherent dreams on the few occasions that I'd actually drifted off. I hadn't been able to get comfortable, not lying, not sitting, and standing wasn't doing me any favors, either.

"Not much longer," I said under my breath. It was the most enthusiastic pep talk I could muster on short notice.

In the dark passageway, I paused to secure the silver belt around my "waist" before carefully picking my way over the scattered, discarded pieces of stone and wood that littered the floor. Most of the castle was newer, but this part was old, even now. I was curious to find out, once I returned to my time, whether or not it still stood, either as a functioning building or as a discarded ruin. I thought it might be slightly heartbreaking if I discovered that there was no remnant of it at all.

Soon, the passageway angled downward, carrying me toward the system of tunnels and catacombs that ran underneath the castle. I took the rightmost fork, which would spit me out through a locked iron gate into the gardens behind the castle. Assuming I had a key, of course. I smiled and touched my belt. It was a gift from Nik and Aset—each link was actually a locket chamber holding a key crafted from solidified At to this or that part of the castle and grounds.

It was still quite dark when I emerged into the gardens, and chilly, but not cold. It was the peak of summer here, disorienting when I considered it was winter back home.

I passed between rows of onions in the bountiful kitchen gardens, then between rows of leeks, then rows of herbs on my way to the walled garden beyond. It was Heru's private sanctuary, where he forbade any but himself—and me—from entering. The garden's decaying stone walls reached a couple feet overhead and were covered almost completely by vines that seemed to both support it and work to pull it down. Within, the garden was overgrown, only a few clear spaces where the plants had been tended recently, but the plants weren't the focal point of this particular garden.

Every few feet along the interior walls, the vines were pulled to the side, a living curtain drawn away to reveal breathtakingly beautiful plaster friezes displaying life in ancient Egypt. The first time I'd seen them, I'd been so stunned that the words tripped over themselves as I told Heru about the passageways under the garage on Bainbridge. The scenes depicted—they were so similar. It was so *him*.

There was one frieze, the one displaying the goddess Hathor and the god Horus—Hat-hur and Heru—as divine consorts. The first time Heru showed it to me, he explained that she was a memory from a dream of a time long ago. I'd touched the side of his face and told him it was not a dream.

Though I'd been here many times before, this would be my first time meeting Aset and Nik in Heru's secret, walled garden. I pushed the door open with a grunt, the old iron hinges groaning and the wood creaking.

Aset and Nik were already there, Aset standing before the mural of the couple Heru and I used to be—would be—*were*—and Nik sitting on the ground, his back against a mossy boulder at the center of the garden. Aset turned partway, watching me enter over her shoulder.

I offered them a quick smile, then turned to push the door closed. I relocked it before stowing my key back in my belt. Turning around, I made my way into the heart of the garden.

Aset met me with outstretched hands, grinning broadly. "And how are you on this morning, dear Lex?" she asked in the original tongue, leaning in to kiss first one side of my face, then the other.

I pulled back and met her eyes. "Well enough, I suppose. And you?"

Aset gave my hands a squeeze. "Oh, you know us. We are as we always are . . ." She released one of my hands to place hers on the crux of my belly. "It shall not be too much longer, I think. Perhaps one more month."

My shoulders slumped and I let out a sound that brought to

mind a mooing cow. Which, coincidentally, was pretty much what I felt like.

Aset laughed, a tinkling, chime-like sound. "When the time is right, it will happen. Not before, and not after."

"But why is *now* not the right time?" I whined.

Again, Aset laughed, and Nik joined her.

"I hate you both," I said, sharing a friendly smile with first mother, then son.

"Nonsense." Aset swatted my arm. "You adore us. Now, come, let us begin your examination so we might return you to my brother before he notices you were ever gone."

Nik stood lookout while Aset took care of the poking and prodding and looking and listening, at least where my body was concerned. He leaned back against that mossy boulder and listened with all his might, hearing everything going on beyond the garden's walls. If anybody was approaching, if anybody was even coming close, we would know.

"I fear it is almost time," Aset said, kneeling beside me while I readjusted my dress's skirt on the ground around me.

I paused and looked at her. "But you said another month . . ."

Aset bowed her head. "But the time is right."

I settled back on my elbows and sighed. "Which means I shall be leaving this time soon. I know I will not give birth here," I admitted to Aset. "I dreamt of my time here once . . . when my Netjer-At qualities were just beginning to manifest. At the time, I did not realize it was me I was watching in the dream, but I now know I witnessed my final moments here—mourning the destruction caused by Apep, saying goodbye to Heru, disappearing . . ."

"This is a violent exit, then?" Aset asked.

"Yes," I said, my voice suddenly thick with emotion. "The most violent yet. There will be much death, here." I stared up at the muted gray sky, counting the vanishing stars and listening to the birds' wake-up songs and the garden critters scurrying and slithering around. "I have struggled with the urge to warn them . . . to warn Heru. They are his people, after all. And I have come to care for a great many of them."

"You cannot warn them of what is to come," Aset said, touching my shoulder. She gave it a gentle squeeze before settling beside me, reclining on her elbows, her skirts mingling with mine. "However insignificant it may seem to spare even a brief human life, doing so could trigger a chain of events that could—"

"I know, I know," I said, emotional exhaustion weighing down my words. "If a butterfly flaps its wings . . ."

Aset eyed me, her expression quizzical. "I am unfamiliar with this saying."

"It is a theory—part of what is called Chaos Theory. Essentially, it claims that minute occurrences can have a major impact on major, um, things." I offered Aset a weak smile. "Sorry, this is a terrible explanation. But anyway, the go-to example is a butterfly flapping its wings, moving the air, and that small change causing increasingly bigger changes that end up affecting the weather." I raised my eyebrows. "Does that make any sense at all?"

Aset nodded slowly. "And it does, indeed, seem an appropriate saying for our discussion—if a butterfly flaps its wings . . ."

I smiled, just a little, even as I felt my heart begin to weep. Perhaps I'd been foolish letting myself get to know the ill-fated humans of this time and place, but initially, their preordained demise hadn't disturbed me—likely because according to my internal clock, the one that was still synched with my native time far in the future, these people were already dust and bone. I'd viewed them as remnants of a past long dead, but now I saw them as living, thriving people with families and hopes and dreams for the future. A future they would never see.

"Shall I tell you of your next adventure?" Aset said, clearly aiming to derail my darkening mood. "A hint of what is to come?"

I shot her a sideways glance. "You want to flap your little butterfly wings?"

"Only gently." She smiled mysteriously. "You, dear Lex, will be coming home."

I perked up. "To Washington?" I knew I would return home while the twins were still babies, according to what Re had seen in the At, but I hadn't realized it would be *before* I gave birth.

Aset's brow furrowed. "I do not know of this Was-een-ton."

"Ohhh . . ." I let my head fall back, feeling especially dense, and more than a little disappointed. "You mean Kemet."

So, it looked like I would be returning to Egypt. I'd have been lying if I claimed not to be excited, even as I struggled with the disappointment of knowing I wouldn't be returning to my true home quite yet. Egypt was my passion; it was in my blood. Hell, I'd married one of the ancient culture's staple gods and had inadvertently *become* another. I thought part of me would always feel like I belonged there, in that rich, ancient land.

"Indeed I do," Aset said. "And you should know, Lex, it will be up to *you* to find us this time around, so make sure you have your satchel well-supplied before you make this next jump."

I laughed under my breath. "I will do what I can," I promised. "This is a longer jump than usual, then?" They'd generally been a couple hundred years at a time, so far.

"It would seem that the twins' power grows as they do—not only do they choose their final destination on safety, but on need. They will be bringing you to a place where they will be safe for the remainder of your pregnancy, and to a time when you will be needed for your final act as guardian of the timeline."

I snorted. "I do not think I would go so far as to call me a 'guardian' of the timeline—perhaps 'stumbler *through*' the timeline would be more fitting."

Aset laughed. "Perhaps."

We were quiet for a moment, enjoying the sounds, smells, and gentle light of the nearing dawn. It was like the whole world was stretching lazily in bed, toying with the idea of waking, rising, and shining.

"Oh, and Lex?"

"Hmmm . . . ?"

"Do not forget your sword. You will need it."

"Someone is coming," Nik said quietly.

"Is it—" I started.

"Lex?" It was Heru. "Lex!"

My eyes bugged out, and I made a shooing motion at Nik and Aset, imploring them to leave, to magically find some way out besides the garden's single door.

Nik shook his head, pointing to me and then to the door.

I nodded, understanding. If I left the garden, Heru wouldn't have any reason to come in, and Aset in Nik's presence would remain a mystery to the world, as it must.

Aset helped me to my feet, and after a quick, quiet embrace and a kiss blown Nik's way, I hurried along the clearest winding path through the overgrown garden, my speed hindered slightly by my waddle. "I'm here," I called as I neared the door. "I'm here, Heru!" I fished the key from my belt, unlocked the door, and pulled it open enough that I could squeeze through, then pulled it shut and relocked it.

When I turned around, Heru was striding through the orchard that neighbored the garden. I didn't have a way to return the key to my belt discreetly, so I dropped it, kicking it under some overgrown weeds with the toe of my boot.

Heru wore his usual guarded mien, but I could pick up on the small nuances that hinted at anger, irritation, and frustration. "I woke, and you were gone," he said, voice low, even. "I had no idea—no hint of where you had gone or why. What was I to think?"

"I could not sleep," I said, brushing off the back of my dress. "And your secret garden called to me." Hopefully he was too upset to realize his key to the garden was exactly where it should be—back in his bedchamber.

Heru's legs devoured the few final yards separating us, and his arms swallowed me up in a desperate hug. He pressed his lips to the top of my head and breathed in and out several times. "Please, refrain from ever doing that again."

I didn't tell him I wouldn't have much of a chance to do it again because I wouldn't be there, in this time with him, much longer. I didn't want him dreading the fast-approaching inevitable. He knew I would be leaving at some point, had to know it would be soon, but I wasn't willing to put him in the same position as me, knowing people he cared about were going to die . . . knowing he could do something to keep that from happening but being unwilling to for the sake of the future he'd yet to live. I couldn't be sure that his resolve to protect the timeline would be as steady as mine.

I smiled against the front of his leather jerkin, a small, sad smile. Maybe Aset was right. Maybe I was a guardian of the timeline. Or maybe I was just a girl trying not to screw too much up while I ricocheted through time.

"I am sorry I frightened you," I said quietly.

Heru exhaled heavily. "Next time, you will wake me?"

My smile, hidden against the leather, turned genuine. It had taken me over two months to break this era's Heru of the habit of ordering me around, but finally, he was learning to request from me, not to demand of me. I thought it was quite an accomplishment, considering I was still working on the same issue with the Heru of my own time.

He pulled back, leaving only his hands on my shoulders. "Let us return, my Lex."

I arched my back as much as the twins would let me, massaging the base of my spine with my thumbs and wishing for some modern painkillers. "Very well. I would like some tea, anyway."

Heru made a face that spoke of disgusting things better spat out. "I do not know how you stomach that stuff. It tastes like dirt."

I laughed. "It does not!" Raspberry leaf tea might not have been as effective as modern drugs, but it at least provided me some relief.

"It does." Heru turned and, with an arm over my shoulders, led me back to the castle.

20

LIFE & DEATH

I woke with a start, then felt a dull tug from deep within my abdomen. I placed my hand on my belly. The twins were stretching around within me like they, too, just couldn't get comfortable.

I felt another tug, quickly followed by a slightly nauseating flip-flopping sensation, like I was hurtling down the drop at Splash Mountain. "Shit," I hissed. The twins sensed Apep.

I scooted to the edge of the bed and hung my feet over, pushing my upper half up off the mattress with sleep-tired arms. "Heru," I said, standing with a groan. "Heru!"

He sat up suddenly, a dagger wielded before him like he was preparing for a backhanded throat-slit. It was a perfect example of why I got out of bed *before* waking him.

"He's here." I pointed to the far side of the room, where my sword hung on an iron hook alongside Heru's two favorites—a massive claymore and a smaller longsword. "You might want to get ready . . ."

While Heru rose, I hobbled over to the wardrobe to retrieve the garments I'd spent all afternoon and evening making. With the help of one of the maidservants, Jane, I'd converted two fine linen nightgowns into simple shifts that would fit in during most ancient Egyptian periods.

I pulled my nightgown off over my head, leaving me naked for a moment, then slipped one of the shifts on in its place. A quick glance over my shoulder showed Heru standing just a few feet behind me, his longsword in its scabbard at his hip, my sword's elaborately strapped harness in his hands, and his eyes filled with heat—either from the peep show I'd just given him or in anticipation of the battle yet to come.

"Thank you," I said, holding out first one arm for him to fit the sword harness over, then the other. I strapped the buckle together over my chest, feeling better with the sword's familiar weight at my back. Unlike my shift, the sword would definitely stand out to the ancient peoples I was about to see. But Aset had said I would need it, and I wasn't about to disregard any of her warnings about my future, because it was already *her* past.

Remembering my dream-echo from over a year ago, and that the woman I hadn't recognized as myself had been wearing a hooded cloak that concealed all but her protruding belly from me, I reached into the wardrobe and withdrew the heavy gray woolen cloak Heru had purchased for me in case of any colder nights. I'd yet to wear it. But I had to wear it tonight.

Draping the cloak over my elbow, I reached into the wardrobe once more and pulled out my trusty, now-worn leather satchel. The spare shift was tucked in there, along with two loaves of dense molasses bread, a small wheel of hard cheese, and a package of dried boar meat. The provisions had been added to my usual supply—a jar of "cure-all" ointment, a flint and steel set, the purse of gold coins, a small mending kit, and a stash of the tea that helped ease my pregnancy pains. I hoisted the strap over my head so it crossed my body, the bag sitting at my hip. I pulled one last item from the wardrobe—my waterskin—and slung its thin leather strap across my body as well.

Standing behind me, Heru took the cloak from my arm and

settled it on my shoulders. I secured the clasp, a small, silver falcon whose talons gripped the opposite side of the fastener, and pulled the hood up. "Alright. I am ready."

Heru knew what had to happen; I'd explained it to him already. Once Apep arrived, he had to stay as close to me as possible. It was imperative that he remain near me for the memory wipe to work. I'd also warned him that whatever happened, he couldn't kill Set. If he did, I would never be born, and everything would be ruined.

Watching him now, seeing the tension and anxiety emanating from him, I knew he itched to be out in the castle hallways, hunting down Apep-Set. I reached up and cupped the side of his face. "Are you ready?"

There was a shout from the hallway beyond the bedchamber door, then a grunt, and then a scream, all in short succession.

Heru's posture changed. He was ready. "I fear we have little choice."

"Can you tell where he is?" I wanted to get the jump through time over with. The tugs from within were increasing, bringing with them nausea and painful, almost throbbing cramps. I rubbed my hands on either side of my bulging belly, hoping to soothe the twins and calm their fretful movements.

Heru was quiet for a moment, his head cocked to the side as he listened. I could hear movement out in the hallway and beyond, but which belonged to Apep-Set, the men he'd brought with him, or the castle servants and guards—the only people who'd remained once Heru sent all of the Nejerets away shortly after I arrived—I couldn't tell. I didn't know this castle nearly as well as Heru, and the stone walls could be tricky with the way sound bounced and rebounded off their uneven surfaces.

"The great hall," Heru said, barely loud enough for me to hear. He drew his sword, then grabbed my hand. "Come."

Instead of heading out the bedchamber door, Heru gripped

the edge of the wardrobe and, straining, dragged it open like a door. Which, as it turned out, was exactly what it was.

Unbeknownst to me, the entrance to another hidden passageway had been concealed behind the sturdy wooden wardrobe I'd stored my things in these past three months. The passageway succumbed to a hungry darkness completely devoid of light—so dark that even my heightened Nejerette vision wouldn't do me any good.

"Do not let go," Heru said, taking a step and pulling me along behind him. Together, we plunged into the darkness.

It quickly became apparent that Heru had the passageway memorized, because he guided me around corners and over dips in the floor and down a narrow, steep flight of stairs with gentle hands and the barest of whispers. Faster than I'd expected, we reached a tapestry hanging along the side of the great hall.

Heru peeked through the crack before turning back to me and bringing his mouth to my ear. "Stay here," he breathed, "and remain silent."

I nodded, strands of my hair catching in his stubble.

He pressed his lips to my cheek, and then he was gone, through the opening and out from behind the tapestry with barely a sound. There was a masculine shout—not Heru's—followed by a thump and a grunt. Not Apep-Set, but one of his followers was out there, putting up an admirable fight.

I heard a guttural gasp, then a sharp crack and the thud of a body hitting the floor. Not a second later, Heru stuck his arm behind the tapestry. Apparently not *that* admirable.

I placed my hand in Heru's, letting him pull me out into the cavernous great hall. He nodded toward the open doorway at the far end, not asking me if we should go that way, merely alerting me to his plan before dragging me along behind him.

We crossed the great hall without detection and slipped out into the broad, arched stone hallway beyond. Narrow, glassless windows lined the opposite side of the hall, letting in a cool breeze along with the silvery moonlight. The square of light coming through the nearest window illuminated a scene from a horror movie—one of the guardsman, his eyes open and sightless, a deep gash cutting across his throat.

I looked up, away, anywhere but at the dead guardsman, at the accusation—the blame—filling his glazed stare. *You could've saved me!*

My eyes landed on a second body further down the corridor . . . then on another, and another.

My fault, all of these pointless deaths. I could've prevented them, *warned* them—done *something*.

I could have *saved* them. These people—they were all dead because of my choice. My silence. It didn't matter that it had all been for some greater good. I might as well have killed them with my own two hands.

Unable to face the truth, I turned to Heru. Anger was written all over his face, the hunger for revenge lighting his moon-silvered eyes. "Do not kill him," I mouthed.

His jaw clenched, but he nodded. Once more, he brought his lips to a hairsbreadth from my ear. "Perhaps you should say something. Draw him out . . ."

I nodded, pulling away. It was always the same, and always different. "No matter how many times we go through this, it always feels too quick," I whispered.

"Louder," Heru mouthed.

I said the first thing that came to mind. "I don't know how he keeps finding me." I hoped Apep would do just that—find me, already. The longer we dragged it out, the more people would die. I wanted it done. I arched my eyebrows higher in a silent question—*loud enough?*

Heru's eyes narrowed as he listened. He nodded slowly, pointing down the hallway, the way we'd come. Apep-Set had heard, and he was heading our way.

I felt a very distinct cramp deep within my abdomen. It looked like the twins sensed his approach as well.

Unable to resist—unwilling to forget—I turned back toward the slaughter. Before I left, I needed to see what my inaction had caused. I owed these precious people that much.

My eyes landed on a pretty, dark-haired woman. Her burgundy and gold livery was askew, revealing her wool stockings, and her neck was bent at an unnatural angle.

A harsh sob clawed up my throat as I rushed forward and, hand on the rough stone wall, knelt beside the dead woman. "Oh, God . . . Jane." My shoulders shook as grief and guilt overwhelmed me. I'd tried so hard to convince myself that these people were already dead—thousand-year corpses, to my twenty-first-century mind—but seeing them here, this woman who'd become my friend, proved just how wrong I'd been.

Maybe it would've warped the timeline. Maybe it would've screwed everything up and made all of the struggle worthless. Maybe it would've destroyed ma'at completely and caused the universe to unravel, killing us all.

But maybe saving their lives—the flap of these beautiful, fragile butterfly wings—wouldn't have changed a damn thing. That possibility would haunt me until the day I died. Could I have prevented this slaughter without greater repercussions? Could I have warned them . . . saved them? Could I have?

"I'm so sorry," I murmured, rocking back and forth over Jane's lifeless body. "This is all my fault . . . all my fault . . ."

"No," Heru said from behind me. "It's his fault, not yours." Hands gripping either of my arms, he helped me up to my feet, then wrapped his arms around me, fingers sprawling over my belly.

I covered Heru's hands with my own, still shaking. Another wave of grief and sorrow washed over me, and desperation took hold. Aset had told me I would have to find her this time—

which meant I'd have to find Heru, too. "I don't know where to go," I said, somewhat incoherently.

"Shhh . . ."

"I thought this would be my last stop, but—" Or, at least, I'd *hoped* it would be. A silent sob wracked through my body, spurred by a sharper cramp. I muffled a cry. "I don't want to leave you again."

"Shhh . . ." Heru's voice was soft and soothing through the wool of the hood. "You must trust that you will find me."

I turned around in his arms and reached up to touch the side of his face. I could feel the twins' power welling within me and had little doubt that my skin glowed with a sheen of multi-hued, smoky tendrils. "I will *always* find you, my falcon"—not long now—"but for now, you must forget."

A door banged open down the corridor, and I caught only the barest glimpse of Set's pale face before my world was overtaken by a burst of rainbow smoke, coiling and swirling around me, and I hurtled further back in time.

21

THERE & GONE

I arrived in Kemet, head hanging, and spirit cracked. A smooth, polished surface was cool beneath my knees and palms. My hair was a curtain shielding me from the soft, sunny glow of the world around me.

I barely had a handful of seconds to catch my breath before a sharp cramp twisted my insides.

"No," I gasped. "Not again." Breathing hard, I stared down at the backs of my hands, waiting for the rainbow smoke, the telltale tendrils of At harkening yet another jump backward in time.

I stared for maybe a minute, maybe a little bit longer. I stared at the backs of my hands, waiting for some sign of my impending jump, until the cramping had abated and I was left on my hands and knees, breathing hard and at a loss for why I hadn't been yanked through time once again.

Cautiously, I sat on my heels, pushing my hair back with one hand while the other cradled my heavy, aching belly. I stared around in complete and utter shock. It wasn't the glow of sunlight that had greeted my arrival. Far from it. I was underground, blocked from the sun by several layers of earth and stone—and solidified At.

I was in my sanctuary in the Oasis, what had become Nuin's tomb during my final day here, last time. One of the original walls stretched out before me, covered in the beautiful pictographs and hieroglyphs I remembered, some ancient predecessor to the scripts of my beloved Egypt—something far older than anything belonging to this world. Something alien.

I knew what these walls said, what the symbols meant, what story they told. This was Nuin's story, his retelling of what happened between him and Apep and how they had come to be here, two lost gods wandering a foreign planet.

"How—" I spun around on my knees, both surprised and not to see the solidified At coffin holding Nuin's perfectly preserved body.

So it's after the collapse, I realized with a rush of relief. I didn't need to fear running into any Nejerets, not here, not now. Everybody was gone, returned to the cities of humans to hide in plain sight. There was no way to say how long ago I'd pulled down the rocky walls of the cliffs surrounding the Oasis, no telling how long Nuin's body had been entombed below the dome of solidified At.

"Oh, no . . ." Logic finally caught up to me. "No, no, no . . ."

There was no way out.

In a matter of days, when my body succumbed to dehydration, Nuin's tomb would double as my own.

A howl scraped free from my chest, and I slapped both of my hands against the side of Nuin's crystalline coffin. "No!" I screamed, the sound transforming to a guttural groan as I doubled over, leaning almost entirely on the coffin.

Another cramp, much sharper this time, throbbed within me. I gripped the underside of my swollen belly with one hand, leaning on the smooth, solidified At with the other. A burst of wetness soaked down the insides of my legs.

"Oh, God . . ."

A sound I didn't know I could make started low in my throat and grew. It was a deep sound, guttural and pained. A sensation unlike anything I'd ever felt dropped me to my knees. I felt like someone was reaching up inside me, twisting and pulling on my insides. It was like somebody was trying to yank them out of me completely.

Knees on the floor and hand pressed against the side of Nuin's coffin, I did the only thing I could—I pushed. I bore down with everything I had.

It couldn't possibly be enough.

I LAY IN THE CORNER OF NUIN'S TOMB, SOLIDIFIED AT walls giving off a gentle glow all around me in response to an expression of my will given some unknown time ago—days? Years? Centuries? I was a mess, exhausted and sweating, my hair matted to my head and blood coating the insides of my thighs, my shift, and the floor beneath me. I was stranded, a prisoner surrounded by impermeable walls.

And I'd never been more blissfully content in my entire life.

I held my babies, side by side on my chest, and stared down at their perfect, rosy faces. They each had a mop of black hair and thick, black eyelashes making little crescent moons on their chubby cheeks.

My little girl, on the left, wiggled her little fist before cracking her eyes open and gazing up at me with the most beautiful green and gold irises. Her eyes swirled with power.

"Hello, darling," I cooed. "Are you hungry, little girl?"

She pursed her lips, almost like she'd understood me. Almost like she was answering.

My lips spread into a somewhat quizzical smile as I wondered if maybe she had. She and her brother, still snoring softly on my chest, were unlike any other children who'd ever been born. I didn't have anything to go by. There was no precedent.

But I didn't really care, so long as I was holding my babies.

"Alright . . ." I sat up a little, still sore, but not nearly so much as I'd been just a half hour earlier. My regenerative abilities were kicking in, it seemed, and I didn't mind one bit.

"I'm going to set you down right here for just a second," I said in a soft, singsong voice, settling my baby girl on my wadded-up cloak. I laid her brother down next to her, tucking the edges of the cloak up around them before reaching over my shoulder to draw my sword. The twins were still connected to the placenta, and I wanted to cut their umbilical cords before they became too cumbersome.

I set the sword on the floor beside me, then tugged my mending kit free from my bag, which had been functioning as my pillow, supporting me while I rested on the floor.

"Just a minute," I told them, smiling. I unwound about a foot from the spool of thread, cutting it with the razor-sharp blade of my sword. I cut the thread again, this time in half, then used the strings to tie off the twins' umbilical cords, just an inch or two from their protruding little infant bellies.

"Just one more second . . ." I gathered both slimy cords together and brought them to the edge of the sword, then glanced at my babies. "I'm almost one hundred percent positive that you won't be able to feel this," I told them. My baby boy seemed content to continue snoozing away, but my girl watched me, swirling green-gold eyes focused and, if I wasn't mistaken, curious.

I bit the tip of my tongue, pressing the two umbilical cords against the edge of the sword blade. They separated easily, without even a minor reaction from the twins. I exhaled in relief.

And then I gasped, horrified, as tendrils of smoky, multicolored At surrounded my babies. Between one breath and the next, one heartbeat and the next, they vanished.

"No," I said, heart breaking. "No!" I clutched the cloak they'd been lying on, but it was too late.

My babies were gone.

PART II - TIME BOMB

KAT

22

LOVE & HATE

One second.

That's how long it takes for Lex to vanish in a cloud of rainbow smoke. For my mom to shove me out of the way. For Apep-Carson to pull the trigger. For my ears to ring with the deafening crack of gunfire. For a bullet that should've hit me to go through my mom's skull instead. For my world to be destroyed.

One fucking second.

From the floor, I watched my mom's head snap backward. Warm splatters struck my face and neck and hands as she fell, her body limp. Boneless. I was shocked into silence, too stunned to scream.

That didn't just happen. It couldn't have. I had to be dreaming. This was a nightmare, and I would wake up any second now and find that Carson or Apep or whoever the hell he was *didn't* just shoot my mom in the head, because things like that don't happen to people. Not to real people.

Not to me—to her. My mom.

I tried to throw myself forward, to go to her, but an arm

snaked around my waist, holding me back. "Not yet, child," Aset said.

Restrained and dumbstruck, I watched Nik and Marcus lunge at Apep-Carson in the millisecond after the gun fired. After my mom took the bullet meant for me.

The instant Nik's fingers made contact with Apep-Carson's At armor, it dissolved into nothing but a colorful, smoky vapor.

Marcus grasped either side of Carson's head and jerked it to the side.

The gun slipped from Carson's grasp, hitting the floor with a clank.

I watched Marcus toss Carson's body toward the empty front doorway like a discarded doll. He was limp, like my mom, his arms floppy. Black smoke was already seeping from his nose and mouth, the rancid soul of Apep leaving his no-longer-viable host.

"Nik," Marcus said, staring down at the body. His hands were on his hips, and he was breathing hard.

"Already on it," Nik said, raising his hands, palms out. A convex sheet of solidified At spread out before him. It glided over Carson's body and the small mass of blackness that had already oozed out of him, once more trapping Apep in a prison of At.

"Let me go!" I strained against Aset's surprisingly strong hold. "It's over! Let me go!"

Aset relented, and her arm fell away.

Tumbling forward, I crawled over the place where Lex had been only moments before to kneel by my mom's body. I was afraid to touch her, certain that if I left her as she was, Neffe or Aset would be able to fix her. They could work their medical magic and doctor her back to life. They could do anything. There was still a chance, so long as I didn't make it worse by touching her. There was still a chance that my mom would be alright. That she wasn't dead. That she hadn't died because of me.

I looked around wildly, skimming over Marcus and Dom and Carson and Nik and the At-orb in his hand and focusing on Neffe, still standing at the foot of the stairs. She just stood there, mouth hanging open, when she should have been helping my mom. What the hell was wrong with her?

"Help her!" I said. "Do something!"

Neffe's eyes softened as she looked at me. She shook her head, a slow, defeated movement.

"Oh, my dear," Aset said as she knelt on the other side of my mom. "There's nothing we can do for your mother." She reached across my mom's chest and took hold of my hand. Her fingers were cool and dry, but her hand was shaking. "She's already gone," she said. Her honey eyes searched mine, overflowing with sympathy. Dripping with pity. "I'm so sorry, Kat."

I hated her in that moment. Why was she wasting energy on pitying me when she should've been trying to save my mom? I didn't deserve pity. I'd let my mom push me out of the way. I'd let her die instead of me.

I yanked my hand free and shook my head. "She's not dead!" She couldn't be. "Do something! You have to help her!"

"I've got a pulse," Neffe said, and I glanced up to where she'd been standing at the bottom of the stairs, hope making my heart leap. *I knew it! She's not dead!* But Neffe wasn't there.

She was kneeling on the floor beside Dom, her fingers pressed into his wrist. She hadn't been talking about my mom. "It's weak," she said, "but he's still with us, the stubborn bastard. Aset, I need you. Nik, Father—will you donate? I think a transfusion's the only way we'll be able to save him."

"Yes, of course," Marcus said.

"Good. I need you to move him—gently. He's barely holding on." She stood and moved out of the way, allowing Marcus and Nik to lift Dom off the floor.

Aset stood to join the organized chaos suddenly filling the entryway.

I watched them, tears streaming down my cheeks. Rage filled me. They weren't doing anything to save my mom. They hadn't even tried.

The others left, and I was suddenly alone with my mom's body and the remains of her killer and all of that rage. I couldn't stand the sight of Carson's body a moment longer, couldn't bear the idea that his stupid, fetid soul would last for all eternity because he had the good fortune to have been born a Nejeret, but my mom's soul would dissipate because she was just a human. Just a Nejeret carrier. It wasn't fair.

It. Wasn't. Fair.

Gritting my teeth, I pushed up off the floor, stormed over to Carson's body, and kicked him with everything I had in me. "I hate you," I said, my toes striking his side again. My slipper offered little protection, and my big toe throbbed with the impact of my second blow. "I hate you!" I kicked him toward the front doorway until he was lodged half in and half out, with his head and one leg stuck on the doorframe.

With a grunt, I dropped to my knees and started shoving at his body. I needed him to be gone—out of the house and away from my mom.

"I hate you!" I shrieked with each push. I repeated it over and over as I shoved and shoved and shoved, and though Carson's body gave a few inches, I couldn't seem to get him all the way through the doorway.

"Kat." It was Nik. He was behind me, but I didn't care.

I gave an extra-hard shove, and something in Carson's leg gave way with a sickening snap.

"Kat!" Nik hauled me backward by my upper arms. "That's enough."

I struggled, a wild thing trying to break free.

Nik spun me around and gathered me into his arms, holding me securely against his chest. There was no breaking free from his iron embrace.

“My mom . . .” I moaned against his T-shirt. “He killed my mom.”

“I know,” Nik said, his arms secure around me. “I know.”

23

HER & ME

I stand paralyzed, staring down the barrel of a black pistol. I don't move as Apep-Carson presses the nozzle to my forehead. I don't even breathe. All I can think is—I don't want to die.

Stillness settles around me. Quiet. The others are now paralyzed, too, like me. Everyone seems to be holding their breath. Like me.

I swear I can feel every single blood cell rushing through my veins. I can feel every molecule of oxygen and carbon dioxide and nitrogen and argon in my lungs. A slight breeze flows in through the open doorway, rustling the tendrils of hair that have escaped from my bun. Sweat inches down the back of my neck.

I don't want to die.

Marcus is closest, a few feet to my right—hands up, like a criminal. Dom is facedown on the floor behind him, closer to the door. He's bleeding, maybe still alive. Maybe not.

I look at Marcus, meet his eyes. I try to tell him with just a look how badly I want to not *die. I'll do anything—give up anything—to not die.*

"Let me pass," Apep-Carson says, "or I'll kill sweet little Kat here."

I can feel my whole body shaking.

Apep-Carson steps forward, the pressure of the gun against my forehead forcing me backward. He takes another step. And another. I don't know how I manage to walk backward without tripping. Without my knees giving out.

I've moved far enough now that I can see my mom. I've never seen her look so terrified in my entire life. The second our eyes meet, my chin trembles, and tears break free, streaking down my cheeks. I don't want to die, but even more so, I don't want my mom to watch me die. It'll kill her.

"Nik," Marcus says.

I look at Marcus, but he's staring at something behind me. At Lex, I realize.

"I know," Nik says. "I'm not fucking blind."

I have no idea what he's talking about, so I return my focus to my mom. I try to tell her how sorry I am with just my eyes. I try to tell her I forgive her and I love her. I try so hard, but all I seem able to do is cry silently as Apep-Carson pushes me backward.

"Don't you go anywhere yet, Mother," Apep-Carson says, then clicks his tongue, tutting. "I really wouldn't, if I were you. You won't stop me."

Hope flutters in my chest. Is someone going to do something? Is someone going to stop him from killing me? Is someone going to save me?

"Who said anything about stopping you, shit-stain?" Nik growls.

Apep-Carson's face contorts with rage. The muscles in his forearm tense, making the veins and tendons stand out. This is it. I'm going to die.

Something slams into me, and I'm thrown to the side. It's my mom. She's looking at me, watching me fall. Disgust is painted across her face, and blame fills her eyes.

BOOM.

My mom's accusing face is shattered into a million pieces of bone and skin and blood.

I GASPED AWAKE, MY HEART THUNDERING AND MY lungs sucking in air. Sheets damp and cold with sweat were tangled around my legs, restraining me. I fought against them, frantic to be free. Panic from the nightmare bled into reality, infecting my mind and telling my body to run, to fight . . . to *do* something.

Except there was nothing to run from. Nobody to fight. At least, not here. Not in my bedroom in the middle of the night. Here and now, I only had myself to wrestle. I only had my memories to contend with, my guilt and self-loathing to battle. Here and now, *I* was my greatest enemy.

I blew out a breath and, with a hand, brushed back the long tendrils of hair stuck to my sweaty face. This had been going on for two months—the nightmare. The panic. The guilt. I relived the worst moment of my entire life every time I closed my eyes. I was exhausted all the time, but there didn't seem to be any way to make it stop.

Resigned to yet another night without sleep, I sat up and reached over to turn on the lamp on the nightstand. I opened the nightstand's top drawer and pulled out a deck of playing cards and a small spiral notepad. Curling my legs up, I pushed the bedsheet to the side and shuffled the cards.

Solitaire had been my go-to method of passing the time lately. I kept score, Vegas style. According to the notepad, I was $4,133 in the hole.

If I was lucky and maintained my focus, I'd be able to get back into the three thousands tonight. It was barely past midnight. Plenty of time until morning.

I started dealing, laying out seven cards in a row, then six, then five . . .

It was going to be another long night.

BANG. BANG. BANG.

"Kat!" Jenny, Lex's "real" sister, called through the bathroom door. "Let me in. Please?"

I stared down at the mountain of hair in the sink, then looked at my reflection in the mirror. Better. Much better.

"I'm seriously about to pee my pants!" Bang. Bang. Bang. "Let me in!"

"There are eleven other bathrooms in this house," I said, raising my voice so her human ears could hear me. "You don't *need* to use mine."

"Fine, but if there's any leakage while I waddle my way down the hall, you're doing my laundry."

I rolled my eyes. She was barely halfway into her pregnancy, just a couple months ahead of Lex—hardly into prime waddling territory. Still, I unlocked the door.

Jenny shoved it open. "Cute hair," she said, brushing past me. She paused at the sink. "Aaaaand, there's the rest of it." She continued on to the partitioned toilet area. "You know that self-administered haircuts, especially drastic ones, are a sign that you've lost it, right?"

I glanced at my reflection in the mirror. My curly brown hair was now roughly shoulder-length, where it had been a whimsical waist-length just minutes earlier. I had my mom's hair—and the rest of her—and I could no longer stand the sight of my own reflection. It was like she was in the mirror, her almond-shaped eyes staring back at me with just as much disgust and accusation as I felt. She'd never worn her hair shorter than her waist. Now, I didn't look quite so much like her.

"It's not that drastic." I glanced down at the hair collected in the sink, feeling a little sick and wishing I could make it disappear.

Jenny flushed the toilet, then stood in the doorway while she adjusted her underwear under her maxi dress. That was all she wore these days; she claimed they had to have been invented by a pregnant girl. "Do you want me to even it up for you?" She held out her hands, wiggling her fingers. "I promise to wash 'em . . ."

I really tried not to smile, but she was just so ridiculous that a tiny one snuck out. "Sure," I said, tucking my weirdly short hair behind my ear and averting my gaze. I glanced at my reflection again, then down at the counter. Damn it, I still saw my mom standing on the other side of the glass. "Not like you can make it much worse."

"Sugar," Jenny said, putting on a ridiculous Southern drawl. "I'm an artist. Worse is my spec-i-al-it-y." Her eyes met mine in the mirror. "But seriously, what are we going for here? Like, a long bob? A choppy bob? An inverted bob? Wash and wear?" She glanced down at the hair-filled sink, then back up at me. "And how am I supposed to wash my hands?"

"Oh, right. Sorry." I retrieved the garbage can and loaded it with the mound of dark curls in a few handfuls. "What style do you think would look best? I just—" I stared hard at the hair I was transferring into the garbage can. "I want to see someone else when I look in the mirror. Not me. And not *her*."

It should've been me . . . That bullet had been meant for me. Maybe if I hadn't ignored my mom's requests to see me, maybe if I'd gone to talk to her before Apep showed up wearing his Carson suit, things would've worked out differently. Maybe if I hadn't acted like a stubborn, resentful child, she'd still be alive.

"She loved you, Kat." She was quiet for a moment. "Look, I know you're mad at her for betraying you and abandoning you and all, but I think she really proved who she was in the end—your mom, who loved you."

Jenny didn't get it, and I hated whining to her about my problems. She had her own stuff going on. She just lost her Grandma a few weeks ago. That, on top of her pregnancy and Lex's glaring absence, well—I wasn't the only one struggling right now.

"I just—" I shook my head. "It's like I don't even know who I am anymore. Everything I thought I wanted—all of my hopes, my plans—somehow, they all involved my mom. I mean, she was *my mom*. It was just her and me against the world for pretty much ever." I set the little waste bin down on the floor and looked at Jenny. "And now she's gone, and it's my fault."

"Kat . . ." Jenny's eyes shone with empathy and sympathy and pity, all things I'd come to hate over the two months since my mom's death. "You know that's not true."

I scrubbed my hands over my cheeks, erasing any sign of tears, and cleared my throat. "So about my hair . . ."

Jenny stared at me for long seconds, then sighed and shouldered me out of the way so she could get to the sink. "You need to talk to somebody, Kat. I'm worried about you."

"Please, J . . ." I met her eyes in the mirror while she washed her hands. "Not right now."

"Fine." She dried her hands, then dropped the hand towel onto the counter.

"But you'll still help me with my hair?" I asked her, biting my lip.

"Of course I will." She laughed under her breath and shook her head. "So here's what I think—you say you don't know who you are anymore. Well, who says you have to figure out 'who you are' from the inside out? Why can't you do it from the outside in? You know, 'fake it till you make it'?"

I frowned and shrugged.

"Who do you want to be, Kat?"

"I want to be . . ." I stared up at the ceiling, thinking. "Tough. No, badass. I want to look like someone who doesn't care what others think of her. Someone who can hold her own and knows it." I met my own eyes in the mirror, for the first time in a long time not seeing hatred in the eyes of the person staring back at me. "I don't want to rely on anybody else." I didn't want anybody else I cared about to get hurt because of me. "I want to be able to take care of my own damn self. Period."

"Okay, sooooo . . . I'm not sure we can really capture *all* of that with a cut and style, but I'll do what I can."

I looked at Jenny in the mirror, meeting her smirk for smirk. And then I passed her the scissors.

I SAT ON THE SECOND-TO-LAST STEP IN THE entryway, staring at the spot on the floor where my mom's body had lain. My head rested against the banister, and I listened to Marcus, Neffe, and Aset talk in the kitchen. I liked listening to them talk, carefree and unaffected by my presence. Lately, voices hushed and conversations died when I entered a room, even if only for a moment. I didn't want to be the girl everyone felt sorry for. The girl they walked on eggshells around. But I was.

"I'm going to head down to sit with Tarsi," Marcus said. I could hear felted chair legs sliding on the kitchen's tile floor. "Any procedures scheduled for this morning?"

"Just dialysis," Neffe said. "And that's in about an hour."

They'd roused Tarset from her induced coma a couple weeks ago, and she seemed to be doing alright. She mostly just slept. Some of her organs were still having issues functioning on their own—like her kidneys, thus the dialysis—but her recovery, however slow, had brightened Marcus's mood considerably. Now, instead of brooding through every meal, me-style, he engaged with the others, sharing stories of Lex's travels through time and conjecturing with Aset and Nik as to what she was doing at this or that exact moment. Right now, she was supposedly in Florence in 1480, frolicking through vineyards and picnicking on hillsides with a fifteenth-century Marcus.

I watched Marcus emerge from the kitchen, his fingers touching the lump under his shirt, just over his heart. It was the little vial of Lex's bonding pheromones. More than plenty, according to Re, to last until Lex returned with the twins.

Marcus opened the door to the basement, glancing my way. He met my eyes for the briefest moment, then passed through the doorway and shut the door.

"I'm glad we woke her," Aset said, her voice hushed. "It's been good for him."

"I still think it may have been too soon," Neffe said. "But I agree. He's been much better since she woke. She's given him purpose . . . something to focus on while Lex is away."

"Let's hope we can keep her recovery moving in the right direction," Aset said. "If her health makes a wrong turn . . ."

I waited a minute or two, listening to the sounds of water running and dishes clanking as someone washed up in the sink and the thin pages of a magazine turning every few seconds. These mundane sounds soothed me, especially when I could hear them without feeling the periodic touch of concerned eyes on me.

But even that grew dull in time.

Standing, I strolled into the kitchen, tucked a shorter-than-it's-ever-been strand of hair behind my ear, and paused at the corner of the island, taking a deep breath. Aset and Neffe sat together at the table in the sun-drenched breakfast nook, soaking up a rare dose of November sunlight while they sipped coffee and skimmed their boring-as-hell scientific journals. Nik stood on the other side of the island at the sink, his back to me while he scrubbed some pans.

I did *not* notice how visibly defined his shoulders and back muscles were through his stupid black T-shirt. Who voluntarily wears shirts that thin, anyway?

"Oh my goodness, Kat!" Aset exclaimed. "Your hair! What did you—why—"

Neffe glanced up from her article, raised an eyebrow, then resumed her reading. "It's not awful."

Aset was practically sputtering. "But—but—all your beautiful hair. It's *gone*."

I didn't get why she was making such a big deal; it wasn't like I shaved my head or anything. I had what Jenny called an 'inverted bob'—something I'd never heard of before an hour ago. Basically, my hair was chin-length, maybe a touch longer than that in the very front and a whole lot shorter in the back. It was layered, choppy, and pretty damn sassy. Good enough for now.

Aset pushed her chair back and stood, heading my way. "Don't get me wrong, dear, it looks adorable. It's just a bit of a shock, that's all. I wasn't expecting—you never mentioned wanting to change your hair so drastically."

I stared at the countertop, where I was digging the nail of my index finger into a small crevice in the granite. "It was kind of a spur-of-the-moment thing."

Nik laughed. "Now you're speaking my language."

I raised my eyes to meet his. "What? Lunatic?"

Nik used to scare me, but ever since he witnessed the scene in the entryway during my full-on, shit-lost moment with Carson's body, well . . . I felt compelled to pick fights with him. He'd seen me at my worst. He'd witnessed the full extent of my crazy, and he'd held me when I'd wanted to die. He could've just left me alone, kicking and screaming and beating on Carson's body, but he'd chosen to step in. He'd chosen to bear witness to my shame. The bastard.

"Play nice, children," Aset said, touching my hair as she passed me on her way out of the kitchen. "I'm heading up to shower." She winked at me over her shoulder. "And I love the new hair. I'll meet you downstairs for dialysis in an hour, Neffe."

Nik leaned his backside against the edge of the counter, crossed his arms, and smirked. "Re likes your hair."

"Re likes your hair," I parroted in that bratty voice used almost exclusively by kids. And by me.

"Mature, Kitty Kat. Real mature."

"Your face is mature," I snapped. Genius comeback, I know,

but I couldn't help it. My tolerance for a lot of things was nonexistent these days—Nik's stupid perfect face and creepy eyes and endless tattoos included—but nothing bothered me as much as that damn nickname.

Neffe huffed out a breath, stood, and stalked out of the kitchen.

I watched her leave, then turned back to Nik, glaring. I always felt better after our little tiffs, like fighting with him was an outlet. I could only beat up on myself so much, and I never fought back. But Nik always did.

His eyes narrowed. "You've got a lot of anger in you, don't you?"

I lifted one shoulder.

"You should find an outlet." I didn't bother telling him this *was* my outlet. His pale blue eyes bored into me, that mocking smirk absent for once. "Trust me, kid. Anger is always starving, always ready to consume you. And all you have to do is let it."

I was tempted to roll my eyes and tell him to shove it. But I didn't. Maybe it was because he was right—I could already feel the anger eating away at me, eroding parts of my soul. I looked at him, maintaining the tense stare connecting us despite the intense desire to look away. "So what do you suggest?"

"Pain helps some people." It was an effort not to let my eyes stray down to the tattoos covering his neck and arms. "And I've always found beating the shit out of someone therapeutic . . . in a controlled setting, of course."

I frowned, considering what he was saying. "Would you teach me? To fight, I mean?" The words were out before I could stop them, and I immediately regretted asking.

Nik shrugged and leaned his back against the wall. I didn't think he could've looked any less interested. An unplugged toaster would have looked more interested than him. "Honestly," he said, "I'm a terrible teacher, and technique's not really my thing. Not that I need perfect technique . . ." He flicked his wrist, a vine of At whipping into existence and snapping so close to my ear that a few short strands of hair fluttered down to the counter. "I've got a bit of an unfair advantage."

My heart thudded in my chest—not frightened, but thrilled.

"But . . ." Nik closed his fist, and the crystalline vine evaporated into wisps of multicolored smoke. "If you really want to learn, I know who to ask."

"Oh?"

His lips curled into a self-satisfied smile as he nodded to himself. He was still looking at me, but it was clear that he no longer saw me. "Meet me in the training room in an hour." His pale eyes scanned me from the shoulders down. "And wear something else."

"What?" I glanced down at my tight jeans and faded T-shirt. It had been black at some point in its life but was now the dull gray color that black dye fades to after too many trips through the washer, but it was also insanely soft. "What's wrong with what I've got on?"

"You need to be able to bend your legs." He turned and headed up the hallway toward the front of the house, stride carefree and hands in the pockets of his black jeans.

"I can bend my legs in these," I called after him.

He let out a derisive snort. "Whatever you say, Kitty Kat."

I huffed out a breath. "Well what am I supposed to wear, then? Spandex?"

"Don't know. Don't care." He reached for the doorknob to the front door and twisted, pulling the door open. "Just don't wear that."

I pressed my lips together and let out a long, frustrated growl. "Dickwad," I grumbled, following his path toward the front of the house and heading up the stairs. To change.

"KATARINA."

"Dominic," I said, enunciating each syllable of my half-brother's name clearly.

I was sitting against the wall on the side of the training room opposite the one and only door to the outside world. The "training room" was actually its own detached building tucked away in the woods behind the main house. I'd never been inside before, and it was pretty damn opposite what I'd been expecting. I'd thought I would be walking into a glorified school gym—the tiny version—with those nasty padded mats that smell like an insipid combination of plastic and other people's sweat. But the training room was nothing like that.

The walls were covered in horizontal strips of wood, some pale, aromatic variety that gave the room a pleasant, earthy smell. It kind of reminded me of a sauna. But the walls weren't empty, like in a sauna—plus it wasn't super hot. Weapons hung on the walls—knives and swords of every conceivable size and shape, staffs and sticks, some as short as my arm and some way longer than I was tall, and other weapons I wouldn't even begin to know how to identify. There was even a column of whips hanging, neatly coiled, on the wall behind me, just a few feet to my right.

The floor was padded, but it didn't emanate that oh-so-lovely gym mat odor, and it was patterned with a series of concentric circles, light gray on dark, the outermost of which was a snake eating its own tale. An ouroboros, I knew from my rudimentary study of ancient Egypt—the snake eating its own tail was a symbol of the cyclical nature of time.

Dom toed off his shoes, bent over to remove his socks, laid them neatly over his shoes, and strode into the center of the room, planting his feet in the heart of the innermost circle and placing his hands on his hips. He was wearing lightweight, loose-fitting black pants and a white V-neck T-shirt. "Nik tells me you wish to train."

I fingered the hem of my capri yoga pants. "Sure." I shrugged. "Whatever."

"If you wish me to train you, little sister, I will do so gladly. But I would have your full commitment. Your implicit obedience."

I balked. "You want me to *obey* you?"

"I see." Dom's chest rose as he inhaled deeply, exhaling through his nose. "It would seem you are not ready." Without another word, he turned and headed back toward the door. He lifted his right foot and pulled on his discarded sock, then lifted his left foot to do the same.

"Wait, Dom. Please, just . . . I'm sorry." I climbed to my feet using the wooden wall behind me for leverage. Unsure what to do with my hands once I was standing, I folded my arms behind my back, gripping my elbows. "I'll do it. Whatever you want. I just—" I stared hard at the head of the snake on the mat. "I need this." My eyes felt glassy, and I wanted to punch myself for my body's go-to reaction of tearing up whenever I was frustrated or angry. "I need help. I—" I swallowed, choking on the words. "I need *your* help. Please . . ."

In my periphery, I saw him set his sock back down on his shoe, remove his other, then straighten. "Very well. Let us begin."

24

FAULT & BLAME

I sat in the center of the training room, my elbow on my knee and my chin resting on my palm. My hair was crusty with dried sweat, and only a small damp spot chilled my lower back where my T-shirt had yet to dry. I blew a chunk of hair away from my eye.

My stomach yawned audibly, begging for food. I had water aplenty, thanks to the bathroom tucked behind an inconspicuous door in the back corner of the room, but food was nowhere to be found. Trust me, I looked everywhere. There were only two other doors in the training room besides the one to the bathroom, each leading to a storage closet. Neither stored food.

I wondered if I would reach the hungry-enough-to-pass-out point by the time Dom returned in the morning. Because I sure as hell wasn't leaving until then, not even to keep my stomach from eating itself. I would pass his stupid test, damn it, even if I starved to death in the process.

The door behind me opened, and I sighed. "There's no way it's morning already . . ."

"No, it's not."

"Marcus." I spun around on my butt and climbed first to one

knee, then up onto shaky legs. I started smoothing down my hair but, realizing it was pointless, tucked what I could behind my ears. "I thought you were Dom."

The ghost of a smile touched Marcus's mouth. "Mind if I join you?"

I took a step backwards, arms extended as much as my fatigued muscles could manage. "You own the place . . ."

That ghostly smile made another appearance. Marcus turned away from me, toed off his sneakers, pulled off his socks, and stepped onto the mat barefoot. He wore silver and white basketball shorts and a plain white T-shirt, the lump from the tiny At vial containing Lex's bonding pheromones visible over his heart, as always. "I hear that Dom is training you?" He crossed the serpent and made his way to the centermost ring of the mat.

I withdrew back to the wall and slid down to the floor. "I guess."

Marcus nodded to himself. "That's good. He's an excellent teacher."

I shrugged. It was only my first day training with Dom, so I had no clue how this whole thing would go. "I can't leave," I told Marcus. "Just so you know. Sorry."

He stood in the center of the mat, feet shoulder-width apart. "What has he tasked you with?"

"Something impossible." At Marcus's quirked eyebrow, I explained, "Dom wants me to count all of the individual objects in the room. I can't leave until I have the right answer, and he made it more than clear that there's only *one* right answer, and that if I get it wrong, we're done—no more training." I huffed a breath. "It's a test, obviously."

"It is. And there *is* only one right answer."

That earned an eye roll. "Yeah, I figured that out about five minutes after he left me in here, oh"—I held my arm up in front of me and squinted at my bare wrist—"about two hours ago. And I know the answer has nothing to do with how many 'things' are in this room. Because, like, what counts? Do the nails in the wall count? Does each board under the mat count? Does everything in the bathroom count? There are a gazillion possible answers, but only one way for me to *not* fail." I crossed my arms over my chest and extended my legs straight out in front of me, crossing my ankles as well. "I have to stay in here until Dom returns in about twelve hours. It's a riddle, and *that's* the damn answer."

"How cruel," Marcus said, chuckling. "And what is the point of such a test?"

"Besides torturing me?" I frowned. "I don't know . . . I guess it tests how committed I am?" I bit my bottom lip, my brow scrunched. "Or determined?" I snorted, laughing under my breath. "Or stupid."

"I have watched Dom train many young Nejerets, and more often than not, his would-be pupils fail this first test."

I stared at him, eyebrows raised in curiosity. "Really?"

Marcus nodded. "Not with a wrong answer, but by arguing that the test itself is unfair. In doing so, they prove that their pride outweighs their willingness to learn."

"Oh."

"It is the first sign of a poor pupil."

I stared at my toes. "But it doesn't say anything about how good they'll be at actually fighting . . ." *Or how* bad *they'll be . . .*

"Ah, but for those who pass, well—determination can turn even the slowest learner or clumsiest pupil into the most adept martial artist."

"You think so?" Maybe there was hope for me, then.

"I know so. Now, if you don't mind, I need quiet so I can focus while I run through the kata."

"Oh, right." My cheeks heated. "Sorry."

Marcus turned so he was facing the door to the outside—to *literally* all the food in the world—and held his fists extended before him, just a few inches from his body. I watched as he started to move, filled with both awe and trepidation. I didn't think I'd ever be able to make my body do what his could. Some of his motions were jerky, like an intended strike with his hands or feet, while others resembled the smooth, flowing motions of a ballet dancer. And his breathing seemed as much a part of the routine as the placement of his arms and legs. He moved around the mat for what felt like an eternity but what I figured must have been an hour and a half or so, never stopping for more than a few seconds and seeming to never tire.

Finally, he stood exactly as he'd begun and bowed to the door, then turned around and bowed to me.

I clapped halfheartedly. "Good job?"

Marcus's lips twitched. Relaxing, he crossed the mat and sat beside me, his breathing impossibly even. This close, though, I could see that he'd worked up a pretty solid sweat. "So what did you think?" He rested his elbows on his upraised knees and clasped his hands together lazily. "Ready to give the kata a try?"

I scoffed. "Sure. And then I'll cure cancer."

"You never know. You might surprise yourself." He threw me a sidelong glance. "I've been teaching Lex—I was, *before*—and she's no fighter, but she's been picking up the forms fairly quickly."

"Yeah, but Lex was a dancer for most of her life. It's practically the same thing."

"Perhaps it has helped, but as I said, she is no fighter—not in practice, and not in spirit. She doesn't have the heart for it. She is, at her core, almost stubbornly passive. Live and let live." His words weren't filled with judgment but rather hummed with reverie. "It pains me to watch her be drawn deeper and deeper into this war."

I turned my head to look at his strong profile full on. His fingers pinched the lump under his shirt and his eyes stared ahead, no doubt seeing things not of this place or time.

"She's strong, Marcus. She'll survive this." I hesitated before adding, "She'll make it back to us."

He grunted faintly and placed his hands on the floor, leaning forward to get up.

"Can I, um . . . ask you something?"

He paused and looked at me. "I believe you just did."

I let the words tumble out of my mouth before I could chicken out. "Have you guys had any luck in tracking down the Kin?" I itched for knowledge of those responsible for dragging my mom down the path that had led to her eventual death. I wanted nothing more than for Marcus to tell me we'd found them all. To tell me we'd wiped them out.

"I know it's hard with the At being pretty much inaccessible," I said, "but hasn't anything my mom told you helped?" Dom had been interrogating her for hours each morning and afternoon during the days leading up to her death. He'd spent the most time with her while she was here, and it was Dom who'd relayed her messages to me every day—her pleas to see me. Pleas I'd ignored. Why hadn't I just sucked it up and visited her? They say time heals all wounds, but this one—this regret and guilt—it festered, worsening every day.

"In a sense," Marcus said, "yes, your mother's information has helped. We know the names of the Kin she interacted with, as well as some of what they can do using their sheuts. We know much about their structure and motives and have even managed to track down where they were when Gen and Carson—Apep—fled, but the Kin have long since moved on."

"Oh." I stared down at my hands.

Marcus was quiet for a moment, frozen in that half-tensed position. "I assure you, Kat, they will pay for what happened to Gen. Unfortunately, progress has been slow because the Council is divided about—"

"When aren't they," I said under my breath.

Much to my surprise, I earned a bark of laughter from

Marcus. "Quite true. But this time, half of us believe the Kin have gone 'underground' to re-amass their efforts against the Council of Seven, while the other half believe they've scattered to the wind, leaderless and without purpose."

"So does that half want to give up?" Even asking the question left a bitter taste in my mouth. I blamed myself for what happened to my mom, but I also blamed the Kin. As I sat there, I felt some of that blame shift away from me and toward them. There was no doubt in my mind that if it weren't for the Kin, she'd still be alive. I suddenly wanted nothing more than the strength, skill, and ability to find them. To hurt them. To make them pay for stealing my mom's life. I didn't *want* the Council to avenge my mom. I wanted to avenge her myself.

"Not a chance," Marcus said, his voice hard. "But it changes the way we would hunt them—and hunt them we will. Make no mistake of that." He pushed up off the floor and stood over me. "Is there anything else?"

I ventured a glance up at him, then returned to staring at my hands, picking at imaginary hangnails. "I just—" I coughed to conceal a convulsive pre-sob. "I was so mad at my mom. I wish I'd visited her while she was here. I wish I'd had a chance to tell her I forgave her, but I was so mad at her . . ." I'd never said it aloud before. It felt good to admit, like a confession that would bring me one step closer to absolution. I laugh-cried and shook my head angrily. "If I'd known . . ."

Marcus placed his hand on my shoulder. "I know, Kat. And I understand. Gen would forgive you, I have no doubt in my heart."

My chin trembled, and I turned my face away from him. I didn't want him to see me cry.

"Perhaps, in time, you'll be able to forgive yourself."

As the tears broke free and my shoulders shook, Marcus removed his hand and made his way across the mat. Moments later, he was gone, and I was alone with only my anger and despair for company.

And a whole damn lot of determination. I would pass Dom's test. I would learn to fight. And I would avenge my mom. The Kin would pay.

25

HUNGER & DRIVE

I locked my bedroom door and sat on my bed, closed laptop before me on the comforter. My heart beat rapidly as I stared at the small black thumb drive resting atop the computer. Dom had considered the thumb drive a gift. I wasn't so sure.

"I'M IMPRESSED WITH YOUR PROGRESS, LITTLE SISTER."

"Oh, um . . ." I met his eyes for the briefest moment, then stared down at the spot where the serpent's tail disappeared into its mouth on the training room floor. Sweat dripped down the back of my neck, and I was still a little out of breath from our latest training session. "Thanks."

Dom lifted my chin with cool fingertips. "Humility balances pride. Shame does not. Don't feel ashamed to take pride in all you have accomplished so far." He smiled, the rare, fond expression softening his severe features. "I am proud of you."

I looked up at him, shocked by his words. I kid you not, my heart swelled so big I literally thought it might explode. I felt all warm and fuzzy and chock-full of a crap-ton of joy.

Because Dom was proud of me.

What was happening to me?

"You deserve a reward for your hard work and discipline these last four weeks," he said, reaching into the pocket of his loose-fitting workout pants. He pulled out a slim, black thumb drive and offered it to me on his palm. "This drive contains the video files from my interrogations of your mother." He rested a hand on my shoulder, apparently unconcerned with the sweat-soaked state of my T-shirt. "I know what it is to have the driving force behind all of one's actions stem from the loss of one's mother. And moreover, I know what it is like to have vengeance become one's central purpose."

My eyes widened. Though a desire for revenge against the Kin had slowly overshadowed my self-loathing over the long weeks of training, I'd never admitted it to anyone. "So . . ." I wiped my palms on my yoga pants. "What happened to your mom?"

"Apep happened." Dom must've read the disappointment on my face, because he added, "Perhaps one day I will tell you my story, but today is not that day. Just know that I understand your reasons for training so hard . . . and I approve." His dark eyes bore into me. "I will continue to help you in any way I can. I only ask one thing of you—plan your vengeance all you like, but do nothing until I deem you ready."

I nodded, unable to speak.

"Good." His stare became more intense, if that was even possible. "The path of vengeance is dark and lonesome, and it often stretches on and on without end. At times, it will seem to you as though you walk this path alone, because none feel the loss of your mother as deeply as you do and none are driven onward by it as resolutely as you are. But you are not alone. I will be with you, if not by your side, then here"—he touched the tips of his first two fingers to my temple—"and here," he finished, placing the palm of his other hand to the left of my sternum, directly over my heart. A moment later, he withdrew his hands.

Tears welled in my eyes. Not because I was sad or pissed or frustrated, but because he cared. My big brother cared about me, and the revelation made me almost giddy. "Thank—" I cleared my throat. "Thanks, Dom." It was impossible for him not to notice the effect his words were having on me, and for once, I didn't care one bit. "Really, I—just, thank you."

. . .

I GLANCED AT THE BEDROOM DOOR, DOUBLE-checking that it was locked, then returned to staring at the thumb drive. I'd missed out on my mom's final days because I'd been too stupid or stubborn or resentful—maybe all three. I doubted I would ever forgive myself for that, whatever Marcus said, but I felt like I owed it to my mom to do what little I could to make up for it.

I blew out my breath and, with shaking fingers, picked up the thumb drive and plugged it into the laptop. I raised the computer screen and turned it on. Within seconds, the desktop appeared, the wallpaper a photo of Lex and me standing in front of the pseudo-Gothic Suzzallo Library at the University of Washington. The icon for the thumb drive hovered directly over the bun atop my head in the photo.

I forced my hesitant finger to direct the mouse to the icon and double-click.

I'd expected a half dozen video files, maybe a little more. I scrolled the folder's view bar downward. "Holy shit . . ." There were a *lot* more than a half dozen.

A quick skim through the file names revealed two types: some with just a date and time, and some with a parenthetical amendment that included my name and a time marker. I clicked on one of the latter at random. The video player opened, and my mom appeared on the screen, sitting at a small, square metal table in what appeared to be some sort of a jail cell. A moment later, Dom came into view and sat opposite her.

She was there, on the screen. Alive.

I held my breath, my finger hovering over the mouse pad.

My mom glanced at the camera, and it was like she was looking at me. Like she could see me. All of the guilt and shame I'd been working so hard on bottling up broke free, crashing over me.

I snapped the laptop shut. A horrific sob tore its way up my throat, and I buried my face in my hands.

Not thirty seconds later, someone knocked on my bedroom door. "Kat, dear?" It was Aset. "Are you alright?"

I groaned into my hands. If there was one thing I'd learned from living in a house with a bunch of Nejerets, it was that privacy was essentially nonexistent. At least the house's other, human occupants—Lex's parents and sister, Jenny—hadn't heard my stupid, ugly sob.

I cleared my throat. "I'm fine!" I scanned the bedroom furniture like it would magically give me somewhere to hide. Hopefully for the rest of my life. "Just stubbed my toe on the dresser," I lied.

"Alright, well . . ." In those two words, Aset made it abundantly clear that my ruse had failed. "Tarsi and I are heading down to do some bloodwork. A hand would be most welcome, if you're not too busy. You know how much she loves drawing with you . . ."

I stared longingly at my laptop but knew I wouldn't be attempting *that* again within the long earshot of Nejerets. Which meant I wouldn't be watching the videos in this house, or even on the compound. But that led to the question—where to go? I didn't want to watch the videos somewhere public. The possibility that tons of people might witness my weakness and misery firsthand was out of the question. Too many people had seen me break down already.

A park, maybe? Or I could just borrow one of Heru's gazillion cars and pull into a parking lot—*any* parking lot.

I frowned and hunched my back. Neither sounded appealing.

The apartment my mom and I'd lived in over the shop for pretty much ever popped into my head, but a second later, I dismissed the idea of going there. Though the vivid image in my mind showed it exactly the same as we'd left it last spring, I knew our things had been moved out months ago—some moved here, into this bedroom, others put into storage elsewhere on the compound. The idea of being there when everything was *wrong* wasn't remotely appealing.

I perked up, feeling a tiny, triumphant smile curve my lips. The apartment might've been eerily empty, but the shop wasn't. It had been closed for months, but it was still there, just as my mom had left it. It was the perfect place to watch the videos in privacy.

"Kat?" Aset's voice reminded me I'd been quiet for too long.

"Oh, um, sorry." I scooted off the bed and slipped my bare feet into cozy, wool-lined boots. "Yeah, I'll be right—" I caught a glimpse of my splotchy, tear-streaked face in the standing mirror by the wardrobe. "I'll be down in a few minutes," I said, amending my response.

"Lovely. I'll let Tarsi know. I'm sure she'll be excited." Aset's retreating footsteps moved down the hallway, then descended the stairs.

I shuffled into the bathroom and turned on the sink. A few splashes of cold water and a couple minutes usually did the trick. I should know—I was a pro at this, after all.

IN THE GRAND SCHEME OF THINGS, I DON'T REALLY matter. Not compared to everything going on with Lex and Marcus and ma'at and the fate of the universe. That fact was made abundantly clear when I drove one of Marcus's many cars off the compound with nothing more than a nod from the Nejerette on duty at the gatehouse. I didn't even have permission to borrow the Lexus. Not that I was breaking any rules, exactly. Probably. I just hadn't asked.

Nobody cared, anyway. Whatever. I didn't mind.

But also, I kind of did.

My pride probably would've been wounded, had I much left,

but Dom had been doing a pretty admirable job of beating any excess pride out of me, figuratively speaking. For the most part.

I skipped several dozen songs on my iPod before giving up and driving the fifteen minutes to the ferry terminal in quiet, just the hum of the engine and the road sounds filling the silence until I parked. I used to love music. My mom had always hated my taste in music. Now I could barely stand my old favorites, either.

While I waited for the ferry to disembark, I stood bundled in my long, puffy down coat at the bow of the upper deck and stared down at the water, thinking it was exactly what Lex would be doing were she in my place. She adored ferry rides, using pretty much any and every excuse to take one. The faux fur lining the rim of my hood tickled my cheeks with each icy-cold gust of wind. I shivered.

Lex was probably lazing about the Tuscan countryside with Medieval Marcus right now, so I doubted she'd really be feeling like she was missing out on this particularly frigid ferry ride. She was supposedly in fourteenth-century Florence now, having just arrived, according to Aset. I smiled to myself, imagining pregnant Lex materializing right in front of Marcus, who in my mind was wearing some ridiculous getup that consisted of tights and one of those puffy-sleeved doublets. Remotely, I hoped she'd found a way to make her phone's battery stretch. I desperately wanted to see pictures when she got back.

Splat.

I glanced down at the deck. About a foot to my right, a fresh, clumpy white blob of bird poop glistened in the crisp December sunlight. I looked up at the seagull swerving back and forth overhead, just beyond the bow. "Not cool, dude."

And I swear that little feathered bastard's beady eye locked on me right before he released a second slimy missile.

I took a step back just in time, the seagull crap landing where my right boot had been a second earlier. "Asshole."

The bird cried out.

With one last glare, I turned and headed into the ferry's warm interior, following the signs to food and drink. I needed something warm. Maybe not coffee. I was already antsy enough; I didn't need to be jittery, too. Hot chocolate, then.

Which, as I found out a few moments later, turned out to be from a packet. But for the hot water and sugar, it was totally worth it. I sat in one of the empty booths near the stern, warm and cozy within the ferry's cabin and hands curled around my Styrofoam cocoa cup. I stared out the window at the expanse of glittering gray-blue water.

It was easy to zone out during the thirty-five-minute ferry ride. The clear winter sky overhead was a crisp, icy blue; the late morning sun was shining, reflected by the ruffled surface of the Sound. In no time, I was in Seattle.

A half hour after leaving the ferry, I was hopping off the bus in Capitol Hill. I crossed the street to the east side of Broadway, where my mom's long-closed shop, *The Goddess's Blessing*, still occupied prime real estate between a novelty shop and a hipster cafe. Marcus owned the building, so it wasn't like my mom and I ever had to worry about losing the shop or our apartment above. It was the biggest way my mom had let him help us out, and she'd made him accept a rent check every month.

I never understood why before, but I got it now. Pride and shame. I was starting to wonder if every human action and interaction could be boiled down to pride and shame.

My key slid into the lock easily. Part of me had expected the keyhole to be clogged or rusty from months of disuse, which seemed stupid in retrospect. I pulled the door open, holding my breath when the little copper bell overhead chimed, alerting nobody of my arrival. The sound sparked a string of bittersweet memories.

I stepped out of the sunlight and into the dark shop, breathing in the stale, dusty air. It was scented overwhelmingly by the rich, spicy, floral, and earthy aromas of the incense and essential oils that had pooled within the stagnant space. Eyes watering, I coughed into my sleeve and turned around to twist the lock on the glass door, then rested my forehead against the metal frame and closed my eyes. "Welcome home," I murmured.

Air from months ago coated the inside of my lungs, a time capsule more real and evocative of the past than anything I'd ever viewed in the At. Of course, maybe it was less about the smell of the place and more that I'd pretty much grown up here.

I made my way past dusty display tables of the stones, figurines, and New Age–chic trinkets my mom had adored to the back of the shop, stomach twisted and achy. Slowly, almost hesitantly, I passed through the heavy beaded curtain of quartz, amethyst, and moonstone beads blocking off the doorway to the back room. This was—had been—my mom's favorite place. She'd spent more time in here than in her own bedroom. Literally. There were nights she would send me upstairs but would remain down here, doing readings, researching, crafting.

And by *crafting*, I'm not talking about glue guns and papier-mâché. You see, my mom was a Nejeret carrier, and carriers are special: not quite like us, but not quite human, either. They're a whole brand of *other*, unique all to themselves. They don't get to live forever or benefit from superhuman healing and heightened senses, but they haven't totally lost the genetic lottery, either—especially not if they know what they are and what they're capable of.

Some people call it a sixth sense, or insight. It's the eyes in the back of parents' heads and the gut reactions some people feel so distinctly they can't *not* trust them. It's the unshakeable sense of déjà vu, the heebie-jeebies, the mother's instinct. It's the sense of knowing, in your heart, what can't be known. The realization that wakes you in the middle of the night. The hairs that stand up on the back of your neck. The urge that makes you pick up the phone just before it rings. It's all part of being a Nejeret carrier.

Many carriers are born, live their lives, and grow old totally unaware of their full potential. Others, like my mom, are raised knowing what they are, fully aware not only of the wondrous world closed to them but of the mysterious in-between that belongs to them alone. And some carriers, like my mom, capitalize on their unique abilities.

Fortunes were her expertise, mostly palm reading and tarot cards, but she discovered early on that she had a talent for sensing physiological vibrations. She could read people better than most Nejerets who'd had thousands of years' experience. Or rather, she could read *most* people. She hadn't been able to read an Apep-possessed Set, my father—*shudder*—and hers.

The thought was truly vomit-worthy.

And my mom must've been fooled by Carson, both before and after he'd been possessed by Apep. My lip curled into a sneer. I wished I could bring Carson back to life just to kill him slowly. His death had been way too fast and far too painless. He deserved worse. More. But I couldn't bring him back to life, so I'd have to settle for hunting down the other members of the Kin instead.

I shrugged off my messenger bag and set it on top of the round table in the center of the room, then pulled a tablet from the bag with shaking hands.

At the sound of a key being fitted into the lock of the shop door, my head snapped up. The bell over the door jingled, and I spun around, fingers clutching the tablet. Through the beaded curtain and the shadowed shop floor beyond, I could see only a dark silhouette backed by blinding sunlight.

"Mom?" It was irrational, I knew. She was dead, *I knew.* But part of me fully expected her voice to be the one that answered. My whole body tensed, waiting. Hoping.

"It's me, Kitty Kat." It was Nik.

I covered my mouth with my hand just before a sob broke free. I leaned back against the table and hugged the tablet to my chest, taking deep breaths. "What the hell are you doing here?"

"What are *you* doing here?"

"Nothing," I snapped. Who did he think he was? This was *my* place. Mine and my mom's. Nik had no right to be here, let alone to pry into my business.

"Not true," he said. "You're definitely doing something. Sharing is caring, Kitty Kat . . ."

"Fuck you."

"Thanks, but teens aren't really my thing."

"Fuck *off*."

"Hmmm . . ." His silhouetted hand traced along the edge of a display table. "Don't think so."

I gritted my teeth. "Why are you here?"

"Curiosity." He wasn't moving and I couldn't see his face, but I had the disturbing impression that he was watching me through the curtain.

I was quiet for a moment. "Yours?" I asked. "Or Re's?"

Nik started across the shop floor, slowly nearing the beaded curtain. "Re thinks you matter. He claims you're important for some reason—you're fated to be the catalyst for something epic."

That was the last thing I wanted to hear. "Like what?"

"Don't know. He doesn't share everything with me." Nik stopped in the doorway, just on the other side of the beads. "All I know is that if you run off and get yourself killed *now*, everything he's worked so hard for will turn to dust and blah blah blah . . ."

Can I just point out how *not* happy I was with the revelation that Re thought I was important. What bullshit. I did my important thing, helping break Lex out of Apep-Set's prison in the At back in June. It was a way more important thing than I'd ever expected to do in my lifetime—help to rescue the literal mother-to-be of the gods, the messiah of our people, the world, and the whole damn universe—and I'd paid the price for mattering. I was stuck in the body of an eighteen-year-old. Forever. And let's not forget that my forever could last thousands of years.

So yeah, I tapped out from doing important things after that. Washed my hands of mattering. Re was free to think whatever the hell he wanted to think about me, but it wouldn't change a thing. I was done. *Done.*

I straightened my spine. "I have no intention of getting myself killed."

"Oh, Kitty Kat . . ." Nik stretched out his arms and planted his hands on either side of the doorframe, then pushed his face through the curtain. "So naïve."

26

WATCH & LEARN

There was nothing I could say or do to make Nik leave. Sure, I could've packed up and left to watch the video files elsewhere, but I had little doubt that he would follow me. It wasn't like I hadn't anywhere else to go, anyway.

"Just don't break anything." I watched him through the beaded curtain while I fished the thumb drive out of the zippered pocket inside my bag. "And don't turn on the lights," I added as his hand hovered over the switch on the wall to the right of the doorframe. "I don't want anyone thinking we're open."

He lowered his hand. It wasn't like he needed any light, anyway. He was a Nejeret; he'd be able to see more than well enough once his eyes adjusted to the dimness.

"Would it be so bad—people thinking you're open?" he asked.

I pulled out a chair and sat—not my mom's vintage violet armchair, but the other, smaller padded chair clients used to use during their readings. It was where I always used to sit when I was there after school, doing homework or playing on my phone when I wasn't covering for my mom out on the shop floor.

"We're not—the *shop* isn't open." I turned on the tablet. "It's probably in some sort of legal limbo now, anyway."

"It's not."

I stared at him through the curtain. He tossed his long, black leather jacket onto the checkout counter, then thumbed through the business cards displayed on the end, his back to me. "What do you mean?" I shook my head. "How do you know—"

"Dom transferred everything of your mom's over to you."

"I—" I swallowed and licked my lips. "What?"

"Seventeen."

"*What?*"

Nik straightened, and he looked at me, his eyes glinting in the shadows. "File number seventeen. Watch it. You'll understand better."

I glanced down at the thumb drive. "You've watched them?"

Nik moved on to the outdated fliers posted on the bulletin board hanging on the wall beside the counter. "Marcus made the whole Council watch them all. His attempt to nudge the other Council members out of inaction."

"It didn't work." It was impossible to keep the bitterness from my tone. If the Council of Seven wouldn't man up and go after the Kin, then I'd do it for them. Actually, I preferred them sitting on their thumbs. It would keep them out of my way.

Nik's shoulders rose and fell. "They're afraid."

I snorted. They'd be stupid not to be—and however slow the Council was to act, intelligence and wisdom were not things they lacked. Which apparently made me a moron, because all I felt was hunger for the hunt . . . excitement for the kill. "Are you afraid?" I asked Nik.

He laughed, a harsh, dry sound. "I'm bored."

I plugged the thumb drive into the tablet's sole USB receiver. "And what—you think following me around is the most direct route to excitement?" I still didn't really know why he was here, other than the bit of insider information he had from Re. What did he want? "*Awesome* plan. How's that working out for you?"

"It's yet to disappoint."

I frowned and muttered, "Well, don't blame me when it does." Reaching into my bag, I pulled out my headphones. "Will you be able to entertain yourself for a couple hours?"

Nik grunted. "We'll manage." *We.* Right, because he wasn't alone. Far from it. He'd been sharing his body with a being with near-infinite knowledge for thousands of years; they probably still had tons to talk about. Like me, apparently.

I tucked the earbuds into my ears, adjusted the tablet's volume, and opened the thumb drive. My eyes scanned the file names, unconsciously searching for number seventeen. As it turned out, it was one of the files with "Kat" and a timestamp written in parentheses at the end of the date-time file name.

Tapping on the video file, I shot a quick sideways glance to the curtain but didn't see Nik. He must've moved into one of the alcoves to study the jewelry in the glass cases or the crystals, stones, and candles on the bookshelves. Whatever. So long as he didn't intrude further, I didn't really mind him being there.

The video opened, engulfing the tablet's small screen. Once again, my mom appeared. She was sitting on the far side of a table, facing the camera, just like before. Only this time, she wasn't in the underground holding cell but in a white-walled room, empty but for the table and two chairs.

I watched with bated breath as Dom came into view and sat in the chair opposite my mom. His body didn't block the camera's view of her, but that didn't stop me from scooting my chair closer. Like it would make any difference.

"Let's continue where we left off yesterday," Dom said, and my mom nodded.

She watched him, attentive. Willing. I could see it on her face. She wanted to help.

I cleared my throat, and I leaned in closer.

"Tell me more about the relationship between Mei and Mari," Dom said.

"What do you want to know?"

I had no idea who or what they were talking about, beyond the fact that Mei had supposedly been the leader of the Kin before Carson freed Apep and she was killed—maybe even by his hand. And I only knew that much because Neffe and Dom had been talking about it one morning at the breakfast table and hadn't heard me come down the stairs. Sometimes it was like they all forget that I, an out-of-the-loop Nejerette with pretty dang good hearing, lived there, too.

After double-checking the timestamp at the end of the file name—16:07—I slid the progress bar to the right, too curious and impatient to wait a whole fifteen minutes for them to get to the relative good part. I needed to know what Nik had been talking about just a moment ago, not to mention what Dom had deemed significant enough to note as being of specific interest to me. Like, now.

". . . and I respected her for that," my mom said. "Mari was the closest thing Mei would ever have to a daughter. Mei loved her unconditionally . . . would've done anything for her."

"So you felt you could relate to Mei?"

My mom didn't say anything, just nodded and turned her face away from the camera. She was crying. My own eyes stung with tears.

Dom pulled something from his back pocket and held it out across the table. When my mom accepted his offering and dabbed under her eyes, I realized he'd handed her a handkerchief.

"Thank you." My mom coughed to clear her throat. "I'm sorry. I don't mean for this to keep happening."

"There is no need for apologies. Truly, I understand."

My mom made a sound that slightly resembled a laugh. "I'm afraid I forgot the question . . ."

"Ah, yes. Did you feel Mei's motherly relationship with Mari made her easy to relate to?"

"Absolutely." I was surprised by the level of conviction my mom could pack into that single word. "Everything she did was to protect Mari. If the Council ever found out about her, they'd view her as an abomination, someone too dangerous to let live. Fear would have driven them to hunt down and destroy her, along with all of the Kin with sheuts, simply for the crime of existing. At least, that's the way Mei saw it."

"You are aware of Nuin's mandate against pre-manifested Nejerettes from having sexual intercourse with men, Nejeret or otherwise, and that the purpose of this mandate was to prevent Nejeret with sheuts from ever being born?"

My mom nodded. "But Mei viewed that as merely an excuse. She taught that Nuin's 'mandate' was a convenient law the Council used to legitimize their fear of the more powerful Kin. There was no proof that it had even been Nuin's wish—no record of it in the At that Mei or any of the other Kin could find."

"I see."

"Do you?" My mom leaned forward, forearms on the table and hanky balled up in her right hand. "Do you really? Because Mei believed it was all a Council ruse—evidence of their corruption. In her mind, she had no choice but to amass an army and overturn the Council of Seven. If she didn't, they would kill her and everyone she loved."

"And you, Gen? Is that why *you* betrayed the Council? Did you fear for your daughter's life?"

"I—" My mom slumped in her chair. "Yes, I did. Kat is also a product of broken mandates. What Set did to me—"

"*Apep*-Set," Dom clarified.

"Maybe Apep was in control, but it's Set's genes that run through my and Kat's blood."

Dom nodded once. "Fair enough."

"I—I feared Kat would become an outcast once her incestuous lineage became commonly known."

"And . . . ?"

"And then after she was forced to manifest . . ."

"Another broken mandate?"

My mom nodded, but it was seconds before she actually spoke. "Kat—my little girl—she became not just one, but two things the Council forbade based on Nuin's ancient laws." My mom stared down at her hands, joined together on the table. "I was afraid for her. I still am. She'll never be accepted, not with the way things currently stand. I couldn't just sit back and let that happen, not when I had the chance to change the world she lived in . . . to make it into a place that would be more open and accepting."

My chin trembled, but my eyes remained glued to the screen. Here was yet more proof that my mom got tangled up in this mess because of me. Because she loved me. And I'd been mad at her, ashamed of her. I'd called her a traitor alongside everyone else.

"I see," Dom said. "Now, I'd like to go back to talking about Mei and Mari."

"Yes. Yes, of course. I'm sorry. I didn't mean to derail us . . ."

"No apology needed. Now, tell me, please, what was Mari's relationship with Mei like?"

"Well, she called Mei 'Mom' most of the time, so . . . I'd say that's how she saw her. Mei was grooming Mari to be her successor. Everyone knew it. I think it's a natural thing for a parent to want to feel like all of their hard work won't go to waste, to know that we'll leave something behind for our children . . . something our children will *want* to take over once we're gone." My mom shook her head and sat up straighter. "I'm sorry, I got sidetracked again. Yes, I believe Mari loved Mei like a mother. But . . ."

"But, what?"

"The past month or so . . . I don't know. Mari seemed off, somehow." Again, my mom shook her head. "Something changed between her and Mei."

"How so?"

"Well, Mari's a little more passionate than her mother. Or maybe vehement is a better word for it. Anyway, you have to understand that Mari was raised to believe the Council of Seven wants to kill her. A few weeks ago I overheard her and Mei arguing. Mari was saying that the Council is evil and that all who follow its rule are tainted and must be 'cleansed,' and that if Mei wasn't strong enough to do it, Mari would take over and do it for her. Her conviction was terrifying."

"Are you suggesting that Mari may have had some involvement with Mei's death?"

"I think it's possible, but that's in the past. You should be more worried about the present." My mom pressed her palms down on the table and leaned forward. "With Mei gone, you should all be worried that Mari will find a way to unite the Kin under her more radical views. If she can mobilize them against you . . ."

Dom shifted in his chair. "I see. I'll make sure your warning is passed along."

"Good." My mom relaxed a little. "Dom, can you tell me—what's going to happen to me?"

There was a long pause, and I held my breath. The answer both mattered and didn't. She was already gone.

"Your fate is in the Council's hands," Dom said finally.

"Oh, alright. Um, w—what do you think that fate is likely to be?"

"I'm sorry, Gen, but I honestly cannot say."

"Oh, well . . . I understand."

"I think we should take a break." Dom scooted his chair back and stood.

"Dom?"

He stopped halfway to the camera and turned around to face my mom.

"Would you mind—I'd like to make a will. Whatever happens to me, I want to make sure Kat's okay."

"Of course," Dom said. "I'll get started this evening and have a draft for you to review at our morning session tomorrow."

"Thank you."

Dom turned away and approached the camera.

"And will you tell Kat—"

"—that you love her and would like to see her?" Dom said, like he'd heard it a million times before. I could only see the side of his black leather belt and the bottom of his tucked-in shirt now. "Of course."

The video went black.

Heart thudding, I wiped the wetness from under my eyes, then pulled up the folder and clicked on the first video from the sixteenth of September, when my mom and Carson first showed up. I pulled my sketchbook from my bag and grabbed a pen from the outside pocket to take notes. I wanted to know everything—more about Mei, this Mari chick who might or might not have killed Mei, and more about anyone else who'd tricked my mom into believing their bullshit. I wanted to know who had been in league with Carson, who else had believed releasing Apep and siccing him on us—and using my mom to gain entry to the compound—was a grand ol' plan.

I was committed. All in. I was going to hunt down anyone who was even remotely involved in my mom's death. I was going to interrogate them. Hurt them. Punish them.

Sitting up straighter, I stared at the tablet's screen and pressed play.

27

BATMAN & ROBIN

I plucked the earbuds from my ears and dropped them on the table, then stretched my arms high overhead and arched my back. It was the first time I'd changed my position in hours. A groan, low and guttural, escaped from somewhere deep inside me. I expected some sort of commentary on the noise from Nik.

When none came, I glanced sidelong at the beaded curtain, eyes narrowed. "Yo, Nik!" I called through the doorway to the main part of the shop.

There was no answer. In fact, I couldn't hear anything other than the usual signs of colorful Capitol Hill life out on the street. No whooshing of breath. No shushing footsteps. I closed my eyes and concentrated. Nothing.

Had he left?

I checked my phone quickly—just a handful of unread texts from Dom, but nothing from Nik—then stood, frowning. It irritated me that he'd left without letting me know. I wouldn't have used headphones if I'd known I was alone. Anyone could've come in here. Anything could've happened to me. Not that I thought anyone was after me; it was simply a matter of common courtesy.

And, of course, the definition of *anyone* and *anything* was much more disturbing now that I'd watched the first four video files. They'd been long, two over an hour, and packed full of useful, totally insane information. The things these people could do with their sheuts . . .

Mind. Blown.

I pushed through the beaded curtain, tucking my hair behind my ear. "Nik?" Darkness had fallen outside, making the shadows within the shop murkier and more deceptive. But still, thanks to my heightened eyesight, I could see well enough in the dark.

A quick scan of the area showed no sign of him. But my mom had designed the layout of the shop with hidden nooks and crannies to make customers feel like there was always something new to discover if they just poked around a little longer. Sure, it enabled the occasional shoplifter, but it had been my mom's theory that the experience—especially the *prolonged* one—would lead to a profit in the long run.

Nik was in the last place I looked—duh—tucked away in one of my mom's favorites of those hidden nooks.

He was kneeling on the worn hardwood floor in the center of an alcove created by three towering bookcases, their shelves laden with Tarot decks, sets of rune stones, fortune sticks, and a wide variety of books on the myriad forms of divination. It was one of the few places besides the back room and the bathroom that passersby couldn't see into through the windows. He was sitting on the heels of his black boots, his back to me and his head bowed.

I understood instantly why I hadn't heard any sign of him, or why he hadn't heard me calling out to him. A thin sheet of At surrounded Nik, shimmering and iridescent.

I walked into the alcove, sidestepping around his little cocoon until I could see his face. His eyes were closed, his features relaxed. His short black hair was messy, but in that way that looked semi-purposeful and really not all that bad.

I'd never seen him like this, totally unaware, his eyelids shutting away his haunting, too-pale eyes. He looked peaceful. Hell, kneeling and head bowed like that, the soft iridescence of the almost-glowing At surrounding him, he looked damn near angelic—the fallen-angel brand of heavenly creatures, of course. I mean, I could still see the tattoos on his arms and neck, after all.

"Nik?" I knocked on the transparent dome, watching his face closely. "Can you hear me?"

There was no response, not even a twitch. Certainly not his usual smirk.

It dawned on me that this was a crazy-rare opportunity, something I couldn't possibly pass up. Much as I hated to admit it, Nik was as stunningly beautiful as Marcus, only his personality and generally dickish attitude hid it most of the time. But not when he was like this.

Like this, he was breathtaking.

"Well . . . don't take this the wrong way or the right way or whatever, but do you mind if I sketch you? Speak now, or forever hold your peace . . ." I held my breath and waited a few seconds, eyes locked on his face. "I'm taking your lack of response as assent. Cool."

I retrieved my sketchbook and pen from the back room, then rushed back to the alcove. "Don't move. Don't move. Don't move," I muttered over and over, like the words might somehow keep him in his apparent trance.

Maybe it worked, because he was still there, exactly as I'd left him.

I tiptoed around his bubble of At and sat on the floor before him, back against a shelf and sketchbook resting on my knee. I studied the lines of his face, his supine posture, the blacks and grays of his ever-fading tattoos. There was so much to see, to study, to capture. Too much.

Like tended to be the case with our kind, Nik was in prime physical condition thanks to a combination of regenerative Nejeret genes and a tireless workout schedule. I often found him with Marcus or Aset in the training room, either just finishing up or just about to start at the beginning or tail ends of my sessions with Dom. I never actually saw him spar with anyone or move through any kind of practice routines, but it seemed like he was always there. At least, all the times that Dom hadn't blocked out the room to train me.

I sketched Nik's hands first, palms upturned and fingers curled in relaxation on top of his thighs. I love drawing people's hands, especially those of people I know. They say so much about a person, and yet it's so easy to *not* notice them. Are their fingers long or squat? Their knuckles bulbous? Their nails flat or curved? Long or cut short? Manicured? Do they have calluses? Scars? Freckles or moles? Are they veiny? There were so many things to look for, to notice . . . so many tiny differences making each person's hands unique.

Nik's hands were sturdy. So very different from Dom's elegant, long-fingered pianist hands. Nik's appeared made for a maker, for a craftsman. They were large, but not with bulging knuckles or sausage fingers, and his nails were flat, close-trimmed, and clean. Being a Nejeret, he didn't have any calluses or scars, but the lines on his palm ran in long, deep grooves, as tended to be the case with the older Nejerets.

I filled two pages with a collage of images of his hands before flipping to a fresh page and raising my eyes to his face. I followed the line of his neck, capturing the supple curve with pen and paper, then his sharp jawline and squared chin. I drew the gentle curve of his bottom lip, finding myself lingering on that lone feature.

The right corner of his mouth tensed, then lifted into that

all-too-familiar smirk. "Kitty Kat . . ."

I watched his lips form the sounds, entranced but not able to actually hear his voice through the At. The barrier melted into a wispy, colorful mist that dissipated before it reached me.

"It's not polite to stare."

My eyes flashed up to meet his. "I, um . . ." I fumbled my sketchbook closed. "You should be more careful. The Kin might have other people like you and Carson. What if one of them came in here and you were all zoned out and—"

"I knew it was you out there." His pale eyes twinkled. "You knocked. Said you were going to sketch me . . ."

"But—but you didn't respond."

"Because I was finishing up my conversation with Re."

"Oh." I chewed on my lip. "Did he say anything . . . about *me*?" I dreaded the answer, but the question had to be asked.

Nik shook his head.

Both disappointed and relieved, I scrambled to my feet, hugging my sketchbook to my chest and sidestepping around the very edge of the alcove. My butt and shoulder blades brushed against the edges of the shelves as I made my way free. "So, um . . ." I alternated between looking at Nik to make sure he stayed in the same place and avoiding eye contact as he tracked my progress.

He watched me, expression bland, bored, even. "Are you finished?"

I froze. "Finished?" I sure as hell wasn't going to keep staring at him and sketching while he was conscious.

"With the videos?" He shifted so his feet were under him and stood gracefully. Facing me, he raised his eyebrows. "Or are you planning on watching more?"

I shook my head, backing away when he started toward me. "I'm done. For today, I mean."

"Good." Nik brushed past me and headed to the checkout counter. He hopped onto the counter with ease and hunched forward, elbows on his thighs. Sometimes he acted so normal—so human—he made it impossible to believe he was over five thousand years old, just a handful of years younger than Marcus and Aset, and far too easy to forget that one of the actual creators of our universe cohabitated with him in his body. "I'm starving. Get your shit together and we'll grab something to eat."

I stared at him, owl-like. "Why?"

His right eyebrow twitched, the silver piercing glinting red from the light of the traffic signal outside. "Because I'm hungry . . ."

I opened my mouth to ask why—why was he still here? Why did he want to get food *with me*? But the questions caught in my throat when I realized that I didn't want him to go away, to leave me alone. I was relieved he was still there. I blamed my sudden change of heart on the disturbing information I'd learned from my mom in those first few videos.

"Oh, um, okay. Cool." I crossed the shop and headed into the back room. "Just give me a sec."

A few moments later, I was hoisting the strap of my messenger bag over my head and passing through the beaded curtain. "I just want to grab one thing," I said, weaving around display tables to the nook in the back corner of the shop where the majority of the books and journals lived. I picked up a distressed leather-bound planner with a dandelion seed head engraved on the cover. It was the kind that had an alphabetized address book section and small binder rings, making it easy to add, remove, and reorganize pages. Perfect for cataloging members of the Kin.

I tucked the leather book into my bag. "Alright," I said, walking to the door. The sound of Nik's boots told me he was following. "Where to?"

"Dick's?"

Grinning, I turned the lock. "I was so hoping you'd say that."

I used to eat at the Seattle staple so often that a burger and fries from Dick's Drive-In qualified as my main food group. "It's been *forever.*" I opened the door, letting in the noise of a bustling Friday evening on Broadway, and stepped outside.

"How many videos did you get through?"

"Four," I said, waiting for him to shut the door. "Four and a half, technically."

Nik chuckled, the sound making the hair on the back of my neck stand at attention.

I fit the key into the lock and eyed him over my shoulder.

"Guess you'll be coming back . . . especially if you want to fill that little hunting book without the others figuring out what you're up to."

I froze, head bowed and key turned partway. How did Nik know that was what the dandelion planner was for?

He laughed under his breath, a dry, humorless sound. "Thought so."

He hadn't known, but he'd suspected. And I'd just confirmed his suspicions. Carefully, I finished locking the door, then faced him. "I have to do it," I said, defiant.

Nik nodded to himself. "Sure."

"Dom knows. He said he'd help me however he can."

"However he can . . ." Nik sneered.

I crossed my arms. "What's that supposed to mean?"

"You'll never be Dominic l'Aragne's main priority, Kitty Kat. He's oath-bound to Heru and Lex. Honor and duty will always come first, with him. You can't depend on him."

"I'm not depending on him," I said. I lied. Cheeks growing hot, I turned away from Nik and strode down the sidewalk toward the intersection. Dom had been the ace up my sleeve.

"You know, self-deceit really is the worst kind of treachery."

I spun around and stomped back to the storefront, stopping just a few feet from Nik. "Oh, just shut up, would you?"

He shrugged and leaned his shoulder against the broad

storefront window.

"The only person I need to depend on is *me*," I said, poking myself in the chest. "That's the only person I want to depend on . . . the only person I *can* depend on."

"Maybe."

I scoffed, arms crossing over my chest once more. "And what's *that* supposed to mean?"

"There's always me . . ."

"You?" My mouth fell open, and I snapped it shut. I snorted a laugh. "Are you kidding me?"

"Fine. Whatever." Nik pushed off the window and strode past me, toward the intersection that would eventually lead him to glorious, greasy food.

I stared after him, struck dumb and feet cemented in place. It took painfully long seconds for me to be able to respond. "Nik! Wait!" I jogged after him, catching up to him halfway across the crosswalk leading to the west side of Broadway. "Were you serious? Do you really want to help me?"

"Honestly, Kat, I don't give two shits what happens to you."

I stopped a couple steps from the curb. A car waiting to turn right honked, and I flashed the driver an equally abrasive hand gesture before leaping onto the sidewalk.

"But Re does," Nik continued, "and I want to know why. He's not talking, so that leaves me with one option—playing sidekick." He strode along, hands in the pockets of his long, black leather coat, not a care in the world.

I jogged a few yards, falling into step beside him as he started across the next crosswalk. "So you're serious. You'll help me?"

He shrugged. "Don't really have a choice."

Ears freezing, I pulled up my fur-lined hood and stuffed my hands into my coat pockets. We walked the length of the block in silence. When we reached the next crosswalk, I peeked at him out of the corner of my eye. "Alright. You can be my sidekick."

28

SECRETS & LIES

I sat beside Nik on the bench at the bus stop while we waited for the bus back to the ferry, hugging myself through my coat and listening to the rain beat down on the glass overhead. I glanced at Nik, then hunched my shoulders and shivered, leaning a smidgen closer to him. He was bigger than me—it was only fair that he share his body heat.

"All that stuff my mom told Dom about the Kin and their sheuts," I said, "were you surprised at all?"

Nik gave the original non-answer—a shrug. He did that a lot.

I shivered against the damp cold. "Did you know all of those things people can do with their sheuts were possible? I mean, it really is like magic—teleporting, freezing time, blocking memories, creating things out of At and anti-At . . . freaking *mind control*. And did you know you could, like, train yourself to be able to do other things with your sheut?" According to my mom, Nejerets born with a sheut had an innate "power"—like Nik and his ability to manipulate At—but they could gain some level of proficiency in other areas through an ass-load of hard work and dedication.

Still, he said nothing.

So, watching his face, I barreled onward. "Could Lex do all of that when she was, you know, trying not to die from sheut overload? And the twins: will they be able to do everything—like will they be the ultimate sheut-wielders, putting all of the Kin to shame?"

"The things Lex could do," he said, "the things the Kin can do—that's only the tip of the iceberg. The twins' power will scare the shit out of everyone, and we'll all be helpless against them. They'll be all-powerful, and the knowledge of the universe will be theirs for the taking, a pseudo-omniscience that will make them all the more powerful. They will be Netjer." His voice took on a hollow, distant sound. "The gods will walk amongst us once more, and the universe will tremble."

I shivered again, but this time it had nothing to do with the cold.

THE BUS WAS FAR FROM FULL WHEN NIK AND I FIRST boarded, but it wasn't so late that we'd completely missed the evening surge of people heading toward the waterfront to catch their return ferry across the Puget Sound. After two stops, seats were limited, and after three, a few people were standing in the aisle.

Ours was one of the long, accordion buses with the rotating middle section. We were sitting on the sideways seats just before the joint. Some people hated those seats—motion sickness, I guess—but I'd always found a secret pleasure in pretending to stare out the opposite window while really watching the people sitting right across the aisle from me.

When the bus's brakes screeched and we came to a halt at the fourth stop, I grabbed onto the metal pole separating my leg from Nik's. The edge of my pinky brushed against his jeans. "Sorry," I mumbled.

He grunted softly in response.

A woman boarded the bus through the door at the front, haggard-looking and toting a small girl of three or four years with a fluffy ponytail almost directly atop her head. Despite the mother's obvious exhaustion, she smiled down at her little girl, her hand gripping the child's protectively, and guided the child ahead of her down the aisle.

Nik didn't even hesitate, though it took me a moment to realize what was going on. He stood, reaching up to take hold of the pole running horizontally overhead when the bus lurched forward. He nodded to the woman, offering his seat to her and her daughter.

I watched him curiously, searching for the telltale signs that it wasn't Nik in control, but Re. Except the eyes that met mine for the briefest moment were that disturbingly familiar pale blue. The more time I spent with Nik, the more I realized I didn't know him at all.

I watched the little girl, now seated beside me, happily distracted by her mom's cell phone. She was playing some game with cats chasing birds and, if I wasn't mistaken from my cursory glance, donuts.

Nik shifted his hand from the pole overhead to the one by my leg and hunched down, leaning closer to me. "Stop staring at the kid," he said, quiet enough that only I could hear.

My eyes flashed up to his. I hadn't been staring. I'd been looking, that's all.

Nik's hand scooted down a few inches until it was really close to mine. Too damn close. And yet it was still that same hand I'd drawn, the same one that looks like it belongs to a craftsman, to someone who uses his hands to make his way through the world. To someone who relies on his own abilities.

It was exactly the kind of person I wanted to be. The kind of person I was trying to be, with Dom's help. *Dom* . . . My stomach knotted when I thought of my half-brother. I didn't think he'd approve of how quickly I'd gone from lusting after revenge to actually going for it. But he'd said I could plan all I wanted so long as I didn't actually *do* anything until he deemed me ready. But what if I couldn't wait that long?

"Are you going to tell Dom what I'm doing?" I asked. "Or Marcus?"

"You said Dom already knew." Nik looked away, staring through the broad windshield at the front of the bus.

"I mean . . . he knows I'll *eventually* go after them . . ."

Nik laughed under his breath and shook his head.

"The Council probably won't like that I'm looking into the Kin on my own," I persisted quietly.

Nik continued to stare out the windshield. "So?"

"But the Council—"

"—doesn't tell me what to do." Nik's eyes were blue ice when they met mine.

"Does that mean you're not going to tell them what I'm doing?" The thought of actually admitting I was hunting the Kin out loud just felt ridiculous, so I didn't.

"Don't worry, Kitty Kat. Your secret's safe with me."

I glanced up just in time to see that familiar, haughty sneer twist his mouth.

"For now."

29

FRIENDS & FRENEMIES

"Again." Dom's voice was harsh, demanding. He wasn't asking; he was telling.

"Seriously?" It was late, and I was beat. My T-shirt was soaked through with sweat, and pieces of my hair were matted to my forehead and cheeks. I was the quintessential hot mess, and I was really missing my long hair right now, because I would've killed to be able to put it up into a ponytail. An elastic headband just wasn't enough.

Dom crossed his arms over his chest and leaned his back against the wall of the training room. "You have not been practicing enough. Therefore, you must practice more, here. Now. Run through the sets again."

"That's not true, and you know it." I, too, crossed my arms. "I spend every free second of my day training." In fact, training was one of the few things keeping me going right now—Dom knew that better than anyone else. Sure, my clandestine vengeance-plotting sessions with Nik at the shop were the other major highlights of my days—we'd been at it for nearly a month—but any plans we came up with were useless without Dom's training. *I* was useless without his training.

"And the other seconds?"

I inhaled deeply, blowing out the breath in an irritated huff. "What is it, Dom? You think I'm up to something? Wasting my life?" Even as I spoke, I did as he'd requested, starting Dom's "sets" from the beginning.

The sets were loosely based on the karate katas I'd watched Marcus move through all those weeks ago, though the forms and routines Dom taught me were more comprehensive, drawing on a multitude of disciplines. They were Dom's own personal brand of martial arts, and they mixed things like karate and aikido with boxing and gymnastics. Even a little tai chi was thrown into the mix. It was kind of like Krav Maga, or so I could tell from the research I'd done, but harder. More intense. *Worse.*

I'd painfully graduated up to sixteen memorized routines, each a series of poses, strikes, and forms that served to strengthen me—offensively and defensively—inside and out. It took me about an hour, maybe an hour and a half to work through all sixteen sets. When I was more proficient, I would be much faster. But then, there would also be additional sets to perform.

I finished the first set with a whoosh of breath and sweep of my arms overhead, resulting in me posing like a Bollywood dancer. I craned my neck to look at Dom. "This is about the fact that I've been going to the shop every day, isn't it?"

I glided through the first few poses of the second set, moving from one position to the next, pushing out my breath in grunts when necessary, but otherwise having a hard time regulating my breathing. I had the feeling I was going to feel this, regeneration-wise, tomorrow. I hadn't eaten enough today, not for this kind of exertion. Whether my regenerative abilities kicking into high gear would result in me looking older or ridiculously skinny, there was no way to tell. But kick in, they would. I had no doubt of that.

Cool. Hopefully I'd look older. After all, a regeneration-based hangover was the only way I'd move beyond my eighteen-year-old body. Ever.

I glanced at Dom over my shoulder. He still hadn't answered my question. He just stared at me with his dark, assessing eyes, his dark hair slicked back and his sharp features carefully guarded against some dark emotion. He was a bundle of darkness, that Dom.

"Watch your posture," he snapped.

I turned my head so I was staring at the wall of staffs and other non-bladed weapons. "Are you mad that I've been going to the shop?"

Still, he didn't respond.

"You're the one who helped my mom set me up as the inheritor of the shop in the first place. I really don't understand why you're pissed that I'm spending time there."

Infuriatingly, Dom just continued to watch me, essentially nonresponsive, as I moved on to the third set.

I was breathing harder now. Again. "What's . . . the problem . . . Dom?"

"Do you not trust me?"

"What . . . are you talking . . . about?" I twisted around, lowering myself into the next form, which always reminded me of the warrior pose in yoga. After a deep inhale and exhale, I dragged my back leg around my other foot, toe pointed, and slid it forward to stand in martial art's equivalent of ballet's fourth position.

"Of course . . . I trust you." I laughed breathily. It sounded forced, even to my ears. "Jesus, Dom . . . I think . . . I've proven that . . . by now." I'd shared more of my inner ugliness with him than I'd ever shared with anybody else, ever—even Jenny, and that girl goes after information like a bloodhound.

"You know that I will be there for you if you need me," Dom said. "Whatever you need from me, little sister, anything, you need only ask."

I let my arms fall to my sides, defeated and exhausted. "I *know*, Dom." I turned to face him. "I do." I inhaled and exhaled heavily and swiped my hair and a fair amount of sweat out of my face. "I just—I feel closer to my mom when I'm there." It wasn't a lie, exactly. It just wasn't the whole truth. "It's painful being there, but it's also like a part of her is still there. And I know it sounds stupid, but that's really what it's all about—her." And hunting down the people responsible for her death.

Dom took a single breath, letting it out in a slow, quiet sigh. It was the sound of disappointment, of resignation. "I never doubted that for a second, little sister. But just know, should you decide to tell me the full truth, I am here, ready and willing to listen."

I opened my mouth, then shut it again, unable to make myself tell him. I hated lying to him, but I wasn't willing to risk him trying to stop me.

My shoulders hunched, my arms hanging uselessly at my sides. I'd never before felt like such a complete and utter asshole.

FOR THE FIRST TIME IN WEEKS, I WOKE FROM A nightmare of *that day*. Soaked in cold sweat, I pulled out my old friend, the deck of playing cards, and played through several hours of Solitaire until, finally, it was late enough for me to get ready and head out to the ferry.

I parked the car in the ferry terminal lot, getting a great spot thanks to being earlier than usual for the nine o'clock boat. I boarded and found my way to the booth Nik and I usually shared on the upper deck. When the ferry started to move away from the dock with Nik's side of the booth still empty, I assumed it meant he wouldn't be joining me, at least not for this leg of the commute.

Sometimes he didn't meet up with me until the bus, sometimes not until the shop, but he always showed up eventually. I had no clue what he did when we weren't together. He often stayed in Seattle when we left the shop, sometimes rode the ferry back to Bainbridge with me, and rarely actually came home. Part of me wondered about what he did during all those nights away. And part of me never wanted to find out.

The only certainty was that on the nights he didn't come home, he always showed up with bruises and minor injuries, some barely visible through all the ink in his skin. The marks would fade after an hour or two, from his body, if not from my mind.

If he didn't show up for the ferry ride today, fine with me. After Dom's guilt trip and the sleepless night, well . . . I felt like being alone anyway.

I leaned my head back and closed my eyes.

"Hey," Nik said, and my eyelids snapped open. He set a large paper coffee cup on the table and slid into the bench opposite mine. He wrapped his hands around the cup, warming his fingers.

"I thought you weren't coming." There was accusation in my voice, even I couldn't ignore it.

"I was getting a coffee." Nik's lips curled into that annoying smirk. "What—are you mad I didn't get you anything?"

I glared at him for another second or two, then returned to staring out the window. The ferry was heavy with commuters heading into the city to join the daily grind, but there were a few families, too—parents with their young kids and too-cool teenagers braving the chill to enjoy the rare winter sun on the deck.

"What's wrong with you?" Nik asked, no hint of concern in his voice.

I didn't look at him this time. "Nothing."

For long minutes, Nik and I sat in silence. Finally, he broke it. "Is it Dom? Unrequited love can be a bitch . . ."

My eyes locked on Nik's, fury heating my blood and disgust churning in my stomach. "He's my *brother*, asshat." I flashed him an undoubtedly ugly sneer. "I don't really know how to say this nicely, so I'm just going to go for it—shut the fuck up."

Nik leaned back in his seat and raised his arms, placing his hands on the back of his head. "Hit a nerve there, didn't I?"

Now that I was looking at him—well, glaring at him—I was able to see what appeared to be fingernail or claw marks running down the length of his neck, from just below his ear to his collarbone, where they disappeared beneath the collar of his T-shirt.

Normally I was so much better about keeping my mouth shut. Okay, normally I was a *little* bit better about keeping my mouth shut. But so far, I'd done a really good job of not asking Nik where he went, what he did, or how he got his ever-changing scratches and bruises. But today, all bets were off.

The only two options I could come up with were that he spent his evenings at some sort of a fight club, where he let people beat the crap out of him, or that he procured the services of a dominatrix, whom he also let beat the crap out of him. Or a dominat*or*? I'd never really considered Nik's sexuality—I hadn't! —but suddenly it seemed like the most fascinating thing in the world. It was immensely more intriguing and less painful to think about than my rotten training session with Dom the previous night.

"What happened to your neck?" I asked, verbal diarrhea pouring out of my mouth.

Nik leaned forward, planting his elbows on the table and, once again, curling his hands around the paper coffee cup. The corners of his mouth pulled up in a slow, purposeful grin, and his eyes locked with mine. "I have to say, Kitty Kat, I'm surprised it took you so long to ask."

I waited for seconds, but it was clear that he wasn't planning on saying more. "That's it? That's your non-answer?" I felt irrationally irritated that he hadn't explained himself, despite knowing full well that he didn't owe me any kind of an explanation. Despite knowing, full well, that I didn't want an explanation. Not really. Whatever weird shit he was into, it was none of my business. My business was weird and shitty enough on its own.

Apparently, Nik agreed. "MYOB," he said lazily.

I narrowed my eyes. "Just don't let your 'business' screw up mine."

Nik chuckled. "Wouldn't dream of it."

30

PLAN & ACTION

"I think that's it." I was sitting across from Nik at the table in the shop's back room, flipping through the pages of the dandelion planner, scanning the information I had on each member of the Kin. Well, on each of the members my mom had known anything about. "We're ready . . . unless there's anything else you think we need to add. Third time's the charm?"

Nik shook his head. "It'd be a waste of time. Can't really afford that, can we?"

He was right. I'd watched the interrogation videos once on my own and once more with him. Another time through would just be time wasted and opportunity lost. The videos were nearly four months old now; the more time we let pass, the less accurate my mom's information would be. Soon, it would be completely obsolete. I couldn't let that happen. She deserved better. And *they* deserved so very, *very* much worse.

I stared across the table at Nik. "I guess that means it's time for action." I just hoped he had some sort of a plan. I mean, he'd been around for pretty much ever; he had a little more experience with this kind of thing than me, especially if he consulted with his spiritual hitchhiker. Re had a little more experience with *every* kind of thing.

Unfortunately, my hopes proved faulty. Zippo from Nik.

"Well . . ." I leaned over the table, flipping through the planner's pages until I reached the M's. "Here's what I'm thinking—Mari's the person we have the most info on, obviously. So we go after her first. Cut off the head of the snake."

I'd filled nearly four full pages, front and back, with information about Mei's "daughter." Mari took up eight times as much space in my little hunting book than anybody else. Most only had a line or two—their name, any distinctive physical features or personality traits my mom had relayed to Dom, and, of course, what sheut powers they were proficient in.

I tapped the first page of the Mari section in my hunting book. "I mean, she was clearly involved with the whole Apep-Carson situation. Hell, she probably killed Mei. And I bet she knows where all the others are. Plus, if we take her out, who'll the others band around? We'll be buying ourselves more time. She's the most logical person to start with." I sat back in my chair. "Except we have no clue what she can do with her sheut."

"Which makes it a tad bit difficult to estimate how dangerous she is," Nik said. "And, considering we still haven't figured out which of them made the anti-At pocket watch . . ."

Taking a deep breath, I decided to just dive in, addressing the really damn scary elephant in the room. "We could just go into this believing her 'special gift' might be the ability to manipulate anti-At?" It was kind of like what Nik could do with solidified At, only a whole lot scarier, since one touch of obsidian-like anti-At could erase a Nejeret from the timeline completely. If it touched me, it would be like I'd never existed.

Nik nodded, very slowly. "But an assumption like that could be just as dangerous should it prove wrong. If you go after Mari believing she can manipulate anti-At and find out that she's capable of doing something else, then you'll be totally blindsided by whatever that other thing might be."

I tilted my head back and forth, considering his point. It was a pretty damn good one. "Okay . . . so, I'd go after her being aware that she *might* be able to control anti-At, or she *might* be able to do any of a gazillion other things. How's that sound?"

Nik was quiet for a moment. "That's all assuming we can even track her down."

I perked up. "We could try joining forces and see if we can find a stable portion of the At. Two bas and a ren working together . . . we might have a shot."

Nik shook his head, frowning. "I'm afraid we will have to find another way."

I exhaled heavily and slouched back in my chair. "Has the Council had any success in tracking down any of the Kin? Or are they still sitting on their thumbs?"

Nik's lips quirked. "They've made precursory attempts, but they haven't gotten anywhere yet." He tapped his fingers on the table, thoughts swirling around behind those pale blue eyes. It pleased me when he spoke about the Council as the "other" to our "we." I couldn't have explained it if I'd sat down and tried, but I liked having Nik on my team. "What if we took a more human approach . . . searched for the Kin some way that the older Nejerets would never consider?"

I nodded to myself. Another good point. The older Nejerets, especially the millennia-old bodies on the Council, were used to relying on their Nejeret gifts, specifically the ability to enter the At and find people in the echoes. They had a really hard time moving on from the ways and traditions they were used to, even when those ways and traditions were duds, like the present, unstable At. Their adoption of new technological developments was downright sluggish. Change is hard. At least, that's what they say.

But humans—they're all about adopting the latest and greatest, newest and most effective technologies. They love finding ways to use technology to enhance their own natural abilities. And I was practically still one of them.

My hopes lifted. Just because the Council had been unsuccessful so far didn't mean I would be, too. I just had to search in ways they hadn't, consider things they never would. I had to think like a human.

I leaned forward, heartbeat picking up. "I have an idea. There's someone we need to go see."

I STARED UP AT THE FACE OF A RESTORED OLD FOUR-story brick school building. It was on the edge of the Industrial District, the I-5 off-ramp curling around the building. No wonder it wasn't a school anymore. Safeco and Century Link Field were visible behind the brick building, beyond the myriad of legs extending from the freeway. The school had been decommissioned decades ago—I looked it up on the bus ride here—and had been recently renovated and converted into an artist's collective. A shallow yard, planted with sculptures rather than living things, filled the several dozen feet between the sidewalk and the front of the building.

Nik stood beside me on the sidewalk, hands in the pockets of his long, black leather coat. "You sure about this, Kitty Kat?"

We were there to see Garrett, a talented young hacker I'd gone to high school with. Garrett was . . . unique. He wasn't really like anybody else I'd ever met. He had a way of getting away with things—things said, things done—that other people couldn't. Things other people would earn a slap for saying or doing. Or a punch. Or a well-timed kick to the balls.

Chewing on my lip, I stared down at my phone, pulling up

the text messaging app. I double-checked the text from my old high school friend, Gracie, and nodded. "This is where she said his workspace is."

"But are you sure you want to do this?"

"I, um—" I shook my head, dispelling the doubts suddenly buzzing around me. "Yeah, of course. When we get in there, can you just hang out in the background? Garrett doesn't really like guys, and if he thinks we're in any way involved, like . . ." For whatever reason, I couldn't bring myself to say "dating."

"Just tell him I'm your cousin." Something in Nik's expression made me want to slap him. He wore a strange mixture of disbelief and amusement, like he couldn't believe I would ever consider the possibility that somebody would think we were involved.

"Fine. Let's get this over with." I marched up the path leading to the former school's double doors, not bothering to look back to see if Nik was following me. At that moment, I really didn't care.

After a quick check of the directory in the lobby, which still very much resembled the main office of a high school, Nik and I headed up to the third floor. According to the map beside the directory, Garrett had a corner studio overlooking Safeco Field and the Industrial District. Not the greatest view, in my opinion. But to each their own.

We headed up two flights of stairs, then down a hallway that displayed artwork on the walls and in large, built-in display cases, much like the school must've done decades ago. Except this artwork was not anything a school would've allowed. There was more anatomy displayed here than in a *Playboy*.

"Interesting place," Nik said.

I glanced at him over my shoulder, and a laugh escaped from me in the form of a soft snort. "Tell me about it."

"You like the arts. Maybe you should apply for a spot here."

"Yeah . . . not really my style."

Nik chuckled, and I frowned. He usually only laughed when he was making fun of me. Which then made me question—was he making fun of me? Had I missed something?

I exhaled heavily. It didn't matter. "I think it's that one down there," I said pointing with my chin to a black door at the end of the hallway. "If you just want to wait out here, I'll see if he can even help us."

"You don't think he can?"

We neared the door. A light glowed through the crack at the bottom of the door, bright neon green. "I *hope* he can. Garrett's the only person I actually know who has real experience with the dark web and other crazy hacker stuff." I shrugged. "He's our best shot. And if he can't help us, maybe he knows who can."

"Alright." Nik leaned his shoulder against the wall beside the door and crossed his arms. "I'll be here if you need me."

I flashed him a quick thank-you smile, then knocked on the door. "Garrett," I called. "It's Kat . . . from Garfield," I added, sounding unsure about my own alma mater. "Gracie told me you were here. There's something I need your help w—"

The door sprang open, and Garrett's electric-blue hair was the first thing I saw. Of course he had blue hair. It was so Garrett.

He wasn't handsome, exactly, but there was just something about him. A twinkle in his eye and a quirk of his mouth that spoke of mischievous things left unsaid. It was more his demeanor than his appearance that enabled him to get away with the borderline inappropriate things he said all too often.

As I stood there, facing him through the doorway, I felt my lips spread into a broad grin. I was genuinely happy to see him. I couldn't believe I hadn't sought him out earlier.

"Kat!" Garrett's grin mirrored mine. "What—" He shook his head slowly. "What are you doing here?" His eyes slid past me, landing on Nik, and his smile wilted. "Who's that?"

I shot a cursory glance over my shoulder. "My cousin." I made a show of rolling my eyes and looking super disinterested. "He wanted to tag along." I leaned in and whispered, "He's always following me around . . ." Had he been human, Nik wouldn't have been able to hear me. But Nik wasn't human. Inside, I was giggling.

"Oh, yeah?" Garrett nodded enthusiastically. "Cool. Alright."

He was a little bit taller than me, and when he leaned in to give me a quick hug, I didn't feel overwhelmed by his presence. Nejerets were always big, it seemed. We were a secret race of people who were larger-than-life, often times physically, not to mention intellectually and reputation-wise. It had been a long time since I'd been around a regular ol' human guy. If you could even call Garrett regular.

"Come in." He stepped back and held out his arm. "I was just finishing something, but it can totally wait till later."

I followed him into his studio, then stopped and stared around in awe. The space was bigger than your usual, say, English classroom, and it was filled with computers and servers and mainframes and things that I didn't have names for but that looked pretty technologically advanced with all their cables and buttons and blinking lights. I'd never seen anything like this before. Everything the Nejerets had was sleek and new and made to fit in your pocket. It was all expensive and top-of-the-line, but it wasn't made for things like this.

"So . . . how exactly is this an *art* studio?"

Garrett strode over to a monitor and clicked a few keys on a keyboard. The monitor went black. "I don't know that I would actually call it an art, per se . . . but I do have a lot of creative freedom in my work." He scanned around the converted classroom and all of the equipment it contained. "And I don't call this a studio. It's my lair."

"You are such a dork."

Garrett looked at me, eyebrows raised and brilliant blue eyes laughing. They matched his hair. "Katarina Dubois, are you flirting with me?" His eyebrows did a little dance. "If so . . ." He leaned on the edge of the monitor with his elbow. "Hey girl . . ."

"Like I said," I laughed, "dork." Being around him, someone who was so odd and good-natured, was a breath of fresh air after being around Nik all the time. It was either sarcasm or harsh reality with him—a good ol' serious-fest. Garrett was the opposite of serious. The anti-serious.

"So, what's brought you to my lair?" Garrett asked. "Not that I'm not stoked to see you. It's just, well . . . I haven't heard from you since you dropped out of school last year." I didn't actually drop out of school—I graduated early. Marcus pulled some strings and, well . . . the rest is history.

I traced my finger over the wires on a circuit board sitting on a table beside a bunch of tiny screwdrivers and other tools for working on miniature things. "I'm . . ." I took a deep breath. "A lot's happened. My mom, she—" I swallowed roughly. "She died."

"Shit . . ." Garrett rubbed his hand through his unkempt blue hair, making it stand on end. "Kat . . . I'm sorry. I had no idea."

"Yeah, um . . . that's actually sort of why I'm here." I looked at him, looked away, back at him, then away again, unable to maintain eye contact for more than a couple seconds. "She was murdered, and I was hoping . . ." I was terrified he would refuse to help me. I didn't have anyone else to go to, not anyone with skills like his, and I *needed* to find the Kin. I owed them pain, with interest.

Was I obsessed? Maybe. Did I care? Not a bit.

"Seriously, Kat, whatever you need, I'll totally do it." He crossed the room to stand in front of me, placing his hands on either side of my shoulders and ducking his head so his face was at the same height as mine. "What can I do? How can I help?"

"Well . . ." I pulled my bottom lip between my teeth.

“There’s someone I need to find. Someone who was involved in what happened, and I want to track her down.” I raised my eyes, finally meeting his for more than a few seconds.

“So this is like a vengeance thing?” Garrett’s bright blue eyes lit up. “Awesome.”

31

KAT & MOUSE

"Oh, yeah . . ." Garrett spun his chair and rolled one desk over. His nimble fingers typed away at a second keyboard, and he occasionally reached up to swipe something left or right or up or down or off the screen entirely with the tip of his finger. "I see you. Tricky, tricky . . ."

"What is it? What did you find?" I'd been standing at the broad window for the past half hour, zoning out while I stared down at the first-floor terrace. Or maybe *zenning* out—what used to be a basketball court had been converted into some sort of a giant Zen garden. Nik lounged in a chair nearby, his boots propped up on a low windowsill.

I rushed over to Garret's complex multisystem interface and gripped the back of his chair. "What did you find?" I repeated, the tips of my fingers digging into the chair's padding.

Garret glanced at me over his shoulder, a grin stretching across his entire face. "A report from the border—the Canadian border. The border guard turned away someone that sounds like your girl . . . about five three, slim, of Asian descent, and extremely hostile."

He rolled back to the first computer, and I had no choice but to release his chair. "Apparently, she threatened the guard with a black sword that she produced out of nowhere—'out of thin air,' the report says—and managed to avoid detainment. But . . ." He glanced at me one more time, his eyes bright and his cheeks flushed. "Before all that, when she thought she'd be able to get through, our violent little magician friend presented her driver's license to the guard."

He turned his chair all the way around and leaned forward, hands clutching his knees. "The name on the license was Mari Smith, and I have a social." He turned back around and reached for the mouse. "And a photo."

On the monitor, a window opened displaying a Washington State driver's license for one Mari Smith. I'd never actually seen a picture of Mari, but this woman on the screen—Asian, pretty, vibrant green eyes—she looked exactly how I pictured her in my mind, and there was no question that she was a Nejerette. No question all.

"It's her," I said, turning to exchange a look with Nik. "It has to be."

Still grinning, Garrett nodded. "All right. Time to track her down . . ."

THERE WASN'T MUCH BESIDES COMPUTER EQUIPMENT in Garrett's lair. Nik and I waited at the only table not completely covered in priceless or irreplaceable tech stuff. I sat, watching Garrett type away—scrolling here or there, switching from monitor to monitor—and did my best to ignore the fact that Nik was staring at me from the other side of the table. I'm not known for my patience.

"What?" I asked, giving Nik a pointed look.

Frowning, he shook his head.

"Oh, come on," I said, annoyed. "You're the one staring at me . . ."

Frown still in place, he shrugged. "The black sword—I think it's safe to say she can control anti-At. Sure you still want to start with her?"

I leaned forward. "We agreed that was the best plan."

"Before we knew what she could do."

"We're sticking to the plan," I told him.

"Fine." Nik looked at me for a moment longer; then his focus shifted to Garrett before sliding to the window. "But you should know your suicidal is showing."

I huffed out a breath and crossed my arms over my chest, glaring at Nik's profile. Gritting my teeth, I forced myself to look away from him, to hold my tongue, to not throw something at him. I returned to watching Garrett, preferring the distraction of his whirring, buzzing, whizzing, and rolling.

"This should do it," Garrett said, more to himself than to us. "Yeah . . . this'll work nicely. Come to daddy . . ."

I met Nik's eyes for a moment, reading judgment and ridicule, then stood once more and crossed the room to stand behind Garrett. "Did you find something?"

"Think so. There's a cell phone linked to a credit card registered to her social." He opened a new window on the screen, a black background with neon green letters. "I, uh . . . developed a program—well, I've been *working* on developing a program, and this'll technically be the first time I use it for more than just, uh . . . tests."

Nik made a noise of derision, but Garrett didn't even notice.

"Next time the phone is used, even if it's just for a text message or to check email, I should be able to get a lock on its location."

"Just because the phone's linked to her doesn't mean she's the one using it," Nik said from across the room.

"Well, yeah, but this is better than nothing." Garrett gave me a look that said *I can't believe you're related to that guy* clearer than words ever could. "So long as the line is still active, this could give you a solid lead."

I gave his shoulder a squeeze. "Thanks, Garrett, really. This is way more than I had to start out with. Couldn't have done it without you."

Garrett rubbed his hand over his blue hair. "Anything for you, Kat."

AFTER FIFTEEN OR TWENTY MINUTES OF WAITING with no ping from Garrett's little high-tech piece of art, I was getting pretty antsy.

"I really wouldn't worry too much about it, guys," Garrett said, still tapping away on his keyboard, doing his own form of hunting. "Some people don't check their phones every few minutes. Some people go hours without it."

I looked from him to Nik, and we both shrugged.

A phone rang, and I jumped. I think we all jumped. I scanned around the room searching for the noisemaker. It rang again.

Garrett hopped out of his chair, standing for the first time in an hour or two, and jogged to the door. I hadn't been able to see it before, but nestled between two shelves of an industrial metal shelving unit, an old landline telephone was anchored to the wall. "Exciting," Garrett sang. "I almost never get calls on this line."

"Should we be concerned?" Nik asked, his voice even. I looked at him, noting his stiff posture.

"No, no, it's probably just Jane, the receptionist. She mans the phones down in the lobby. If a potential client calls in looking for someone with one of our particular talents, she'll redirect them to the appropriate studio." He shot a quick glance back at us. "It happens every month or two. Could be a new client . . ." He picked up the phone. "Howdy. Garrett 'the Gadget Man' Green, here. What can I do you for?"

I watched him, listening hard. My enhanced Nejerette hearing wasn't strong enough to pick up on the other side of the conversation. I could hear the other person's voice, barely, and certainly not well enough to make out what they were saying.

I glanced at Nik, eyebrows raised. He shook his head. He couldn't hear them either. Which meant whoever it was had to be speaking very quietly.

We both watched Garrett as he said *hello*s and *okay*s and *got-it*s.

"No," Garrett said. "No, I'm not alone."

Nik and I exchanged another glance.

"Katarina Dubois and, um . . . her cousin?"

I straightened in my chair, senses on high alert. Across from me, Nik stood very slowly.

"Garrett . . . ?"

He held out a hand, one finger up. Hang on. He scrambled for something on the bookshelf, then searched through all of his pants pockets before finding a pen in his front left pocket. "Yeah, okay. I'm ready."

Nik started around the table, craning his neck to get a better view of whatever Garrett was writing down.

"Can you see?" I whispered.

Nik shook his head.

"Uh-huh," Garrett said. "Yeah, got it. Which one?" He was quiet for a moment, the other voice humming in the background, just out of ear's reach. "Oh, right—that one. Okay, and then where?" Again, he was quiet for a long moment, listening and writing. "Really?" His pen stopped. "Are—are you sure I have to do that?"

I stood, getting a really bad feeling. "Garrett?"

He glanced at me, and shook his head. "Alright. I'll do it."

He hung up, then turned to face us, holding out what appeared to be a grease-spotted napkin covered in writing. "I have to relay a message to you." His voice sounded off, somehow. Calm, but just . . . off. "The guy on the phone—he knows what we're up to."

"Who was on the phone?" Nik asked, slowly making his way toward Garrett. Almost stalking him.

"Dunno," Garrett said, heading my way. "But he knows where your girl is." Garrett passed Nik, just out of arm's reach, and when he reached me, he handed me the napkin. "That's her location. Apparently she's hiding out in one of the tent cities."

I looked down at the napkin, mouth hanging open. "How . . . ?" I raised my eyes to meet Garrett's. His were wild, frantic.

"I don't want to . . ." His voice was strained. He lifted a shaking hand, reaching for me, but I leaned away. "He said I have to . . ." Sweat was beading on his forehead and dripping down the sides of his face. "I can't *not* do it."

"Garrett, what's wrong?"

He took a step backward, then to the side. "He said this is a warning. Stop looking for them. They're giving you Mari—a trade."

"A trade for *what*?"

"Blood for blood." Without warning, he leaned forward and broke into a dead sprint straight for the window.

Glass smashed and wood splintered. Garrett's yell as he fell was the most horrible thing I'd ever heard in my entire life.

Until his body hit the Zen garden two stories below.

I stumbled to the broken window, hand over my gaping mouth, holding in a scream.

"We should go," Nik said from beside me.

I stared down at Garrett's broken body. His legs and arms didn't look right anymore; they were bent at odd angles. A pool of blood slowly seeped out all around him. And yet his bright blue hair was still the same, dazzling against the bland sand.

"Kat!" Nik tugged on my arm.

Blinking, I looked at him, not understanding what just happened.

"We have to go. Now!"

32

NIK & RE

I stood at the door to the shop, pulling and pushing and not understanding why it wouldn't open. I just wanted to get inside. Away from the world.

"I'll get it," Nik said, shouldering me out of the way. A moment later, he opened the door and I stumbled into the familiar space, only to be greeted by a tidal wave of emotions. It was like walking through that doorway, that in-between, had shattered the numbness of shock, and reality crashed over me. Surrounded by the familiar, I couldn't ignore the horrifying memory any longer.

Garrett . . .

"Oh God . . ." Clutching my chest with both hands, I bent double, gasping for breath and sobbing and really close to throwing up. "Oh God . . ." I sucked in air, but it didn't seem to do me any good. My chest felt too tight, not giving my lungs the room to expand.

Nik touched my shoulder. "Kat?"

I flung his hand off and shied away, knocking into a display table and sending candles and crystals toppling. "Don't touch me!" I hugged my middle, my arms the only things holding me together. I was poison—first my mom, and now Garrett. I didn't want to infect Nik, too. "Don't touch me," I repeated hoarsely.

I hated that Nik was always the one who was there when I broke down. He always bore witness to the moments when the universe proved it enjoyed nothing more than fucking with me.

"Don't touch me . . ." I inhaled in more of that useless air. Each breath suffocated me. "Oh God . . ."

I flinched when Nik's hand landed gently on my upper arm, but I didn't brush him off this time. With a sob, I flung myself at him, gripping the front of his leather jacket so hard that some of my nails bent backwards. "He's—he's dead." I stared up at Nik, feeling like I was floating. "He's dead because of . . . because of me." The guilt was back, drowning me.

"Kitty Kat . . ." Nik wrapped his arms around me and placed a hand on the back of my head, pressing it against his shoulder. He stroked my hair and rubbed my back and just held me.

I cried against his shoulder, a soggy, sobbing mess. I kept trying to speak, but every time I tried, the words would get caught in my chest and a new wave of guilt, sorrow, and regret would pour out of my mouth instead.

First my mom, now Garrett—they were both dead, because of me. How was I supposed to live with that knowledge? How was I supposed to go on?

One word—revenge.

It's in moments like this that the hunger for vengeance is a beautiful thing. And I was suddenly starving.

After some time, when the more violent sobbing gave way to silent tears, Nik put his hands on either side of my face and tilted my head back. He brushed the tears from under my eyes with his thumbs. It did little but clear the way for new tears.

"I—I killed him."

"No, Kat." Nik shook his head ever so slowly. "*They* did. You know the Kin have the power to do this kind of thing."

"But—"

He leaned in and planted the gentlest of kisses against my lips. "No, Kitty Kat. You didn't kill anyone today."

He kissed me again, and it was like I could take a full breath for the first time in an hour. My chest relaxed, and I inhaled fully. His lips touched mine for the third time, and I melted into him, grateful for this unique brand of comfort that only Nik could give me. When his lips were touching mine, the only thought in my mind was that I wanted more.

"No!" Gripping my shoulders, Nik shoved me away.

I fell backward against a display table.

"What the hell is wrong with you?" He turned away from me, his back hunched, his head bowed, and his fists clenched at his sides. "If you ever try anything like that again, I swear I'll—"

"But—" I stared at him, fingers on my lips and eyes wide, head shaking. "But you—*you* kissed me."

He swung his head around to glare at me, fury burning in his moonstone eyes. Re was in charge. "I wasn't talking to—" He turned away from me. "Oh, never mind."

"I didn't—" My cheeks burned with mortification, with anger. I reached for the closest thing, an amethyst geode chunk about the size of a baseball. "Get out," I said, holding the geode up, threatening to throw it at him.

He looked at me like he didn't even know me. But then, considering that it was Re staring out through Nik's eyes, maybe he didn't. His irises faded back to blue, and I waited for some sort of an apology, or at least an explanation. None came.

"Get out!" To emphasize how much I meant it, I threw the geode. It smashed into the bookcase behind him, shattering bottles of essential oils. Shards of glass and fragrant liquid sprayed everywhere. "Get out, Nik!" I shouted, voice breaking at the end. I picked up a candle and threw it at him, chest heaving. "Don't you *ever* come near me again." I threw another candle.

He ducked out of the way.

"Get out." I picked up a geode, a bigger one this time. "Now." I raised the geode to throw.

Without a word, Nik turned and left the shop. Without even a backward glance.

"I don't need you," I said when he was gone. I fingered the napkin with the directions to Mari's hideout, safely stowed in my coat pocket. "I'll do it on my own." It was what I'd always wanted anyway.

33

TICK & BOOM

I brushed my hair out of my face with the back of my wrist as I relaxed. My muscles trembled with fatigue from running through the sets for a third time in a row, but I felt calm, focused.

It had been barely a day since Garrett's death . . . since Nik and the kiss and Re . . .

I'd spent the long hours in the empty apartment above the shop, pacing in the dark, lying on the floor while I stared up at the ceiling, and finally, when I was on the verge of losing my mind, running through Dom's sets. Each time I worked through the poses, I decluttered my mind a little more until clarity and purpose were all that remained. My mom. Garrett. The Kin. Vengeance.

Today was the day. I couldn't put it off any longer. I wouldn't survive another day of inaction. The Kin owed me a debt; it was time for them to pay in full.

There was no way to know if Mari was still in the tent city where Garrett's psychic killer had claimed she would be. Who knew if she'd ever even been there. Hell, maybe it was a trap. It didn't matter. I was consumed by a single desire, and if I didn't act on it soon . . . well, that simply wasn't an option. I would act on it. Today.

Even if it killed me.

Once the sun was up, I headed down to the shop to arm myself from the small stash of weapons I'd collected in a chest in the back room in preparation for this day. It wasn't much, but it would have to do. I fastened two sheathed combat knives to my belt, one on either side. The left knife was longer, with a seven-inch blade, while the right was a more standard five inches. I was already wearing a leather bracelet that wrapped around my wrist four times, the sturdy cord moonlighting as a garrote. I tucked a squat T-handled knife into my front right pocket and an expandable baton into the side of my black combat boots.

Sure, a gun might've been easier and more effective than everything else combined, but I neither had one nor had any practice with one. It would be more of a liability than anything else. Besides, I was going for stealth. For maximum damage with minimum outcry. I planned to fly under the radar for as long as I could to take out as many of the Kin until either the job was done or I was dead.

I shrugged into my long down coat, double-checked that the napkin with the instructions for finding Mari was in the right pocket, and set my phone on the backroom table. I didn't know if anyone could use its GPS hardware to track me. I didn't want to find out.

After taking a deep breath, I pulled up my hood and I passed through the beaded curtain, heading for the door. And stopped mid-step in the middle of the shop.

"What the—" A sword was resting on the checkout counter, scabbard, sword belt, and all. My heart rate doubled.

I took two steps toward it, then stopped to glance around the dark shop. "Hello?" I focused on listening for a heartbeat, breathing, anything. "Nik?" I quickly checked all of the little nooks and crannies, anywhere someone might hide.

There was no one. Not Nik. Not anyone.

Warily, I made my way back to the checkout counter. To the sword. A katana, from the size and shape of the scabbard housing the blade.

Nik must've come back at some point last night while I'd been upstairs. I might—*might*—not have heard him. The thought that he'd returned spurred a flutter in my chest.

The sword's long, slender scabbard was antique-looking—antique, but not old, its silver embellishments only slightly tarnished. The hilt was tightly wrapped in leather stripping, the pommel silver with the silhouette of a bird emblazoned into the metal. A yellow sticky note had been stuck to the hilt: *Thought you might need this.* The writing was clean, nondescript. It could've been Nik's. It had to be.

I shook my head, not understanding. Had he really come back? I hoped the answer was yes, though I didn't understand why it meant so much to me if he had.

With one hand on the scabbard, the other on the hilt, I cautiously pulled the sword free. The blade slid out of the scabbard with zero resistance. It gleamed, nearly transparent and shimmering with an iridescence that made it almost seem to glow.

"Holy shit," I said under my breath.

The entire blade was made of At, which meant it would be absolutely indestructible.

It had to be from Nik. According to my mom in the videos, nobody else could do what he could do with his sheut—except for Carson, but that douchebag was dead. Nobody else could've made this sword.

Nik was still helping me, even after the explosion between us the previous afternoon.

I didn't know whether to laugh or cry. I felt like doing both.

After a quick Google search on my phone, I figured out that the sword belt with all of its extra leather straps was really a shoulder harness. I found a nice little three-part graphic that walked me through how to put it on, then once again donned my coat. A mirror-check in the bathroom assured me the hilt wasn't visible if my hood was up. Good enough.

I'd already unlocked the shop door when, against my better judgment, I turned around and headed into the back room. I snatched my phone off the table and sent a text to Nik: *Thanks for the sword.* See, I can have manners. Sometimes.

The bell over the door jingled, and I froze, listening to the crunch of glass and geode debris under shoes. Unexpectedly, I smiled. He'd come back, again. He'd said I could depend on him, and he'd meant it. I hadn't truly believed him until now.

I passed through the beaded curtain. "I just sent you a—"

But it wasn't Nik who stood just inside the shop door. It was Dom.

I froze. "What are you doing here?"

"I came to warn you." Dom took a step toward me. "Kat—"

"No." I crossed my arms. I couldn't handle this right now, not from him. I was so close to actually *doing* something. Dom was the only person who might—just maybe—be able to talk me out of it. I couldn't let that happen. "Just stop, Dom. You're not my father. I'm not your responsibility, so please, just leave me alone."

"I—" I wasn't sure if it was anger that paralyzed his tongue or something else. Whatever it was, he was shaking with it. Because of the words I'd hurtled at him.

I'd never felt so ashamed before, and I hated myself for wanting to turn around, run away, and go find some dark, dank corner to hide in. I set my jaw and squared my shoulders. It would all be worth it soon. Either that, or it would all be over. And then it wouldn't matter anymore.

"I may not be your father," Dom said, "but we're still family."

My chin trembled, but I clenched my teeth to still it.

"I could stop you from doing whatever it is you have planned."

I met his eyes. "But you won't." I knew it in my bones.

He shook his head, disappointment in his dark eyes. "This is your battle. I will not interfere. But I will warn you, little sister—all is not what it seems."

My eyes narrowed. Reluctantly, I took the bait. "What do you mean?"

"In all the time you've spent with Nik, has he shared with you the fact that Re has access to the At?"

I scoffed and shook my head. "Nobody can use the At right now. It's broken."

"Not true," Dom said. "Re can access it whenever he wishes. The instability does not impact him. The echoes are, as always, his for the viewing."

"What—but he said—" I shook my head. Nik had said using the At to find Mari and the other members of the Kin wasn't an option. "You're lying," I told Dom. "I'd have heard about it by now."

Dom shook his head again. "It's something the Council has been keeping under wraps."

My eyes became glassy. Nik lied to me? Why? I held my head high, betrayal burning right alongside defiance in my gut. "Then why are you telling me this now? Won't the Council be pissed that you're sharing their precious secrets?"

"Because I don't want you to die," Dom said, his words a whiplash across my soul.

I flinched, but didn't respond.

"Little sister . . . Nik is powerful, I know, and that makes him a tempting ally. But Re is unpredictable. He shares only bits and pieces of what he's seen in the At, even with the Council. It is essential that you keep that in mind every time either he or Nik tells you anything. Their motivations are unclear. As powerful as the pair are, they are equally dangerous."

There was a long stretch of silence between us. I worked to regulate my breathing, waited until I felt confident that my voice wouldn't tremble. I cleared my throat. "It doesn't even matter. We're not working together anymore."

"But you still walk the same path—the one he and Re helped guide you down—with or without them by your side."

I stared at Dom, struggling with the truth in his words. I wrestled it into submission, then locked it away.

"You are acting on emotion, not reason. I fear that if you continue down this path, you *will* die."

"I don't care," I said, brushing past him. I yanked the door open and strode down the sidewalk. I wanted nothing more than to be away—from Dom. From that place. From my life.

From the realization that part of me hoped he was right. Part of me wished for the quiet of death.

34

MOTHERS & DAUGHTERS

Sword strapped to my back and mostly hidden under my coat, I stepped onto the curb of the final block and slowed. The slightly run-down neighborhood was a combination of tiny homes, several-story brick apartment buildings, and small commercial spaces. At the end of the dead-end road, a tall chain-link fence blocked the way to a steep downward slope covered in overgrown grass and the corpses of last year's blackberry boom.

I supposed the fence had been put up as an attempt to keep the riffraff living in the tent city at the bottom of the hill away from the people living and working up here. I hadn't even considered the possibility that there might be a better way to access the mobile city of the homeless; it was simply the only access point I knew about.

Eyes scanning the length of the fence, I stopped at the cement dividers blocking the end of the road. My feet seemed to be fighting against my brain, against my desire to go on, to see this through. To finish it.

A moment later, my traitorous mind threw in its lot with my stubborn feet. *There's no way to get past the fence . . . might as well turn back now . . .*

"No," I said, teeth gritted. I shook my head and balled my hands into tense, shaking fists. I needed to do this—needed it far more than I'd ever needed anything else. If I turned back because a dumb little fence was in my way, I might as well just lie down and die.

But it's not just the fence holding you back . . . it's Dom . . . it's Nik's lies . . .

"Just cut through the damn thing," I said, hoping voicing my intentions would silence any internal doubts. I stepped over the divider and drew the At sword. After all, what was the point of having what was essentially a magic sword if I didn't put it to good use?

The At blade cut through the chain links with surprising ease, and I was on the other side in a matter of minutes. I leaned back, looking first to the left, then to the right, searching for a passable way down the steep hill. And, what do you know, there was a trail snaking down the right side of the slope—well-traveled, by the looks of it.

Apparently I wasn't the only one bypassing this fence these days.

Holding onto the cold chain links, I sidestepped until I reached the path. There was a drop-off of a couple feet but a landing of a yard or so that was as level as I could hope for. I maintained my grip on the fence, walking my hands down while I reached past the drop-off with my right boot. When my toe touched solid—if a little soggy—ground, I blew out a breath and finally let my hands release their death grip on the fence.

I turned around, flexing and releasing my fingers. The trail was a little muddy from the previous night's rain, but not so bad that it was unpassable. I started down it and, after two skids, decided sidestepping would give me better purchase on the ground. It took me a while to reach the bottom of the hill, but I managed to do so without falling, thanks to my slow pace.

"Okay," I said, straightening my coat and feeling behind

myself to make sure the sword was still concealed. Satisfied, I pulled up my hood and surveyed the sea of tents spreading out before me.

So far as I could tell, only one person had noticed my stumbling and bumbling arrival—a young-ish man wearing jeans and a navy-blue raincoat, hood pulled up over his Mariner's hat, a short beard concealing the bottom third of his boyish face. He sat in a folding chair by a small campfire, watching me quietly. He wasn't at all what I'd expected to find in a place like this. I wasn't sure what I'd expected, but he wasn't it.

I raised a hand in greeting.

He nodded, which I took as consent to enter his territory.

I picked my way through the overgrown grass, weeds, and dead blackberry vines creeping in on the edge of the clearing. I passed between two tents—one gray and green, the other a faded, once-vibrant golden orange—and stopped a few feet away from the watcher.

"Hi," I said, tucking my hands into my pockets.

Again, he nodded. "Quite the entrance . . ." His voice was soft, restrained, and he had a gentle Southern drawl. "You ain't Kin, so what's a Council Nejerette like you doin' in these parts?"

"I—" I stared at him, mouth hanging open but no words spilling out. He was Nejeret? A member of the Kin? This scruffy-looking homeless guy? Now that I knew what he was, it seemed obvious, and I didn't know how I'd missed it. I closed my mouth and stood a little straighter, a little taller, fingers itching to reach over my shoulder for the sword hilt. "I'm looking for Mari. We have business."

"I see, well . . ." The Nejeret stood and took a step toward me.

I stepped backward.

He held up his hands in placation, then returned them to his coat pockets. He was shorter than I'd expected and looked utterly harmless with the way he was standing there all *loo-di-doo*. "I ain't goin' to hurt you; just tryin' to show you the way."

I eyed his pocketed hands. "You aren't worried I'm here to hurt her?"

"Are you?"

"No." We both knew it was a lie.

He laughed, then shrugged. "Mari can take care of herself." His focus shifted slightly to my right, almost like he was looking at the sword hilt hidden in my hood. "Might serve you well to keep that in mind."

I licked my lips, shaken but not swayed. "Thanks."

"She's just two fires that way," he said, raising an arm and pointing to the south. He flipped out his thumb. "And one east. Purple tent. Can't miss it."

I nodded. The directions Garrett had written on the napkin in my pocket mentioned a purple tent. "Thanks," I said again, nodding to him as I moved past him.

"Remember what I said," he called after me.

I gave him a thumbs-up.

So Mari could take care of herself? Well, so could I.

I only passed a few more people as I made my way through the tent city. Some were clearly Nejeret—Kin—while others were markedly human. I could see why Mari and her people had chosen to hide out here, in plain sight; it really was one of the last places I'd have considered looking. For Nejerets, a people capable of amassing insane amounts of wealth due to our ability to see the future—usually—it seemed almost incomprehensible that they would allow themselves to sink to this level. Smart.

When Mari's purple tent came into view, just on the far side of that eastbound campfire, my heart rate picked up. This was it—the moment of truth. The beginning of the reckoning.

Only one person sat at the fire, back to me and hood pulled up.

"Mari." I stood between two of the tents encircling the fire. "I'm looking for Mari."

"Then look no more," the fire-tender said, not pushing the hood of her raincoat back, not turning around on her upturned stump, not seeming the least bit interested in me at all. "You've found her."

I drew my sword, the shimmering blade emitting a crystalline ring as it came free from the steel-lined scabbard, and licked my lips. I could do this. I could *do* this. I took a deep breath, willing my hands to stop shaking.

"So, for curiosity's sake, how did you find me?"

I stood there, sword brandished before me. "Someone tipped me off."

"I see."

"I don't think you do. My name is Kat—Kat Dubois. Genevieve Dubois was my mom."

Mari laughed, a hard, cold sound. "So you're working with them, then?"

I took a step toward her. "I'm working with *me*."

"Oooh . . . scary. The lone warrior," she said, mocking me. "Well, let's get on with it, then. Go ahead, do your mommy proud. Kill me."

"You're insane," I said. And despite warning bells ringing in my head, I raised the sword and lunged at her.

She moved incredibly fast, spinning on the upturned stump and springing to the left. A sharp, searing pain stabbed into my side, stealing my breath. My momentum vanished, my strength evaporating. The sword tilted downward until the tip pointed to the campfire, then slipped free of my fingers entirely.

"Now you can join her in nonexistence," Mari hissed, her eyes mirroring the blind anger, hatred, and determination that must have shown in mine only a moment ago.

This is what you wanted, my mind whispered. I rejected the thought.

"Consider this payback for what your mom did to mine."

"Wha—" I gasped. "What . . . are you . . . talking . . . about?"

"She killed my mother," Mari snarled, her face so close to mine that her spittle landed on my cheek.

"No—no she . . . didn't." I gritted my teeth, pushing through the pain. "My mom thought . . . *you* did."

Mari's jade-green eyes opened wide, the corners of her dainty mouth tilting down in a frown. She released the hilt of the dagger she'd stabbed into my side, just under my ribcage, and I stumbled backward. I sank down to the mucky ground, a hand planted in the mud to keep me upright.

"But—" Mari fell back onto the log. "But Bree said . . ." Mari shook her head. "Said she saw Genevieve leaving my mother's room. She was the last one, right before Bree found my mom . . ."

"And what . . . about . . . Bree?"

Mari's mouth opened and closed, then opened again. She did a pretty good impression of a fish out of water.

"Could . . . Bree . . . have . . . done it?" It seemed so obvious to me. "Where . . . is Bree . . . now?"

Mari covered her mouth with her hand. "She's gone. She went with the others—the rogues."

I fell backward into the mud.

"Oh, God!" I heard the squelch of Mari's knees sinking into the earth beside me. A moment later, her tensed face came into view, hovering over me.

I could hear the splat-splat-splat of boots running in the mud. Her people coming to aid her, I assumed. So close, Mari's eyes were the most startling shade of green I'd ever seen on a living person. It's funny, the things you notice when you're dying.

"I'm sorry," Mari said, those jade eyes filled with conviction. "I'm so sorry!"

"It . . . hurts." Tears leaked from the corners of my eyes, and my eyelashes fluttered.

"I'm sorry," Mari repeated. "I don't know what to—"

"Kat!" It was Dom.

I let out a sob, groaning when the action jostled the thing sticking out of my side. I turned my head toward the sound of his approaching footfalls. At first, I thought I was seeing double, because I could've sworn there were two of him running between the tents.

But then one of him thrust his hands out and strands of At, living, liquid quicksilver, shot out of his palms. The vines extended over me, reaching. Searching.

With incredible, excruciating pain, I turned my head once more, this time to watch the vines' progression. They wrapped around Mari, over and over, lifting her up into the air. Her feet didn't touch the ground, her pointed toes reaching, nearly skimming the mud, but not quite. Around us all, a dome of solidified At sprang into being.

"What—who are you?" Mari gasped a breath. "You're not Kin."

Nik ignored her. "Make her tell us if there's a way to reverse it," he said to Dom. "I'll do what I can for Kat."

I watched Dom approach Mari, his eyes locked on me, not her. There was so much pain etched into the sharp lines of his face. And so much rage.

Nik dropped to his knees on the other side of me, but I no longer had the strength to turn my head. I glanced down as far as I could, watching his hands—those beautiful, strong, sturdy hands—hover around the hilt of the black, obsidian-like dagger sticking out of me.

Anti-At. Mari had stabbed me with a knife made entirely of anti-At. Which meant I wouldn't just die. I would be erased, absolutely and completely.

"No," Nik said. "Kat, I—he didn't tell me . . . I didn't

know . . ." Hands shaking, he moved his fingers within a hairsbreadth of the dagger.

I blinked rapidly and took a shallow, halting breath. I didn't understand what he was talking about. But then, that was probably because I was dying.

"She says there's a way, Nik," Dom called, and I focused back on him. He was blocking my view of Mari, until he turned to the side to look at Nik. At me. "You have to isolate every remaining particle of that black poison and bind it with At. The damage that's done is done, but it should prevent any further unraveling." He turned back to Mari. "Anything else?"

She shook her head, her face ashen. "I'm sorry. I thought she was working with the rogues. I didn't know . . ."

Dom abandoned her, leaving her hovering in a tangle of At vines, and stumbled toward us. "Can you do it?" he asked Nik, sinking to his knees beside me.

"I don't know," Nik said. "Maybe. Now shut up. I have to concentrate."

"Dom?" I sucked in a halting breath. Look at me, being rebellious even as I lay dying.

Dom took my hand in both of his and leaned in close. "I am here, little sister."

I closed my eyes and smiled, just a little. My mind had never been so clear. I didn't want to die; I could see that now. But if I had to, at least Dom was there with me. When I spoke, my voice was the barest whisper. "I'm sorry."

35

ENEMIES & ALLIES

Mari's anti-At blade might have damaged my soul, but thanks to Nik, it didn't kill me. I sat on the counter by the register, peering around the shop. It hadn't been an actual, working shop in almost a year now. Maybe it was time to fix that.

At the prick of a needle gliding through my swollen, torn flesh, I sucked in a breath. "Jesus, Dom . . ." I looked down. That was a mistake, so I stared up at the ceiling instead. Him sewing up my stab wound was almost as bad the actual stabbing. I wasn't sure if I'd be able to handle much more of Dom's gentle doctoring. "Is this really necessary? I mean, I'll heal anyway . . ."

Dom gave the suture a tug, and I gasped. Stitch tied off, he glanced up at me with his dark, guarded eyes. "It is not necessary, no, but you will heal three times as fast this way." He trimmed the thread, then went to work on the next suture. "Whatever comes next, we should all be at top strength."

I focused on the doorway to the back room. The heavy strands of beads were drawn to one side and held back by a decorative hook in the wall. Nik was sitting at the table back there, staring straight ahead, eyes unseeing. It wasn't the expression that he usually wore when his consciousness was turned inward, communing with Re. This was different. This was new . . . and really damn unsettling.

Mari was here, too, strange as it seemed, considering she was target numero uno just a few hours earlier. At the moment, she was in the bathroom tucked around the corner, cleaning off her tent city grime. She'd brought a duffel bag with her—clean clothes, she'd explained, plus a few odds and ends.

None of us were sure what was going to happen next with Mari, or with me, or with anything, really. The "rogues"—what she called the sheut-toting members of the Kin who'd gone AWOL after Carson broke Apep out of his original At prison—knew where she'd been hiding out, and that reality was enough to keep her away from the tent city and the rest of her people for now. Possibly indefinitely.

My eyes returned to Nik of their own volition. In my mind, I weighed the words he'd spoken earlier, the claims he'd made. He'd had my trust, and he'd shit it. But then he'd gone and saved my life. I wasn't sure if that evened the score or not. I wanted to believe him, but I didn't know if I could anymore.

"You have to understand," he said, eyes wild and desperate as they switched from looking down at me to up at Dom in the rearview mirror and back. "I didn't know this would happen. I never thought Re's interest in you revolved around you dying."

We were in the Lexus, Dom driving back to Capitol Hill and Mari sitting in the front passenger seat. I was in the backseat with Nik, my head on his lap and his wadded-up T-shirt pressed against my stab wound, just trying to move as little as possible. I stared up at Nik as he spoke, studying the changes in his expression, measuring the truth in his words.

"I swear, Kat, I didn't know he wanted you to die."

"But I didn't die." At least, not yet.

Nik looked down at me and brushed a few stray strands of hair from my face, his hands coming to rest on either side of my head, almost cradling me there in his lap. I'd never seen so much pain in his pale blue eyes, so much anger. So much anything. *Indifference was his usual modus operandi, that and being a dick.*

"He won't shut up," Nik said. "He just keeps shouting that you should be dead." He swallowed roughly, then turned his head to look out the window. "I've felt him slipping—becoming more erratic . . . taking bigger risks. He used to share everything he learned in the At with me, but he rarely shares anything these days. I've been keeping him subdued with pain—he hates pain—but now . . ." He shook his head, squeezing his eyes shut. "He's screaming for me to fix it. To finish it . . ."

I stiffened. "To do what?*"*

Dom brought the car to a stop. He pushed open his door, got out, then yanked Nik's door open. "Out. Switch seats with Mari."

"I won't do it," Nik said. "I won't hurt her."

"But he *might." Dom's voice brokered no arguing. And then there was his face . . .*

"I'm in control."

"Good," Dom said. "Stay that way. And switch seats with Mari."

NIK HAD BEEN ZONED OUT EVER SINCE.

"This is the last one," Dom said, guiding the curved needle through my skin one last time.

"Bummer," I said, voice strained. "I was just starting to enjoy it."

Dom breathed out a laugh and paused, the needle having just passed all the way through me. He bowed his head, quiet for a long moment. When he finally looked up at me, raising his eyes to meet mine, my chest tightened. "I was so afraid—"

"Don't," I said, cutting him off. "Please, Dom. If you—you'll make me cry, and I think that'll hurt like a bitch."

Dom smiled, softening his sharp features. "So . . . no more

visits to the At for you." Mari's knife might not have killed me, and Nik may have saved me from certain nonexistence by binding all of the anti-At particles with regular At, but there would still be lasting side effects. The initial contact had severed my ba from the At—I would never again be able to ascend to that higher plane to watch time play out around me in the echoes. "How are you handling it?" Dom asked, tying off the final suture.

"Oh, you know . . ." I started to shrug, but cringed when the movement tugged on the stitches. "I don't think it's really sunk in yet."

"I would imagine not." Dom cleaned the wound one last time and bandaged me up. "Let me know when it begins to itch," he said. "I'll need to remove the stitches."

I nodded, gingerly slipping off the counter.

The bathroom door opened just a few seconds after my feet touched the hardwood floor, and Mari came around the corner. She looked like an entirely different person—long, sleek black hair pulled back into a high ponytail, navy slacks, lilac blouse, and high-heeled pumps. This was a successful young businesswoman, not someone you'd find in a tent city inhabited by Seattle's transient population.

She dumped her duffel bag by the wall behind the checkout counter and headed for the table in the back room. "I can't possibly explain to you how good it feels to be clean." She started scooting my mom's violet armchair away from the table.

"Not that one," I said, knowing it was rude and not caring. That was my mom's chair. If anyone was going to sit there, it was me.

Mari glanced at me, eyebrows raised. "Oh, um . . ."

"The corner," I said, pointing to a small padded chair tucked away there under a stack of books, twin to the one Nik occupied. Slowly, I made my way into the back room, Dom following behind me. I could practically feel him hovering. "Just move everything to the floor. It's fine," I told Mari. Clenching my teeth, I eased down into the violet armchair. I was surprised by how *right* I felt, sitting there.

Mari dragged the smaller chair to the table, then sat. "So . . . what next?" I didn't know how old she was—that factoid hadn't been in the videos with my mom. Based on the way she spoke, I'd have guessed she was on the younger side, but I couldn't say for sure. After all, just look at Nik—he sounded as young and modern as me, most of the time, but he was old as dirt.

"I believe a free exchange of information might be the best way to proceed," Dom suggested. He stood behind me, his hands resting on the top of the armchair.

I glanced up at him. "There's another chair in the—"

He shook his head. "I'm fine standing."

After Mari nodded, Dom and I started sharing all that had happened after my mom and Carson came to us on Bainbridge. So much talking—so many deep breaths—quickly became painful for me, and Dom took over completely.

"My God," Mari whispered when Dom finished telling her about the day my mom was killed. "That's insane . . ."

Eyebrows raised, I nodded my agreement.

Mari leaned forward in her chair, her forearms resting on the edge of the table and her hands clasped together. "I'm so sorry, Kat," she said, eyes on me. "I really thought Genevieve . . ." She shook her head, her eyes downcast. "Perhaps it's best if I start at the beginning." She took a deep breath. "You see, Carson and I were involved." She paused, looking back and forth between Dom and me like she was waiting for judgmental gasps and pointed fingers.

"We know," Dom assured her. "Gen told us."

I snorted softly. "And trust me, I understand." A twisted sneer curled my lips. "I—Carson and I had a thing, once."

Mari's gaze locked with mine, and in that moment, something clicked between us. "I thought I loved him." She made a choking noise. "I *did* love him, which is so much worse because it just proves how much of a fool I was."

"Love makes fools of us all," Dom said.

"Maybe . . ." Mari let out a disparaging laugh. "Thinking about it—about *him*—makes me sick to my stomach."

"Yep . . . *totally* understand," I said.

Mari smiled at me. "Carson was Kin by birth, his true nature hidden in the At by several of our people, as is the way with all of us. He recruited Genevieve, suggested poisoning the Meswett's sister as a way to prove her loyalty and worthiness to us—which we didn't approve, by the way, but accepted as adequate proof after the fact. And because Carson knew you all, he became an integral part of our rushed mission to retrieve the Apep sphere." Again, her focus switched back and forth between Dom and me. "Which I swear we never intended to open."

Dom and I exchanged a glance. "Why go to all the trouble of stealing it, then?" he asked.

"Leverage—we were going to use it as a threat to get the Council to listen to us, but . . ." She sighed. "Our biggest mistake was putting Carson on duty guarding the Apep sphere. At shift change, some of the other guards reported seeing him talking to the sphere, but when questioned on the matter, he claimed he was dictating notes for a research project into a voice recorder."

"He was talking to Apep," I said, staring at Nik. He still wore that far-off, lost expression. "His sheut power made it so he could hear *through* the At."

"As I suspected," Mari said. "I don't know whether it was his intention all along or if his conversations with Apep poisoned his mind, but Carson slowly built a circle of close 'friends' who, over time, withdrew from the mainstream Kin teachings. They . . . I'm not proud to admit it, but they really worked me over. They convinced me that my mom's ways were too lax and inclusive—too passive—and that the tyranny of the Council of Seven could only be fought with violence. Unlike my mother, I didn't want to work with the Council anymore. I had no interest in reforming them. I wanted to overthrow the Council completely."

"Which is why *my* mom thought you killed Mei," I said.

"I know, and I doubt the shame will ever leave me." Mari hung her head. "She must've been so disappointed . . ."

I almost couldn't believe how easy it was to relate to this woman—this Kin Nejerette—who I'd been dead set on destroying just a few hours earlier. I felt the urge to reach out to her, to pat her on the shoulder or even hug her. I suppressed it, leaning back in my chair. "Trust me, Mari, I can relate."

A humorless laugh escaped from her, and slowly she raised her head. Her eyes were bloodshot, making the jade irises stand out that much more, but her jaw was tensed. She wasn't about to blubber about all of her troubles. I admired her for that.

Mari took a deep breath, then continued her story. "We found the shards of the At sphere on the floor near where it had been stored." Mari shook her head. "He must've wanted us to find them, or he would've returned them to the other side. He wanted us to know that not only was our leverage gone, but Apep was once again free to terrorize the world, and because of us, he had a damn powerful host."

"And afterwards?" Dom asked. "You mentioned 'rogues'—the ones who've since abandoned you, your people, and your cause. Were you referring to Carson's trusted comrades?"

My focus shifted to Dom. He was slipping into interrogator mode. It was impossible to miss the transition after watching so many hours of recordings of him interviewing and questioning my mom. But when his eyes flicked my way, meeting mine for a moment, I blinked back to Mari.

She laughed under her breath. "As it turned out, Carson had a lot more friends than I'd known about. Nearly a fifth of my people vanished overnight, and I've been bleeding people steadily ever since." She looked at me, her reddened eyes filled with hopelessness. "The Kin are down to about two-thirds of our original numbers, and it's been sheer desperation and a whole lot of promises and compromise that's kept even that number intact." Her gaze slipped off me, unfocusing. "They don't trust me anymore, not completely. And the rogues want me dead, because they think I betrayed Carson by not following him. There's no way to win."

"So they're the ones who told us where to find you?" I asked, thinking back to that afternoon in Garrett's studio—his *lair*. Had it really only been yesterday? It felt like years had passed between then and now. Like years, and like no time at all.

Mari nodded. "Had to be them."

"They killed my friend. Made him jump through a window."

Mari's gaze snapped to my face. "That would be Nikolaj—he's always been able to bend another to his will with his voice. It doesn't work on Nejerets, but . . . it's dangerous nonetheless. He and Carson were *very* close."

"So you really didn't have anything to do with that?" I asked.

She laughed that increasingly familiar dry, sarcastic laugh. "What, and sic a crazy chick with a death wish and a big-ass sword of At on myself? Do you have any idea how terrified I was sitting there with you behind me, knowing you were seconds from trying to kill me?"

"I—" I shook my head, her confession shocking me into silence. She'd seemed so calm and collected, so sure of herself. I'd been the one bumbling into the encounter, practically throwing myself onto her anti-At dagger.

I laughed under my breath. Maybe I should thank her for stabbing me, because it woke me up when nothing else could. I'd had a death wish, but Mari's blade had cured me of that, for good.

"The pocket watch," Nik said, his voice strained. All eyes snapped to him. It was the first time he'd spoken since switching seats with Mari in the car, the first time his eyes held any kind of focus. He stared at Dom, just above my head. "Ask about the pocket watch."

I craned my neck to look up at Dom. His expression darkened, his sharp features hardening and his hawkish gaze locked on Mari. "You made the pocket watch that was sent to the Meswett, obviously . . . the one made of anti-At." His voice was quiet, pointed, and far from gentle. "Unless there is another like you?"

"No, there's only me. Mine seems to be a talent one must be born with; it cannot be learned."

"Why did you want to unmake the Meswett?"

"I didn't—" Mari shook her head vehemently, eyes wide and filled with confusion. "I have no idea what you're talking about."

"You don't recall creating such a watch?"

"No, no, I do—I just never sent it to *anyone*." Mari looked at me, then returned her focus to Dom. "It was a practice piece. I'd been working on making more and more complicated things, honing my skill. I was *bored*. Then, one day, a few of the things I'd made were just . . . gone."

"And that was the end of it? You didn't try to find them, these things that can unmake a Nejeret from the ba out?"

"Of course I did," Mari snapped. "But when my mother found out about it, she told me not to worry about it because those missing pieces of 'anti-At,' as you call it, play a part in the future."

"Which Mei knew because she could travel through time," Dom clarified.

Mari nodded. "Mother had this thing she called the 'one true path'—it was the way to a specific future she'd visited, one where Kin and Council found a way to work together, where we weren't outcasts relegated to hiding in the shadows any longer. She said—"

"The Council," Nik said. His fingers were curled into such tight fists that his nails gouged his skin and blood seeped from his palms. I had no doubt that we were witnessing his attempt to keep Re subdued—through pain. "Take her to the Council."

He slammed his fist on the table, and his eyes flashed from pale blue to opalescent white. "No! They should be wiped off the face of this earth!"

His irises switched back and forth between shades, over and over and over, until his gaze grew distant once more. He muttered under his breath in a language I didn't understand. It had an almost alien sound, like the syllables hadn't been meant for human tongue, lips, teeth, or vocal chords.

Really freaking disturbed, I stood and backed away from the table, throwing furtive glances Dom's way. His face displayed the same horror I felt.

If Nik was losing it—if *Re* was losing it—then I feared for all of our futures. Re had been the showrunner for so long, calling the shots and guiding our way when nobody else would or could. But this—this person looked like he belonged in a padded cell, somewhere he wouldn't be able to hurt himself or others. I was more worried about the others. I was more worried about *me*.

"What's going on?" Mari asked, her expression more confused than horrified. I figured the horror would set in once she learned who, or, rather, *what* Nik was—the host to one of the cocreators of our universe. Who was apparently losing it, big-time.

"I have no idea." I looked at Dom while I said it, but he offered me no reassurances, only shaking his head. "Do we take her to the Council, or . . .?" I was having a hard time determining which was Re's desire and which was Nik's.

"Do it," Nik or Re or whoever was in charge whispered between clenched teeth. It was the single most terrifying deliverance of two words, of four letters, I'd ever heard in my entire life. He dragged his eyes upward, meeting mine. They were blue, for the moment. "The Council. Take her—"

The color flashed to that inhuman white again. "No!" His irises flickered between the two colors, between the two personalities—the two souls—in a never-ending, dizzying pattern. He closed his eyes and dropped his head to the table, resting his forehead on the backs of his hands.

Dom and I stared at each other, the breaths and heartbeats stretching out uncounted. He nodded first, and I answered the same way.

"Okay . . ." I shifted my gaze to Mari. "Looks like you're coming with us. Any objection?"

Wide-eyed, Mari shook her head. "I don't really have a choice. It's go with you guys or start running. Nikolaj and Bree and the others—they're so much more powerful together than I am alone, and staying with my people just puts them in danger . . ." She looked utterly defeated and absolutely desperate.

Nik's choice—bringing her to the Council—had to be our best option. If we brought her to Bainbridge, she and the Council could come to some sort of an agreement, maybe even figure out a way to work together rather than against each other. Then the Kin and Council Nejerets could join forces against these "rogues." It seemed like the best plan; I couldn't imagine why Re was fighting against it so hard.

"I would have you understand one thing," Dom said. "There is no way for us to guarantee that the Council will not imprison you or use you to draw out the remainder of the Kin."

She slid her fist down the length of her sleek black ponytail. "You know, we haven't just been twiddling our thumbs in that shithole, my people and I. We've been collecting data and documentation. If my people don't hear from me by the end of the day today, they'll release a file containing irrefutable evidence proving the existence of Nejerets." Her gaze was steady on

Dom. "The whole world will know about us, for better or for worse, and the fallout will be chaos—for us, for you, *and* for the rogues." She pressed her lips together in a grim smile. "I'll give you one guess as to which side is more likely to survive in that scenario."

"You wouldn't," said on my exhale.

Mari's gaze shifted to me, her green eyes diamond hard. "People depend on me—their lives are my responsibility. I will do what has to be done."

I held my hands up, like that motion of surrender alone might appease her. Tread carefully, I reminded myself. It might've seemed like we had a lot in common, but clearly we were very different people.

"Warning noted," Dom said, not sounding the least bit surprised.

I stared at him, frowning.

"I shall make sure the Council of Seven is aware of your conditions before we arrive. Before we leave here, you may use the landline to alert your people that you are all right. I only ask that you keep us aware of any changes to your contingency plan so we don't accidentally trigger your people into doing something they will regret."

I realized my mouth was hanging open, and closed it.

"Do we have an agreement?" Dom asked.

Mari nodded.

Slowly, Nik raised his head off the table. I checked his eyes first—pale blue—then scanned the rest of his face. Not too strained, too tensed . . . almost peaceful. Until his jaw twitched. He was barely holding it together.

Reading the question in my eyes, he forced a razor-thin smile. "I'm fine, Kitty Kat." He shivered, the jerky motion making the table shake. "For the moment."

36

SUSIE & SYRIS

"Are you even listening?" Why, oh why, couldn't I just keep my mouth shut?

Marcus crossed his arms over his chest and shook his head infinitesimally.

A quick sweep of the other Council members, especially the ones on the video screens, told me that Marcus was the least offended by my outburst—at least, besides my "dad," Set. *He* seemed to be trying to hide a smile.

I exchanged a look with Mari, who didn't seem surprised by the Council's reaction to her conditions. I, however, was flabbergasted.

After another quick scan of the Council members, I settled my stare on cold, hard Ivan. How he was related to Alexander—or Lex, Alice, or Jenny—was beyond me, but he was. "You're kidding, right? This is a joke. You're not seriously willing to gamble that Mari's people don't actually have the documentation to back up their threat, are you?" I made an ugly, guttural noise deep in my throat. "How are you even still talking about this?" Oh my God, why was *I* still talking? "You should be *doing* something. Just listen to her and stop being so damn closed-minded!"

Ivan's gaze slid past me, landing on Marcus. "I do not understand the reason for this one's continued presence." *This one* being me.

Honestly, neither did I. It had been one of Mari's initial conditions that I remain with her when she visited the Council. She'd said she trusted me, that we shared a bond none of them would understand. She'd claimed she wanted me as her Council liaison and that she would only work with them, talk to them, if I was with her. That was almost a month ago, thus my exasperation. The Council are a bunch of slugs.

"Katarina tracked down the leader of the Kin before we found even a single member," Marcus said. "As General of our people, I say she has earned a position at our wartime council. If you disagree, speak now." *Or shut up* was left unsaid.

There was silence all around. Hell, I was tempted to "speak now" because it was so obvious to me that I didn't belong there, but . . . I *wanted* to be there. You know, watch history happen and all that. So I kept my stupid mouth shut.

"Wonderful," Marcus said. "Now, perhaps if Mari were willing to produce the documents she claims to have, the Council could move past this matter and onto actual negotiations."

I looked at Mari, eyebrows raised. I honestly didn't know if she had the stuff to back up her claims. I figured she did, because that would be one hell of a bluff—hard, documented evidence of our kind compiled into a neat, transmittable, *broadcastable* file.

"I've been waiting for you to ask," Mari said. She reached into her pocket and produced a small, neon green thumb drive, which she set on the table. "I keep a copy of the folder and files with me at all times—all of my people do. We also keep backups on various clouds . . . secured, of course," she said with a small smile. With the tip of her pointer finger, she slid the thumb drive across the table to Marcus. "Go ahead, check the files. Take as long as you need. For the sake of my people's safety and livelihood, I'm eager to move forward with negotiations when you're ready."

"I move that we close Council chamber doors during review to all but active Council members," Ivan said.

Marcus nodded. "Very well, we'll—"

Chaos erupted on the conference room table in the form of multicolored smoke that cleared to reveal two plump, pink, naked newborn babies.

Everybody sitting around the table—me, Mari, Nik, Set, Heru, Dom—stood to some degree or another at the sudden arrival of the two infants. Eyes were opened wide, jaws had dropped, and shock had stolen our voices.

One of the babies—the girl—hiccupped and started fussing quietly. The boy just kept on sleeping.

I gulped a breath of air, heart still racing. "Is that—"

"The twins," Nik said, cutting my question off. It was the first time he'd spoken to me in nearly a month. "Yes."

After a few more seconds of stunned silence and staring, Mari, of all people, leaned forward and gathered the little girl in her arms, cradling her against her chest and cooing softly. She gave me a pointed look, her eyes shifting between me and the baby boy.

I held up my hands defensively. "I wouldn't even know where to start," I told her. I looked to Marcus for help—he'd raised lots of kids. Surely he knew what to do . . . or at least how to hold it—the baby. After all, the kid *was* his.

But Marcus wasn't looking at the lonely little boy snoring softly on the table. He was staring at Nik.

Dominic took care of the neglected baby situation by carefully slipping his hands under the boy's head and bottom and sliding him closer until he was cradling the little guy close, almost an exact mimic of Mari.

"Where's Lex?" Marcus's voice was quiet, his words precise.

I turned my head, looking from him to Nik. It was a damn good question, because her babies were here, but Lex was nowhere in sight.

Nik blinked, his eyes fading from pale blue to shimmering white. "I cannot say, because I do not know." Suddenly, he was glaring at me. "Because the At is now permanently misaligned . . . because Katarina refused to die."

PART III - OUT OF TIME

LEX

37

GHOSTS & MEMORIES

I lay on the polished At floor of Nuin's tomb until the last, hidden vestiges of my survival instincts awakened within me. Delivery had been bloody and damaging enough to my body to trigger my reactivated regenerative abilities, and after a long nap, I barely ached at all anymore. I also looked like I'd dropped about twenty pounds—from my pre-baby weight. Regeneration was a gift with a hefty price.

Driven by desperate hunger, I sought out the food stored in my satchel. I wolfed down the first loaf of molasses bread like it wasn't some dense, slightly sticky thing akin to a protein bar. It eased the hunger pains, if only a little.

I'd never truly understood what it felt like to be starving. It's something I used to stay all the time—I'm starving. I'm so hungry I could eat a horse. If I don't eat something soon, I might die. I understood it now.

I attacked the wheel of cheese next, not even bothering to peel off any part of the rind. I figured it probably wasn't poisonous, and even if it was, I was really only delaying the inevitable right now. Best-case scenario, the rind gave me more calories, a little more time to wallow in self-pity, thinking about my babies and all the things I wouldn't get to experience, wouldn't get to see, as I wasted away in this underground tomb.

The bitterest disappointment came from knowing I wouldn't get to raise my children. I hadn't failed. The twins had been born, whole and healthy, and, so far as I knew, had returned to their native timeline. To my native timeline. I didn't even blame them for leaving me behind. They were just babies; they hadn't known any better.

I astounded myself with the ferocity with which I devoured the wheel of cheese, moving on to the second loaf of molasses bread once it, too, was nothing but a fond memory. I forced myself to take my time, reducing the loaf to just a corner chunk and crumbs in a luxurious several minutes.

Sighing, I stared at the last bit of bread, wishing it would sprout a whole other loaf. All I had left now was that small nugget and the packet of dried boar meat sitting on the floor beyond my knee. I opened the oilcloth. Six strips. I picked one up, tearing off half with my teeth and chewing methodically. I was aiming for efficiency; I couldn't afford any wasted energy. When the boar meat had gone the way of the cheese, I polished off the last bit of the molasses bread.

I no longer felt starving, but I was far from sated. The water filling my waterskin was lukewarm but still refreshing, and it mimicked the sensation of a full belly for a blissful moment. But soon that, too, was gone.

I sat on the floor for several minutes, staring at my bag and wondering if tales of boiled leather soup had been true and whether or not leather needed to be boiled at all in order to be edible. My stomach growled.

Frustrated, I stood on shaky legs and wandered into the large, arch-ceilinged chamber directly beyond Nuin's tomb. It was the first addition I'd made to the underground structure when I'd expanded upon it some unknown years ago, creating my sanctuary. I'd inscribed countless words on the walls, communicating with Marcus across the chasm of time in the only way I could.

I started reading from one wall at random, hating the words because they'd been written by a version of me who still had a future, who still had things to look forward to. These words had been written by me in a time when I didn't know that this was how I would end.

But does it have to be?

I didn't want to die here. I wanted anything besides me dying here, underground and alone while my children grew up, motherless. My body would remain in here, locked away until Marcus opened the tomb in several thousand years.

Wait a minute . . .

That never happened. Or wouldn't happen. The future had already been written—because it was *my* past. And one single certainty about that future-past shed a glowing beam of hope straight into my heart.

Marcus hadn't found my body in this tomb. Marcus hadn't found *any* body in here except for Nuin's. Especially not *mine*.

Which meant there was a way out. I just had to find it.

I MUST HAVE DONE AT LEAST SEVEN CIRCUITS AROUND the complex of underground chambers, each more frantic than the last. There were thirty-three rooms, each unique, and each lacking even the faintest hint of a way out. Which I'd already known, because I'd built almost the whole damn place and I hadn't included any sort of a hidden escape tunnel.

But I hadn't built the *whole* place; the entry chamber—Nuin's actual tomb—had been built by him untold eons ago. That fact made laps around my mind as I returned to the entry chamber.

"It has to be something in here." I stood in the central doorway set in the wall opposite the steep stairs leading up to the one and only exit. I'd sealed the exit myself, keying the solidified At barrier to the unique combination of Marcus's and my bonding pheromones. If I'd had a vial containing some of his pheromones—like he had of mine—then I'd have no problem leaving. The door would dissolve as soon as I touched it, and that would be that. Would be. If I had a vial of his pheromones . . .

I scanned the glowing, pearlescent walls, seeing the symbols etched into the surface and looking for any outliers. Anything that stood out as a possible button or latch or keyhole or *anything*. When the visual scan proved fruitless, I switched to a more tactile approach, running my hands up and down the wall's surface. I made sure to feel around and within the engraved depression of each and every symbol.

Nothing.

With the tips of my fingers, I traced the seam where wall met floor all the way around the room.

Nothing.

Desperate, exhausted, and a little dizzy, I examined every inch of the rectangular dais displaying Nuin's perfectly preserved body at the center of the room. "Come on . . . come on . . . come on . . ." I repeated the words over and over, a mantra keeping me going in spite of the yawning ache in my belly and the weakness settling into my limbs and the fog invading my mind as my energy stores depleted.

But still, I found nothing. No way out. No clue. Not a damn thing.

A dull headache thrummed in the base of my skull, reminding me not-so-subtly that I'd gone too long without food and water. I rested my forehead against the transparent At barrier encasing Nuin's body and closed my eyes. "How?" I said, voice cracking. "How do I get out?"

I opened my eyes and stared at Nuin's familiar, peaceful features. He looked so much like Marcus, and my mind was so weary that it was easy to confuse who was actually lying there, lifeless perfection taunting me. Tricking me. Fooling me that it was Marcus instead of Nuin.

"How do I get back to you?" I whispered. Tears welled as I stared at his face. As I missed his touch. As I started to accept that this was it for me. This was how I would die.

"How?" This time the word was barely understandable, dripping as it was with misery and self-pity. I would never get to hold my babies again. I would never see them grow up. I would never witness the wonder that was *them*. With a sob, I sank down to my knees. "How . . ."

"Courage, dear Lex."

My spine stiffened, and my breath lodged in my chest. That voice—it was an impossible voice. It was a voice that no longer existed. It was the voice of the dead. The gone.

Slowly, I lifted my head and looked through the transparent sarcophagus. Nuin still rested within in his sleeplike death. So how had I heard his voice?

Neck frozen in place, I peered out of the corner of my eye, searching for the speaker. Searching for a ghost.

He stood halfway up the stairway, hands clasped behind his back and resplendent robe shimmering with brilliant colors.

"Nuin?" I clambered to my feet, focus shifting from the very real body mere inches from me to the same man standing on the stairs. "How—are you real?"

He smiled his kind, familiar smile and started down the stairs. Once his descent was complete, he paused and held his arms out at his sides. "I am here."

I couldn't tear my eyes from him. "But you're also in here." I patted the top of the sarcophagus. "So how can you be real?"

He raised his eyebrows, steepling his fingers under his chin. "Reality is such a fluid idea, don't you think?"

I licked my lips. "I don't—" I shook my head. My brain wasn't capable of making sense of what I was seeing.

"Real . . . unreal . . ." Nuin clasped his fingers together and lowered his hands. "Does it truly matter?"

He'd talk me in circles if I let him, and I didn't have time for that. "I guess not." I eyed him. "Why are you here?"

His face broke into a genuine, heartwarming smile. "To help you, of course."

I blinked, opened my mouth, then shut it again.

"You are stuck, dearest one. You feel you have no way out. You are giving up." His smile turned sly. "But you should not. There is something you are missing."

I shook my head and took a step toward him. "But I've looked everywhere. Literally. If you know of something I missed . . . I'm all ears."

"I'm all ears," he repeated, laughing under his breath. "English is such a funny language."

I raised my eyebrows. "Nuin . . . ?"

He shook his head, still chuckling. "The answer is not out here," he said, closing the distance between us. He raised his hand, resting his palm over my heart. "But in here."

I searched his rainbow eyes. "I don't understand."

He lowered his hand. "Think about it, my Alexandra. There are no doors . . . no passageways or tunnels. The solidified At is just as impenetrable as ever, and you don't have any of Heru's bonding pheromone to trigger the release . . ." His eyes locked with mine. "What is the only possible way in or out?"

Yet again, I shook my head.

Nuin frowned, the expression thoughtful. "Let me rephrase—what would a person *need* in order to get in or out of here?"

I drew my lower lip between my teeth, eyes narrowing. "My and Heru's bonding pheromones . . ."

"Besides that. What else might someone possess that would allow them passage out of here?"

"I don't know," I said, head aching and exasperation and hunger wearing down my patience. "I guess Nik would be able to get in here." My eyes widened as Nuin's coaxing smile spread into a grin. "Because he has a sheut," I added. "The only other way in or out of here is with a sheut."

Slowly, Nuin nodded, and I mirrored the motion. "Indeed, it is."

My shoulders slumped. "But I don't have a sheut."

"No?" Nuin rubbed the side of his jaw. "Is that a fact? Is that something that we know with a certainty? Just as we *know* you don't have access to any of Heru's bonding pheromone and that your body will not be found in here when Heru gains access in the twenty-first century—do we *know* that you don't have a sheut?"

"Well . . ." I frowned. "No, I guess I don't *know* it, but . . . I think I'd be able to tell if I randomly sprouted a sheut."

"Would you, now?"

My frown deepened. "Is that even a thing that can happen? Could someone *grow* a sheut?"

"Is that not what Aset did when she brought Nekure into the world? Did she not grow a sheut along with a child?"

"I—" I stared at him, mouth gaping open as my sluggish thoughts caught up and I thought, once again, of my own children. A spike of longing speared through my chest. I was desperate to hold them in my arms again. I raised one hand to my forehead and rubbed my temples, focusing on the most pressing issue. "Are you saying that the sheuts my children would've had are somehow still in me?"

"They were displaced by my and Apep's sheuts, and they didn't simply vanish." He leaned in like he was about to share a secret. "A sheut, once created, can never be destroyed." He straightened. "So, where else could they have gone?"

"I—" I shook my head, absolutely dumbfounded. "I don't know." But even as I struggled with disbelief, with hope in the face of near defeat, I felt my body weakening further. I leaned against Nuin's coffin.

"Yes," the other Nuin said, "your increasing weakness is a problem. You will need more energy if you're to have any chance of accessing and controlling your sheuts." His eyes slid to the corner of the chamber where I'd rested after giving birth. It looked rather gruesome now.

I followed his line of sight. He was staring at the placenta.

The blood drained from my face. "You're not saying . . ."

"It is the only thing left within these walls with any nutritional value."

"But—"

"You want to get out of here, do you not?"

"Yes, but . . ." I stared at the globby sack of flesh and blood that looked way too much like a gory jellyfish, bile rising up my throat.

"And you wish to see your children again? And Heru?"

"Of course, but—" I gagged involuntarily.

"So what is the problem? This is the only way."

I swallowed. Barely. "But . . . I don't have any way to cook it." Dying was the last thing I wanted in the entire world. Next to last was eating that thing raw.

Nuin transformed, his robe morphing into a black wool coat and dark gray trousers, and his eyes bleeding from multihued and swirling to a glowing, black-rimmed gold.

I sucked in a breath. "Marcus?"

"Want and need, Little Ivanov." The corner of his mouth twitched, his eyes burning with intensity. "Want and need . . ."

My knees gave out, and I fell to the floor, my head hitting the smooth At with a thwack. Stars burst to life, drowning out the soft glow emanating from the walls, and quickly faded to darkness.

38

PERCEPTION & REALITY

I woke to the scent of frying meat. It smelled sort of like beef, but more metallic and mineraly than your standard ribeye. It reminded me of the scent of beef liver, which Grandma Suse cooked once a year on her not-so-late husband's birthday. Apparently it was one of Alexander's favorite dishes. I'd only eaten it a couple times as a little girl, but I remembered not hating it. I also remembered not loving it.

"I see you're up, lazybones."

My eyes popped open, and I sat up—gingerly, as necessitated by the pang of pain throbbing on the side of my head, an unwelcome accompaniment to my dehydration headache and the hunger pains gnawing away in my stomach. "Grandma?"

I stared around the tomb, unsurprised to discover that Nuin's body was my only companion. Her voice had been a dream. She couldn't be here. "She hasn't even been born yet," I reminded myself.

"Oh, come now, Lex . . ." Grandma Suse came bustling through the doorway opposite the stairs wearing her favorite apron—the white and pink one that looked like a ladies' tennis outfit—and carrying a plate piled high with piping-hot, perfectly seared beef liver. "Never let the facts get in the way of a good story."

I couldn't help but smile. I scooted around on my butt and rested my back against the dais. "What are you doing here?"

She bustled over, the crystal beads on the chain of her eyeglasses sparkling as they shifted and reflected the wall's gentle glow. "I'd think that was obvious. You look hungry enough to eat a whole elephant, sweetheart." She smiled and offered me the plate. "This won't be nearly so bad, I promise."

I accepted the plate with a thanks and a smile, settling it on my lap before looking back up at my grandma. "I miss you," I said, chin trembling. "I miss all of you."

"Oh, honey . . ." Grandma Suse lowered herself to the floor with creaks and groans and sat beside me. "I'm always with you. Wherever you are, just close your eyes and listen with your heart, and you'll hear my voice, cheering you on."

I swiped a stray tear from under my eye, then swept a preventative wipe under the other and sniffed.

"Go on, Lex, sweetie, eat up before it gets cold."

With a weak smile of thanks, I picked up the fork and knife from the plate and cut into a chunk of meat. "Will you tell me a story, Grandma? Like you used to?"

"Oh, gee . . . I suppose I can handle that." She pursed her lips. "Now let's see . . ."

I chewed for a moment longer, then swallowed my first bite. It was softer than I'd expected and way more metallic tasting than the liver she'd cooked had ever been. "How about the story of how you and Grandpa met?"

"Alexander?" Grandma laughed out loud, patting her knee. "Oh, sweetie, you're not old enough for that story." I was about to protest, reminding her that I'd just given birth, but she settled her hands in her lap and spoke first. "Have I ever told you about the day Alice was born?"

"Mom?" I frowned. "If you did, it was a *long* time ago, because I don't remember it at all." I took another bite.

"Well then, let me refresh your memory." She smiled, a light of warm remembrance filling her rheumy brown eyes. "I was just filling the tub for a good long soak when my water broke . . ."

"FEELING BETTER, SWEETHEART?" GRANDMA SUSE asked when I set the empty plate on the floor beside me.

I nodded, leaning my head back and sighing. "*Much* better."

She leaned forward and patted my knee. "Good." With a hand on the corner of the dais, she pulled herself up to her feet. "You rest now, Lex. Gather your strength. You have a lot to do today." Fondly, I watched her sort of hobble up the stairs, then walk straight through the At barrier blocking the doorway out to the Oasis like it wasn't any more substantial than air.

My smile wilted as reality sank in. I was delirious. She hadn't really been here. And that hadn't been beef liver . . .

I forced myself to look down at my hands, regretting it the instant I did.

Blood coated my fingers and palms and dripped down my wrists. I gagged, but managed to hold the placenta in with a hand over my mouth and eyes squeezed shut. Full-blown hallucination or not, one element had been real—I felt better. Stronger.

It didn't matter *how* I'd regained that strength, only that I had. Only that I now had a chance.

While I sat and digested—and did my best not to think about what I was digesting—I considered my possibilities, sheut-wise, assuming not-Nuin had been right. There were only three sheut powers I could come up with that would allow me to get out of the tomb—the ability to manipulate physical At, the ability to make spatial jumps, and the ability to travel through time. I figured I had to have one of those powers, by default. Lucky for me, I had practice with all three.

I touched the wall and thought *lights off* with all my might.

Darkness, complete and utter, surrounded me.

"Shit!" I hissed, thinking *on* with a franticness that was matched only by a sudden rush of excitement. When the glow returned to the walls, extra-bright, I raced up the stairs, slamming my hands against the blockade and willing it away.

Nothing happened.

"Come on," I breathed, thinking harder. Willing the At barrier away harder. I gritted my teeth. "Come on . . ."

Still, nothing happened. It didn't matter how many times I tried or how hard I focused. The only change I managed was painting the opalescent At with smeared, bloody handprints. The barrier wouldn't budge.

Turning around and leaning my back against the un-openable door, I looked around the chamber below, like something down there might make any of this make sense. I ran my fingers through my sweat-crusted hair, cringing when the sticky blood tangled it further.

"Gross . . ." I brushed my hands off on the sides of my shift; it was already ruined anyway. "Okay, what am I missing?"

I stared down at Nuin's coffin, hoping he would reappear and give me more guidance. Except I was fairly certain he'd just been a figment of my imagination—him and Marcus and Grandma Suse—conjurations of my subconscious mind, projected outwards to give the appearance of someone being there to help me. I'd read about things like that happening to people when they were in dire situations—lost in a cave or stranded at sea. Who's to say being marooned in time is any different?

"Alright, Lex," I said. "Think like Nuin, come on . . ." One hand on my hip, I tapped the opposite index finger against my lips while I thought aloud. "I was assuming that being able to make At glow was tied to the ability to physically manipulate it, but that's clearly wrong, so . . ."

I nodded to myself, turning the glow of the walls on and off once more to confirm that I could do it. "*That's* clearly the power afforded me from one of the sheuts . . . but I had twins, so there should be two sheuts." I narrowed my eyes. "It could be totally different, a completely unrelated power, and it has to be something that can get me out of here."

Turning around, I stared at the At barrier barring my way and thought not *through*, but something more like *other side*.

Unyielding blackness surrounded me once more. For a moment, I thought I'd accidently turned the wall's glow off again. But then I remembered what lie beyond the tomb's door —the Oasis. Cut off from the outside world completely by an At dome covered with a layer of rock and sand, it was just a bigger, darker tomb. I'd shifted through space, landing on the other side of the door.

I jumped back into Nuin's tomb, a plan already forming in my mind. I took the steps two at a time and quickly repacked my bag with what little I had left. After adjusting the leather straps, I buckled the sword harness back over my chest and drew my sword, willing it to glow as the walls' light died out. And once again, I ascended the stairs.

The spatial shifts seemed to tire me the most, so I decided to take it slow, traveling by foot as much as possible, using my sword as a torch lighting my way. Besides, I was out of practice, and spatial shifts were sort of a precision skill—at least, when emotion wasn't the driving force behind them. I had no idea how much distance I could cover or if longer leaps would tire me more than short hops. I was used to the sheut of a full-fledged Netjer, which I was guessing packed a lot more punch than my minor sheut. Better safe than sorry.

The last thing I wanted to do was kill myself by accident, not when it was looking like I had a real shot at surviving this . . . of seeing the twins again. Especially because I had a pretty good reason to believe that the ability to move through space *and* time were linked. Because that was what Mei could do.

At the top of the stairs, I turned, gave Nuin a small salute, and shifted out of the tomb, taking the first, tiny step in the unfathomably long journey home.

39

SUN & MOON

There had been a moderately high creep-out factor in Nuin's tomb, what with his body being down there and the whole "buried alive" issue. And yet, it was a flickering match to the roaring inferno of creepiness that was the abandoned Netjer-At Oasis. Visible only by my sword's otherworldly glow, the Oasis was alive with shadows that moved just beyond the edge of my vision. Every heartbeat brought another trick of the eye. I held every other breath, thinking I'd heard something ahead or behind me.

I was tempted to hightail it up to the tunnel and shift through the final At barrier separating me from the outside world. And I would have, if not for what awaited me outside the Oasis. Sand. And heat. And nothing else for hundreds of miles.

Even with my newly discovered sheuts and the abilities they afforded me, I wasn't willing to venture out into the Sahara without stocking up on what little provisions this haunting underground city could provide—namely water. One glance at the nearest tree told me it had died long ago and that the plentiful gardens and orchards scattered about would be little more than skeletons of what had once been. But the stream that snaked through the Oasis flowed with pure, crisp water fed by a plentiful and reliable underground spring. It was the reason Nuin had chosen this place as the tucked-away Nejeret homeland in the first place.

As quietly as possible, I picked my way across the decrepit garden stretching between the entrance to Nuin's tomb and his breathtaking palace, passing by the massive arched doorways on my way to the stream just beyond. The sounds echoing throughout the dome were an eerie reminder of just how hollow this place truly was.

I glanced up and shivered. Nuin's crystalline palace disappeared barely ten feet up; the delicate towers, archways, and spires that extended higher, reaching for the top of the dome, were entirely consumed by the unrelenting darkness. Even my heightened Nejerette vision was no match for the complete and utter lack of light.

One glance up was enough. I focused on the ground from there on out.

I reached the stream a few minutes later, taking a paved path down to the water's edge. I dropped my bag on the ground, unbuckled my sword harness, set the sword down beside the bag, and crouched to fill up my waterskin. I gulped down almost the entire thing, then refilled the waterskin once more and stoppered it with the attached cork.

Peeling my soiled, blood-crusted shift over my head, I dropped it on the ground and knelt by the stream. I splashed tepid water onto my face and scrubbed my hands, but it didn't seem to be doing much good. I didn't have soap for a proper washing-up, but I did have the next-best thing—a whole lot of water, the whole Oasis's worth.

The lip of the stream was only a few inches higher than the water's surface. I dangled my feet in the stream first, then slid the rest of the way in, lying back to dunk my head. The water flowed gently around me, proof that there was still life in this place. It gave me hope that there was still a chance to resurrect the Oasis, my people's home.

I floated there, on my back, kicking my feet every few seconds to remain in relatively the same place. With my eyes closed, it wasn't so creepy, floating there in the long-dormant Oasis. It was peaceful. Therapeutic, even.

When I was as clean as I would get, I climbed out of the water and dried off with my heavy woolen cloak. I slipped into the clean linen shift a moment later, then suited back up and drained and refilled the waterskin one last time before leaving the stream. Sword lighting the way, I crossed the nearest bridge to the far side of the stream and hiked up the long, winding At-paved pathway to the tunnel.

The shift through the barrier blocking the tunnel's exit was easy enough. I landed on the other side, bracing for a blast of dry heat. The crook of my arm shielded my eyes from the onslaught of bright Sahara sunlight.

Except . . . a cool breeze ruffled my linen skirt, and faint pinpricks tickled my ankles as individual grains of sand brushed by.

Frowning, I lowered my arm and peeked through one barely cracked eyelid, then opened my eyes. The stars were so bright to my light-starved vision that I had to squint. For a moment, it seemed as though the night sky was a solid sheet of silver, not unlike the unearthly glow given off by my sword. Having no need for more light, I sheathed the blade.

My eyes began to adjust, and the heavenly bodies separated into clusters, then into a billion pinpricks of light. There was no moon in sight, only the stars stretching from horizon to horizon, a sea far vaster than the one I was about to set out across.

I scanned the ocean of dunes extending to the horizon in every direction. Figuring it would be best to start slow, I focused on a dune that was due east, about halfway between the Oasis and the horizon a couple miles away. One mile seemed like a good distance to start with. A safe distance.

Staring at the dune, I gathered my will and thought, "*There!*" with all my might.

In the blink of an eye and the poof of swirly rainbow smoke, I shifted through space.

When I landed, I spun around, searching in the distance for the mound of sand and limestone covering the domed city. It took me a moment to find it, but the hill of rubble was there, maybe a mile away. I grinned. I could do this. I could *really* do this.

Spurred by my success, I aimed for a dune on the very brim of the horizon. Two miles. If I could jump that far without wearing myself out, I could settle in for a series of two-mile jumps. It was a little over two hundred miles to Men-Nefer, so far as I'd calculated on my original trip by foot from the ancient city of Memphis to the Netjer-At Oasis. About a hundred jumps. It would be like counting to one hundred while jumping rope. Easy peasy.

The first two-mile jump was almost as effortless as the one-miler. Almost. I was a little out of breath, but no more so than I would have been after running up a couple flights of stairs.

The second two-mile jump left me breathing hard. After the third, I was so out of breath I had to bend over and put my hands on my knees. Little spots of darkness and light danced across my vision, and I felt a little lightheaded.

I sat down on the peak of dune four with a huff and uncorked my waterskin. Seven miles.

Maybe I needed a new plan. Or any plan beyond "get to the only city in ancient Egypt I've ever visited." I didn't even know if Heru or Aset or Nik were there. Hell, I didn't even know *when* I was, beyond sometime before the 10th century. Was I in Roman Egypt or Ptolemaic? Would I return to Men-Nefer to find that the Persians were in charge or the Nubians? Or would I discover that I was stranded in the heart of Egypt's most well-known ancient era, the New Kingdom?

The more I realized I didn't know anything about what I was attempting to jump into—literally—the more apparent it became that there was only one place for me to go: the Hathor Temple in Men-Nefer.

Aset had set up the ancient order of priestesses devoted to the goddess Hat-hur—to *me,* essentially—on my direction after I rescued her from her abductor. When I first arrived in Old Kingdom Egypt nearly a year ago, my time, the priestesses had been expecting me. And they'd been waiting for me millennia later, ready to prepare me for my journey into the ancient past. Whatever era I was in currently, I hoped I could count on the temple being a safe haven. The priestesses could help me get my bearings. I could get some much-needed R & R while I figured what the hell I was going to do next. It wasn't a sure thing, but it was all I had.

After one more sip of water, I corked the bottle and stood. I couldn't do a hundred more of those little two-mile shifts, hopping my way across the Sahara. I wouldn't make it, not if three shifts over a scant seven miles had knocked me on my butt.

But five twenty-mile jumps—that should do the trick. I could take a long break between each and would reach the temple in far less time.

Decided, I focused on the horizon, then closed my eyes and imagined I was a bird soaring high overhead. I envisioned how much further I needed to move this time, creating a mental image of a bird's-eye view of the desert and pinpointing my landing spot, ten times further away than my last spatial shift. With a deep breath, I focused my will. *Go.*

"Holy shit," I gasped, hands and knees sinking into the gritty sand and head hanging as the smoky, multihued tendrils of At dissipated all around me. I was dizzy and out of breath. And next time would be worse. What about the time after that? And the one after that?

I wouldn't make it. I knew it, somewhere deep inside me. And if I didn't make it to the temple, I sure as hell would never make it home to my family.

Sitting back on my heels, I brushed my hair out of my eyes with sand-coated fingers. I jutted my lower jaw and stared up at the sky. On the horizon almost dead east, the moon was rising, a solid disk of silver.

According to some of the ancient lore, the sun and the moon were considered the two eyes of the sky god, Horus—the mythological version of my very real bond-mate, Heru. His left eye, the moon, was said to be weaker than his right eye, the sun, because the desert god, Seth—the mythological version of my formerly possessed father, Set—stole Horus's left eye during the battle for the divine throne after Osiris's death. Seth is said to have damaged the eye, and though it was eventually returned to Horus, it was forever weakened, never to outshine the sun.

Well, the moon was strong enough for me. It was a gleaming beacon spurring me onward. I would make it home to Heru—to Marcus. To our children. I would make it home. I *would*.

"Alright," I muttered, once again pulling out my waterskin. "I can do this." I chugged the rest of the water, corked the bottle, and didn't even bother with standing. I'd probably collapse or pass out after this next jump, anyway. Maybe it would be too much. Maybe it would kill me. Maybe. But I had to try.

Closing my eyes, I imagined the inner sanctuary of the ancient Hathor temple. I pictured the interior walls, coated in plaster and covered in brightly painted reliefs depicting the goddess watching over worshipers and revelers, blessing the land, and interacting with the other gods, namely her consort, Horus. I could see it all so clearly—the three small recesses set into the walls at chest height, the tall, narrow doorway leading out to the temple hall, the dim moonlight shining in through that single opening . . .

For the first time since using this new sheut, I felt the swirling tendrils of At snake around me. I felt them tear me out of reality, keeping me whole and sane only by way of their protective embrace. I felt the chaos beyond them, the disorder of possibility tap-tap-tapping, searching for a way in. And I felt my cocoon of smoky At shatter as reality slammed back into place.

The ground lurched and tilted beneath my hands and knees, and I had no choice but to lie down on my side to recover some semblance of stability. Had I missed? Because it sure as hell felt like I'd landed on a boat in the midst of a violent storm.

Remotely, I heard the slap of sandals on a stone floor, but I couldn't bring myself to turn my head to look, let alone open my eyes. A moment later, rushed words were being thrown down at me. A young woman, by the sound of her voice, though I had no idea what she was saying.

I waved my hand in her general direction. "Is this the temple of Hat-hur in Men-Nefer?" I asked in the original tongue.

She was quiet for a moment. "It is," she said, though her response sounded unsure.

"I am her," I told her. "I am Hat-hur."

"You—I—are you certain? *You* are the Golden One?"

I gave her a thumbs-up. "Yes, quite certain. Just give me a moment and I shall introduce myself properly." I inhaled and exhaled heavily. "I have had a long day."

40

CHANCE & FATE

"How long have I been asleep?" I'd been awake for all of three seconds, but I was impatient for the priestess sitting at my bedside to answer. I was impatient, but my stomach was desperate. "And might there be anything to eat?"

I was famished, and I felt lightheaded. No headache, though, which meant bonding withdrawals had yet to kick in. I couldn't have been out for more than a couple hours, then, and while I felt as though I could sleep for days, the need for nourishment had overridden my exhaustion and roused me. I was still underweight, thanks to my regenerative abilities healing the damage to my body during childbirth and my minor head wound shortly after. Food was my number-one priority, getting home to my babies a close second.

The priestess—a different one from the skeptical young woman who'd found me in the inner sanctuary—offered me a reserved smile and a bow of her head. She was middle-aged, her onyx shoulder-length hair decorated with a delicate headband of woven gold thread and turquoise and quartz beads that reminded me of the one I'd worn the last time I was here, and she wore a simple, slightly loose-fitting white linen shift.

"There is food already set out for you, Golden One," she said, her mastery of the original tongue impressive; she had almost no accent whatsoever. She glanced over her shoulder, and I followed her line of sight to a table set out with a relative feast of fruits, bread, cheeses, and other things hidden in dishes that I couldn't see clearly from my reclined angle. "I shall send for the roast and stew, if it pleases you. We did not wish for the scents to wake you."

I stared at her for several seconds. That was how long it took my sluggish, sleepy mind to puzzle out that she was waiting for a response. "That—" I cleared my throat and propped myself up on my elbows. "That sounds lovely. Thank you."

Again, the priestess smiled almost hesitantly. She stood and turned away from the bed, but I grabbed her wrist before she could leave.

"How long was I asleep?" I could see it was still night through the rectangular windows cut in the uppermost quarter of the wall, high above the table. But depending on the time of year, night could last a mere nine hours at this latitude or nearly fourteen—and five hours was a big difference when racing against the clock. I didn't feel any hint of the bonding withdrawal headache yet, which had always been the first symptom for me, but I knew that once it started, I'd only have a matter of days to either get home or find Heru and soak up some of his bonding pheromones. If I didn't, I would die and so would my chances of ever seeing my children again.

Get home. I could barely think about what that would entail. Traveling through time, that was a given—but if my recent stint in spatial shifts was anything to go by, my sheut's time-jumping juice would prove to be equally weak, at least in comparison to what I was used to. I'd barely managed to cross two hundred miles in a night; how would I manage millennia between now and when the withdrawals killed me?

"The sun was born and died twice while you rested, Golden

One," the priestess said, only risking meeting my eyes for the briefest moment.

My heart stumbled, and for few seconds, I no longer felt hungry. "Two days," I breathed, releasing her wrist. "I was out for two full days?" It wasn't possible. That meant it had been three or four days since I'd last seen Heru. Bonding withdrawals should've been in full swing by now.

"Y—yes, Golden One." The priestess bowed her head once more. "I shall return shortly," she said and rushed out of the room.

"Wonderful." I fell back onto the hard mattress and stared up at the plain white plaster ceiling, barely managing to fight off panic by focusing on the sound of my heart beating, on the whoosh of air in and out of my lungs.

"You are quite different from what I expected," a woman said from the doorway. I recognized her voice as belonging to the younger priestess from before.

I tucked my arm behind my head, propping it up.

The priestess stood in the doorway, hands clasped before her. She wore a nearly identical shift and headband as the older, shyer priestess, the only deviation being the gold-plated amulet of a sun disk cradled in cattle horns on the front of her headband.

"You *must* be related to Denai," I said. The head priestess I'd spent so much time with the last time I was here had had a particular je ne se quoi about her, something that this young priestess had in spades.

Her eyes widened. "I am Anai, head priestess of this temple. Denai was my grandmother." She took a step into the room. "How did you know?"

I smiled, glad I finally had a clue as to the time period—we were in the First Intermediate Period, sometime during the Ninth or Tenth Dynasties, probably nearing the year 2100 BCE. "I spent a great deal of time with Denai once, many years ago," I told Anai. "You remind me of her." I suppressed a laugh. "Though perhaps a little more spirited." I didn't tell her that one day, thousands of years from now, I would meet another head priestess of this order named Anai, possibly one of this Anai's descendants.

"I—you really are—my grandmother spoke of you often." Anai crossed the room and sat in the chair at my bedside, bowing her head. "Please, Golden One, tell me how I can serve you."

"Pshhh . . ." I waved a hand dismissively. "By not doing all the bowing and scraping, for starters." I sat up and turned so my legs dangled over the edge of the bed. The slightest amount of weight on my shaking legs told me I wouldn't make it to the table of food on my own. "And a shoulder to lean on would be much appreciated, as well."

Anai lifted her head, her expression quizzical but her eyes determined. "Of course, Golden One." She slipped an arm around my waist and used her other hand to grip mine.

"'Hat-hur' is fine," I told her as we slowly made our way to the table. "'Golden One' is nice and all, but it is just so . . ." I made a "yuck" face, which earned me a giggle.

"Very well, Hat-hur." Anai left me at the table, my hands on the tabletop to keep me standing, while she retrieved the chair from the bedside. In true Egyptian fashion, there wasn't an extravagance of furniture in the room—just the bed, the chair, and the table. "There," she said, resting a hand on my shoulder. "You may sit now."

"Thanks." I grabbed a fig from the nearest dish and popped the entire thing into my mouth. In my defense, it was on the smaller side, as figs go. I held a hand over my mouth as I chewed and looked up at Anai. "Are you hungry?" I motioned to the spread with my other hand. "Feel free to join in."

I swallowed, tossing a torn-off piece of flatbread into my mouth. While I chewed that, I leaned forward and retrieved an earthenware pitcher from the center of the table and gave it a sniff. Wine—light, fruity, and barely alcoholic. I poured it into an alabaster goblet, quickly falling into a pattern of shoving food into my mouth and washing it down with gulps of wine.

Anai watched me from the end of the table, a tiny nugget of cheese in her hand and her eyes opened wide.

"Sorry," I said between a gulp of wine and another bite. "I still seem to be recovering from—" My explanation caught in my throat as I thought of the twins, my precious newborns, who could be with anybody right now. With my hunger partially sated, the need to find them became all-consuming. *They're with Marcus,* I told myself. *Please let them be with Marcus . . .*

I cleared my throat. "I was injured, and though my kind heal quickly, it uses up a lot of energy."

"I see," Anai said, taking the tiniest nibble of cheese.

I continued my gorging, though at a slightly more moderate pace. I took a short break while a couple priestesses brought in warm dishes—a thick, savory lentil soup, some sort of roasted fowl, and a spicy stew that tasted like beef, only gamier. It seemed to take forever to sate my hunger, but in time I was finally, blissfully full.

I stood, legs feeling strong and steady but eyelids drooping. I was tempted to fight against the regenerative sleep, but I wagered that once the bonding withdrawals hit, I would need to be at full strength. And I would have to survive the withdrawals if I were to have any chance of making it home to my family.

So I ambled back to the bed and practically collapsed onto the hard, thin mattress, already asleep by the time my feet left the floor.

"ANAI?"

"I am here, Golden—Hat-hur."

I opened my eyes, turning my head to look at her. She'd returned to the chair at my bedside. I had no idea how long she'd been sitting there, patiently watching over me while I slept, let alone how long I'd been asleep. I was almost afraid to ask. At least, I still felt no sign of bonding withdrawals. "How long was I asleep this time?"

"It is midday," Anai said, glancing at the open-air windows near the top of the wall. The light streaming in through the openings was crisp, bright, and golden. "You have been asleep for six or seven hours."

I took a deep breath, blowing it out as I sat up. Could've been worse. I stretched, easing the aches and kinks caused by the thin mattress and from sleeping without a pillow. I'd never grown accustomed to the hard headrests used by these ancient people, and I'd been too tired to bother making any kind of a pillow before passing out.

My stomach groaned, but with a usual hunger, not that desperate appetite specific to the regenerative process. It looked like I was healthy enough; it was time to get on with my journey.

I picked away at a spread of food nearly identical to the first, taking bites between packing in preparation to leave. I wrapped up less-perishable food items in the oilcloths saved from my previous stash of provisions and tucked them into my bag, then washed up using the small washing stand and toiletry chest in one corner of the room. Finally, I donned my sword harness.

She eyed the sword, one eyebrow raised. When she made that expression, she looked so very much like her grandmother; I hid a smile. "Will you be meeting the others of your kind in Abdju?"

"Abdju?" It was the ancient Egyptian name for Abydos, one of the oldest cities in this land. It was located in Upper Egypt—or *southern* Egypt—and, most notably to this era, was the location of Pepi I's funerary temple, which would blossom into a great temple of Osiris in the years to come. I had no idea why she would expect me to go there.

"When last Aset visited," Anai said, "she mentioned that the Netjer-Ats would be gathering in Abdju for the succession."

I paused in adjusting the harness's straps—I'd filled out a bit during my stay here—and stared at Anai. "Apologies, but I have been out of touch for some time. *What* succession?"

"Now that Osiris has passed on," Anai said, "it is time to lay him to rest and decide on the next leader of the Netjer-Ats." Remotely, I wondered if that was why the temple at Abdju would one day become a cult center for the worship of Osiris—because he'd supposedly been laid to rest there. "Aset explained that the contest was between Heru and Set, though she felt certain Heru would emerge victorious."

The blood drained from my face, and my heart went cold.

That succession. The one where Heru *did* win, but two days after he was instated as leader of the Council of Seven, he was attacked by Set and nearly killed. The one where he'd only survived because Aset had stepped in, distracting Set while her people carried Heru off to safety. The one where Aset was supposed to have died. At least, according to the rest of the world.

"How long ago was Aset here?" I asked, my voice hollow.

"A month ago, perhaps . . . maybe longer?" So, in ancient terms, at least thirty days, but maybe more.

It couldn't be a coincidence that I was here, now. According to Marcus, Aset had sacrificed herself to save him, but what if that wasn't the whole story? Marcus—Heru, at the time—had been blinded in Set's attack, not to mention wounded so severely that he'd been near death. He'd hardly been in any position to remember everything that had happened. To remember if I'd been there.

And I no longer believed in coincidence. This past year had cured me of that. If I was here, now, there was a reason.

I finished adjusting the leather harness. "The Netjer-Ats are meeting in Abdju, you said?"

Anai nodded.

I lifted my bag's strap over my head, settling it on my shoulder, then followed with my waterskin. "Do you know where, exactly?"

"The Temple of Osiris, of course." So apparently the transformation of Pepi I's funerary temple had already begun.

"Of course," I said under my breath. It didn't really matter—the shift there was going to stretch my limits regardless. Abdju was about four hundred miles south of Men-Nefer, over four times as long as my farthest spatial shift, the one that had all but knocked me unconscious.

I crossed the room to stand before Anai, taking her hands in mine. "Thank you, truly, for everything." I leaned in, kissing her on either cheek and leaving her absolutely stunned. "I apologize for leaving in such a hurry, but there is somewhere I must be. It is a matter of grave importance."

"I—it was a pleasure to serve you, Golden One."

"Farewell, Anai." I took a couple steps backward, dropped to one knee, and placed one hand on the floor while gripping the hilt of my sword, just over my shoulder, with the other. "May all of your daughters be as strong and loyal as you." Bowing my head, I closed my eyes and focused on, instead of a place, a person: Aset.

She was the one who had stopped Set from killing Heru, not me. I couldn't risk screwing things up by replacing her in such a significant event, but I also couldn't risk assuming that I hadn't been there at all. Like I said, me and coincidence broke up a while back.

I took a deep breath, then another. And shifted.

41

HORUS & SETH

I landed on a rough stone floor, hunched over and breath stolen. Behind me, a woman grunted, closely followed by the clang of metal striking not metal, but maybe stone, and a masculine laugh. Was I too late? Had the fight for Heru's life already started? I spun, drawing my sword, and lunged forward half-blindly.

"Nekure!" Aset shouted.

A moment later, vines of At sprouted from the floor, and I was caught up in a web of otherworldly origins. The thin, unbreakable vines snaked around my ankles, waist, shoulders, and wrists. One even slithered so far upwards as to hold my sword in place.

I blinked, confused. They were fighting; I was here to help. So why was Nik restraining *me*?

"Is it really you, Lex?" Nik said, laughter in his voice. "What are you doing here? And why are you attacking us with a sword?" He whistled. "And what a sword . . ."

"You should like it," I said, breathing hard but not fighting against his restraints. "You made it—or *will* make it."

"Really?" He walked around me, eyes only for the sword held

upright before me. "I have never seen anything like it. What do you call it—this shape?"

"A katana. It originates in a land far from here . . . and in a time far from now."

"I like it."

"What is it about men," Aset said, wiping her face and neck with a linen towel as she approached, "always so focused on their swords . . ." She was flushed, as was Nik, and my brain finally caught up to what I'd misinterpreted as the attack on Heru. They'd been sparring. She stood in front of me, her eyes searching mine. "Release her, Nekure. Clarity has returned to her mind."

"Of course," Nik said, his vines of At retracting in that same slithering motion.

Unfortunately, without their support, my legs gave out.

"Nek—"

Nik's arms wrapped around me in a backwards bear hug. "I have her."

"Bring her to the table," Aset said. "She needs food and rest."

I slumped in a chair at a narrow pedestal table and accepted the ceramic goblet Aset placed before me. "No food, please. I could not possibly eat any more right now." I still felt full from my last somewhat rushed feast. "I just need a moment to regather my strength." Which, I was fairly certain, was true. I didn't feel nearly so bad as I had when I'd arrived at the Hathor temple, despite having shifted so much farther. I chalked it up to having started off in much better shape. It gave me hope for the rest of my journey home.

"So you say," Aset said, sitting opposite me. Nik stood behind her, leaning his shoulder against the wall.

I sipped the water and glanced around, not seeing any enormous columns or stunning reliefs. "This is not the Osiris Temple." We were in a sitting room, the sparse wooden furniture pushed up against the walls and a wide reed mat laid out on the floor.

"That is true," Aset said. "This is not the Osiris Temple, but it is a short walk from this villa." She cocked her head to the side. "Were you expecting to appear there?"

I nodded, brow furrowed. "I thought—" I looked from Aset to Nik and back. "Has the Council decided yet? Have they chosen Heru as their next leader?"

"They have. My brother was coronated two days ago." Aset's eyes narrowed and she leaned forward a little. "Where have you come from, Lex? We did not expect to see you for a very long time yet. Why are you here?"

I set the goblet down. "It is a long story, but I think I am here because of the attack on Heru, which should be—" But when their faces showed only confusion, I frowned. "You do not know?" I looked at Nik. "He did not warn you?"

Aset and Nik exchanged a glance.

"I need to speak to Re," I said, hastily adding, "please."

Nik shrugged, and a blink later, his irises shone opalescent white. He pushed off the wall and bowed his head. "My dearest Alexandra, so lovely to see you again so—"

"Cut the crap, Re," I said to him in English. I stood, hands on the table. "Why haven't you told them about the attack? It could happen at any time. They need to be ready."

He appeared, as usual, unaffected by my little outburst. "It is true; I've noticed signs that Apep is wresting control from Set. The eyes are so telling . . ." He frowned dismissively. "But I didn't want to worry these two. Did you know, just before you arrived, I was going to suggest that we search him out. He's staying here in the villa with us, so we should hear any scuffle that breaks out."

"Scuffle," I said, voice low and cold. "It's a bit more than a scuffle."

"I suppose it is, at that." He nodded thoughtfully. "Tell me, dear Alexandra, how are you enjoying your new sheuts?"

"Wait—you knew? You knew I would end up with the twins' discarded sheuts, and you never said anything? Over the thousands of years . . ." I closed my eyes and took a deep breath. *Not the time,* I told myself. *Really not the time.* I took another deep breath, shaking all the while. "Can we have Nik back?"

"You know, I think I'll run things for this little adventure. I've yet to have a real fight in this body yet, and I find the prospect thrilling. Plus, I know what needs to happen, and also what can't." Like that Apep-Set can't die, or that Nik has to keep his sheut power under wraps, since nobody besides Heru and us could know about it until Aset and Nik come out of the proverbial coffin in my time.

"Fine," I said, returning my attention to Aset. She'd been watching our incomprehensible exchange with interest. "Set—well, *Apep* is going to attack Heru any moment now," I told her, switching back to the original tongue, "and according to the account Heru told me thousands of years from now, *you* are the one who saves him. I no longer have the power to block or alter memories, so it *must* be you who truly rescues him." I stepped away from the table and started pacing. "He will be attacked and blinded fairly quickly, as he will not expect anything like that from Set, and he will be badly wounded." I wrung my hands. "You cannot afford to be too late. If you are . . ."

Aset's curiosity had faded as resolve set in. "I understand. Do you know where this will happen?" Because she knew as well as me that we couldn't rely on Heru's location in the At—not with my anomalous presence warping the timeline's reflection in the echoes.

Hopeful, I looked to Re-Nik, but he shook his head. "No," I told Aset. And finally I understood why I was there. Why I *had* to be there. "But I can find him."

I stopped pacing and faced Aset. "I can shift to him, then

back here, and describe where he is. I should have a general sense of the direction, so that should make it easier." I strode over to the bench where Aset had laid my sword, picking it up and sheathing it over my shoulder in one smooth motion. "I need something to hide my face, a veil or a headscarf—do you have anything like that? We cannot risk Heru seeing my face."

The moment I uttered the words, the gears of reality clicked into place, and I felt sick to my stomach. The twins weren't here to wipe Heru's memory of me this time around. I couldn't risk letting him seeing my face—letting him remember me—in any time between now and the moment I returned home. Which meant I couldn't be near him, not really. I'd been so focused on simply staying alive that I hadn't thought everything all the way through.

I'd been planning on returning to my native time pretty much the same way I'd left it, hopping through the eras from Heru to Heru, feeding the bond and wiping his memory when I left. Except the innate power granted to me by *my* sheut—or sheuts—couldn't do that. Maybe with time and a lot of training . . . but time was the one thing I was extra short on.

I lowered myself onto the bench. If I couldn't risk being close enough for him to see me, then I couldn't feed the bond. Bonding withdrawals would set in eventually, and . . .

"I do not," Aset said, oblivious to my mood shift. "We could cut something from a dress or—"

"Here." Re-Nik placed a misshapen piece of gleaming solidified At on the table. "This should work. Come here so I can fit it to your head."

It's a mask, I realized. Numbly, I stood and crossed the room, stopping to stand directly before Re-Nik. He placed his creation over my face, using Nik's sheut to secure it behind my head. It resembled a Venetian mask, something that might be worn during Carnival—not obstructing my vision at all and leaving my nostrils, mouth, and jaw free.

"Lex," Aset said, finally picking up on my distress. She took hold of my hand. "This will work. We will find him and save him, and all will be well."

I glanced down at her, sorrow overflowing in my heart. "Your whole life is about to change, and I am so sorry for that." I gave her hand a squeeze. "Everyone will think you are dead after this. They will, and I know it is not fair, but it is what must be."

"So it is time for that already?" Aset gave my hand a return squeeze, then let it go and stood, turning away. "Re warned us that this would be our fate the first time he took control of Nekure's body. He said we would have roughly a human lifetime to get our affairs in order before we would have to withdraw from the Nejeret world and go into hiding." She laughed quietly, a laugh that I thought was meant only for her. "I had not realized how fleeting their lives are."

"It will not be forever," I said in lame consolation.

"I know." She cleared her throat, but it did little for the increasing huskiness in her voice. "It will be a great adventure, do you not think? And how wondrous that my son and I have a chance to play such a large part in all of this." She laughed that soft laugh again, and this time I joined her, all the while fighting back my own welling tears. "We get to help you save the universe." Her head drooped. "What more could we ask for?"

I moved to stand before Aset and took both of her hands in mine. "You *will* have great adventures—the places you will see." I forced a smile. "The two of you will be the protectors of the timeline, guarding my passage as I get yanked back further and further in time. You will always be there, and I will always need you. I could not have made it this far without you and Nekure, and I will never *ever* be able to repay you for all you have done. But I can promise you this—you *will* have your lives back one day, and when you do, you will be needed and loved more than most people ever dare to hope for. And my babies—" My chin trembled. "They will need you as much as I ever did."

"Lex, what are you—"

I shook my head. "Later. We have an appointment, remember?"

She licked her lips. "Yes, yes, of course. Go, find my brother. We shall be ready when you return."

I nodded, and a moment later, I was gone.

Focusing on Heru, I reappeared in the shadowed space between two wide, round columns etched with elaborate hieroglyphs. I was still kneeling, which was good, because the shift left me momentarily unsteady. One hand on the column to my left, I stood and surveyed the dim area around me. There were more columns, what appeared to be two lines of them running down a wide, cavernous hall. The walls were covered with a layer of plaster, yet to be decorated.

I knew exactly where I was—the Osiris Temple. So where was Heru?

Footsteps. I heard them approaching from the far end of the hall, where a narrow doorway led to a darker passage. I pressed myself against the column, making myself as inconspicuous as possible.

A second set of footsteps joined the first, this pair moving more quickly.

"Heru!" Set said, followed by more words that I couldn't discern. He was speaking in the common tongue, and I wasn't fluent enough to follow. Though I'd learned some during my months in Old Kingdom Egypt, I hadn't learned enough.

When Marcus first told me about the truth behind the famous myth, the Contendings of Horus and Seth, he shared the story of Set attacking him. It had been two days after Heru was instated as the head of the Council of Seven. Set had been acting strangely hostile for some time, and he'd approached Heru in the guise of truce and friendship. False truce and friendship.

From the sound of their voices now, it was time.

Fighting the instinct to shout a warning to Heru, I squeezed my eyes shut and shifted back to the villa where Aset and Re-Nik waited.

"Now," I said before the rainbow smoke had cleared. "It is happening now . . . in the temple." I collapsed into one of the chairs.

Aset and Re-Nik hesitated at the doorway.

"Go! I can catch up, but he needs you *now*."

They didn't waste another second. And I was left alone, breathing hard and gulping water. When this was all over, I'd need a good long rest before I even thought about jumping through time to return home.

That was, of course, assuming I didn't die of bonding withdrawals first.

42

FIGHT & DIE

After Aset and Nik left, I sat and recuperated for only as long as I absolutely had to. When my breath was caught and my thirst quenched, I assumed what was quickly becoming my standard shifting position—down on one knee, one hand on the ground to stabilize me and the other gripping the hilt of my sheathed sword. Just in case . . .

I landed in that darker passageway connected to the colonnaded hall. The shouts and grunts and thuds coming from the hall itself were insanely loud, echoing off the temple's plaster and stone walls in a seemingly endless, chaotic jumble of sound. The fight had begun.

I closed my eyes and forced myself to take several long, slow, deep breaths. I would be of no use to anyone if I ran into the skirmish all wobbly-kneed and fuzzy-brained.

Heru shouted out in agony, and my resolve disintegrated. I was on my feet in a heartbeat. Aset and Re-Nik raced up the passageway and passed me, just barely beating me into the hall.

Heru lay sprawled on his back on the stone floor in the center of the chamber, the two rows of thick columns running along either side of him. Dressed in head-to-toe black, four men held down each of Heru's limbs with a dagger through his wrists and feet. Apep-Set knelt at his head, his own dagger poised almost surgically over Heru's face. Slashes crisscrossed my bond-mate's eyes and streaked down his cheeks. His head thrashed from side to side, only adding to the cuts.

Set shouted something incomprehensible, though somewhere in the deep recesses of my mind, instinct told me it was along the lines of "Hold still!"

Aset reached them first. She shrieked, launching herself at Set and using her momentum not just to roll him away from her brother but to fling him against one of the pillars. His dagger flew out of his hand, chipping the plaster wall before pinging to the stone floor.

I lost track of what happened next in their fight, because I was suddenly locked in a battle of my own. One of Apep's sycophants ran at me, his black hood falling back, revealing a mostly shaved head and plaited side-lock. It was a priest's hairstyle. Having abandoned his dagger in Heru's wrist, he brandished a long, smooth wooden staff.

I raised my sword, angling it to the side to block his first blow. My sword's insanely sharp At blade sliced through the staff like it was butter. It took off his arm just above the elbow almost as easily.

Re-Nik was engaging two of Set's other priests, and I probably would've been in trouble if I'd had to deal with the other two simultaneously. One of mine was down an arm by the time the second decided to come after me. He screamed, staring at the spurting stump, eyes bulging.

"You picked the wrong side," I told him, kicking him backward into the newcomer.

Both men stumbled backward, the able-bodied priest throwing his hysterical, one-armed companion to the side. He didn't show any concern for the injured man. As he scrambled to his feet, his eyes never left me.

He was smarter; he tossed his staff away and yanked the two daggers impaling Heru's feet free, settling into a defensive position on the far side of Heru's body.

I could hear Aset's grunts as she fought with Apep-Set and Re-Nik's victorious hoot as he downed one of his foes, but I didn't dare take my eyes off my opponent. I stepped over Heru, avoiding one of several substantial patches of blood. A quick glance down told me he was still breathing, if he wasn't exactly *moving*. The blood loss must have knocked him unconscious.

For now, he was alive. We'd need to get him out of here and into a healer's hands soon if he was to stay that way.

I heard another victory cry from Re-Nik, and a few seconds later, he headed my way.

"Get Heru out of here," I yelled just as the priest lunged at me. I deflected his first dagger with my sword. "At this point—" I spun out of the way of the priest's secondary underhanded strike in a sort of two-legged pirouette. "I'm expendable. He's not."

"I shall return shortly!" Re-Nik shouted, ending with a grunt as he hoisted Heru's unconscious body up into his arms.

Set's single remaining priest chose that moment to try another attack. I dodged his offhand strike by ducking, but he spun around, sweeping back with the dagger in his right hand and catching me off guard. I barely deflected the blade, and the tip slid across the front of my thigh, slicing in a good centimeter deep.

"Ah!" I stumbled back a few steps but forced myself not to look down. My eyes were only for the priest.

Aset cried out, and Apep-Set shouted victoriously. We were running out of time. Heru was safe, but the timeline would be just as screwed if Aset died here instead.

"Hey, asshole," I said to my priest, knowing full well he couldn't understand me. I held up my sword and willed the blade to glow.

The priest's eyes bugged out, an effect that was only enhanced when my sword swept under his outstretched right arm and bit through the flesh under the side of his ribcage. I dragged the sword up his body as high as I could, yanking it free when it hit the bottom of his sternum.

Turning on my heel, I stalked toward Apep-Set. He was crouched over Aset, her top half blocked by a pillar.

I stopped dead in my tracks the moment her face came into view. Her eyes—they were gone. Just empty, bloody caverns.

"No . . ."

"She would not let me take her brother's eyes, so I had to settle for hers instead." Apep-Set grinned like a devil. "I cut out her tongue, too—she always did talk too much."

"You—you killed her." *But I promised her . . .*

"I did." He stood slowly, keeping his knees bent and the dagger upraised and ready. For me. "But fear not, masked one, you will not have to mourn her for long."

"You *killed* her." *But I* promised *her . . .*

"And now you are boring me."

Raising my sword, I charged at him. Fury blinded me, and I no longer cared that Set couldn't die, that killing him now would be killing me by preventing me from ever having been born. It didn't matter. I wanted him dead. I wanted to feel my blade tearing into his flesh and bone more than I'd ever wanted anything in my life—more than I'd wanted Marcus or Heru, and more than I wanted to get home.

Bloodlust. It was a term I'd never understood before. I did now.

"Pretty sword," Apep-Set said an instant before he sidestepped and buried a knife in my side. He held me, suspended on his knife's blade, and leaned in.

I stared up at his face, unable to blink. Unable to breathe.

"And pretty eyes—red has always been my favorite color."

I coughed, tasting blood, thick and salty on my tongue.

This was it—or it could be. I could let it end, all of it. I was so tired, and maybe the birth of the twins would still stand, even if Aset wasn't there to guide my way as I journeyed backward in time. Nik would still be there, and Re, and Heru was alive. It was possible that ma'at had still been restored, that the universe was safe and stable once more. There was a possibility that I could die now and everything would be fine.

It was so very tempting just to give up, to give in. To let go.

But I promised Aset . . .

Apep-Set lowered me to the temple floor almost gently.

"You were . . . right," I said between gasping breaths. "I will . . . not . . . mourn Aset . . . for long . . . I think . . ."

Apep-Set nodded sagely. For once, the darkness in his eyes didn't seem menacing or psychotic, and Set's features—he just looked tired . . . tired, and sad. "Your wound is not immediately lethal, but it will kill you. Would you like me to leave you this way, or shall I ease your burden and end your pain?"

My lips spread into a wide grin, and I started chuckling. And coughing up blood, but chuckling all the same. I sucked in a halting breath and focused my will. "I choose . . . option number three," I gasped at the exact moment that the world disappeared in a maelstrom of swirling, rainbow smoke.

I reappeared in the exact same place on the floor, only a minute or two earlier. Before Apep-Set killed Aset. Because, damn it, I'd promised her she would have a life when this was all over.

I was behind Apep-Set, and I still had the breathtakingly painful stab wound in my side. I'd replaced my former self in the timeline. The same ba can't overlap in time—it's a temporal paradox, one of the few true impossibilities. I had no doubt that my priest was confused about my sudden disappearance from the opposite side of the hall. It was my one and only advantage.

With a hand on the wall, I climbed up to my feet and snuck up behind Apep-Set. I had little fear of him noticing me; he was too busy holding Aset up by her neck with one hand, slowly strangling the life out of her.

Gritting my teeth, I gripped the hilt of my sword with both hands and bashed the butt into the base of Set's skull. He dropped to the floor like a sack of bricks. Aset fell just as hard.

I scrambled over Set's body, struggling to yank Aset away from him. Her legs were tangled with his, and I had to physically lift his left leg to unhook her foot from his calf.

"Come on, Aset," I murmured. "You're going to be fine."

I dragged her a few yards away from Apep-Set, laid her on her back, and held my finger under her nose. Nothing, not even the faintest stirring of air. I fumbled along the side of her neck, feeling for a pulse. Again, nothing.

"She's dead." The words sounded foreign to my ears, despite having passed through my vocal cords.

At the sound of movement, I glanced up. The last priest stood between the nearest two columns, his pair of daggers hanging limply from his hands and his stare stuck on Set's motionless body.

I held up my sword at the priest and willed it to glow.

He took a step backward.

I pointed the sword at him, then at Set's body, then at the door. I might not have spoken his language, but I could still tell the bastard to drag his master the hell away from here.

He lifted Set's body more easily than I'd expected, and within seconds, the two were gone.

"You are not dying on me," I told Aset, kneeling beside her. I couldn't tell how extensive the damage was to her throat, but nothing looked misshapen, only bruised and a little swollen. "Do you hear me?" I leaned over her, adjusted the angle of her head, and cleared her airway. "You are *not* dying on me. Not today. I need you too much." Sealing my mouth over hers, I exhaled. Breaking away, I took a deep breath and did it again.

I sat up straighter and stacked my hands, placing my palms

on her chest to begin compressions. "You"—I pumped her chest with my hands, gritting my teeth to battle the sharp pain in my side—"are . . . not . . . going . . . to . . . die . . . to . . . day. Do . . . you . . . hear . . . me? Do . . . you?"

"My Alexandra . . ." Re-Nik rushed back into the hall. "Heru is with healers—he'll be fine. I told the others that Aset had been slain, and that it was too late for her, but that they should focus their efforts on hunting down Set." He passed between two columns, heading straight for us. "What happened—"

Aset gasped, sucking in an enormous breath, then coughing violently.

"I—I brought . . . her back," I said, even as I fell to the side.

Re-Nik caught me. "You are wounded."

I nodded, and darkness closed in all around me.

43

STAY & GO

When I came to, my mask was gone and I was lying on my back, covered by a linen shroud. Whatever supported me rocked gently to and fro, and I could hear the quiet slap-lap of water and the whispered creaking of wood all around me.

I tried to sit up and instantly regretted it. Pain speared the left side of my body, shooting outward. It left me paralyzed and whimpering. A hand gripped mine, small and soft, but strong nonetheless. Another held me down by the shoulder.

"Hush now, Lex," Aset said, her voice soothing. "I am here. You are safe and will be well, in time." I could see the outline of her through the shroud. She appeared to be wearing a golden yellow headscarf over her head and wrapped around her face.

"I do not . . . have time." The twins. Heru. I had to get home to them, and I needed to do it before the bonding withdrawals killed me.

She unhooked a portion of the headscarf, revealing her face. "I would argue, rather, that you do not have a choice."

"You do not . . . understand." Once again, I tried to rise, but the minor pressure Aset put on my shoulder was more than enough to keep me down.

"I understand plenty," she said, drawing the shroud back and uncovering my face. Without the barrier, I could see that her headscarf was embroidered with sage-green vines and tiny white flowers, and that she'd changed into a long wrap dress of the same pale green, embroidered with fist-sized bunches of yellow or white blossoms. Her outfit struck me a cross between a traditional Indian sari and the garb of an ancient Greek woman.

"I understand that you need food and rest," Aset continued, "or the regeneration will kill you even as it heals your wound. There is nothing more I need to know until this most urgent danger has passed." As she spoke, she brought a conical copper funnel to my lips with one hand, holding up a large ceramic pitcher with the other. "This will be awkward, but I dare not move you while your lung repairs itself." She held the funnel over my mouth. "Open, please."

I glanced at the pitcher. "What is it?"

"Ewe's milk mixed with honey and fig paste." She smiled minutely. "Truly, it is quite good, and the sugars will speed your recovery."

Eyeing her dubiously, I opened my mouth. Thankfully, she poured only a small mouthful through the funnel, then righted the pitcher and waited for me to swallow.

"We are on a boat?" I said once the concoction was down. It was smooth and sweet, and slightly warm from the sun high overhead. Rays of brilliant sunlight peeked through the miniscule gaps in the woven reed mat shielding our portion of the boat.

Aset waited for me to open my mouth, then poured another mouthful through the funnel. "We are." Her gaze flicked up, beyond my head. "My dutiful son is ferrying us upriver to Lunet —Pepi's old winter palace there was abandoned years ago." A sad smile curved her lips. "The others will believe Nik has gone on a pilgrimage back to the Oasis, returning my body to the place where it belongs." She looked down at me. "And any humans who see us passing will leave us be, assuming we are carrying one of the dead to her final resting place."

The shroud suddenly made a lot more sense. "Me? *I* am . . . the dead . . . am I not?"

"Indeed," Aset said with a nod, once more pouring some of the fortified milk down the funnel.

I swallowed. "Why . . . are you dressed . . . as a Sumerian woman?" I asked, guessing at her outfit's origins.

Aset glanced down at herself. "Akkadian, in fact. I borrowed this from Ishtar. We were in a hurry, and it was the best I could come up with." She shrugged one shoulder. "We could not very well have any witnesses claiming to have seen me strolling along with Nekure while he was supposedly carrying my dead body . . ."

Nik chuckled, and I craned my neck in an unsuccessful attempt to see him without moving the rest of my body. "I approve of your loose definition of the word 'borrow,' Mother."

Tutting, Aset repositioned my head and poured another helping of the milk down the funnel. "Ishtar was careless with her belongings, leaving them so unattended." Aset sniffed. "Besides, she has so much clothing I doubt she will notice a single item is missing. And my need was greater than hers. I could hardly march out of the temple as I was." She grinned. "Truly, this is quite a bit more exciting than I had anticipated . . ."

I swallowed, snorted a laugh, and groaned.

"Careful, dear Lex." Aset set down the pitcher and funnel to rest a cool hand on my forehead. "I cauterized your wound to stop the bleeding but nearly doubled the internal damage in doing so. Your lung was pierced by the tip of Set's knife, and he nearly sliced your spleen in half. It was by sheer luck that he missed your intestines."

I sighed. "No wonder . . . I hurt . . . so badly."

"And are having such a hard time speaking," Aset said. "So I suggest you stop trying."

I attempted to roll my eyes but found that my eyelids were drooping closed.

"Sleep now, dear Lex. There will be plenty of time for talking when you are better."

"No," I tried to tell her, but I only got so far as parting my lips before sweet, painless sleep dragged me away.

I WOKE WITH A START AND SHARP INHALE. I SAT UP ON instinct, eyes popping open and left arm tight against my side in anticipation of pain. Only a dull ache throbbed deep within. It was both a pleasant surprise and an ill omen of time lost.

"Aset?" I called, scanning around me. I was in a small room with stone walls and no windows, unless the holes in the patchy, decaying ceiling counted. Only small bits of plaster remained, clinging to the decrepit skeleton of the roof, and several large openings afforded me a glimpse of a clear night sky. "Nik?"

"I am here, Lex," Aset said, rushing into the room through what appeared to be the only doorway. "I am here."

I shot a second cursory glance around the room. "This is Pepi's abandoned palace?" She'd said it was in Lunet—the ancient name for Dendera, some sixty miles east of the Osiris Temple in Abydos.

Aset knelt at my side, pulling down the thin linen sheet that had been covering me and peering closely at my naked torso.

Instinctively, I crossed my arms over my bare chest.

"Stop that," Aset said, tugging at my forearm. "You are blocking my view of the wound."

Lowering my arms, I looked down, squishing my left breast

out of the way. A pink, puckered scar about two inches long and barely a quarter of an inch wide was all that remained of what had been a life-threatening injury.

My stomach grumbled. "How long was I asleep?"

"Two days," Aset said, straightening and looking me in the eye. "You must eat, then rest more. I believe it will take two, maybe three more rounds to return you to full health." She reached to the side and handed me my waterskin. "Drink while I retrieve some food."

I grabbed her forearm as she started to stand. "Aset, if I go through two or three more rounds of regenerative sleep, I will surely die. The bonding withdrawals . . ."

"Dear gods," she said, covering her mouth with her hand. "I forgot all about that." She sat back down and leaned in close, her eyes searching mine. "How bad are the withdrawal pains? How long do you think you have left until they incapacitate you?"

"I—well—" I frowned, surprised to find that, when I looked for it, I found no hint of a withdrawal headache. In fact, the only pain I felt was the dull throb in my side. "They have yet to start."

Aset's lips spread into a hesitant smile. "This is a good thing, is it not?"

Slowly, I shook my head. "I—I do not know. By my count, it has been six or seven days since I last spent time with Heru. The withdrawals should have started by now. They should be *bad* by now."

"And yet they are not." Her smile faded.

I scoured her face for answers. "I gave birth about a week ago, just after I arrived in this time."

Aset's eyes widened.

"Do you think—is it possible that the act of giving birth somehow broke the bond?"

"Truly, Lex, I could not say." She touched her hand to the

side of my face, tilting her head just a little. Compassion and concern shone in her eyes, silvered by the moon and starlight leaking in through the ceiling. "Where is the child?"

I focused on a barren corner of the room and recrossed my arms over my chest, hugging myself. The pain of missing them dwarfed that of the stab wound. "Children—I had twins, and they are gone. They jumped away shortly after—" I swallowed a sob, then took a deep, shaky breath. "I can only hope that they have returned home, to their father." I looked at Aset. "And to you. But I do not know for sure, which is why I must return there as soon as possible."

"Lex, who was with you during the birth?"

"No one." My eyes wandered back to that lonely corner. "I was alone in the Oasis. They brought me there . . . it was the safest place."

"Oh, dear child," Aset murmured, wrapping her arms around me in a sturdy embrace. "I am so sorry you had to go through all of that alone."

Enveloped in her motherly warmth, I felt my will break, and I gave in to an outpouring of tears. They were tears of sorrow and grief, of desperation and fear. They were tears of holding on, and of letting go. They were tears of, just for that moment, weakness. Of giving up.

How many times had I been on the verge of giving up since this all started? Too many to count.

Maybe next time would be the time I actually did it. But not this time.

CURLED UP ON MY SIDE AND EYES CLOSED, I BASKED IN the hazy lull of waking up, doing my best to ignore the hunger gnawing away in my belly. I pictured my babies, remembering how they'd felt nestled on my chest, so tiny and soft and floppy.

"Are you planning on lying there starving yourself all day?" Based on her voice, Aset was somewhere behind me. "Or are you going to rouse and eat so you can regain the strength you will need to return to your family?"

Groaning, I pulled on my big-girl pants and rolled onto my back, opening my eyes so I was staring up at patches of purple and orange sky through the holey roof. I wasn't lying on a bed, exactly. Or at all, really, but regenerative sleep didn't care—it would knock me out and sweep me away even if I were lying on a glacier, naked and freezing. The reed mats beneath me were far from comfy, but they raised me off the ground enough that I wasn't rolling around on loose grains of sand. It wasn't much, but it was something.

"Are you still without any symptoms of the bonding withdrawals?" Aset asked from the doorway.

I looked at her sidelong and nodded. The anxiety that simple fact wound within me was nearly as debilitating as the withdrawals themselves. I felt like I had a time bomb stashed away deep inside me, ticking away . . . waiting . . .

I returned to staring up at the ceiling.

"Re and I discussed your situation at length while you slept, and he has proposed two possible scenarios."

I glanced at the doorway. "Where is he? Or Nekure, I mean."

"He is busy in the At, cloaking our presence in the echoes as far into the future as he is able. But that is of no matter, right now. Not to you." She waved a hand dismissively. "Re thinks either the bond between you and Heru was broken during the act of childbirth—some sort of a natural failsafe to ensure that the wellbeing of your children is your primary concern, rather than that of your bond-mate—"

"But that implies some evolutionary basis for whatever is happening to me." I shook my head. "That would require hundreds if not thousands of iterations of my scenario—bonded

Nejerette bearing children—to have occurred before me." It wasn't impossible, just not very likely.

Aset entered the room and knelt beside my bedroll. "Which is precisely why I believe this to be the less-likely scenario," she said, helping me sit up. She retrieved my waterskin from the floor beside her and handed it to me.

"So what is the *more*-likely scenario, then?" I asked, uncorking the bottle and tipping it back. I was suddenly so thirsty that I thought there might not be enough water in all of Egypt to quench my need. The thirst far outweighed any embarrassment I felt at being bared to the hips before Aset.

"That you are most likely experiencing a temporary condition, whereby the mechanisms that usually regulate your brain and body function are in flux—due to childbirth, of course . . ."

"Of course," I mumbled.

". . . and that, in time, your body's systems will settle down, returning you to your normal state."

"My normal, pheromone-dependent state, you mean," I clarified.

"Indeed," Aset said, straightening and bowing her head.

"So, basically, I *might* have no deadline. But it is *maybe* more likely that I only have a postponed deadline, and I still need to get back to my time—to my *Heru*—before the withdrawals kill me."

Aset flashed me a pitying smile.

"Then we have to assume the latter and hurry this regeneration process along."

Aset's smile broadened, her amber eyes lighting up. "Very well. I shall return shortly with food."

WHEN I ROUSED AFTER MY NEXT REGENERATION cycle, I felt hungry, but not famished, and I dared to hope that the regeneration process was over. I sat up, feeling more than a little refreshed and pleased to note that I still felt no hint of the telltale withdrawal headache.

"She returns from the dead once more," Nik said, his lean frame little more than a dark shadow silhouetted in the doorway. It was night again, and the full moon had waned to half its former size, visible through the holes in the ceiling.

I snatched the linen sheet up to cover my chest. "Aset?" I asked, voice froggy from sleep.

"Bathing down by the river. How are you feeling? Up to getting out of bed?" When I nodded, he pointed to a spot beyond the head of my bedroll. "Your dress is folded up, just there." He turned to the side. "I will be out here by the fire. Just follow the glow . . ."

"Alright." I cleared my throat, reaching for the waterskin. After nearly draining the thing, I set it down and found my dress exactly where Nik had said it would be. I slipped it on over my head, pleased that the movement didn't cause any twinge of pain in my side. It meant it was time for me to go. I wanted—no, needed—to get home, regardless of whatever was going on with my end of the bond between Heru and me.

But I had to do two things before I left.

Barefoot, I walked into a narrow hallway where the ceiling was still mostly intact. I could just make out hints of a shadowy design on the crumbling plaster. I followed the glow of flickering firelight off the far wall to a doorway leading to a larger room with a ceiling completely open to the stars. In the middle of the space, Nik crouched beside a small fire, alternating between tending a makeshift spit and stirring something in a small iron pot.

"Whatever you are cooking smells wonderful," I said, wandering into the open-air room.

Nik pointed to the two large lumps skewered on the spit.

"Rabbit." He shifted his finger so he was pointing at the pot. "And rabbit stew."

"Love the variety." I chuckled and sat cross-legged on the floor to his left. "Nekure?" I asked, biting my lip.

"Hmmm?" He paused his stirring and looked at me, eyebrows raised and open expression lit by the dancing flames.

"I mean this in the least offensive way possible, but can I talk to Re?"

His lips curved upwards at the corners, just a little, and he resumed tending the stew. "Afraid not. He is in the At right now."

"Oh." I stared at the pot, mesmerized by Nik's slow, hypnotic stirring.

"It is kind of nice, now, having some time without him."

I looked at Nik's face. He was resolutely staring at the pot of stew.

"He never used to go into the At alone before, but now . . ."

"Does it bother you, sharing your body with him?"

Nik shrugged. "Not usually, but . . . it makes certain things uncomfortable. I am never alone, not in here," he said, tapping the side of his head. "He cannot see everything I am thinking, but . . ." Nik let out a deep sigh. "I can always feel him there, even when he is not communicating with me."

"Does he ever sleep?"

Nik glanced at me, just for a moment. "He detests pain, so whenever I am injured, he tends to go—" Nik frowned. "Not to sleep, exactly, but something like that. *Dormant* might be a better word for it."

"Huh," I said to myself, thinking that little bit of information explained a lot about the man Nik would become millennia down the road. I inhaled, then held my breath for a few seconds. "If I asked, would you make a few things for me? Out of At, I mean?"

He brightened, grinning. "For you, anything."

I laughed. "Charmer."

His eyebrows lifted. "What do you need?"

"A bracelet and a small statuette of the goddess Hat-hur."

Nik's eyes widened. "A statuette?" He twisted around, reaching into a reed basket a few feet behind him. He pulled out a drawstring leather purse about the size of a bowling ball, and from that, he withdrew a very familiar little statuette carved from alabaster. "You mean like this?"

Now *my* eyes widened, and I held my hand out for the tiny stone goddess. "Where did you get that?" Because I had little doubt that it was the same statuette Genevieve had gifted me over a year ago, my time . . . over four millennia from now, Nik's.

"My grandfather gave it to Mother a while back, having noticed the special interest she had taken in the Hat-hur cult."

Marcus had once told me the statuette used to belong to his sister and that it had been a gift from their father. A gift Osiris had given Aset because of all the time she was spending setting up the order of priestesses who would make *my* journeys through time a success. A tiny laugh escaped from between my lips, and I shook my head as the seemingly unrelated threads of time wove together.

"What?" Nik asked. "What is it?"

"Nothing, really . . . just that it is so strange how something can seem random when viewed from one perspective, but when looked at from another angle, a clear pattern emerges." I met his eyes, holding the statuette out to him. "Would you be able to make a smaller, At version of this *within* the original?"

"I could . . ." He accepted the statuette, looking from it to me and back. "But for what purpose?"

"Trust me when I say that it is a long story, but it will be essential to me making my first jump backwards in time."

Nik's eyes narrowed. "Very well."

"Wonderful," I said, clapping my hands together. "And as for the bracelet . . ."

I STOOD BEFORE ASET AND NIK, BAGS PACKED AND ready to go. Everything that needed to be done had been done, and I was, once again, fit as a fiddle. It had taken several attempts for me to get the charm on the statuette just right, using the subtler and more complicated of my sheut powers to attune the smaller statuette hidden within the stone to my ba and anchoring it to the correct time and location—end of the Sixth Dynasty, the Hathor Temple in Men-Nefer. Guiding Nik through the hieroglyph etchings on the bracelet listing all of the dates and locations he and Aset would meet up with me in their future had been nearly as complicated, and much more tedious.

Now, I was leaving two of the people I trusted most in the world with all the direction they needed to find me as they traveled along the slow path while I hop-skipped through time. I had a solid plan, jumping forward in time in hundred-year increments, using the Hathor Temple in Men-Nefer as my constant, my home base. It would take forty-one jumps through time, including forty-one periods of rest between. Depending on how long I had to rest between jumps, it could take as little as a few days, or it could take months. There was no way of knowing without trying.

"Thank you," I told them, one of each of their hands in either of mine. "I love you both dearly." I gave their hands a squeeze. "I could not have come this far without you."

Aset offered me a sad smile. "Perhaps . . . perhaps not, but thankfully, *that* we will never know." She leaned in and placed a light kiss on my lips. "Be well, dear friend," she said as she pulled away. "I know in my heart that you have it within you to make it home to your family. Just remember that they are waiting for you—that *we're* waiting for you."

I nodded, tearing up, then looked at Nik.

He grinned his familiar, mischievous grin, but his heart wasn't in it. I could tell by the shimmer of worry in his pale blue eyes. He leaned in, planting another light kiss on my lips. "Safe travels, Lex."

"You, too."

Releasing their hands, I took a step back, flashed a shaky smile, and jumped into the future.

44

TIME & PLACE

Three jumps. Three hundred years. For once, zero problems.

I leapt into the 1700s BCE, the heart of the Middle Kingdom, with relative ease. I always jumped to and from the inner sanctuary of the Hathor Temple, and each time I landed, a new priestess greeted me within seconds, realized who and what I was, and carried out the requisite bowing and scraping that one apparently *must* do when one meets one's God. Only when that was done did I proceed to scarf down whatever food they could offer me before resting for a couple hours.

I could feel myself wearing down. Even with the brief breaks, each succeeding jump was harder. I made a deal with myself that after five jumps—five hundred years—I would give myself a full day of rest.

After the fourth jump, I landed in the 1600s, nearing the end of Egypt's Middle Kingdom, with a dull headache. I was hyper-aware of the persistent throb at the base of my skull, at the slight ache in my joints. I told myself it was just the temporal jumps wearing me down—nothing a good long rest wouldn't fix.

But after I rested, the headache was worse. The achy joints were worse. I couldn't ignore the truth. Bonding withdrawals had begun.

This changed things. I no longer had weeks to get home. I barely had days, if my last bout with the withdrawals was any indication. I settled on shorter resting periods—fifteen or twenty minutes, a half hour at most—with maybe one or two longer periods of a couple hours. Full days were out of the question.

After my fifth jump forward in time, I landed in the temple's dark inner sanctuary smack-dab in the middle of ancient Egypt's golden age, the New Kingdom. If my jumps had been even remotely accurate, Hatshepsut was the current pharaoh, one of the few women to have ever claimed that title.

I knelt on the temple's stone floor, head hanging. I was dead tired. One of those longer, day-long breaks sounded pretty damn tempting. It didn't matter that it was also pretty damn impossible. The withdrawal symptoms were noticeably worse. Not debilitating, but definitely worse.

At the sound of footsteps, I craned my neck to see the doorway.

A man stepped up onto the ramp leading to the inner sanctuary, not quite what I was expecting—certainly not a priestess. He was slim and bare-chested, wearing a white linen kilt that nearly reached his ankles. His head was shaved, and his bare face was unfamiliar save for one distinctive element—its unquestionable, ageless perfection. He was Nejeret.

He stopped halfway up the ramp and looked from me to the doorway, then glanced over his shoulder, his expression utterly bewildered. Looking at me once more, he said something, but I didn't understand New Egyptian, at least not the spoken variety.

"Who are you?" I asked in the original tongue, narrowing my eyes. "What are you doing here?"

The Nejeret's eyebrows rose. "I would ask you the same," he said.

I stood and took a step toward the doorway, but my knees buckled. I stumbled forward, catching myself with a hand on the plaster wall.

The Nejeret rushed forward, reaching for my elbow. "Are you unwell?"

I pulled my elbow out of his grip and took a sideways step along the wall to put some distance between us. "Who are you, and what are you doing in my temple?"

His eyebrows rose once more, and a moment later, his lips spread into a broad grin. "You are Hat-hur? One-time wife to the Great Father?"

I eyed him warily. Nobody should have remembered that, nobody except for my priestesses, Aset, and Nik. "Who are you?" I repeated.

The man's smile faltered, giving way to a look of wide-eyed awe. He touched the fingertips of one hand to his chest and bowed his head. "I am Senenmut, head scribe to Heru, leader of the Council of Seven, sent here by Heru himself to record the accounts of, well, *you* from the temple walls."

My eyes widened. "You—you're Senenmut?" I was as surprised to find him here as he was to find me. I'd seen him once before, in the At, but only for a few seconds before Apep-Set appeared and imprisoned my ba.

"Indeed." Senenmut nodded, then raised his head, his eyes meeting mine. "Is the mythical Hat-hur familiar with my name?"

I nodded once, slowly. "I am familiar with you, yes."

Senenmut was the man who'd engraved the two tablets that originally set me on this course—one containing directions to the hidden, underground temple where our people's greatest artifact, the ankh-At, had been stored, the other inscribed with Nuin's final words. With his last prophecy. It had always been a mystery as to how Senenmut had discovered the forgotten prophecy. Now, it was starting to make sense.

Senenmut was able to inscribe the forgotten prophecy onto that tablet because *I* told him the prophecy. Because, at this moment, I was the only living person who remembered it. Once again, threads I'd believed tied in a chaotic jumble revealed themselves to be woven into a beautiful, intricate pattern—one only had to view it from just the right angle.

I rested my forehead against the plaster wall. In a bit . . . I could think more about the mysteries of time travel in a little bit. Right now, I needed food and rest. "Have you seen any of the priestesses?"

Senenmut entered the inner sanctuary, reaching out tentatively in case I pulled away again. I didn't. His grip on my elbow was sure but not overly tight, and I let him guide me out through the doorway. "Come, Golden One, who consumes praise, who desires dancing, who shines on the festival, who is pleased to dance all through the night . . ."

His words tickled something on the edge of my memory. There was a sense of familiarity in the recited verse.

"Your priestesses are busy with festival preparations." He smiled, a little shyly. "It is good timing on your part, for there is much to eat . . . and, appropriately, most is meant as an offering to you."

I looked at him, the verse clicking. "The festival of drunkenness?"

"The very one."

I frowned. What I would've given to be able to witness one of the ancient Egyptians' most famous religious events. The festival of drunkenness was said to be a purely spiritual time when the ancient peoples would gather at the temples—especially the Hathor temples—and drink until they passed out in the hopes of inducing a divine epiphany. Orgies were said to be involved as well. But I wouldn't be confirming that tidbit, not today.

"I cannot stay," I said regretfully, the archaeologist in me dying, just a little, as the mother in me beat her into submission. "But I would have you sit with me while I rest. There is something I must tell you, Senenmut . . . something you must record."

45

NOW & NEVER

"Oh, God," I breathed, stumbling into the back wall of the inner sanctuary. The stone beneath the plaster was warmer than the air, so I figured it was early in the night, the stone still retaining some of the day's heat. Legs trembling, I turned around so my back was against the wall and sank down to the floor.

I'd made ten more century-long jumps over what I estimated was about a day. I was exhausted, and my head pounded. The bonding withdrawals were worsening, right on schedule.

I wrapped my arms around my knees, hugging them to my chest as I battled tears. Defeat stalked me, but I wasn't giving up. I was just overwhelmed.

"Hello?" The voice was female and pleasant, and she spoke in the original tongue. The more snippets of time I spent in this temple, the more I suspected speaking in Nuin's ancient language had gone from tradition to flat-out rule. My intermittent appearances necessitated it, and I'd never appreciated the ability to communicate thoroughly and completely more.

"I am here," I called softly. "In the sanctuary."

A girl appeared in the doorway, little more than a shadow

while my eyes adjusted to the darkness. She wore the usual simple white linen shift that denoted her as a priestess of this temple, but she was the youngest I'd yet to encounter. She couldn't have been more than twelve or thirteen years old.

"N—nobody was in here a moment ago," she said, voice shaky. "I checked."

"Oh?"

"Which means you—you must be *her* . . . the Golden One."

Here we go again . . .

I nodded but realized a moment later that she probably couldn't see the movement. "I am Hat-hur." Twisting, I placed my palm against the plaster wall behind me and dragged myself up to my feet. "I need food and a bed—just for a few hours. Can you arrange that?"

She was quiet, staring at me with huge, shadowed eyes.

I sighed and pushed my hair out of my face, combing my fingers through the slightly greasy strands. "Or can you take me to someone else who can?"

The girl nodded, backing up a step when I moved forward. "Denai—" She took a few more backward steps as I approached the doorway. "She is just this way," the girl said, turning and running down the ramp. When she paused to look back at me and found me slowly hobbling after her, she stopped to wait. "Denai is the head priestess. She says I will take her place one day, and her name. She says that it is my destiny."

"Really?" I focused on putting one foot in front of the other. The ramp was mud brick and had devious little cracks and divots.

"She says I have been chosen by the gods. On my twenty-third name day, I will begin to manifest into a Netjer-At."

My steps faltered, and the young priestess rushed forward to catch me by my elbow.

"The nameless goddess stowed my mother away here when she was pregnant so the other Netjer-Ats would not know about me." Side by side, we settled into a slow, creeping pace. "She knew my mother would not survive my birth and told Denai to raise me to be strong in my mother's stead, like our goddess Hat—" The girl hesitated. "Well, like *you*."

"Did she truly?" I stifled a smile. Aset, you flatterer.

The girl nodded. "But sometimes I fear that *they* will find me, and—" She took a deep breath. "I fear they will hurt me," she said in a quieter voice. "Sometimes I think that something must be wrong with me. Why else would the nameless goddess have hidden me away here?"

We passed through a side doorway in the outer sanctuary and entered a dark, colonnaded hall. I'd been here so many times before, walked between these columns with so many different priestesses on my way to the living quarters. But this time felt different. It felt significant. This *girl* was important, and I needed to figure out why.

"Tell me," I said, "what is your name?"

"Me? Oh, I am called Aramei," the girl-priestess said. It was totally unhelpful; hers was a name I'd never heard before in reference to any Nejerette.

"Hmmm . . ." I frowned. "Did the 'nameless goddess' tell Denai anything else?"

"Just that she will be watching over me and—" Again, the young priestess and future Nejerette hesitated.

"And what?"

"It is the most serious of secrets." And it was clear that she was dying to share it with someone—anyone. I feared she'd choose the wrong person. Any person would be the wrong person if there was any chance that the secret would be captured in the At. But *I* didn't exist in the At . . . not yet, at least.

"I will not tell a soul," I said, crossing my heart with my index finger. "Besides, what could it hurt? In a few hours, I shall be one hundred years in the future . . ."

Aramei pursed her lips, like that act alone might hold the secret in. It didn't. The secret tumbled out in a rushed whisper. "The nameless goddess is my grandmother."

I stumbled over nothing but sheer shock. This girl—this Aramei—was Aset's granddaughter? That would mean she was Nik's daughter. What did that make her? Would she be a regular Nejerette? Would she be like Nik, with a sheut? Or would she be *more*, like my lost twins?

"Are you alright?" Aramei tightened her hold on my arm.

"Yes, yes," I said, patting her hand. "Exhausted and famished, but well enough. I must say, Aramei, that is quite the secret." For millennia, the Council monitored the At in search of those they considered "abominations"—any Nejerets born of two Nejeret parents, like Nik. Long ago, Nuin set several unbreakable laws in place, the prohibition of such abominations chief among them. It was the reason the Kin had lived in secrecy for centuries, since their inception by Mei.

I considered holding my tongue, but didn't. I couldn't *not* warn this girl. "And I agree with A—the nameless goddess. You must not tell anyone else your secret. You must *never* tell anyone else. Not ever."

"ARAMEI?" IT WAS THE FIRST THING I SAID UPON landing after my next hundred-year jump. It was still the Late Period in Egypt, and I was still in the inner sanctuary of the Hathor temple. After my next jump, I would be entering Ptolemaic Egypt, when the Greeks ruled over ancient Kemet. I wasn't sure what, exactly, that would mean for the running of the temple.

"Aramei? Are you here?" I leaned against the frame of the doorway, staring out at the empty outer sanctuary. There were fewer offerings than usual scattered around the edges of the room and a general sense of abandonment about the place.

I heard the clack of hard wood against stone accompanied by the shuffle of footsteps. It was coming from the side doorway that led to the living quarters.

An elderly priestess appeared in the doorway, gray hair arranged in elaborate plaits and white linen shift baggy on her skinny, slightly hunched frame. She leaned heavily on a hooked, gold-plated walking stick.

"It has been ages since last I heard that name," she said, voice raspy. "Are you she, then?"

"I am Hat-hur."

"We have been expecting you."

My eyebrows rose. "You have?"

The old priestess gave a single nod. "We keep records of when you visit. According to the stars, it has been time for a while now." Cane arm shaking, she held out her free hand toward the doorway behind her. "Come, there is food prepared and a bed made up for you."

I descended the ramp, head pounding but body slightly less exhausted than last time. I'd allowed myself a four-hour rest, a luxury I could hardly afford. This time would have to be briefer —one hour at most.

"And what of Aramei?" I asked the old woman as I approached. "Is she not the head priestess?"

She shook her head. "Aramei was head priestess when I first joined the order. She took over the running of this temple shortly after your last visit. She was a great woman—she took me in as a small child, called me daughter and groomed me to succeed her since she, herself, was barren. I had not yet bled for the first time when she disappeared, leaving a child in charge of the most important temple in the history of mankind." There was bitterness in her voice.

I stopped before the elderly priestess. "Have you any idea what happened to her?"

She shook her head. "Only that she abandoned me . . . abandoned us."

"And the nameless goddess—what does she say of Aramei's disappearance?"

"She did not know. She claimed she could no longer sense Aramei, that she had ceased to be and therefore must be dead, but—"

"But what?"

The old priestess focused on my face with rheumy eyes. "I saw her once, years after she disappeared. I woke in the middle of the night to find her sitting at the foot of my bed. She smiled at me and told me—" Her voice caught. "She told me she was proud of me—so proud. And then I blinked, and she was gone."

I frowned, brow furrowed. "Might it have been a dream?"

"Perhaps," the old priestess said, wiping her free hand over her wrinkled cheek. "But it did not have the feel of a dream." She coughed a laugh, a rattling, phlegmy sound. "Oh, but listen to me going on about the long-dead past. Come, eat and rest." She ushered me through the doorway into the colonnaded hall. "My bones are tired and my journey is nearly at an end. But yours, I gather, is far from over."

I LEFT MY PURSE OF GOLD WITH THE ELDERLY priestess, hoping it might help the temple navigate what I suspected were difficult times, then made the next seven jumps in quick succession. The rapidly worsening bonding withdrawals urged me onward despite my mounting exhaustion. I could feel my sheut's power draining even as I felt time slipping away. How much longer did I have left until the withdrawals incapacitated me? A day? Less?

I allowed myself a luxurious hour-and-a-half nap in the fourth century CE but stuck to strict half-hour rests between my next five jumps. I barely made the last one, blacking out upon entry into ninth-century Egypt.

I woke in a bed, head resting on a flat pillow and room flooded with golden light streaking in through the openings near the top of one wall. I was in the temple living quarters, and I had no idea how long I'd been there. My only point of reference was the splitting headache. It was hours worse. But how many? How much time had I lost to sleep?

It didn't matter. Only one thing did—I was still alive. The bonding withdrawals hadn't killed me yet, which meant I still had a chance to get home to my babies. To Marcus.

I sat up, a single truth becoming abundantly clear. Next time would be worse. Next time the exhaustion might knock me out until the withdrawals *did* kill me. Which meant my next jump had to be the final jump.

I turned, dangling my legs over the side of the bed and stretching in a vain attempt to alleviate the throbbing ache in my joints. I stood and hobbled over to the small table that had been set up with fruits, breads, and cheeses and alternated between shoving food into my mouth and getting myself ready for the next jump. The final jump.

I was just buckling my sword harness when a young woman in the usual white linen priestess shift entered the room. "You are awake," she said.

I glanced up, then continued adjusting the leather straps into a comfortable position. "I am."

"And—you are leaving?"

"I am." Finished with the buckle, I took a deep breath and looked at the priestess. "I will not return for hundreds of years. The nameless goddess will guide you when the time comes. You will tell your sisters this?"

She nodded.

"Good. And tell them thank you," I added. "For everything." I dropped to one knee, placed my hand on the floor, and bowed my head, willing the power within my sheut to well one last time. I'd been limiting myself to hundred-year jumps; I had no idea how far my reach truly was. Hopefully far enough. The power within me became a tumbling snowball, something too great and powerful to stop. My jump was imminent, my children and Marcus and *home* preeminent in my mind.

"Lex! Wait!"

I looked up just in time to see the most unlikely of faces behind the priestess—Aramei, full Nejerette now, but easily recognizable. She pushed the priestess out of the way and lunged across the room toward me. But she was too late.

I was already gone.

46

ALMOST & THERE

Sometimes when I'm falling asleep, I jerk awake, certain I've fallen out of my bed. It's one of the most disorienting sensations, especially when I wake to find that I'm still safe and snug in my bed. I know it's not unique to me, and I suppose it might even be the reason we say "falling asleep." Who knows . . .

But I woke like that, in some unknown time and place. I jerked upright, slimy muck beneath me and a brilliant sun shining in the clear blue sky overhead. I squinted against the glare, groaning at the brain-shattering pounding in my head that resulted from opening my eyes. My stomach lurched at the onslaught of pain, and I leaned to the side, hands against a grassy slope, and vomited.

"Ugh . . ." I wiped the back of one hand over my mouth. Dizzy and aching, I forced myself to look first to the left, then to right. The world tilted this way and that, totally unpredictably, but I was coherent enough to tell that I was beside a paved road that curved around a hillside . . . and that I was in a ditch. I had, quite literally, passed out in a ditch somewhere.

"What would you think of me now, Mom?" I wondered aloud, my voice tight with pain.

It took my withdrawal-rattled brain seconds to catch up to the enormity of being in a ditch beside a paved road. People didn't start paving roads like this until the eighteenth or nineteenth centuries. Which meant I was home, or damn near close to it.

An engine rumbled, but my view of the vehicle was obscured by the grassy hillside. I watched it round the corner, raising my hand to block the sun. My eyes were having a hard time focusing on anything beyond a few yards away, but my heart beat merrily in my chest and relief flooded my body. I was *home*. My children . . . Marcus . . . they were so close.

The car came to a skidding halt a short way past me, and I was finally able to focus on it. My excitement evaporated. The vehicle looked more like a horseless carriage than any kind of car I was used to. It was old—like, Model T old—and even more disconcerting, it looked brand-new. Either the driver was coming from an antique car show, or . . .

"Lass?" The driver left his car door open and approached me cautiously. "Are you alright, lass?" He was Scottish, male, and dressed in a brown tweed suit, but I couldn't tell more than that. Just like the car, I was having a hard time focusing on him as he moved closer. "Lass?"

"I—I am fine," I said, stumbling over the English words. It had been so long since I used them. "I'll be fine."

The man crouched at the edge of the road, elbows on his knees. "Might there be somewhere I can drop you off?"

"Where am I?" I asked. "What year is it?" I needed to find Marcus. It was the only way to alleviate the pain, and doing that was quickly becoming all I could think about.

"You're in Scone . . . in Scotland," the man said with a frown. "And the year is 1909. Please, lass, where can I take you? Surely you've got people wondering where you've gone."

There were people waiting for me, likely wondering where I'd gone and if I would ever make it home, but I couldn't get to them, not in my current state. The bonding withdrawals were so bad I wasn't even confident I would be able to stand. Jumping forward one last time was out of the question . . . unless I could find my bond-mate and absorb some of his pheromones . . .

I racked my addled brain for any information I'd tucked away about Marcus during this time period. He'd lived in Scotland with the majority of his line, having established Clan Heru what must have been shortly after I left him here in the tenth century. He'd returned throughout the years, as his lack of aging necessitated both reclusiveness and relocation every few decades, and he'd spent the first third of the twentieth century with his clan here in Scone. I might not have made it all the way home, but I'd made it to him. Close enough for now.

"Clan Heru," I said slowly. "The castle is nearby."

"Aye," the man said. "I know well enough the location of Castle Uaireigin." He squinted down at me. "Are you one of them, then? 'Tis hard enough to tell through the mud."

I wasn't sure if he was asking if I was Nejeret or if I was a member of Clan Heru. I wasn't sure it mattered. "Please, sir, I was out walking and must have hit my head. If you could just bring me to the castle, or near to the castle, I can manage the rest."

"Aye, I'll bring you to the gate of Castle Uaireigin, but the rest is up to you." He extended his hand down to me. "I'd prefer to remain a stranger to Clan Heru."

I nodded, accepting his hand and relying heavily on his strength to hoist me up and out of the ditch. Once I was standing, he released my hand and gave me a quick once-over. "Felt the need to go for a walk in your dressing gown, did you, lass?"

"I—" Swaying a little, I wrapped my arms around the front of my body, doing what I could to cover my chest. The linen shift wasn't transparent, but it wasn't substantial enough to hide everything. "I am not sure . . ."

The driver's expression darkened. "Perhaps more has befallen you than a mere bump on the head . . ."

It took me a moment to capture his meaning. Finally, I shook my head. "I do not know, sir," I said lamely.

He studied my face for a moment, and when he spoke, I had the feeling he'd been considering saying something else entirely. "Come along, lass." He held his arm out to the car maybe a dozen yards away. I stumbled, but he caught my arm. "Careful . . ."

"Thanks," I said breathily.

"Please do not think me rude for not introducing myself or inquiring about your name," he said as he situated me in the front passenger seat. "With Clan Heru, well . . . it's just safer this way."

"It's fine." I offered him as much of a smile as I could manage. It was a valiant attempt with pathetic results. "I prefer anonymity as well."

"Lovely." He settled in the driver's seat. "Shall we be off, then?"

I nodded, head spinning and feeling like it was about to explode. I couldn't get to Castle Uaireigin—to Marcus—fast enough.

LEANING AGAINST THE STONE WALL BESIDE THE TALL iron gate blocking off the driveway to Castle Uaireigin, I watched my knight in a shining automobile drive away. The car was out of sight, hidden by bends in the road and tall, leafy trees, far before the sound faded.

"Lex." The voice was husky and almost familiar. I spun around, lightheaded and world lurching, and found I recognized the woman standing a dozen feet away. Or rather, the Nejerette.

"Aramei?" I held onto one of the gate's iron bars with a death grip. It was either that or fall down. Aramei was older now, just as I'd seen her during the brief glimpse this last time in the Hathor temple. She was about my height and lanky, much like her father, and her dark hair was pulled back into a sporty ponytail. She was wearing boot-cut jeans and a fitted, button-down plaid shirt—not really era-appropriate attire.

She nodded once. "But please, call me Mei."

I blinked, dumbfounded. "I guess that explains why you're dressed like that," I said. My own dress was out of date, but from the other end. "How—" I started to ask, but stopped myself. She was a time traveler . . . and the leader of the Kin. She was also supposedly Nik's daughter—Aset's granddaughter. And she was dead, in my time. But I couldn't tell her that. I settled on asking, "Why are you here?"

"To stop you." Mei's smile was kind, almost sad. "You can't do this, Lex. If you go in there and find Heru, you'll change everything. You'll *ruin* everything we both worked so hard for."

My head pounded, and all I could think about was getting closer to Marcus. The pain was all-encompassing, driving logic from my brain. "But the withdrawals . . . I'm dying . . ."

Mei took a step toward me. "As you are now, yes, you're dying. But that won't change by seeing him. You'll only delay the inevitable. You'll still die—a slow unraveling of your threads in the timeline—and then you'll cease to be. Your children will *cease to be*."

"My children . . ." I leaned my head against the gate, the smell of the iron filling my nostrils. "I'm so tired, and I hurt so much."

Mei touched my arm. "I know."

"How did you find me?"

"I felt the ripples of what you were about to do. Desperation can drive us to distraction, and I fear that is what it is doing to you."

"So what, I should just lie down and die?" I laughed bitterly. "After everything?"

I knew she was right, that I couldn't go see Marcus, that I couldn't go be near him and absorb however much of his bonding pheromone I needed to regain my strength so I could make this final jump home. Marcus would remember me; it would change the timeline from this point forward. I knew she was right, somewhere deep within the far recesses of my brain, in the logical, reasonable areas that had been locked away, imprisoned by the pain. By the desperation.

"You could," Mei said. "You could die, here and now, and it wouldn't matter. Universal balance would remain restored, thanks to the continued existence of your children." She gave my arm a squeeze. "But you saved my life once, a very long time ago. I didn't understand it until I was older and learned of what I could do—of what it truly meant to be a Nejerette out of time—but you saved my life that day you visited the temple. You appeared out of nowhere, a true goddess to my child's brain, and scared me into keeping my promise. I never told another soul about my lineage . . . I never spoke of it aloud again. There was no way for anyone to know that I was like my father. My silence was the only reason I survived.

"You *could* die here." She rested the side of her head against the gate, mirroring me, and smiled. "But you don't have to—not here, maybe not at all. I can jump through time with you. I can take you home. Your children are waiting for you."

I watched dark spots move in all around me, giving me tunnel vision until all I could see was Mei's smooth Nejerette features. *My children* . . . Deep in the far recesses of my mind, from that prison cell of pain, a coherent thought swam free. "Do it."

PART IV - TEMPUS FUGIT

KAT & LEX

47

KAT

"Hey." It was Mari. She was behind me, further up the beach.

I closed my eyes and tilted my head back, asking the spirit of the Puget Sound—of the seagull standing sentinel nearby, of the ebbing and flowing saltwater, of the seals barking some ways down the beach—to lend me even a shred of patience.

It wasn't that I disliked Mari; on the contrary, we clicked. She was on the younger side, less than a century old, and in pretty much any other situation, I thought we'd be good friends. But in *this* situation, being friends with her only set me further apart from the rest of the Nejerets. I'd been born one of a kind, the daughter of incest—a most grievous crime amongst Nejeretkind—and I'd only escalated my differences further when I'd forced my Nejeret traits to manifest by going into the At a couple years too early. Grievous Nejeret crime number two.

Now, thanks to Mari and her anti-At dagger, my ba was completely cut off from the At. Even with the twins' existence returning ma'at to the universe and stability to the At once more, I would never again enter it. I would never see the vibrant colors of time and space swirling all around me. I would never watch scenes from the past or from the possible futures play out right before my eyes. I would never, not ever, be a normal Nejerette.

I already felt like I didn't belong, and spending time with Mari, the emissary of the Kin, turned me into a full-blown outcast.

"What are you doing?" Mari sat down beside me on the piece of driftwood. "I hope I'm not interrupting . . ."

"It's fine." I set my pen in the seam of my sketchbook and flipped the cover closed. "I was just drawing."

"Oh? Can I see? I'm a terrible artist . . ."

Shrugging, I handed her the sketchbook. "The stuff you make out of anti-At is pretty good." Aside from the part where touching anything she made would kill a Nejeret from the soul out.

"That doesn't count," she said. "It's easy to make something pretty when you can just think it into existence."

She opened the sketchbook's cover but didn't immediately go to the page I'd been working on, marked by my pen. She started at the beginning, flipping through pages of ink and pencil drawings, pausing whenever she reached the ones splattered with color from oil pastels or chalk. "These are really good." She paused on a collage of hands sketched in ink. "Whose hands are these?"

"No one's." I reached out and flipped to the page I'd been working on a moment ago. "This one's supposed to be the At," I said, tapping the half-finished sketch with a fingernail. "I want to get it right before I forget what it was like."

Mari closed the sketchbook ever so gingerly and handed it back to me. "Oh."

And now I'd upset her. It was her fault that I was like this, but it was also my fault—for being a rash idiot—and I knew she regretted having permanently damaged my ba. She felt bad, and now I felt bad for making her feel bad. It was stupid.

"So, um . . ." I searched the gray-blue water for something, *anything* to change the subject. I blurted the first thing that came to mind. "Do you know how to fight?"

Mari shot me a sidelong glance. "A bit. My mom wanted me to know how to defend myself. She said that in a group of people where everybody has exceptional powers, it often comes down to the most mundane skills to set us apart." She laughed to herself. "There was a girl who used to hold classes for those of us who wanted to learn. So, thanks to her, I know just enough to be more of a danger to myself than to anybody else."

"Do you maybe want to spar sometime?"

Mari met my eyes for a moment, then returned to staring out at the sea. "Yeah, okay." She nodded. "I'd like that."

"Cool. Um . . ."

My phone buzzed, and I fished it out of my back pocket. It was one o'clock, time for the Council to reconvene. Which is why I wasn't surprised to find a text from Dom, reminding me not to be late for babysitting duties. It was my turn to watch the twins while Marcus locked himself away in the conference room with Mari, Nik, Set, and the remotely present Council members to continue their never-ending discussion of the rogues, the Kin, and the future of Nejeret society.

"I gotta get back to the house," I told Mari, and she nodded. She needed to head there soon, too.

I tapped out a quick text to Dom letting him know I was on my way, then shoved my sketchbook and pen back into my bag and settled the strap on my shoulder. Fifteen minutes later I was sitting in an armchair in Marcus's suite, Susie, Lex and Marcus's daughter, nestled in my arms and a bottle in one of my hands.

It had taken weeks for Marcus to choose names for the twins —we'd just called them BG and BB for baby girl and baby boy until he'd come to a decision—but when he finally did, we all felt his choice in names was absolutely perfect. BG became Susan, or Susie to most of us, named after Lex's recently departed grandmother, and BB became Syris, named for Marcus and Aset's father, Osiris. They were good names, strong names, with memorable and significant namesakes.

"Are you ready for it, little missy?" I waggled the bottle a few inches from Susie's face. "I think this might be the best, yummiest bottle yet . . ."

Nearby, Marcus made a slow circuit around the sitting room, Syris snuggled against his chest. The infant boy hated sleeping; he would fight it with all his might, but once he was asleep, he was out. Marcus had a knack for being able to coax his son to sleep, and I was grateful he was taking the time to do it before he left for the meeting, because baby-charming was a gift I didn't have.

We both looked to the door when it opened. Aset entered the room, expression grim.

Little Tarset was holding Aset's hand, her cheeks pink and onyx pigtails askew. The ancient four-year-old broke free and ran straight for me. "Baby!" She was obsessed with the twins.

Marcus headed for his sister. "Take Syris for me. The others are waiting on me."

Aset crossed her arms over her chest and raised her eyebrows. "I'm older than you."

As Tarset climbed onto the sofa beside me, I looked at Marcus, then Aset, then back at Marcus. Something was happening. Something big and important and really damn tense. The kind of thing that made me want to be anywhere but here.

"What's this about?" Marcus resumed his slow pacing, snuggling the baby boy close but never taking his eyes off his sister's face.

"You are their father," Aset said. "And yet you put the Council first. Your children are more important than the Kin or the rogues or any other Council matter. Syris and Susie are the most important things in the entire world, but you can't seem to carve more than a few minutes of each day out for them.

Why, Heru?" She planted herself directly in front of him. "Why?"

Marcus inhaled and exhaled deeply. "When the deliberations are over . . ."

"The deliberations can go to hell for all I care," Aset said. "Syris and Susie need you *now*."

Marcus's features hardened right before my eyes. I held my breath, hoping my silence would make me disappear.

"Lex needed them." Marcus's words were clear, quiet, careful. Cold. "She needed them, and they abandoned her. If they'd never been born—"

"Bite your tongue," Aset snapped. "They didn't leave her out of choice. It was just something that happened . . . a reflex. Lex told me so herself."

"But will she ever tell *me*?" Marcus asked, his features softening and his golden eyes shimmering with grief. "Will she ever say anything to me again? Will I ever see her again?"

"Oh, dear brother . . ." Aset sighed and held out her arms for the baby. "She has the ability and the will to make it back to us. We must have faith in her."

Gently, Marcus transferred his son into Aset's arms. "Once the Council has come to a decision on this matter with Mari and the Kin, I'll step down and you can take my seat." He stared down at his fussing little boy. "For Lex."

Aset nodded. "For Lex."

I MOVED SMOOTHLY FROM ONE POSITION TO THE next, sometimes slow, sometimes fast, sometimes blowing out my breath or even grunting, always concentrating with every fiber of my being. Going through Dom's sets was better for calmness and clarity than meditation. It was impossible to think about anything but what my arms and legs would do next. The poses were becoming second nature, but even so, moving through them required absolute focus. It was, hands down, my favorite thing to do. The sound of the waves rolling up and down the beach only added to my tranquility.

Aset had released me from babysitting duty after a couple hours, and this was my second round of the day. I'd fallen into the habit of running through the sets first thing in the morning and last thing at night. It was late afternoon, so today was turning out to be a three-a-dayer. It happened more often than I'd ever admit, but Dom only frowned when he found me running through the sets in the training room or out on the beach in the afternoon; he never advised me to stop.

At the sound of footsteps on the rocky beach, I spun around, settling instinctively into a defensive position.

"Kat!" Mari hopped over a long piece of driftwood on her way down the beach. "You won't believe what just happened!" Before I could even think about guessing what she was so excited about, she blurted, "I did it! The Council finally agreed —the Kin don't have to hide anymore."

I relaxed my stance, a smile taking over my face. I couldn't have stopped it if I'd wanted to. "Dude, that's awesome!" I took three enormous steps and threw my arms around her. "I'm so happy for you! What does this mean? Can you go home?"

Mari stiffened, and a second later, her arms fell away from me. "I have no home."

"Don't be stupid." I took a small step backward and shook her by the arms. "You know what I mean . . . will you be able to go back to your people? I know how much you miss them."

Mari shook her head, her green eyes gleaming like sea glass. "The rogues are still out there, hunting us . . . hunting *me*. My people have been lying low, staying off the Internet and phone lines as much as possible, but I've received messages—several have disappeared. I can only assume the worst."

"Well, did the Council agree to anything else? Are they going to help you with the rogues?" I rolled my eyes. "Are they going to finally get off their asses and *do* something?"

Mari let out a single, bitter laugh. "So they say . . . but only because some of their people have gone missing, too. It's the reason they agreed to stay our impending executions in the first place." Her lips spread into a flat, grim mockery of a smile. "They finally realized that they need the Kin just as much as we need them."

My hands fell away. "What does that mean? What did they agree to?"

"The Kin has been granted a single seat at the Council." She shrugged and turned to stare out at the Puget Sound. "Once the rogue threat is taken care of, they've agreed to reassess the structure of the Nejeret governing body."

My eyebrows climbed up my forehead, and my mouth fell open. "Are you serious? That's huge."

One corner of Mari's grim smile curved upwards, turning it into more of a smirk. "Maybe they need us more than we need them," she said, pride shining in her eyes. "This is the first step toward the future my mom saw. I didn't believe it was possible for us to work together, but . . ."

I touched her shoulder. "Maybe this is the first step toward eliminating things like *us* and *them*," I said.

"Maybe, but—" She cocked her head to the side, then looked over her shoulder.

I glanced the same way, my stare sticking on Nik—he stalked down the trail through the woods toward the beach. Toward us. "You shouldn't be here," he practically growled.

So it wasn't Nik, but Re; I hadn't seen either for a couple days. His arms were covered in zebra stripes of cuts in various stages of healing—likely Nik's attempt to continue to keep Re subdued. *Failed* attempt, it seemed.

His lips retracted, baring his teeth in an open snarl. "You

shouldn't be here," he repeated, lips barely moving and teeth locked together.

My heart was pounding, but I managed to keep my breathing even. My body shifted, one of my feet sliding backward on the rocks, just an inch or two, my arms relaxing at my side. It was a casual defensive position, allowing me to be ready for a hundred types of attacks. "There's plenty of beach to share," I said, impressed by how even and calm my voice sounded. Inside me, there was terrified little girl begging me to turn and run as fast and far as I could.

Re-Nik reached the mouth of the trail and stepped onto the beach, just the driftwood and several yards separating us now. "You were supposed to die," he said. "Dom was supposed to kill Mari. The Council was supposed to launch an attack on the Kin living in squalor." In the blink of an eye, two daggers made of crystalline At formed in either of his hands. "But none of that happened, because Nik has feelings for you. Because he wouldn't let you die."

Mari stepped in front of me. "Stop," she commanded, a black spear suddenly in her grasp, pointed at Re-Nik. It was a good thing she stepped in, because I was currently paralyzed and speechless.

Mari stepped forward, the spear growing until the point almost touched him, just under his chin. "I don't have to stab you. I don't even have to break your skin. All I have to do is touch you with this and everything that you are, were, or might be will disappear. It'll destroy Nik's ba—I don't know what it'll do to your ren." She rolled her shoulder. "Want to find out?"

Re's daggers disappeared into wispy, rainbow smoke. Slowly, he raised Nik's hands in surrender.

"Hands down," Mari said. "Turn around, and don't bother trying to hide behind your precious At. I'll just surround it with anti-At, and then you'll be stuck for good." She inched her spear closer to him, and he leaned back. "You're going to see the Council."

Pale blue bled back into Nik's irises, and he nodded. "He's gone . . . retreated to the At for safety. I'll go with you." He turned away from us. "No struggle, I swear."

We trudged back to the main house in relative silence, Nik in the lead, Mari following close behind him, her anti-At spear at the ready, and me bringing up the rear.

"Marcus!" I called out as soon as we were through the front door. "Something's wrong with Re!"

"There's nothing wrong with me, child."

I sucked in a breath. So Re was back. Peachy.

"But you—you are a virus, eroding more and more of reality with every breath you take." Re-Nik turned his head, letting me see his profile. "You were a sacrifice. Why couldn't you just die?" He faced ahead once more.

I stood in the doorway, mouth hanging open and eyes stinging.

Marcus appeared at the top of the stairs, hands on his hips. "Explain. Now."

"It's Re," I told him. "He's lost his mind. He just tried to kill me."

Marcus's focus shifted to Re-Nik, though his expression remained the same—very much *not* amused.

Re-Nik bowed his head. "It's true—he won't shut up about it."

And just like that, Nik was in control . . . for the moment.

"He's snapped," Nik said. "He won't stop raving—everything with Mari and the Council deliberations over the Kin—none of it would have happened if Kat had died that day. The rogues and Kin would still be focusing on one another, and their feud would eventually wipe out both groups. He thinks—" Nik shuddered. "He thinks he can right things by killing her, even now. He sees her as an aberration, this person who not only doesn't show up in the At anymore, but whose continued existence drives reality further and further from what's reflected there."

"But killing her now wouldn't change anything," Mari said, spear still held strong. "The Council's decision has already been made; there's already an agreement."

Nik balled his hands into fists at his sides. "Trust me, he's not listening to reason anymore." Nik raised his head, looking at Marcus. "If Mari hadn't been there when we came after Kat . . ." Another shudder racked his body. "He's fighting me. I don't have much time, but I think what happened to Apep after Re split his sheut from the rest of him is happening to Re now. His sanity is slipping; his logic is warped."

"Can you control him?" Marcus asked. "Is there a way for you to keep him locked away within you?" The two men stared at one another, Marcus looking down on his nephew, on his creator.

Nik's gaze slid over to me, and my heartbeat stumbled over itself. After a long moment, he nodded. "He'll never try anything like this again, I swear it."

"Very well." Marcus stepped to the side, welcoming Nik up the stairs.

Nik ascended, and Mari and I followed. I'd just entered the conference-room-turned-council-chambers when there was a flash of rainbow smoke, and two figures appeared.

"I have returned to you the Meswett, Alexandra Larson," one said—a woman. She was holding up her companion, who *could* have been Lex, but limp and head drooping like that, it was hard to tell. "Her sheut is badly damaged, and she is near death. I have been to the future. I know the one and only way to save her. Grant me amnesty and I'll tell you."

"Granted," Marcus said, pushing up from his seat so hard and quickly that the chair slammed against the wall behind him, making the mounted monitors tremble. He hurried around the table, reaching the pair while I was still struggling to process what was going on.

"Mom?" Mari said.

I looked at her, then back at the pair.

So much happened all at once. I didn't know what to do, so I just scooted out of the way and pressed my back against the wall. Mari joined me.

Marcus helped Mei ease Lex down to the floor.

"You," Mei said, pointing to Nik. "Come. You must turn her into At for the time being. It will be years until we have the means to save her."

I looked at Nik. He stood behind a chair on the opposite side of the table from me, utterly immobile. His eyes were locked open and focused on Lex, but the irises were flickering, pale blue one second, opalescent white the next.

"Nik!" I shouted. "Help her!"

He looked at me with those disturbing, flickering eyes, and I sucked in a breath. It was wrong, whatever was going on inside him. So very wrong.

Mei's calm, collected countenance broke. "Father! Please . . ."

And then he blinked, and it stopped. His irises settled, one blue, one white. He stood taller, his head held high. "We will do this thing you ask of us, Daughter." He didn't sound like Nik *or* Re, but some eerie combination of the two. "It will be a fitting final act . . ."

I didn't have the time or wherewithal to consider his—their—words. I just stared at Lex, now lying stretched out on the floor, unconscious or . . . or worse. Mei had backed away, and Marcus knelt beside Lex's body, alternating between pumping her chest and blowing into her mouth.

"Heru," the strange combination of Re and Nik said, taking a single step toward the heartbreaking scene. "Stop." He knelt on the opposite side of Lex's body.

"No!" Pump. Pump. Pump. "She'll die!"

"She is already dead."

A soft, collective gasp cascaded through the room, followed by the silence of held breath. The silence of expectation, and of dread. Mari's hand found mine, and I gripped her fingers tightly.

"Her ba is badly damaged. If you manage to revive her now, her body will only give out once more. You must let us preserve her in At, as our daughter said. When the twins are old enough and have mastery over their power, they should be able to repair the damage to her ba." The *thing* that had once been Nik took hold of Marcus's wrists and pulled them from Lex's chest. "Do not touch her again, unless you, too, wish to be transformed into At."

Almost as soon as he released Marcus, his hands were on Lex, one on her forehead, the other on the middle of her chest. It happened slowly, like ice crystals creeping across a window. Too slow to see the change, but fast enough that within minutes, she no longer looked like a flesh-and-blood person, but a pristine statue carved of quartz.

"It is done," he—they—said, removing his hands from Lex. A moment later, Nik's body went limp, and he fell to the side.

"I'm here." Aset's quick footsteps rushed up the hallway. "What hap—" Her words died when she reached the doorway.

"Attend to your son," Marcus said, fingers tracing over Lex's stone-like face. "There is nothing more we can do for her now."

Blinking, I swallowed, my mouth feeling incredibly dry. I looked at Mei. "Did you say 'father'?"

I'D BEEN WALKING FOR HOURS, WANDERING ALONG the trails winding all around the compound. When I reached the beach, I was ready for a nice, peaceful rest sitting on a piece of driftwood, lavishing in the serenity of the Puget Sound. Except the beach was already occupied.

I paused at the mouth of the trail, watching Mari and her mother, Mei. They sat side by side on some driftwood, not speaking. Just being. It was a beautiful scene, and I was struck with a surge of jealousy. Mari had her mom back, but I never would.

Mei had explained to us all in the quiet after the chaos of her and Lex's arrival that she'd stepped out of time just a few seconds before her death—an event which she would be returning to at some point because, according to the natural progression of the timeline, it already happened. Someday, when she had tens, hundreds, maybe even thousands more years under her belt, she would return to that moment, and she would die.

But not yet. Apparently, she still had much to do. She seemed to know everything, or at least all that would happen in the next couple decades, so long as we continued down her "one true path." The twins would grow up and learn to control their Netjer powers and, in time, be able to revive Lex. Nik, too, she claimed would be restored to full health, minus the soul of one ailing god. Apep would remain locked away in his sphere of At in the safe Marcus had buried somewhere here within the compound's walls, the rogues would be hunted down and dispatched, and we'd all hold hands, sing "Kumbaya," and toast marshmallows around a campfire. At least, that's what she claimed. Well, maybe not that last bit.

We had no way of knowing if she spoke the truth, because—thanks to me—the At was no longer an accurate reflection of reality. As Re had said while raving, the echoes showed a world in which I'd died in that tent city. It was awesome. I'd been hoping for one more thing to set me apart from the rest of the damn world.

Not wishing to disturb Mei and Mari's mother–daughter

moment, I started to turn around to head back up the trail, but a twig snapped under my boot.

Both Mei and Mari turned their heads to look at me.

I lifted a hand to wave. "Sorry."

Mei smiled. It was warm and motherly and clawed at my heart. "Please, Kat, come join us. There's something I must tell you both."

Frowning, I shrugged and started down the beach toward them. Once I was sitting on the driftwood beside Mari, Mei stood and faced us, hands clasped before her. She was supposedly Nik's daughter—his only one, Aset claimed—born to a woman both he and Re had fallen in love with two millennia ago. Their daughter, Aramei, had been hidden away in an ancient Hathor temple—Lex's temple—until, one day, she vanished. There was no sign of her in reality or in the At. Because she was a woman out of time. She'd never showed up in the At again. Kind of like me.

Now, standing there before us with the gray-blue water of the Sound stretching out beyond her, I thought I could see the resemblance between her and Nik. It made my heart hurt. I missed him.

"I hope you like the sword," Mei said to me with a kind smile.

"The sword?" I shook my head, confused. But then I understood, and my eyes widened. "You left it on the counter for me?" I'd thought it had been Nik.

Mei nodded. "It was with Lex, when I found her."

Still, I shook my head. "But why did you bring it to me?"

"Because you needed it," she said. "Because the *one true path* needed you to have it."

I stared at her, dumbfounded.

"And now there is a task the one true path requires the two of you to complete." Her gaze fixed on me, a hard glint in her gray eyes. "You'll need your sword."

48

LEX

Groaning, I swallowed with some difficulty; my throat was so dry. I cleared it and peeled my eyelids open. My eyes felt crusty and grainy, scratching as they opened. The light in the room was blinding, gleaming off sterile white walls and forcing my eyes shut once more. The upper half of me was propped up, either by pillows or a hospital bed, I wasn't sure. Near my left hip, something warm and vibrating restricted my arm's movement. On my right side, someone was holding my hand, my fingers fully enclosed in a sure, two-handed grip.

Once more, I forced my eyes open. It was Marcus's hands holding mine, his shaved head bowed and his broad shoulders hunched. He looked slighter than usual. But then, I had no idea what he'd been through during my travels in time.

"Marcus?" My voice was a mere rasp, barely audible.

He raised his head.

I blinked, my eyes opening wide despite the bright light. "You're not—" I cleared my throat once more, hoping that if I did it enough times, my voice might eventually return to normal. "You're not Marcus."

I stared at the young man. His eyes were strange, his irises a glowing, seething mass of blues and purples and reds with hints of golds and greens in the depths, not to mention streaks of opalescent white and inky blackness. They were the eyes of a Netjer. The eyes of a god.

Except the only Netjers currently in existence in our universe were my children, and they were still babies. It had only been a matter of weeks since I gave birth to them.

"Who are you?"

"I know this must be a shock, but—"

"Lex?" My head snapped to the right. Marcus stood beyond the foot of the bed in an open doorway, his usual gray slacks and white button-down shirt looking unusually wrinkled. There was a stain on his shirt, down near his belt buckle, that looked an awful lot like coffee. He stood in that doorway and stared at me, his lips parted and eyes guarded.

I sat up the rest of the way, pulling my hand free of the stranger's grip and waking up one of the two tabby cats sleeping on the bed. It stared at me with guarded eyes, just like Marcus. I returned its stare, not quite sure I understood what I was seeing. The cat looked like Rus . . . but fully grown.

I looked at Marcus. "What's going on? How—" I shook my head, pleading with my eyes for him to make everything I'd seen in the moments since waking make sense. "Who's he?" I asked, pointing to the stranger with my chin.

"Lex," Marcus said, stepping into the room, "that's Syris . . . your son." After two more steps, I raised my hand for him to stop.

I looked from Marcus to the stranger and back, once again shaking my head. "No, that's not possible. It's only been weeks." I licked my lips with a sandpaper tongue. "I was *just* pregnant. I just gave birth. I was just holding my babies in my arms . . ." I looked at the stranger once more, my throat constricting and heart thudding.

His resemblance to Marcus was impossible to ignore, but I

thought I could also see pieces of myself in him, in the tilt of his eyes and in the slope of his nose. With recognition, reality started to sink in, and I squeezed my eyes shut and shook my head.

"Lex . . ." Marcus's voice was a soft hush.

My chin trembled, and though I felt like parting my lips would be playing with fire where tempting tears was concerned, I had to know. I had to ask. "How?"

"You've been frozen in At for the past sixteen years," Marcus said, taking another step toward the bed.

"No. Just stop. I can't . . ." I gestured for him to stay put with my hand, then looked at the stranger. Syris. My son. "You grew up," I said, voice trembling. Tears escaped, gliding down my cheeks. "You grew up without me."

"They had to, Lex." Marcus closed the distance to the bed. He sat on the edge, displacing the cats, and wrapped his arms around me. He pulled me close, rubbing my back. "It was the only way to save you."

I sobbed against his shoulder, a brutal, guttural sound torn from my chest. *My babies . . .*

Syris took hold of my hand once more, his strong fingers cradling mine delicately, almost like he thought they might break in his grip. "We were just babies when you first returned. You'd nearly exhausted one of your sheuts and, in doing so, had badly damaged your ba. You were dying—well, you were technically dead. And we were too little; we couldn't do anything to help you, so they had to freeze you in At. But me and my sister—we've been practicing controlling our powers practically since we could walk. We knew, even then, what we had to do. We just couldn't do it until, well—until yesterday."

I turned my head so my cheek was pressed against Marcus's shoulder and I could see Syris. My son. I wondered how long it would take for that to sink in.

"I'm still me, Mother." He offered me a tentative smile. "I sat with you every day." His nostrils flared. "I told you all of my problems . . . all of my fears and worries—"

"Oh my God!" a young woman cried, launching herself onto the bed almost as soon as she entered the room. "I can't believe you're really awake." Her voice broke as the words tumbled out. "After all these years, Mother, we finally got you back." Her face was sandwiched somewhere between my neck and Marcus's chest, muffling her voice. She was a teenager, but she became a little girl once again, just for a moment. *My* little girl, and I didn't even know her name.

My sense of hearing spiked all of a sudden, my sight dimming from that brilliant, almost overwhelming sensitivity to something slightly manageable. I picked up on one side of a conversation that was happening far from this room, somewhere else in the . . . well, wherever we were. It was Dominic's voice, talking to someone else I couldn't hear.

". . . think it's past time you returned." He must've been talking on the phone. "Even more reason to give up the fight." There was a pause, and then he said, "Good. Let me know when you're scheduled to arrive. I'll have a car waiting."

"Who—" I sniffled. "Who's Dom talking to?"

"It's Kat," Marcus said against my hair. He was still rubbing my back with one hand, though his other arm had found its way around our daughter's shoulders. "She's been . . . away for quite some time now."

I sniffled again, hoping somebody had a tissue nearby, because I was definitely going to need one. "Away? Where? Why?"

Marcus sighed. "It's a long story."

49

KAT

I tossed a pocket-sized leather book onto Gerald Meyer's body. It landed on his blood-soaked sweater with a soft splat, directly over his heart.

"He was telling the truth," I told Mari, disgusted with myself. I dropped down to one knee and slid first one side of my sword blade along the clean portion of his sweater near the hem, then the other, wiping off the blood. His blood. "The guy was obsessive about keeping track of his contact with other Nejerets." The proof was in the book—names, dates and times, locations, topics of discussion. "He wasn't a rogue; just a deserter."

I watched Mari out of the corner of my eye. She was spinning an unused black dagger on the palm of her hand. It was a nervous tic of hers, an indicator that she was pissed.

Good. So was I. "We didn't need to kill him." I sheathed my sword over my shoulder and looked at her full-on. "He was scared . . . a little erratic, maybe, but not dangerous."

Mari closed her palm, her fingers curving around the hilt of the dagger—a dagger only she could touch without dire ramifications. Without, in time, becoming unmade. "He abandoned my people." She glared at me. "A deserter's just as bad as a rogue."

I laughed bitterly and shook my head. "It's been how long now? I think you can drop the 'my people' bit." The Council had dissolved over a decade ago, giving way to the Senate, a representative body of nineteen Nejerets elected by *our* people—all of us—every ten years. There was no more "us and them," not where Nejerets were concerned.

Gerald's body made a gurgling noise—not a noise of life, just one of those weird things dead bodies do. Hang around them long enough and it's bound to happen.

"We didn't need to kill him."

Mari sneered. "Don't tell me you're going soft on me. You were all about this position, remember?" Like I'd had a choice . . .

I glanced at her, then back down at poor, dead Gerald. I was just glad I'd killed him before Mari could. She liked to play—to punish, as she put it—teasing her victims with the threat of that anti-At dagger before putting them out of their misery with a plain, steel blade. She couldn't actually risk unmaking someone, especially not a rogue. Doing so would cause the timeline to weave around their absence, creating a new pattern—a new *now*. Her mom would kill her for screwing with the timeline. Figuratively, of course. Me, I'm much more literal than dear, sweet old Mei.

As I stared at Gerald's slack face, studying his perfectly smooth Nejeret features, part of me wondered if there were even any other rogues left out there. Was there anyone left for me to hunt? Or, at least, anyone whose death wouldn't leave me feeling like I was killing a little bit more of my humanity every time I snuffed out another life?

My phone vibrated my back pocket and I stood, fishing it out of my jeans and turning away from Mari. "Dom? What is it?" It had been years since I'd heard from him—my older brother, my mentor, my best friend—years since he'd given up on my blackened soul. He'd never said as much, but I'd seen it in his eyes the last time we parted.

"Are you busy?" His familiar accent sounded foreign to my ears.

"No, I'm free. Just finished a hunt." I walked away from Gerald's body, toward the kitchen, liking the idea of putting the island between me and the evidence of what I'd just done. There was silence on the other line. "Dom? Is everything alright?"

"More than alright, little sister. She's back. Lex—" His voice was thick with emotion. "She just woke up a few minutes ago, and . . . Kat, she's really back."

"Holy shit," I said against my fingers. Mei had claimed to have learned during her travels through time that the twins would be able to heal Lex when they were sixteen years old, once their sheuts reached maturity and they gained full mastery of their powers, allowing them to repair her fractured ba. Sixteen years—had it really been that long already?

"I think it is past time that you returned."

I stared up at the apartment's popcorn ceiling, blinking away the sting of tears. "I can't keep doing this, anyway. It's become . . . it's just not the same. It doesn't feel right anymore."

"Even more reason to give up the fight."

"Yeah." I cleared my throat. "I'll catch the next tube." The gravity tubes would be faster than a plane, even if they were insanely expensive. My funders had insanely deep pockets. "I'm near Reykjavík, so it'll take me, what, like five hours to get back to the Seattle station?"

"Let me know when you're scheduled to arrive," Dom said. "I'll have a car waiting."

"Will do." I ended the call.

"You can't go," Mari said, stalking toward me. "We're not done yet. There are still seventeen more names—"

I drew my sword and pointed the crystalline blade at her,

stopping her in her tracks. I was the better fighter. We both knew it. I didn't have the crutch of a sheut to lean on; it was just me and my sword.

Dagger still in hand, Mari planted her fists on her hips. "My mom said the future wouldn't be safe until we finished, and the Senate agreed that it's our mission to wipe every single potential rogue off the face of the earth."

I looked at her for a fraction of a second longer, then strolled past her to the front door. "Fuck the Senate."

I twisted the doorknob, yanking the front door open and not caring when the knob slammed against the inside wall. The sky was dark outside, the stars winking in and out of sight as thin clouds passed by.

"But—but you can't leave me. You swore you'd get vengeance for your mom."

I paused on the landing just outside the apartment and sheathed my sword. "The last five have been deserters, not rogues," I said over my shoulder. "And not a single one of those names left on the list have been identified as rogues. My vengeance is done. Whatever you do now, that's for your vendetta. Don't put that shit on me."

"You—traitor! Coward!"

I only saw one way to respond. I raised my right hand high overhead and gave Mari the finger. And then I walked away.

50

LEX

I shifted in the lightly padded chair so I was leaning forward, elbows on the edge of Nik's bed and chin resting on my palms. He was in a room that was connected to the lab in the basement of the main house on Bainbridge, much as I'd been.

"I'm so sorry," I told the man stretched out under the covers. His face wasn't peaceful, as though he were sleeping. Rather, he appeared locked in a constant internal battle. And then there were his eyes, open but unseeing. One iris was Nik's natural, pale blue, the other an unearthly opalescent white. For the past sixteen years, he'd been trapped in At-qed, the prolonged hypometabolic state our physical bodies slipped into when our bas were off, sifting through the echoes in the At.

Except Nik's pseudo At-qed state didn't make sense, not really. His ba wasn't anywhere in the At; we'd looked high and low. The At itself was a strange place now, a misaligned echo of an alternative timeline—one where Kat died shortly after I was yanked into the past and Mei was dead and gone. But that didn't explain why we couldn't find Nik or Re somewhere on that higher plane, despite his body being stuck in what was very clearly a state of At-qed. So where were they?

"If I'd known this would happen—that Re would lose it and you'd be a prisoner in your own body . . ." Sighing, I closed my eyes, squeezing out the tear that had been lingering in my lower lashes for minutes. "If I'd known, Nik, I would've warned you about it before you offered yourself to him."

"No, you wouldn't have."

I straightened and twisted around in the chair to see Kat standing in the doorway. My eyes widened and my lips parted as I sucked in a startled breath. The woman standing there was barely recognizable as the girl I'd known nearly two decades ago.

She still looked eighteen, her body slim and curves slight. Her dark hair had been bleached and cut short, the longest layers barely reaching past her chin. She wore fitted jeans tucked into worn, black combat boots that laced halfway up her calves, a cropped black tank top that revealed a couple inches of her toned midriff, and a fitted red leather jacket. Designs had been inked into her skin on the backs of her hands, her neck, and on what I could see of her abdomen.

But those were just the physical changes. Her once-soft brown eyes were darker, harder. The gleam in her eyes made the outfit and tattoos seem right, whereas the Kat I'd known would've looked like she was wearing a costume. Just another reminder that while to me it felt like not even a year had passed, the world had gone on for much longer around me.

"You wouldn't have warned him," she said, leaning a shoulder against the doorframe. "You had a mission, Lex—saving the universe—and warning Nik was a risk you wouldn't have taken." She pushed off the doorframe and walked into the room, gait easy and somehow restrained. "There's no reason to feel guilty. He knew what he was doing." She sat on the opposite side of the bed, her eyes locked on Nik's tensed face. I wasn't sure she was really talking to me anymore.

I watched her as she stared at Nik, not a hint of what she

was feeling showing up on her face. She was so very different . . .

"I hear you've been busy," I said. My eyes slid to the sword hilt peeking up from behind her shoulder. "How's the sword been working out?"

She looked at me, a flash of surprise knocking down nearly two decades of walls for a fraction of a second. She blinked, and her guarded mask returned. "I forgot it was yours. Mei dropped it off at the shop years ago. Do you want it back?"

I shook my head, smiling to myself. "It saved my life a time or two, but I'm sure you're much better with it than I am." I shrugged. "Besides, what use would I have for it now? But you—"

"I'm done working as the Senate's assassin," she said, eyes sliding back to Nik's face. "It's changed me . . . too much already. I need to stop while there's still anything of *me* left."

"Oh thank God," I said in one quick exhale.

Kat looked at me, that startled expression cracking through the mask once more.

"I mean, I was determined to be supportive and everything, but all I could think about was your mom and how pissed she'd have been if I *didn't* try to talk you out of this assassin gig."

Kat stared at me for long seconds, her expression unreadable. Until, between one heartbeat and the next, the corner of her mouth quirked upward. "She sure could throw a fit, couldn't she?"

I smiled, glad to see that there was still something of my sweet little half-sister in there after all. Older sister now, I supposed. "Sometimes when I remember her," I said, "my mind gives her red hair—it just fits her personality so well."

Kat chuckled under her breath, but a few seconds later, her expression sobered, and her gaze wandered back to Nik. "She's why I did it in the first place, you know." She glanced at me, just for a moment. "Revenge and all that . . ."

I nodded. "Dom filled me in."

Kat rolled her eyes, and I suppressed the urge to grin. "I'm sure his recap was filled with sighs of disappointment."

"No . . ." Confused, I shook my head, eyes narrowed. "He seemed pretty damn proud, actually. Worried and guilty, too, but mostly just proud."

"Really?" Hope flashed in Kat's eyes. This close, I could see that though the brown of her irises had darkened to a nearly black color—likely a result of her Nejeret traits manifesting completely—there were bright specks of gold scattered throughout.

I smiled at her, laughing softly. "Really."

"Oh, well, um . . ." She stood and started sidestepping her way around the bed. "I should find him . . . say hi."

"You really should."

Kat spun around and jogged to the doorway, then headed to the right and was gone, only the sound of her boots on the polished tile floor lingering.

I shook my head. So *very* much had changed. But not everything.

"OH GOD," I SAID, PANTING AND ROLLING ONTO MY side to reach for the glass of water on the nightstand. "I think I'm dead. You killed me." I gulped some water, then glanced at Marcus over my shoulder. "Death by pleasure . . . not a bad way to go."

Marcus raised one eyebrow. "You look quite alive to me, Little Ivanov." He grinned wickedly. "Shall I finish you off?"

I took another sip of water before setting the glass on the nightstand and easing back down to the bed, my back to Marcus. "I think I'd go into a regenerative coma," I said, resting my head on my folded arm.

"Just one more time." Marcus's hand slid from my waist to the curve of my hip, his fingers tracing inward along the crease between my thigh and torso. "And then I promise I'm done . . . for now." He teased my inner thigh with his fingertips.

I whimpered. "Marcus . . ." I thought I was asking him to stop, but my hips shifted seemingly of their own accord, and his fingers slid along my most sensitive places. I arched my back and sucked in a breath as a lightning bolt of pleasure zinged out to every nerve ending in my body.

Marcus's body curved around me from behind, his lips finding my neck and his knee parting my legs. He entered me in one smooth thrust. The arch of my back deepened, and my eyes closed.

In that moment, I was capable of just one thing—feeling. Marcus's arm slipping beneath me to curl around my body, his hand coming to rest on my neck, holding me in place. His lips hovering just behind my ear, his breaths hot and urgent. His hips rocking against me, and his fingertips caressing me in rhythm with his ever-deepening thrusts.

"I will . . . always . . . need you . . . just one . . . more . . . time . . ." With the final word, he extended tendrils of his ba into me, touching me deeper and filling me more completely with his soul than he ever could with his body.

I cried out, the sensation, the closeness, the pleasure overwhelming me until it was all that existed in the world. And when it faded, there was nothing but the quiet darkness of unconsciousness.

I BLINKED, DROWSY AND A LITTLE DISORIENTED. "I fell asleep?" I said, rolling over so I was facing Marcus.

His lips twitched, curving into the tiniest of smiles. "My

fault. I may have pushed you beyond your limits with that last little soul-touch."

"I didn't mind." Heat suffused my chest, neck, and cheeks with the confession.

Marcus chuckled, the sound low and throaty, and raised his hand to brush his knuckles over my cheek and along my jawline. "We'll have to ease up a bit, unless we're going for the saturation point again. Not that I would be opposed to having another child." His pitch lifted at the end, just a hint, turning his words into a question.

I rolled onto my back, exhaling a sigh, and stared up at the ceiling. "I'm not ready." A quick glance was all I needed to catch his careful expression. "The twins . . . I know it's been years for you, but it hasn't even been a month for me. I *just* had them."

"I understand," he said. When I didn't respond, Marcus turned my head with gentle fingertips on my jaw, making me look at him. "Truly, Lex, I do. Just know that when you're ready to try again, I am, too."

Tears welled in my eyes, and my chin trembled. Marcus's arms were around me before the tears could break free, and he pulled me closer, pressing his lips against the top of my head.

"I love you," I said against his chest. "I love you so much."

"But not as much as I love you, Little Ivanov."

I snorted softly. "You can't know that."

"Perhaps not . . ." There was a hint of laughter in his voice. "But I've loved you longer. You can't argue with that."

And he was right. I couldn't.

51

LEX

"It's a party, Lex." My mom pinched my arm. "Parties are for smiles, not frowns."

I gave her a sidelong look, the one she knew all too well from my teenage years. I'd been back for weeks, but it was still disorienting to see her now, a genuine grandmother and unequivocal old woman. The deep lines on her face, the droop of her eyelids, the sag of her jowls, even the sound of her voice . . . I'd become Rip van Winkle in the span of nine months—I'd gone away, only to return to find that the world had kept on turning, that the people I loved had kept on aging, without me.

Or, in Grandma Suse's case, had died. I was still having a hard time coping with that aspect of my new reality.

I glanced at my sister. She was sitting on a picnic blanket with her nearly grown son, Jackson, a future Nejeret, and her two younger kids, Bobby and Judy, named after her Nejeret husband's parents who'd been killed by rogues over a decade ago. Jenny looked more like my mom than my mom did now, as strange as that may sound.

"It feels . . . I don't know . . ." I scanned the yard.

We'd set up a grand barbecue and picnic on the back lawn.

Everyone I loved was there, from my human family to the Nejerets who'd embraced and looked after them in my absence. Dominic and Kat were chatting animatedly, Kat showing him some parody of a sword fight with a half-eaten rib, and Neffe was sharing a picnic blanket with her current beaux, one of the former Kin. Marcus was locked in a deep discussion with my father at the barbecue, and Aset was in the center of the lawn with Tarset, teaching the soon-to-manifest young woman some ancient dance. I found the twins on the periphery of the merriment, heads bent together as they walked toward the main house.

"It just feels off somehow," I said lamely.

"Perhaps your mind is still stuck in a pattern of expectant waiting broken only by intermittent moments of fight or flight," Alexander suggested. He was sitting on the other side of my mom on the bench of our picnic table.

I watched the twins head into the house through the back door, then looked at my grandfather, frowning. "You're probably right." I leaned my head on my mom's shoulder.

My mom slipped her arm around my waist and squeezed. "It's so nice to have you back, sweetie. I can't tell you how hard it's been. Your father . . . for a while there, I wasn't sure he'd pull through, but Syris and Susie helped. He's always been a sucker for babies—and with Susie, it was almost like getting to raise you all over again."

I smiled, a defense mechanism to fend off the sorrow I felt every time it hit me just how much I'd missed out on.

"She's so curious, and they're both so smart—the 'wonder twins,' Jenny calls them . . ."

As if on cue, Syris and Susie emerged through the back door. Susie led the way, what appeared to be a baseball held almost ceremoniously before her in her cupped hands.

I straightened, squinting more out of habit than any real

need to see. My vision couldn't really get any clearer. "What's that in her hands?"

Behind her, Syris followed carrying a similar object, except his was black.

"Oh my God," I breathed. "That's the Apep orb."

"Then the other must contain Re," Marcus said, resting a hand on my shoulder.

I glanced up at him for a fraction of a second. I couldn't bring myself to look away from the twins and what they were holding for longer than that. If the sphere Susie was holding contained Re, then . . .

"What about Nik?" I whispered.

Kat ran past the twins toward the house, Aset close on her heels. I felt torn, wanting to follow but needing to know what was going on with Syris and Susie and the two Netjer souls they were literally holding in the palms of their hands.

"I thought you said Apep was locked away in a safe wrapped in a layer of At and buried under a ton of cement," I said to Marcus, not taking my eyes off my approaching children.

"It was." Marcus's voice was low, his tone even. He was pissed.

The other picnic-goers quieted and stared as the twins passed by, heading straight for us. But the twins—they only had eyes for Marcus and me.

"Don't be cross, Daddy," Susie said, a sweet smile coaxing out her shallow dimples. "We needed Apep's ren . . . and Re's. It's time for us to take them home." My teenage son and daughter stood side by side before us with contrasting expressions. Susie looked excited, eyes bright and color high in her cheeks. Syris, on the other hand, looked both anxious and worried. He looked like maybe, just maybe, he might be sick.

He looked like I felt. "Home?" I mouthed, my voice paralyzed.

"To the Netjer home universe," Syris clarified.

I could feel my head slowly shaking back and forth and could do nothing to stop it.

"We have to go there anyway," Susie said. "It's the only way for us to learn more about what we are and what we can do."

"You're leaving?" I said numbly. But I'd only been back for a couple weeks. We'd barely had enough time to get to know each other.

"Not by choice," Syris said, raising the orb filled with Apep's inky, seething soul. "Apep and Re will continue to unravel if left in this state, and that can't be allowed to happen. Sure, ma'at has been restored and the universe is in balance and everything —for the most part—but, in time, it will begin to deteriorate again right along with Apep and Re."

Slowly, I shook my head. This couldn't be happening. Their birth was supposed to fix everything. It was supposed to be over. It wasn't fair; we'd only been a family for a couple weeks.

"But it will," Susie said, misreading the reason for my head-shake. "Apep and Re created this universe. They're the souls of this place, as integral to it as your ba is to your body. Syris and me . . . we can hold it together without them, and in time we'll share a bond with this universe as strong as theirs is, but the universe will change to fit us, and there's no way to predict *how* it'll change." Her eyes grew glassy. "There's no way to know if this world—if any of you—will even survive the changes."

Syris handed the Apep orb to his sister, then stepped forward and took my hands in his. "Mother, you risked so much for us—for all of us. You must let us return the favor."

"But you're just kids," I said, voice breaking. "I just had you a month ago." I couldn't have stopped the tears from spilling over the brim of my eyelids even if I'd wanted to.

Marcus gave my shoulder a squeeze. "Will it be dangerous?"

Syris's focus shifted higher as he looked at his father. "We don't know, but we'll keep you updated." Looking at me once more, he released my left hand and lifted it to close his fingers around my lapis lazuli falcon pendant. When he released it, the pendant felt hot against my skin and hummed with a barely perceptible vibration. "As long as you're wearing this, I'll be able to reach your mind."

I brought my free hand up to grasp the pendant much as he had.

Syris looked at Marcus. "We've cut off access to the At. It's so unreliable—" He shook his head. "As it is, it does more harm than good."

"That's really the other reason we're going," Susie said. "We're not sure how to fix it, and we thought the other Netjer might have some ideas, or maybe once Apep and Re are restored to full health . . ." She shrugged. "I mean, we've never created a universe, so we're hardly experts. There's bound to be another Netjer who knows more about these kinds of things."

The back door to the main house slammed open, and Kat and Aset came thundering out. "Where is he?" Aset shouted, running ahead. "Where's my son?"

Susie and Syris exchanged a glance. "He's gone," Syris said, closely followed by Susie's "He's fine, though."

Aset slowed to a walk just a few yards away. "Then where is he?"

Susie hugged the two orbs close against her. "He needs some time, Auntie. It's been thousands of years since he was alone in his own mind, and he wanted to get away—to figure out who he is like *this*—before he saw anyone."

"But I'm not just *anyone*," Aset snapped, taking a step toward Susie. "I'm his mother."

"Yes," Syris said, moving to block his sister. "And we get that, we really do." His eyes flicked to me, just for a moment. "We'll never be able to thank you or Nik enough for everything you did to help our mother, but we created something for you . . . something we sort of stumbled upon when we were figuring out how our powers worked. It's a gift we thought *might* at least start to show you how grateful we are."

"Just tell me where my son is; that's the only thank-you gift I need."

"I'm sorry, Auntie, but we can't do that," Susie said, shaking her head.

"Can't or won't?"

"We're merely respecting Nik's wishes," Syris said. "I'm sure he'll return eventually." When Aset didn't respond, only glared, he fished a quarter-sized disk out of his pocket. It shimmered in the afternoon sunlight, appearing to be made of smoky quartz, except the slightly iridescent core shone with writhing, golden tendrils. Syris held the coin of At flat on his palm, extending it to Aset.

She eyed it, both wary and curious. "What is it?"

Syris grinned. "A sheut, Auntie. Just a minor one, like Mother has, so it won't kill you or anything."

"But it will make you very, *very* special," Susie added.

"That's not possible," Aset whispered. "You can't just *make* a sheut."

"Says who?" Susie rotated the orbs in her hands. "We learned how to do tons of 'impossible' things over the years." She grinned. "I could create a whole new galaxy if I wanted to, Auntie. Do you really think creating a lil' old sheut would trip me up?"

"Stop showing off, Suse," Syris said, scolding his sister.

Susie rolled her eyes. Heaven help me, but I was the mother of teenage gods. We were all doomed.

"I only said that I *could* create a whole new galaxy," Susie said, "not that I knew how to do it. And it's not like creating the sheut was easy *or* that we know what you'll be able to do with it, so . . ." She shrugged. "It's pretty cool, though, right?" Her eyes focused on the girl—woman—behind Aset. "And you, Aunt Kat, don't think we forgot about you."

"What?" Kat eyed both of my children, clearly suspicious. "Why?"

"In a sense, your mom died so ours could live," Syris said.

"So *we* could live," Susie amended. "If she hadn't done what she did, hadn't caused that momentary distraction that allowed them to trap Apep, well . . . we owe her, big-time. Which means we owe you."

Kat stared at them, her expression as guarded as ever but her eyes gleaming. "Are you saying—" She wet her lips with her tongue. "Is there a way to bring my mom back?"

Susie shook her head, sympathy written all over her pale, striking features. "That *is* impossible; what has happened had to happen, and she's been gone for far too long. Her energy is already dispersed." She exchanged a glance with her brother, and the corners of his mouth quirked upwards in a near perfect replica of his father's frequent almost-smile.

"We would give you this, though," Syris said, reaching into his other pocket and pulling out a second At coin. He held the two otherworldly things out to Kat and Aset, waiting for his aunts to accept the gifts. "All you have to do is touch it. The rest will happen on its own."

Kat reached out, biting her lip as her fingertips hovered an inch from the waiting sheut. She inhaled deeply, and held her breath. And picked up the disk.

The tiny At creation shimmered, dissolving into her palm. A second later, it was gone.

"That's it?" She looked from Syris to Susie and back. "It's done?"

Both twins nodded.

She narrowed her eyes. "So how do I use it, then?"

Syris and Susie exchanged another glance. "You'll have to figure that part out on your own," Syris said. "It might take a while for it to fully sync with your ba, but we're sure you'll figure out what you can do in no time."

Kat looked at him dead-on. "So you don't know. You just offered me this thing and you have no idea what it'll do to me?"

"Well, it won't hurt you," Susie said defensively.

"We can't know *everything*," Syris added. "We're only sixteen."

"I can't believe I'm doing this," Aset said, exhaling heavily and grabbing the other At coin. It dissolved in her hand, exactly as Kat's had.

Hands now free, Syris turned to his sister and relieved her of the soul-containing orbs.

"Daddy," Susie said, taking a step toward us. "We already gave you your gift, so please don't feel left out."

"What—" I looked from my daughter to my bond-mate and back. "What are you talking about?"

"When we removed the damaged sheut from you, Mother, we had to put it somewhere, and Daddy said he would take it.

"No," I said, barely able to inhale enough air to voice the word. I shook my head vehemently, gripping Marcus's forearm with one hand and pleading up at him with my eyes. They'd removed the sheut that allowed me to travel through space and time, leaving me with the other, seemingly less useful sheut. "It's too dangerous. You could get lost, or stuck, or—"

"I'll be careful, Little Ivanov."

"Besides, Mother," Susie said, "it's still repairing itself, so it'll be a while before he can actually use it, and with the At closed off, he won't be able to travel through time, just space, so . . ."

"But—"

"Mother," Susie said, "it's going to be fine. *Trust* us, please. Trust him."

I closed my mouth, swallowing further protestations.

"Our last gifts are for you," she said, kneeling before me. "You, who sacrificed so much so we could have a chance at life . . . so the universe and all of the life teeming within it could continue on." She pulled a small velvet drawstring bag from her back pocket and handed it to me. "You lost precious years with your mortal family." She smiled, swirling green and golden eyes shimmering with emotion. "We want to give you those years back . . . with interest."

I stared down at the bag in my hand, wondering how what felt like a small stash of marbles could do any such impossible thing. "I don't understand."

"There are five silver marbles in the bag, enough for Grandma and Grandpa, Aunt Jenny, and Bobby and Judy."

"But, how will that—"

Susie's smile widened to a grin. "Each one contains a new, moldable ba, ready to soak into its new host and turn them into a Nejeret."

I stared at my mostly grown daughter, eyes wide and unblinking, and inhaled shakily. My sister and her human kids—my mom and dad—they wouldn't fall victim to the passage of time. They would live forever, like me—*with* me—continuing on in the form of their everlasting ba, even after their physical bodies perished.

On my exhale, I clutched the little bag of immortal souls to my chest and gave in to the unavoidable urge to cry. For once, my tears weren't of sadness or pain or loss or defeat. Not this time. For once, I cried tears of joy.

I SAT ON THE BENCH OF THE PICNIC TABLE, MARCUS on one side of me, holding my hand, my mom on the other, her arm curled around my shoulders. My mother and bond-mate, doing what they could to offer comfort while I stared at the patch of grass my children had disappeared from just a few minutes ago. They'd said their farewells, given promises to return as soon as they could, and then they'd melted into glowing beings of iridescent light and vanished with Re and Apep.

My children . . . they were gone. I thought I should be crying, but I didn't seem able. I felt hollow and wrung out.

I'd thought we were done; I'd thought this was all over—the universe was saved. I'd thought my future would be filled with family birthday parties and excavations and working in the restructured Nejeret government—you know, normal things. I'd thought we would finally get to be a family. Maybe we still would, one day.

But not yet.

"They'll come back, sweetie," my mom said, leaning the side of her head against mine. "And now your dad and I will live long enough to see their return." She held out her arm, examining the back of her hand like she was showing off a ring. "I think I'm already less wrinkly." She lowered her hand to her lap. "You know, I've felt like I was still thirty for the past forty-five years, but to look it again . . . I don't know if I quite believe it's going to happen." She sighed heavily. "I just wish my mother had lasted long enough . . ."

My eyes wandered from the spot of grass left vacant by my kids to the picnic blanket where Alexander sat alone, knees drawn up and arms latched around his legs. He was staring off at nothing, and I had no doubt that his mind had gone in the same direction as my mom's.

I scooted to the edge of the bench and released Marcus's hand. My fingers gripped the knees of my jeans. "I think I need to walk for a bit. Clear my head . . ."

My mom's arm fell away from my shoulders.

"Do you want company?" Marcus asked.

I turned to him, offering him what I could of a smile and leaning in to plant a light kiss on his lips. "No. I'd like to be alone . . . just for a little while."

The concern in his golden eyes faded until only a hint

remained. He knew me well enough to understand that this was how I processed things, how I figured out and worked through my feelings—in solitude—and he returned my smile, his a much better attempt. "Go on, then."

I gave his thigh a squeeze, then stood and arched my back in a stretch. The picnic-goers were still there, scattered around the lawn on blankets and folding picnic tables, but the collective mood had shifted from carefree and celebratory to subdued and contemplative. There was still so much we didn't understand about our existence, about our universe and whatever others were out there.

The twins' revelation that they were visiting the Netjer home universe had shaken a lot of people. We'd all known Re came from somewhere else, but most of us hadn't really considered what that meant, myself included. Our own universe was inconceivably large, its multiple planes of existence and parallel realities far too complex for even my kind to understand in our never-ending lifetimes.

I headed for the woods that surrounded the park-like backyard, aiming for the pathway that led to the beach. The Puget Sound always gave me peace of mind when nothing else could.

When I reached the break in the woods, where stepping over a fallen log transitioned my boots from a path of compacted dirt and pine needles to crunching pebbles, I was surprised to find that someone had beaten me there. Kat stood in the shallows of the shore, her bare feet almost emerging from the frigid saltwater as it receded. The wind picked up and flung about pieces of her short, bleached hair.

"I wondered how long it would take you to find your way out here," she said, not turning to me or raising her voice above a murmur, but knowing I'd hear her all the same.

I meandered down the beach, stopping just behind the kelp line. The rhythmic whoosh of the gentle waves rushing up the rocky beach was already soothing my soul. "Will you go after

Nik?" I had no doubt that Aset had asked Kat to help her find him.

Kat shook her head. "He doesn't want to be found. I can respect that."

"Can Aset?"

Kat laughed, no hint of humor in the sound. "Would you, if he were your son?"

I acknowledged her point with a tilt of my head, my fingers automatically finding the crystalline falcon pendant, my only link to my children. "What will you do, then? Will you stay here?"

Again, Kat shook her head. "I'm different, now. The things I've done—I don't belong here, not anymore."

"Kat—"

"It's true, Lex. A lot has changed since you left. I'm not the weak girl you used to know." Her voice was filled with regret, with longing. With resignation. "She died a long time ago."

I crossed my arms over my chest, hugging myself against the chilly ocean breeze. "You were never weak."

Kat turned her head just enough that she could see me out of the corner of her eye. "I'm not going to go back to the party. Will you tell Dom I said . . ." She frowned. "Just tell him thanks . . . and sorry. He'll understand."

I nodded. "Where will you go?"

She turned back to the endless stretch of gray-blue water. "Home. It's time for me to go home."

EPILOGUE

"I talked to Kat this morning," I told Marcus. "While you were out in the vineyard. I was actually surprised she answered. The call was a bit of a Hail Mary." My hand was in his as we strolled across a rolling Tuscan hillside, a blanket rolled up under my other arm. We'd been staying at the farmhouse just outside of Florence for the past month, decompressing. Marcus was taking a break from the Senate, Aset filling his seat in his absence. It was the first time we'd been alone for more than a day or two since we first met a year and a half ago. Even in other time periods, there were always people around us.

"Oh?" Marcus glanced at me, eyebrows raised. I didn't think I'd ever seen his face so relaxed; it made him even more beautiful—painfully so. "And how is she?"

"She seems . . ." I frowned. "Busy. And distant. She said she hasn't been avoiding my calls, but . . ." I trailed off with a shrug.

"She is setting up a whole new business," Marcus said. A tattoo parlor, in fact, where the shop used to be. He gave my hand a squeeze, then released it. "She *should* be busy." He stopped walking. "How about here?"

I looked around and grinned. We were roughly in the same spot where we'd picnicked the afternoon we'd allowed ourselves to get carried away with, well, *ourselves*. The city below was more sprawling than before, but it was still recognizable as that same bustling place I'd viewed from up here so many centuries ago.

"This is perfect," I said, unrolling the blanket and shaking it out so it would lay flat on the tall grass. "I don't know," I said, returning to the subject of my youngest sister, "I just worry about her."

Marcus set down the picnic basket he'd been carrying in the middle of the blanket and knelt beside it. I joined him, watching as he pulled out item after item—a baguette, a few plastic-wrapped hunks of cheese, a couple salamis, a bundle of napkins and knives, a wooden cutting board—until he found the two plastic wineglasses, the corkscrew, and the bottle of Verdicchio tucked away in the bottom of the basket. He quickly went to work uncorking the wine.

I tore the end off the baguette and nibbled on it. "I can't help but feel like she's shutting us out. Maybe if Nik were around . . ."

"They have both been through quite a bit," Marcus said, tugging the cork free. "If they need some time, then they need some time. Luckily, time is something they both have more than plenty of."

My heartbeat picked up as I watched him pour wine into one of the plastic glasses. I'd been anticipating this moment all morning, ever since I became certain.

Marcus offered me the glass. When I didn't take it from his hand, he looked at me.

I shook my head, ever so slowly, and smiled.

Marcus's brow furrowed, and his eyes searched mine. After a few heartbeats, his brow smoothed and a broad grin spread across his face. "Little Ivanov? Are you saying—"

"I'm pregnant."

His hand was shaking as he set the glass and bottle of wine on the ground beside him. He didn't notice when the glass fell over, spilling the wine into the grass and dirt; he was too focused on me. He leaned across the picnic basket and took hold of my face, kissing me and laughing and possibly even crying a little all at the same time. It was pretty much the best reaction I could've imagined.

"How long have you known?" he asked when he finally released me.

"I received a call from the doctor's office this morning, just after I got off the phone with Kat."

Marcus shook his head slowly, wonder filling his golden eyes, making them glow like the sun.

"Mother? Are you there?"

My mouth fell open, and I slapped my hand to my chest, my fingers gripping the At falcon pendant hanging there. "Yes!" My eyes locked with Marcus's. "It's Syris," I told him, chin trembling, then reached for his hand and brought it up to the pendant so he could hear our son as well. "We're both here," I said. It was the first time we'd heard from the twins in a couple weeks. They usually checked in every few days. "Where have you been?"

"I'm sorry, Mother!" Susie said. *"It's my fault. I accidentally created a time vortex, and . . ."*

As I stared into Marcus's eyes, listening to our divine children recount their most recent exploits in an entirely different universe, a swell of pure, unadulterated serenity rose up around me and I felt an intense sense of rightness. This was what it had all been for—all the pain and suffering, all the fear and worry and not-knowing. This perfect, joyous moment, on this hillside. It had all been for this.

And it was worth it.

The end

Thanks for reading! You've reached the end of *Ricochet Through Time (Echo Trilogy, #3)*, and this concludes the Echo Trilogy, but Kat's story is only just beginning. *Ink Witch (Kat Dubois Chronicles, #1)* continues Kat's story. And don't worry, Lex is in there, too.

GLOSSARY

- **Akhet** The first of three seasons in the ancient Egyptian year. *Akhet* is the inundation season, when the Nile floods, and is roughly correlated with fall in the northern hemisphere.
- **Ankhesenpepi** Nejerette. Nuin's eldest daughter and queen and consort to many Old Kingdom pharaohs, including Pepi I and II.
- **Apep (Apophis)** Netjer or "god." One of two Netjers responsible for maintaining balance in our universe, the other being Re. Apep was historically worshipped *against* as Re's opponent and the evil god of chaos.
- **At** Ancient Egyptian, "moment, instant, time"; The *At* is a plane of existence overlaying our own, where time and space are fluid. *At* can also be used to refer to the fabric of space and time.
- **Ankh** Ancient Egyptian, "life".
- **Ankh-At** Nuin's power. Includes (at least) the power to travel through time, to create and remove memory blocks, and to manipulate the At on this plane of existence.

- **Aset (Isis)** Nejerette. Heru's sister. Aset was worshipped as a goddess associated with motherhood, magic, and nature by the ancient Egyptians.
- **At-qed** State of stasis a Nejeret's body enters when his or her ba departs for the At.
- **Ba** Considered one of the essential parts of the soul by the ancient Egyptians. In regards to Nejerets, the ba, or the "soul," is the part of a person that can enter the At.
- **Bahur** Arabic, "of Horus" or "of Heru".
- **Blade** A ruling Nejeret's chief protector and companion.
- **Council of Seven** The body of leadership that governs the Nejerets. The Council consists of the patriarchs of the seven strongest Nejeret families: Ivan, Heru, Set, Sid, Moshe, Dedwen, and Shangdi. The Meswett, Alexandra Larson Ivanov, is also an honorary member of the Council.
- **Dedwen** A member of the Council of Seven. Dedwen was worshipped as a god associated with prosperity, wealth, and fire by the ancient Nubians.
- **Deir el-Bahri** Located on the west side of the Nile, just across the river from Luxor in Upper (southern) Egypt. Several mortuary temples and tombs are located in Deir el-Bahri, including Djeser-Djeseru, Queen Hatshepsut's mortuary temple.
- **Djeser-Djeseru** Ancient Egyptian, "Holy of Holies". Queen Hatshepsut's mortuary temple in Deir el-Bahri.
- **Hatshepsut** (ruled 1479—1457 BCE) Female Pharaoh during the Middle Kingdom of ancient Egypt. One of Heru's many wives, and mother to the Nejerette Neferure.
- **Hat-hur (Hathor)** Ancient Egyptian goddess associated with love, fertility, sexuality, music, and

dance. According to the Contendings of Heru and Set myth, Hathor is the goddess who healed Heru's eye. She is often depicted as a cow or a woman with cow ears or horns, and a sun disk is frequently cradled by the horns.

- **Heru (Horus)** Nejeret. Osiris's son, Nuin's grandson, Aset's brother, and former leader of the Council of Seven. Heru stepped down from his role as leader to function as the Council's general and assassin, when necessary. Heru was worshipped as the god of the sky, kingship, and authority by the ancient Egyptians. He is often depicted as a falcon or falcon-headed.
- **Ipwet** Human, Nejeret-carrier. Nuin's primary *human* wife at the time of his death.
- **Ivan** Nejeret. Leader of the Council of Seven. Alexander's father and Lex's great-grandfather.
- **Kemet** Ancient Egyptian, "Black Land". Kemet is one of the names ancient Egyptians called their homeland.
- **Ma'at** Ancient Egyptian concept of truth, balance, justice, and order. To the Nejeret, *ma'at* refers to universal balance.
- **Men-nefer (Memphis)** Ancient Egyptian city. *Men-nefer* was the capital city of Egypt during the Old Kingdom.
- **Meswett** Ancient Egyptian (mswtt), "girl-child". The Meswett is the prophesied savior/destroyer of the Nejerets, as supposedly foretold by Nuin upon his deathbed, though none actually remember it happening. The prophecy was later recorded by the Nejeret Senenmut.
- **Moshe (Moses)** Nejeret. Member of the Council of Seven. Central figure in most western religions.
- **Neferure (Neffe)** Nejerette. Daughter of Hatshepsut

and Heru.

- **Nejeret (male)/Nejerette (female)/Nejerets (plural)** Modern term for the Netjer-At.
- **Netjer** Ancient Egyptian, "god".
- **Netjer-At** Ancient Egyptian, "Gods of Time".
- **Netjer-At Oasis** The ancient, historic home of the Nejerets, deep in the heart of the Sahara Desert.
- **Nuin (Nun)** Netjer/Nejeret. One of two Netjers responsible for maintaining balance in our universe, the other being Apep. Also known as the "Great Father", Nuin was the original Nejeret and the father of all Nejeretkind. Nuin was worshipped as a god associated with the primordial waters and creation by the ancient Egyptians.
- **Old Kingdom** Period of Egyptian history from 2686—2181 BCE.
- **Order of Hat-hur** An over 5,000-year-old, hereditary order of priestesses run by Aset and devoted to aiding the goddess Hat-hur (Lex) during her temporal journeys.
- **Osiris** Nejeret. Heru and Aset's father and leader of the Council of Seven until his murder a few decades after Nuin's death. Osiris was worshipped as a god associated with death, the afterlife, fertility, and agriculture by the ancient Egyptians.
- **Pepi II (Pepi Neferkare)** Pharaoh of the 6th Dynasty of ancient Egypt, 2284-2180 BCE. Final ruler of both the 6th Dynasty and of the Old Kingdom.
- **Peret** The second of three seasons in the ancient Egyptian year. *Peret* is known as the season of emergence, during which planting and growth took place.
- **Re (Ra)** Netjer. One of two Netjers responsible for maintaining balance in our universe, the other being

Apep. *Re* was historically worshipped as the ancient Egyptian solar deity.

- **Ren** Considered one of the essential parts of the soul by the ancient Egyptians, closely associated with a person's name. In regards to Nejerets, a *ren* is the soul of a Netjer, like Re or Apep, much like a *ba* is the soul of a Nejeret or human.
- **Senenmut** Nejeret. Scribe of Nuin's prophecy and architect of the underground temple housing the ankh-At at Deir el-Bahri. Senenmut was the "high steward of the king" to Queen Hatshepsut as well as Neferure's tutor. Senenmut was killed by Set after the completion of the underground temple.
- **Set (Seth)** Nejeret. Nuin's grandson, father of Dom, Genevieve, Kat, and Lex, and member of the Council of Seven. Possessed by Apep, Set went rogue when the Council of Seven chose Heru as their leader after Osiris's death around 4,000 years ago.
- **Shangdi** Nejerette. Member of the Council of Seven. Shangdi is worshipped as the supreme sky deity in the traditional Chinese religion.
- **Shemu** The third and final of three seasons in the ancient Egyptian year. *Shemu,* literally "low water," is known as the season of harvest.
- **Sheut** Considered one of the essential parts of the soul by the ancient Egyptians, closely associated with a person's shadow. In regards to Nejerets, a *sheut* is the power of a Netjer, like Re or Apep, or the less potent power of the offspring of a Nejerette and Nejeret.
- **Sid (Siddhartha Gautama)** Nejeret. More commonly known as "Buddha" to humans.
- **Wedjat (Eye of Horus)** Ancient Egyptian symbol of protection, healing, strength, and perfection.

CAN'T GET ENOUGH?

NEWSLETTER: www.lindseyfairleigh.com/join-newsletter
WEBSITE: www.lindseyfairleigh.com
FACEBOOK: Lindsey Fairleigh
INSTAGRAM: @LindseyFairleigh
PINTEREST: LindsFairleigh
PATREON: www.patreon.com/lindseyfairleigh

Reviews are always appreciated. They help indie authors like me sell books (and keep writing them!).

ALSO BY LINDSEY FAIRLEIGH

ECHO TRILOGY

Echo in Time

Resonance

Time Anomaly

Dissonance

Ricochet Through Time

KAT DUBOIS CHRONICLES

Ink Witch

Outcast

Underground

Soul Eater

Judgement

Afterlife

ATLANTIS LEGACY

Sacrifice of the Sinners

Legacy of the Lost

Fate of the Fallen

Dreams of the Damned

Song of the Soulless

THE ENDING SERIES

Beginnings: The Ending Series Origin Stories

After The Ending

Into The Fire

Out Of The Ashes

Before The Dawn

World Before

World After

FOR MORE INFORMATION ON LINDSEY FAIRLEIGH & THE ECHO TRILOGY:

www.lindseyfairleigh.com

Reviews are always appreciated. They help indie authors like me sell books (and keep writing them!).

ABOUT THE AUTHOR

Lindsey Fairleigh a bestselling Science Fiction and Fantasy author who lives her life with one foot in a book—so long as that book transports her to a magical world or bends the rules of science. Her novels, from Post-apocalyptic to Time Travel Romance, always offer up a hearty dose of unreality, along with plenty of history, mystery, adventure, and romance. When she's not working on her next novel, Lindsey spends her time walking around the foothills surrounding her home with her son, playing video games, and trying out new recipes in the kitchen. She lives in the Pacific Northwest with her family and their small pack of dogs and cats.

www.lindseyfairleigh.com

Made in the USA
Las Vegas, NV
05 July 2023

74251479R00249